LAST NIGHT AT
CHATEAU MARMONT

LAST NIGHT AT
CHATEAU MARMONT

LAUREN WEISBERGER

WHEELER
WINDSOR
PARAGON

This Large Print edition is published by Thorndike Press, Waterville, Maine USA and by BBC Audiobooks Ltd, Bath, England.

Copyright © 2010 by Lauren Weisberger.

The moral right of the author has been asserted.

Wheeler Publishing, a part of Gale, Cengage Learning.

Wheeler Publishing Large Print Hardcover.

The text of this Large Print edition is unabridged.

Other aspects of the book may vary from the original edition.

Set in 16 pt. Plantin.

LIBRARY OF CONGRESS CATALOGING-IN-PUBLICATION DATA

Weisberger, Lauren, 1977–
    Last night at Chateau Marmont / by Lauren Weisberger.
      p. cm. — (Wheeler Publishing large print hardcover)
    ISBN-13: 978-1-4104-2639-0 (hardcover)
    ISBN-10: 1-4104-2639-4 (hardcover)
    1. Musicians—Fiction. 2. Success—Fiction. 3. Celebrities—Fiction.
4. Gossip—Fiction 5. Women—Societies and clubs—Fiction. 6. Young
women—New York (State)—New York—Fiction. 7. Female friendship—
Fiction. 8. Manhattan (New York, N.Y.)—Fiction. 9. Chick lit. 10. Large
type books. I. Title.
PS3623.E453L37 2010b
813'.6—dc22   2010029405

BRITISH LIBRARY CATALOGUING-IN-PUBLICATION DATA AVAILABLE

Published in the U.S. in 2010 by arrangement with Atria Books, a division of Simon & Schuster, Inc.

Published in the U.K. in 2011 by arrangement with HarperCollins Publishers.

U.K. Hardcover: 978 1 408 48721 1 (Windsor Large Print)

U.K. Softcover: 978 1 408 48722 8 (Paragon Large Print)

Printed in the United States of America

1 2 3 4 5 6 7 14 13 12 11 10

For Dana, my sister and best friend
forever

1
PIANO MAN

When the subway finally screeched into the Franklin Street station, Brooke was nearly sick with anxiety. She checked her watch for the tenth time in as many minutes and tried to remind herself that it wasn't the end of the world; her best friend, Nola, would forgive her, *had* to forgive her, even if she was inexcusably late. She made her way through the rush-hour throngs of commuters toward the door, instinctively holding her breath in the midst of so many bodies, and allowed herself to be pushed toward the stairwell. On autopilot now, Brooke and her fellow riders each pulled their cell phones from their purses and jacket pockets, filed silently into a straight line and, zombielike, marched like choreographed soldiers up the right side of the cement stairs while staring blankly at the tiny screens in their palms.

"Shit!" she heard an overweight woman

up ahead call out, and in a moment she knew why. The rain hit her forcefully and without warning the instant she emerged from the stairwell. What had been a chilly but decent enough March evening only twenty minutes earlier had deteriorated into a freezing, thundering misery, where the winds whipped the rain down and made it utterly impossible to stay dry.

"Dammit!" she added to the cacophony of expletives people were shouting all around her as they struggled to pull umbrellas from their briefcases or arrange newspapers over their heads. Since she'd run home to change after work, Brooke had nothing but a tiny (and admittedly cute) silver clutch to shield herself from the onslaught. *Good-bye, hair,* she thought as she began to sprint the three blocks to the restaurant. *I'll miss you, eye makeup. Nice knowing you, gorgeous new suede boots that ate up half my weekly salary.*

Brooke was drenched by the time she reached Sotto, the tiny, unpretentious neighborhood joint where she and Nola met two or three times a month. The pasta wasn't the best in the city — probably not even the best on the block — and the space wasn't anything all that special, but Sotto had other charms, more important ones:

8

reasonably priced wine by the full carafe, a killer tiramisu, and a downright hot Italian maître d' who, simply because they'd been coming for so long, always saved Brooke and Nola the most private table in the back.

"Hey, Luca." Brooke greeted the owner as she shrugged off her wool peacoat, trying not to shake water everywhere. "Is she here yet?"

Luca immediately put his hand over the phone receiver and pointed with a pencil over his shoulder. "The usual. What's the occasion for the sexy dress, *cara mia?* You want to dry off first?"

She smoothed her fitted, short-sleeved black jersey dress with both palms and prayed that Luca was right, that the dress was sexy and she looked okay. She'd come to think of that dress as her Gig Uniform; paired with either heels, sandals, or boots, depending on the weather, she wore it to nearly every one of Julian's performances.

"I'm so late already. Is she all whiny and mad?" Brooke asked, scrunching handfuls of her hair in a desperate attempt to save it from the imminent frizz attack.

"She's a half carafe in and hasn't put the mobile down yet. You better get back there."

They exchanged a triple cheek-kiss — Brooke had protested the full three kisses in the beginning but Luca insisted — before Brooke took a deep breath and walked back to their table. Nola was tucked neatly into the banquette, her suit jacket flung across the back bench and her navy cashmere shell showing off tightly toned arms and contrasting nicely with her gorgeous olive skin. Her shoulder-length layered cut was stylish and sexy, her blond highlights glowed under the restaurant's soft lights, and her makeup looked dewy and fresh. No one would ever know from looking at her that Nola had just clocked in twelve hours on a trading desk screaming into a headset.

Brooke and Nola didn't meet until second semester senior year at Cornell, although Brooke — like the rest of the student body — recognized Nola and was equal parts terrified of and fascinated by her. Compared to her hoodie-and-Ugg-wearing fellow students, the model-thin Nola favored high-heeled boots and blazers and never, *ever* tied her hair in a ponytail. She'd grown up in elite prep schools in New York, London, Hong Kong, and Dubai, places her investment banker father worked, and had enjoyed the requisite freedom that goes along with being the only child of extremely busy parents.

How she ended up at Cornell instead of

Cambridge or Georgetown or the Sorbonne was anyone's guess, but it didn't take a lot of imagination to see she wasn't particularly impressed by it all. When the rest of them were busy rushing sororities, meeting for lunch at the Ivy Room, and getting drunk at various Collegetown bars, Nola kept to herself. There were glimpses into her life — the well-known affair with the archaeology professor, the frequent appearances of sexy, mysterious men on campus who vanished soon thereafter — but for the most part, Nola attended her classes, aced everything she took, and hightailed it back to Manhattan the moment Friday afternoon rolled around. When the two girls found themselves assigned to workshop each other's short stories in a creative writing elective their senior year, Brooke was so intimidated she could barely speak. Nola, as usual, didn't appear particularly pleased or upset, but when she returned Brooke's first submission a week later — a fictional piece on a character struggling to adapt to her Peace Corps assignment in Congo — it was filled with thoughtful, insightful commentary and suggestions. Then, on the last page, after scrawling out her lengthy and serious feedback, Nola had written, "P.S. Consider sex scene in Congo?" and Brooke had laughed

11

so hard she had to excuse herself from class to calm down.

After class Nola invited Brooke to a little coffee place in the basement of one of the academic buildings, a place none of Brooke's friends ever hung out, and within a couple weeks Brooke was going to New York with Nola on weekends. Even after all these years, Nola was too fabulous for words, but it helped Brooke knowing that her friend sobbed during news segments featuring soldiers coming home from war, was secretly obsessed with one day having a perfect white picket fence in the suburbs despite being openly derisive about it, and had a pathological fear of small, yappy dogs (Walter, Brooke's dog, not included).

"Perfect, perfect. No, I think sitting at the bar is just fine," Nola said into the phone, rolling her eyes at Brooke. "No, no need to make a reservation for dinner, let's just play it by ear. Okay, sounds good. See you then." She clicked her phone shut and immediately grabbed the red wine, refreshing her own glass before remembering Brooke and filling hers too.

"Do you hate me?" Brooke asked as she arranged her coat on the chair next to her and tossed her wet clutch beside her. She took a long, deep drink of wine and savored the feeling of the alcohol sliding over her tongue.

"Why? Just because I've been sitting here alone for thirty minutes?"

"I know, I know, I'm really sorry. Hellish day at work. Two of the full-time nutritionists called in sick today — which if you ask me sounds suspicious — and the rest of us had to cover their rotations. Of course, if we met sometime in my neighborhood, maybe I could get there on time. . . ."

Nola held up her hand. "Point taken. I do appreciate you coming all the way down here. Dinner in Midtown West just isn't appealing."

"Who were you just on with? Was that Daniel?"

"Daniel?" Nola looked baffled. She stared at the ceiling as she appeared to rack her brain. "Daniel, Daniel . . . oh! Nah, I'm over him. I brought him to a work thing early last week and he was weird. Super awkward. No, that was setting up tomorrow's Match dot-com date. Second one this week. How did I get so pathetic?" She sighed.

"Please. You're not —"

"No, really. It's pathetic that I'm almost thirty and still think of my college boyfriend as my only 'real' relationship. It is also pathetic that I belong to multiple online dating sites and date men from all of them. But what is *most* pathetic — what is bordering on inexcusable — is how willing I am to admit this to anyone who will listen."

Brooke took another sip. "I'm hardly 'anyone who will listen.' "

"You know what I mean," Nola said. "If you were the only one privy to my humiliation, I could live with that. But it's as though I've become so inured to the —"

"Good word."

"Thanks. It was on my word-a-day calendar this morning. So, really, I'm so *inured* to the indignity of it all that I have no filter anymore. Just yesterday I spent a solid fifteen minutes trying to explain to one of Goldman's most senior vice presidents the difference in men on Match versus those on Nerve. It's unforgivable."

"So, what's the story with the guy tomorrow?" Brooke asked, trying to change the subject. It was impossible to keep track of Nola's man situation from week to week. Not just which one — a challenge itself — but whether she *desperately* wanted a boyfriend to settle down with or *loathed* commitment and wanted only to be single and fabulous and sleep around. It changed on a dime, with no warning, and left Brooke constantly trying to remember whether this

14

week's guy was "so amazing" or "a total disaster."

Nola lowered her lashes and arranged her glossed lips into her signature pout, the one that managed to say, "I'm fragile," "I'm sweet," and "I want you to ravish me" all at the same time. Clearly, she was planning a long response to this question.

"Save it for the men, my friend. Doesn't work on me," Brooke lied. Nola wasn't traditionally pretty, but it didn't much matter. She put herself together so beautifully and emanated such confidence that men and women alike regularly fell under her spell.

"This one *sounds* promising," she said wistfully. "I'm sure it's only a matter of time until he reveals some sort of colossal deal breaker, but until then, I think he's perfect."

"So, what's he like?" Brooke pressed.

"Mmm, let's see. He was on the ski racing team in college, which is why I clicked on him in the first place, and he even did two seasons as an instructor, first in Park City and then in Zermatt."

"Perfection so far."

Nola nodded. "Yep. He's just about six foot, fit build — or so he claims — sandy blond hair, and green eyes. He just moved to the city a few months ago and doesn't

15

know a lot of people."

"You'll change that."

"Yeah, I guess. . . ." She pouted. "But . . ."

"What's the problem?" Brooke refreshed both their glasses and nodded to the waiter when he asked if they'd both like their usual orders.

"Well, it's the job thing. He lists his profession as 'artist.' " She pronounced this word as though she were saying "pornographer."

"So?"

"So? So what the hell does that mean. *Artist?*"

"Um, I think it could mean a lot of things. Painter, sculptor, musician, actor, wri—"

Nola touched her hand to her forehead. "Please. It can mean one thing only and we both know it: unemployed."

"Everyone's unemployed now. It's practically chic."

"Oh, come on. I can live with recession-related unemployment. But an *artiste?* Tough to stomach."

"Nola! That's ridiculous. There are plenty of people — loads of them, thousands, probably millions — who support themselves with their art. I mean, look at Julian. He's a musician. Should I never have gone out with *him?*"

Nola opened her mouth to say something but changed her mind. There was an awkward moment of silence.

"What were you going to say?" Brooke asked.

"Nothing, it's nothing. You're right."

"No, really. What were you just about to say? Just say it."

Nola twirled her wineglass by the stem and looked like she'd rather be anywhere but there. "I'm not saying that Julian isn't really talented, but . . ."

"But what?" Brooke leaned in so close that Nola was forced to meet her eyes.

"But I'm not sure I would call him a 'musician.' He was someone's assistant when you met. Now *you* support him."

"Yes, he was an *intern* when we met," Brooke said, barely even attempting to hide her irritation. "He was interning at Sony to learn the music industry, see how it works. And guess what? It's only because of the relationships he built there that anyone paid him any attention in the first place. If he hadn't been there every day, trying to make himself indispensable, do you think the head of A&R would've taken two hours of his time to watch him perform?"

"I know, it's just that —"

"How can you say he's not doing any-

thing? Is that really what you think? I'm not sure if you realize this, but he has spent the last eight months locked away in a Midtown recording studio making an album. And not just some vanity project, by the way; Sony actually *signed* him as an artist — there's that word again — and paid him an advance. If you don't think that's proper employment, I really don't know what to tell you."

Nola held her hands up in defeat and hung her head. "Yes, of course. You're right."

"You don't sound convinced." Brooke began chewing on her thumbnail. Any relief she'd felt from the wine had completely vanished.

Nola pushed her salad around with a fork. "Well, don't they give out, like, a ton of recording contracts to anyone showing a modicum of talent, figuring it'll only take one big hit to pay for all the smaller flops?"

Brooke was surprised by her friend's knowledge of the music industry. Julian always explained that very theory when he downplayed his label deal and tried to, in his words, "manage expectations" about what such a deal really meant. Still, coming from Nola, it somehow sounded worse.

"A 'modicum of talent'?" Brooke could only whisper the words. "Is that what you think of him?"

"Of *course* that's not what I think of him. Don't take it so personally. It's just hard, as your friend, to watch you kill yourself working to support him for so many years now. Especially when the odds are so low that anything will come of it."

"Well, I appreciate your concern for my well-being, but you should know it was my choice to take on the extra private school consulting work to help support us. I don't do it out of the kindness of my heart, I do it because I actually believe in him and his talent, and I know — even if no one else seems to think so — that he has a brilliant career ahead of him."

Brooke had been ecstatic beyond description — possibly even more than Julian — when he'd called her with the initial offer from Sony eight months earlier. Two hundred fifty thousand dollars was more than they'd collectively made in the previous five years, and Julian would have the freedom to do with it what he wanted. How could she have possibly foreseen that such a massive infusion of cash would put them in even greater debt than they already were? From that advance Julian needed to pay for studio time, hire high-priced producers and sound engineers, and cover the entire cost of his equipment, travel, and backup band. The money was gone in a few short months, long before they could use so much as a single dollar toward rent, utilities, or even a celebratory dinner. And once all those funds were being used to help Julian make a name for himself, it didn't make sense not to see the project through. They'd already spent thirty thousand dollars of their own money — the entirety of their savings that had once been earmarked for a down payment on an apartment — and they were burning through more credit every single day. The scariest part of the whole thing was what Nola had so brutally spelled out: the chances of Julian ever making good on all that time and money — even with the Sony name behind him — were almost nil.

"I just hope he knows how lucky he is to have a wife like you," Nola said, more softly now. "I can tell you, I sure wouldn't be so supportive. Which is probably why I'm destined to be single forever . . ."

Thankfully their pasta dishes arrived and the conversation shifted to safer topics: how fattening was the meat sauce, whether or not Nola should ask for a raise at work, how much Brooke disliked her in-laws. When Brooke motioned for the check without ordering the tiramisu or even a coffee, Nola looked concerned.

"You're not upset with me, are you?" she asked, putting her credit card in the leather folder.

"No," Brooke lied. "I've just had a long day."

"Where are you headed now? No après-dinner drink?"

"Julian's actually got a . . . he's performing," Brooke said, changing her mind at the last second. She'd rather not have mentioned his gig at all, but it felt strange lying to Nola.

"Oh, fun!" Nola said brightly, draining the last of her wine. "Want company?"

They both knew she didn't really want to go, which was okay, because Brooke didn't really want her to go. Her friend and her husband got along just fine, and that was good enough. She appreciated Nola's protectiveness and knew it came from a good place, but it was hard thinking your best friend was constantly judging your husband — and he was always coming up short.

"Trent's in town actually," Brooke said. "He's here on a rotation of some sort, so I'm meeting him there."

"Ah, good old Trent. How's he liking med school?"

"He's done actually; he's an intern now. Julian says he loves L.A., which is surprising — born-and-bred New Yorkers *never* like L.A."

Nola stood up and put her suit jacket back on. "Is he dating anyone? If I remember correctly, he's boring as hell but perfectly cute. . . ."

"He just got engaged, actually. To a fellow gastro intern, a girl named Fern. Intern Fern, the gastro specialist. I'd rather not imagine what their conversation entails."

Nola scrunched up her face in disgust. "Thanks for that visual. And to think, he could've been all yours. . . ."

"Mmmm."

"I just want to make sure I still get proper credit for introducing you to your husband. If you hadn't gone out with the Trent man that night, you'd still just be another Julian groupie."

Brooke laughed and kissed her friend on the cheek. She fished two twenties out of her wallet and handed them to Nola. "I've got to run. If I don't get on the train in the next thirty seconds, I'm going to be late. Talk tomorrow?" She grabbed her coat and clutch, offered a quick wave to Luca on the way out, and bolted through the door.

Even after all these years, Brooke shuddered when she thought how close she and Julian came to missing each other. It was June 2001, a mere month after she'd graduated from college, and Brooke was finding it almost impossible to acclimate to her new sixty-hour workweek, split almost evenly between her nutrition grad coursework, logging internship hours, and a make-ends-meet barista stint at a neighborhood coffee joint. While she'd had no illusions about the difficulty of working twelve hours a day for $22,000 — or so she'd thought — she hadn't been able to predict the sum strain of long workdays, insufficient salary, too little sleep, and the logistics of sharing a seven-hundred-square-foot Murray Hill one-bedroom with Nola and another of their friends. Which is why, when Nola implored Brooke to join her for live music on a Sunday night, she'd flatly refused.

"Come on, Brookie, you need to get out of the apartment," Nola had argued while pulling on a tight black tank top. "There's some jazz quartet performing and they're supposed to be really good, and Benny and Simone said they'd save us seats. Five-dollar cover and two-for-one drinks. What can you possibly not like about that?"

"I'm just too tired." Brooke sighed, clicking listlessly through the channels from the girls' living room futon. "I still have to write a paper, and I have to be at work in eleven hours."

"Oh, save the drama. You're twenty-two, for chrissake. Suck it up and go get dressed. We're leaving in ten."

"It's pouring outside and —"

"Ten minutes, not one second longer, or you're not my friend anymore."

By the time the girls had made it to Rue B's in the East Village and tucked themselves into a too-small table with friends from school, Brooke was regretting her weakness. Why did she always cave to Nola? Why on earth was she packed into a smoky, crowded bar, drinking a watery vodka tonic and waiting to see a jazz quartet she'd never heard of? She didn't even particularly *like* jazz. Or, for that matter, any live music, unless it happened to be a Dave Matthews or Bruce Springsteen concert where she could merrily sing along to all the songs. This was clearly not that kind of night. Which is why she felt a mixture of both irritation and relief when the leggy, blond bartender banged a spoon on a water glass.

"Hey, guys! Hey, y'all, can I have your attention for a minute?" She wiped her free hand on her jeans and patiently waited for the crowd to quiet down. "I know you're all excited to hear the Tribesmen tonight, but

24

we just got word that they're stuck in traffic on the LIE and aren't going to make it in time."

Rousing boos and jeers ensued.

"I know, I know, it sucks. Overturned tractor trailer, complete standstill, blah, blah, blah."

"How about a free round as an apology?" called out a middle-aged man sitting in the back while holding up his drink.

The bartender laughed. "Sorry. But if anyone wants to come on up here and entertain us . . ." She looked directly at the man, who just shook his head.

"Seriously, we've got a perfectly good piano. Anyone play?"

The room was silent as everyone glanced around at each other.

"Hey, Brooke, don't you play?" Nola whispered loud enough for their table to hear.

Brooke rolled her eyes. "I got kicked out of the band in sixth grade because I couldn't learn to read sheet music. Who gets kicked out of the middle school band?"

The bartender was not giving up easily. "Come on, folks! It's freaking *pouring* outside, and we're all in the mood to hear a little music. I'll cave and throw in free pitchers for the room if someone can entertain us for a few minutes."

"I play a little."

Brooke followed the voice to a scruffy-looking guy sitting alone at the bar. He was in jeans and a plain white T-shirt and a knit hat even though it was summer. She hadn't noticed him before but decided he might — might — be reasonably cute if he showered, shaved, and lost the hat.

"By all means . . ." The bartender swept her arms toward the piano. "What's your name?"

"Julian."

"Well, Julian, she's all yours." She resumed her position behind the bar as Julian climbed onto the piano bench. He played a few notes, messing around with the timing and rhythm, and the audience lost interest pretty quickly and went back to their conversations. Even when he did quietly play an entire song (something ballad-y she didn't recognize), the music was more like background noise. But after ten minutes he played the intro notes to "Hallelujah," and he started to sing the lyrics in a surprisingly clear, strong voice. The room fell silent.

Brooke had heard the song before, having been briefly obsessed with Leonard Cohen, and had loved it, but the full-body chills were brand-new. She scanned the room.

Were other people feeling this way? Julian's hands moved effortlessly across the keys as he somehow infused each word with intense feeling. Only when he'd murmured the final drawn-out "hallelujah" did the crowd react: they clapped, whistled, screamed, and almost uniformly jumped out of their seats. Julian appeared embarrassed, sheepish, and after an almost imperceptible bow, he began to walk back to his bar stool.

"Damn, he's good," breathed a young girl to her date at the table behind them, her eyes fixed on the piano player.

"Encore!" called an attractive woman who clutched her husband's hand. The husband nodded and echoed her call. Within seconds, the cheering had doubled in volume and the entire room was demanding a second song.

The bartender grabbed Julian's hand and pulled him back toward the microphone. "Pretty amazing, isn't he, guys?" she yelled, beaming with pride at her new discovery. "What do you say we convince Julian here to play us one more?"

Brooke turned to Nola, feeling more excited than she had in ages. "Do you think he's going to play something else? Would you ever believe that some nobody sitting at a random bar on a random Sunday night —

the guy who's there to hear someone *else* perform — can sing like that?"

Nola smiled at her and leaned in to make herself heard above the crowd. "He is really talented. Too bad he looks like that."

Brooke felt as though she'd been personally insulted. "Looks like what? I like that whole scruffy thing he has going on. And with a voice like that, I think he's going to be a star one day."

"Not a chance. He's talented, but so are a million other people who are more outgoing and a whole lot better-looking."

"He's cute," Brooke said a little indignantly.

"He's East Village–gig cute. Not international-rock-star cute."

Before she could leap to Julian's defense, he returned to the bench and began to play again. This time it was a cover of "Let's Get It On," and again, somehow, he managed to sound even better than Marvin Gaye — a deeper, sexier voice, a slightly slower rhythm, and an expression on his face of intense concentration. Brooke was so lost in the experience she barely noticed that her friends had resumed their chitchat as the promised free pitcher of beer made its way around their table. They poured and swallowed and poured some more, but Brooke

28

couldn't take her eyes off the disheveled guy at the piano. When he walked out of the bar twenty minutes later, bowing his head to his appreciative audience and offering the smallest hint of a smile, Brooke seriously considered following him. She'd never done anything like it in her life, but it felt right.

"Should I go introduce myself?" she asked everyone at the table, leaning far enough forward that conversation couldn't continue.

"To whom?" Nola asked.

"To Julian!" This was exasperating. Didn't anyone else realize he'd already stepped outside and would soon disappear forever?

"Julian, the piano man?" Benny asked.

Nola rolled her eyes and took a swig of beer. "What are you going to do? Chase him down and tell him that you can overlook his potential homelessness as long as he'll make sweet love to you atop his piano?"

Benny began to sing. "Well it's nine o'clock on a Sat— Sunday, regular crowd shuffles in. . . ."

"There's a scruffy man sitting next to me, making love to our friend Brooke," Nola finished, laughing. They clinked beer mugs.

"You're both hysterical," Brooke said as she stood.

"No way! You're not following him, are

you? Benny, go with her. Piano Man could be a serial killer," Nola said.

"I'm not following him," Brooke said. But she did make her way to the bar and, after digging her nails into her palms and changing her mind five times, she finally worked up the courage to ask the bartender if she knew anything else about the mystery performer.

The woman didn't look up as she mixed a batch of mojitos. "I've seen him in here before, usually when we have a blues or classic rock band playing, but he never talks to anyone. Always alone, if that's what you're asking . . ."

"No, no, I, uh . . . no, it's not that at all. Just curious," she stammered, feeling like an idiot.

Brooke had turned back toward the table when the bartender called out, "Told me he plays a regular gig at a bar on the Upper East Side, a place called Trick's or Rick's, something like that. Tuesdays. Hope that helps."

Brooke could count on one hand the number of times she'd gone to see live acts. She had never tracked down and followed a strange guy; and, with the exception of ten or fifteen minutes waiting for friends or dates to arrive, she didn't spend a lot of time solo in bars. Yet none of this stopped her from making a half dozen phone calls to find the right place and, after another three weeks working up her nerve, actually getting on the subway one scorching hot Tuesday night in July and walking in the front door of Nick's Bar and Lounge.

Once she sat down, finding one of the last seats in the very back corner, she knew it had been worthwhile. The bar was one of a hundred just like it lining Second Avenue, but the crowd was surprisingly mixed. Instead of the usual Upper East Side mob of recent college grads who liked downing beer after loosening their brand-new Brooks Brothers ties, the group tonight seemed an almost odd mix of NYU students who'd made the trek uptown, couples in their thirties who sipped martinis and held hands, and hordes of Converse-wearing hipsters rarely seen in such concentrations outside the East Village or Brooklyn. Soon Nick's was packed beyond capacity, every seat filled and probably another fifty or sixty people standing behind the tables, all there for only one reason. It shocked Brooke to realize that the way she'd felt when she heard Julian play a month earlier at Rue B's wasn't unique. Dozens of people already knew about him and were willing to travel from all over the city to see him perform.

By the time Julian claimed his seat at the piano and began his checks to make sure the sound was okay, the crowd was buzzing with anticipation. When he began, the room seemed to settle into the rhythm, some people swaying ever so slightly, some with their eyes closed, all with their bodies leaning in toward the stage. Brooke, who had never before understood what it meant to get lost in the music, felt her entire body relax. Whether it was the red wine or the sexy crooning or the foreign feeling of being in a crowd of complete strangers, Brooke was addicted.

She went to Nick's every Tuesday for rest of the summer. She never invited anyone to join her; when her roommates pressed her on where she went each week, she invented a very believable story about a book club with school friends. Just being there, watching him and hearing the music, she began to feel like she knew him. Up until then, music had been a side note, nothing more than a distraction on the treadmill, a fun dance song at a party, a way to kill time on long drives. But this? This was incredible. Without so much as a hello, Julian's music could affect her mood and change her mind and make her feel things that were completely outside the realm of her daily routine.

Until those solo nights at Nick's, her weeks had all looked the same: first work, then the all-too-rare happy hour with the same group of college friends and the same nosy roommates. She was happy enough, but at times it felt suffocating. Now Julian was all hers, and the fact that they never exchanged so much as a glance didn't bother her in the least. She was perfectly content just to watch him. He made the rounds — a bit reluctantly, it appeared to her — after each performance, shaking hands and modestly accepting the praise everyone lavished on him, but Brooke never once considered approaching him.

It was two weeks after September 11, 2001, when Nola convinced her to go on a blind date with a guy she'd met at a work function. All their friends had either fled NYC to see family or rekindled relationships with exes, and the city was still pinned by acrid smoke and an overwhelming grief. Nola had hunkered down with some new guy, spending nearly every night at his apartment, and Brooke was feeling unsettled and lonely.

"A blind date? Really?" Brooke asked, barely looking up from her computer.

"He's a sweetheart," Nola said one night while they sat side by side on the couch watching *SNL*. "He's not going to be your future husband, but he's super nice, and he's cute enough, and he'll take you somewhere good. If you stop being such a frigid bitch, he might even hook up with you."

"Nola!"

"I'm just saying. You could use it, you know. And while we're on the topic, a shower and a manicure wouldn't kill you either."

Brooke held out her hands and noticed, for the first time, bitten-down nails and raggedy cuticles. They really did look gross. "What is he, one of your discards?" she asked.

Nola sniffed.

"He is! You totally hooked up with him and now you're passing him along to me. That's vile, Nol. And I have to say, surprising. Even *you're* not usually that bad."

"Save it," Nola said with a massive roll of her eyes. "I met him a couple weeks ago at some work fund-raiser; he was there with one of my colleagues."

"So you *did* hook up with him."

"No! I may have hooked up with my colleague —"

Brooke groaned and covered her eyes.

"— but that's not important. I remember his friend was cute and single. A med student, I think, but honestly, you're not really at a point to be discriminatory about such things. So long as he's breathing . . ."

"Thanks, friend."

"So you'll go?"

Brooke grabbed for the clicker back again. "If it will make you shut up right now, I'll consider it," she said.

Four days later Brooke found herself sitting at an outdoor Italian café on MacDougal Street. Trent was, as Nola promised, a perfectly sweet guy. Reasonably cute, extremely polite, nicely dressed, and boring as hell. Their conversation was more bland than the linguini with tomato and basil he ordered for them both, and his earnestness left her with the overwhelming desire to plunge a fork into her eyes. Yet for a reason she didn't understand, when he suggested they move on to a nearby bar, she agreed.

"Really?" he asked, sounding every bit as surprised as she felt.

"Yeah, why not?" And really, she thought, why not? It's not like she had any other prospects or even the expectation of watching a movie with Nola later that night. The next day she would have to start outlining a fifteen-page paper that was due in two weeks; besides that, her most exciting plans were the laundry, the gym, and a four-hour shift at the coffee shop. What exactly was she rushing home to?

"Great, I have just the place in mind." Trent sweetly insisted on paying the check and, finally, they were off.

They'd only walked two blocks when Trent crossed in front of her and pulled open the door to a notoriously raucous NYU bar. It was possibly the last place in downtown Manhattan anyone would take a date he wasn't planning to roofie, but Brooke was pleased they'd be going somewhere loud enough to prevent any real conversation. She'd have a beer, maybe two, listen to some good eighties on the jukebox, and be under her covers by midnight — alone.

It took a couple seconds for her eyes to adjust, though she immediately recognized Julian's voice. When she finally focused on the front stage, she stared in disbelief: he sat in his familiar pose at the piano, fingers flying and mouth pressed against the microphone, singing her favorite of his originals: *The woman sits alone in a room / Alone in a house like a silent tomb / The man counts every jewel in his crown / What can't be saved is measured in pounds.* She wasn't sure how long she stood rooted in the doorway, instantly and completely absorbed in his performance, but it was long enough for Trent to comment.

"Pretty great, isn't he? Come on, I see a couple seats over there."

He took her arm and Brooke allowed herself to be pulled through the crowd. She arranged herself in the chair Trent pointed to and had barely placed her purse on the table when the song ended and Julian announced he'd be taking a break. She was vaguely aware that Trent was speaking to her, but between the noise of the bar and the vigil she was keeping on Julian's whereabouts, she didn't hear what he was saying.

It happened so fast she could barely process it. One second Julian was unhooking his harmonica from its piano-top stand and the next he was standing over their table, smiling. As usual, he was wearing a plain white T-shirt and jeans with a knit cap, this one an eggplant color. There was a light sheen of sweat on his face and forearms.

"Hey, buddy, glad you could make it," Julian said, clapping Trent on the shoulder.

"Yeah, me too. Looks like we missed the first set." Someone had just abandoned a chair at the next table, and Trent pulled it over for Julian. "Take a load off."

Julian hesitated, glanced at Brooke with a small smile, and sat. "Julian Alter," he said, offering his hand.

Brooke was about to respond when Trent spoke over her. "Christ, I'm such an idiot! Who taught me my manners, you know? Julian, this is my, uh, this is Brooke. Brooke . . ."

"Greene," she said, pleased with Trent for demonstrating in front of Julian how little they knew each other.

She and Julian shook hands, which seemed like an awkward gesture in a crowded college bar, but Brooke felt only excitement. She examined him more closely as he and Trent exchanged jokes about some guy they both knew. Julian was probably only a couple years older than her, but something made him look more knowing, *experienced,* although Brooke couldn't pinpoint exactly what. His nose was too prominent and his chin a touch weak, and his pale skin even more noticeable now, at the very end of summer, when everyone else had a season's worth of vitamin D. His eyes, while green, were unremarkable, even murky, with fine lines that crinkled around them when he smiled. Had she not heard him sing so many times, seen him throw his head back and call out lyrics in a voice so rich and filled with meaning — had she just ran into him like this, wearing that knit cap and clutching a beer in a loud, anonymous bar — she never would have looked twice, nor thought him the least bit attractive. But tonight, she could barely breathe.

The two guys chatted for a few minutes while Brooke sat back and watched. It was Julian, not Trent, who noticed she didn't have a drink.

"Can I get you guys a beer?" he asked, looking around for a waitress.

Trent immediately stood up. "I'll get them. We just got here and no one's come by yet. Brooke, what would you like?"

She murmured the name of the first beer that came to mind, and Julian held up what looked like an empty water cup. "Can you get me a Sprite?"

Brooke felt a stab of panic when Trent left. What on earth were they going to talk about? Anything, she reminded herself, anything but the fact that she'd followed him all over the city.

Julian turned to her and smiled. "Trent's a good guy, huh?"

Brooke shrugged. "Yeah, he seems nice. We just met tonight. I barely even know him."

"Ah, the always-fun blind date. Do you

39

think you'll go out with him again?"

"No," Brooke said without any emotion whatsoever. She was convinced she was in shock; she barely knew what she was saying.

Julian laughed and Brooke laughed with him. "Why not?" he asked.

Brooke shrugged. "No reason in particular. He seems perfectly pleasant. Just a little boring." She hadn't meant to say that, but she couldn't think straight.

Julian's face broke in a massive smile, one so bright and beaming that Brooke forgot to feel embarrassed. "That's my cousin you're calling boring." He laughed.

"Ohmigod, I didn't mean it like that. He's seems really, uh, great. It just —" The more she stammered, the more amused he appeared.

"Oh, please." He interrupted her, placing his wide, warm hand on her forearm. "You're absolutely, exactly correct. He's a really great guy — honestly, as sweet as they come — but no one's ever described him as the life of the party."

There was a moment of silence as Brooke racked her brain for something appropriate to say next. It didn't much matter what it was, so long as she managed to keep her fan status under wraps.

"I've seen you play before," she announced, before clapping her hand over her mouth in reflexive shock.

He peered at her. "Oh yeah? Where?"

"Every Tuesday night at Nick's." Any chance of not appearing downright stalkerish had just come to a crashing end.

"Really?" He seemed puzzled but pleased.

She nodded.

"Why?"

Brooke briefly considered lying and telling him that her best friend lived nearby or that she went every week with a group for happy hour, but for a reason she herself didn't entirely understand, she was completely truthful. "I was there that night at Rue B's when the jazz quartet canceled and you did that impromptu performance. I thought you, uh, I thought it was awesome, so I asked the bartender for your name and found out you had a regular gig. Now I try to go whenever I can." She forced herself to look up, convinced he'd be staring at her with horror, and possibly fear, but Julian's expression revealed nothing, and his silence only made her more determined to fill it.

"Which is why it was so weird when Trent brought me here tonight . . . such a weird coincidence . . ." She let her words trail off awkwardly and was filled with instant regret at all that she had just revealed.

When she worked up the nerve to meet his eyes once again, Julian was shaking his head.

"You must be creeped out," she said with a nervous laugh. "I promise I'll never show up at your apartment or your day job. I mean, not that I know where your apartment is, or if you even have a day job. Of course, I'm sure music is your day job, your real job, as it should —"

The hand was back on her forearm and Julian met her eye. "I see you there every week," he said.

"Huh?"

He nodded and smiled again, this time shaking his head a little as if to say, *I can't believe I'm admitting this.* "Yeah. You always sit in the far back corner, near the pool table, and you're always alone. Last week you were wearing a blue dress, and it had white flowers or something sewn on the bottom, and you were reading a magazine but you put it away right as I came on."

Brooke remembered the sundress, a gift from her mom to wear at her graduation brunch. Only four months earlier it had felt so stylish; wearing it around the city now made her feel girlishly unsophisticated. The blue did make her red hair look even more

42

fiery, so that was good, but it really did nothing for her hips or legs. So engrossed was she in trying to remember how she'd looked that night, she hadn't noticed Trent return to the table until he pushed a bottle of Bud Light her way.

"What'd I miss?" he asked, sliding into his seat. "Sure is crowded tonight. Julian, dude, you know how to pack 'em in."

Julian clinked his cup with Trent's bottle and took a long drink. "Thanks, buddy. I'll get you back after the show." He nodded to Brooke with what she swore — and prayed — was a knowing look and walked toward the stage.

She didn't know then that he would ask Trent for his permission to call her, or that their first phone conversation would make her feel like she was flying, or that their first date would be a defining night in her life. She never would have predicted that they would fall into bed together less than three weeks later after a handful of marathon dates she had never wanted to end, or that they would save up for nearly two years to drive cross-country together or get engaged while listening to live music at a divey little place in the West Village with a plain gold band he'd paid for entirely on his own, or get married at his parents' gorgeous seaside

Hamptons home because really, what were they proving by refusing a place like that? All she knew for sure that night was that she desperately wanted to see him again, that she would be at Nick's in two nights come hell or high water, and that no matter how hard she tried, she couldn't stop smiling.

2
SUFFER ONE, SUFFER ALL

Brooke stepped into the hallway of the maternal medicine ward at NYU Langone Medical Center and pulled the curtain closed. Eight down, three to go. She rifled through the remaining files: a pregnant teenager, a pregnant woman with gestational diabetes, and a first-time mother struggling to nurse newborn twins. She checked her watch and did a few calculations: if all went as smoothly as she anticipated, she might actually get to leave at a decent hour.

"Mrs. Alter?" Her patient's voice called out from behind the curtain.

Brooke turned back inside.

"Yes, Alisha?" Brooke pulled her white scrub coat tightly around her chest and wondered how this woman wasn't shivering in her paper-thin hospital gown.

Alisha wrung her hands and, staring at her sheet-draped lap, said, "You know how you said the prenatal vitamins were really important? Like, even if I haven't been taking them since the beginning?"

Brooke nodded. "I know it's hard to look on the bright side of severe flu," she said, walking over to the girl's bedside, "but at least it got you in here and will give us a chance to get you started on the vitamins and discuss a plan for the rest of your pregnancy."

"Yeah, so about that . . . is there, um, like some sort of samples you could give me?" Alisha refused to meet her eyes.

"Oh, I don't think that should be a problem," Brooke said, smiling for her patient's sake but irritated with herself for neglecting to inquire whether or not Alisha could afford the prenatals. "Let's see, you've got another sixteen weeks . . . I'll leave the full supply with the nurses' station, okay?"

Alisha looked relieved. "Thanks," she said quietly.

Brooke squeezed the girl's forearm and stepped back outside the curtain. After getting Alisha's vitamins, she half-sprinted to the dietitians' dreary fifth-floor break room, a windowless cubicle with a four-seater Formica table, a mini fridge, and a small wall of lockers. If she hurried, she could cram down a quick snack and a cup of coffee and still make it to her next appointment on time. Relieved to find the room empty and the coffeepot full, Brooke pulled a Tupperware container of precut apple wedges from her locker and began to smear them with travel-sized packets of all-natural peanut butter. At the exact moment her mouth was full, her cell phone rang.

"Is everything okay?" she asked without saying hello. Her words were muffled from the food.

Her mother paused. "Of course, honey. Why wouldn't it be?"

"Because, Mom, it's pretty busy here, and you know I hate talking at work." The overhead intercom drowned out the second half of her sentence.

"What was that? I couldn't hear you."

Brooke sighed. "Nothing, never mind. What's up?" She pictured her mother in her signature khaki pants and Naturalizer flats, the same style she'd worn her entire life, pacing the galley kitchen of her Philadelphia apartment. Despite filling her days with a never-ending stream of book clubs, theater clubs, and volunteer work, it still seemed like her mother had way too much time these days, most of which was filled with calling her children and asking them why they weren't calling back. While it was lovely her mother got to enjoy her retirement, she'd been a lot more hands-off with Brooke when she was teaching from seven to three each day.

"Wait just a minute. . . ." Her mother's voice trailed off and it was momentarily replaced by Oprah's before that, too, abruptly ended. "There we go."

"Wow, you turned off *Oprah*. It must be important."

"She's interviewing Jennifer Aniston again. I can't stand to listen to it anymore. She's over Brad. She's thrilled to be forty-whatever. She's never felt better. We get it. Why do we have to keep talking about it?"

Brooke laughed. "Listen, Mom, can I call you later tonight? I only have fifteen minutes left of break."

"Oh sure, honey. Remind me then to tell you about your brother."

"What's wrong with Randy?"

"Nothing's wrong with Randy — something's finally right. But I know you're busy right now, so let's just talk later."

"Mom . . ."

"It was thoughtless of me to call in the middle of your shift. I wasn't even —"

Brooke sighed loudly and smiled to herself. "Do you want me to beg?"

"Sweetheart, if it's a bad time, it's a bad time. Let's talk when you are more relaxed."

"Okay, Mom, I'm begging you to tell me about Randy. Literally pleading. Please tell me what's up with him. Please?"

"Well, if you're going to be so insistent . . . fine, I'll tell you. Randy and Michelle are pregnant. There, you forced it out of me."

"They're *what?*"

"Pregnant, sweetheart. Having a baby. She's still very early — only seven weeks, I think — but their doctor says all looks well. Isn't that just wonderful?"

Brooke heard the television go on again in the background, quieter this time, but she could still make out Oprah's recognizable laugh.

"Wonderful?" Brooke asked, setting down her plastic knife. "I'm not sure that's the word I'd use. They've only been dating for six months. They're not married. They're not even *living* together."

"Since when are you such a prude, my dear?" Mrs. Greene asked, clucking her tongue. "If you'd ever told me that my educated, urbane, thirty-year-old daughter would be such a traditionalist, I never would've believed it."

"Mother, I'm not sure it's exactly 'traditionalist' to expect that people try to limit baby-making to committed relationships."

"Oh, Brooke, relax a little. Not everyone can — or should — get married at twenty-five. Randy's thirty-eight and Michelle is almost forty. Do you really think anyone cares at this point about some silly little legal document? We should all know well enough by now that it hardly means a thing."

Brooke's mind circled through a number of thoughts: her parents' divorce nearly ten years earlier, when her father left her mother for the school nurse at the high school where they both taught; the way her mother sat Brooke down after her engagement to Julian and told her that women could be perfectly happy these days without getting married; her mother's fervent wish that Brooke wait to start a family until her career was fully established. It was interesting to see that Randy, apparently, operated under a completely different set of guidelines.

"Do you know what I really find amusing?" her mother asked without missing a beat. "The thought that maybe, just maybe, your father and Cynthia will have a baby, too. You know, considering how young she is. Then you'd have a brother *and* a father who are expecting. Really, Brooke, how many girls can say that?"

"Mom . . ."

"Seriously, sweetheart, don't you think it's pretty ironic — well, I'm not sure 'ironic' is the right word, but it's pretty coincidental — that your father's wife is a year younger than Michelle?"

"Mom! Please stop. You know Dad and Cynthia aren't going to have any children — he's going to be sixty-five years old, for god's sake, and she doesn't even want —" Brooke stopped, smiled to herself, shook her head. "You know, maybe you're right, and Dad and Cynthia will jump on the bandwagon. Then Randy and Dad will be able to bond over feeding schedules and naptime. How sweet."

She waited for it and wasn't disappointed.

Her mother snorted. "Please. The closest that man came to a diaper when you two were babies was watching a Pampers commercial. Men don't change, Brooke. Your father won't have anything to do with that child until it is old enough to express a political opinion. But I do think there's hope for your brother."

"Yeah, well, let's hope so. I'll call him tonight to congratulate him, but I have to —"

"No!" Mrs. Greene screeched. "We never had this conversation. I promised I wouldn't tell you, so act surprised when he calls you."

Brooke sighed and smiled. "Great loyalty, Mom. Does that mean you tell Randy everything even when I swear you to secrecy?"

"Of course not. I only tell him when it's interesting."

"Thanks, Mom."

"Love you, sweetheart. And remember, keep this to yourself."

"I promise. You have my word."

Brooke hung up and checked her watch: five minutes to five. Four minutes to get to her next consultation. She knew she shouldn't call right then, but she just couldn't wait.

She remembered as soon as she dialed that Randy could be staying after school to coach the boys' soccer team, but he picked up his cell on the first ring. "Hey, Brookie. What's going on?"

"What's going on with *me?* Not a goddamn thing. What's going on with *you* is a much more relevant question."

"Jesus Christ. I told her no less than eight minutes ago, and she *swore* she'd let me tell you myself."

"Yeah, well, I swore I wouldn't tell you she told me, so whatever. Congratulations, big brother!"

"Thanks. We're both pretty excited. A little

freaked out — it happened a lot faster than either of us expected — but excited."

Brooke felt her breath catch. "What do you mean 'faster'? You *planned* this?"

Randy laughed. She heard him say, "Give me a minute," to someone in the background, a student probably, and then he said, "Yeah, she went off the pill last month. The doctor said it would take at least a couple months for her cycle to regulate before we'd even be able to tell if pregnancy was a possibility due to her age. We just never figured it would happen immediately. . . ."

It was surreal to hear her big brother — an avowed bachelor who decorated his house with old football trophies and dedicated more square footage to his pool table than he did to his kitchen — talk about regulated cycles and birth control pills and doctor's opinions. Especially when all bets would've been on Brooke and Julian as the likeliest candidates to make a big announcement . . .

"Wow. What else can I say? Wow." It really was all she could say; she was worried Randy would hear her voice catch and interpret it the wrong way.

She was so excited for Randy, she felt a lump in her throat. Sure, he managed to take care of himself just fine, and he always seemed happy enough, but Brooke worried about him being so alone. He lived in the suburbs, surrounded by families, and all of his old college buddies had long since had children. She and Randy weren't really close enough to talk about it, but she'd always wondered if he wanted all that or if he was happy with his single life. Now hearing his excitement confirmed how badly he must have longed for this, and she thought she might cry.

"Yeah, it's pretty cool. Can you imagine me teaching the little guy how to throw a pass? I'm going to get him a kid-sized pigskin right from the outset — none of that Nerf crap for my boy — and by the time he's grown into his hands, he'll be ready for the real deal."

Brooke laughed. "So you obviously haven't considered the distinct possibility that you could have a girl, huh?"

"There are three other pregnant teachers at school, and all three of them are having boys," he said.

"Interesting. But you are aware that, although you all share a work environment, your future child and their future children are not required by law or physics to be the same gender, right?"

"I'm not sure about that. . . ."

She laughed again. "So are you guys going to find out? Or is it too early to ask that question?"

"Well, being that I know we're having a boy, I don't really think it's relevant, but Michelle wants to be surprised. So we're going to wait."

"Aw, that's fun. When's the little one due?"

"October twenty-fifth. A Halloween baby. I think that's good luck."

"I do too," Brooke said. "I'm marking it in the calendar right now. October twenty-fifth: I'll be an aunt."

"Hey, Brookie, what about you guys? It'd be pretty nice to have first cousins be close in age. Any chance?"

She knew it was hard for Randy to ask her such a personal question so she was careful not to jump down his throat, but he'd hit a nerve. When she and Julian had married at twenty-five and twenty-seven, respectively, she'd always figured they'd have a baby around her thirtieth birthday. But here they were, already past that and nowhere near even starting to try. She'd broached the subject with Julian a few times, casually so as not to put too much pressure on either of them, but he'd been just as casual with his response. Namely, that a baby would be great "someday," but for now they were doing the right thing focusing on their careers. So although she did want a baby — actually wanted nothing more, *especially* now, hearing Randy's news — she adopted Julian's party line.

"Oh, someday of course," she said, trying to sound nonchalant, the exact opposite of the way she felt. "But now's just not the right time for us. Focusing on work, you know?"

"Sure," Randy said, and Brooke wondered if he knew the truth. "You've got to do what's right for you guys."

"Yeah, so . . . listen, I'm sorry to run but my break's over and I'm late for a consult."

"No worries, Brookie. Thanks for the call. And the excitement."

"Are you kidding me? Thank *you* for the incredible news. You made my whole day — my month. I'm *so* excited for you guys! I'll call later tonight to congratulate Michelle, okay?"

They hung up and Brooke began the trek back to the fifth floor. Incredulous, she couldn't stop shaking her head as she walked. She probably looked like a crazy person, but that would hardly draw attention at the hospital. Randy. A father!

Brooke wanted to call Julian and tell him the news, only he'd sounded so stressed earlier, and there really wasn't time. With one of the other nutritionists out on vacation and an unexplained influx of births that morning — nearly twice the usual amount — her day felt like it was moving at warp speed. It was good: the more she moved, the less time she had to wallow in her exhaustion. Besides, it was exciting and challenging when they got hit like this, and although she complained to Julian and her mother, she secretly loved it: all the different patients from every walk of life, each in the hospital for hugely varied reasons but still in need of someone to fine-tune a diet to their specific condition.

The caffeine hit exactly as planned, and Brooke banged out her final three appointments quickly and efficiently. She had just finished changing from scrubs into jeans and a sweater when one of her colleagues in the break room, Rebecca, announced that their boss wanted to see her.

"Now?" Brooke asked, watching her evening begin to disintegrate.

Tuesdays and Thursdays were sacred: they were the only days of the week she didn't need to leave the hospital and head uptown to her second job, a position as a visiting nutritionist for the Huntley Academy, one of the most elite all-girls private schools on the Upper East Side. The parents of a Huntley alumna who'd died in her twenties of severe anorexia had set up a fund at the school for an experimental program where a nutritionist was available on site to counsel the girls on healthy eating and body image awareness twenty hours a week. Brooke was the second person to staff the fairly new program, and although she'd originally accepted the position solely as a way to supplement her and Julian's income, she had found herself growing more and more attached to the girls. Sure, the anger, the awkwardness, the never-ending obsession with food sometimes wore her down, but she always tried to remind herself that these young patients didn't know any better. Plus the job had the added bonus of giving her more experience working with adolescents, something she lacked.

So Tuesdays and Thursdays she worked only at the hospital, from nine to six. The other three days a week her schedule shifted earlier to accommodate her second job: she worked at NYU from seven in the morning until three in the afternoon and then took two trains and a crosstown bus to get uptown to Huntley, where she'd meet with students — and sometimes their parents — until close to seven. No matter how early she forced herself to bed, and regardless of how much coffee she sucked down when she woke up, she was perpetually exhausted. The dual-job lifestyle was absolutely grueling, but she estimated she needed only one more year of work before being both qualified and experienced enough to open her own private pre- and postnatal nutrition practice, something she'd dreamed about since her very first day of graduate school and the very thing she'd worked diligently toward since then.

Rebecca nodded sympathetically. "She asked if you'd stop in before you left."

Brooke quickly packed up her things and headed back to the fifth floor.

"Margaret?" she called out, knocking on the office door. "Rebecca said you wanted to see me?"

"Come in, come in," her boss said, shuffling some papers on her desk. "Sorry to keep you late, but I figured there was always time for good news."

Brooke sank into the chair opposite Margaret and waited.

"Well, we've finished calculating all of the patient evaluations, and I'm happy to report that you received the highest marks of the entire dietician staff."

"I did?" Brooke asked, barely believing she'd come in first among seven.

"It wasn't even close." Margaret absent-mindedly slicked on some ChapStick, smacked her lips, and returned her gaze to her papers. "Ninety-one percent of your patients evaluated your consultations as 'excellent,' and the remaining nine all ranked them as 'good.' The next best on staff had an 'excellent' rating of eight-two percent."

"Wow," Brooke said, aware that she should be aiming for a little modesty but unable to stop smiling. "That is great news. I'm so happy to hear it."

"So are we, Brooke. We're extremely pleased, and I wanted you to know that your performance doesn't go unnoticed. You'll still be assigned cases in the ICU, but as of next week, we'll be replacing all of your psych shifts with neonatal. I'm assuming that's okay with you?"

"Yes, yes, that's wonderful with me!" Brooke said.

"As you know, you're only the third most senior on staff, but no one else has your background and experience. I think it'll be a perfect fit for you."

Brooke couldn't keep herself from beaming. Finally, that extra year of coursework in child, adolescent, and newborn nutrition in grad school, plus her optional double internship — both in pediatrics — had paid off. "Margaret, I can't thank you enough for everything. That is just the best news ever."

Her boss laughed. "Have a good night. I'll see you tomorrow."

As she walked to the subway, Brooke sent up a silent thanks, both for her semipromotion and, almost better, the fact that she didn't have to deal with any more dreaded psych shifts.

She jumped off the train at the Times Square stop, quickly weaved her way through the masses of people underground, and strategically emerged onto the street at her usual Forty-third Street stairwell, which was closest to their apartment. Not a day went by that she didn't miss their old apartment in Brooklyn — she'd loved nearly everything about Brooklyn Heights and hated almost everything about Midtown West — but even she had to admit that both their commutes were a little less hellish.

She was surprised when Walter, her tricolored spaniel with a black eye-mask patch over one eye, didn't bark when she inserted her key into the apartment door. Nor did he race to greet her.

"Walter Alter! Where are you?" She made kissing noises and waited. Music was playing from somewhere in the apartment.

"We're in the living room," Julian called back. His reply was punctuated by Walter's frenetic, high-pitched woofs.

Brooke dropped her bag just inside the door, kicked off her heels, and noticed that the kitchen was significantly cleaner than she'd left it.

"Hey! I didn't know you were getting home early tonight," she said as she sat down next to Julian on the couch. She leaned over to kiss him but Walter intercepted her and licked her mouth first.

"Mmm, thank you, Walter. I feel so welcome."

Julian muted the television and turned to face her. "I'd be happy to lick your face too, you know. My tongue probably can't compete with a spaniel's, but hey, I'm willing to try." He grinned and Brooke marveled at that fluttery feeling she got when he smiled like that, even after all these years.

"Tempting, I have to say." She ducked around Walter and actually managed to kiss Julian's wine-stained mouth. "You sounded so stressed earlier, I figured you wouldn't be home until so much later. Is everything okay?"

He stood and walked to the kitchen, returning with a second wineglass, which he filled and handed to Brooke. "Everything's fine. I realized after we hung up this afternoon that we haven't spent an evening together in almost a week. I'm here to remedy that."

"You are? Really?" She'd been thinking the same thing for days but hadn't wanted to complain when Julian was at such a crucial point in the production process.

He nodded. "I miss you, Rook."

She wrapped her arms around his neck and kissed him again. "I miss you, too. I'm so glad you came home early. Want to run out for some noodles?"

For their budget's sake, she and Julian made it a point to cook as often as possible, but they both agreed that the cheapie corner noodle joint didn't really count as eating out.

"Do you mind if we stay in? I was looking forward to a quiet evening with you tonight." He took another sip of wine.

"Sure, fine with me. I'll make you a deal. . . ."

"Oh no, here we go. . . ."

"I will go slave over a hot stove to prepare you a delicious and nutritious meal if you agree to rub my feet and back for thirty minutes."

" 'Slave over a hot stove'? You can make a chicken stir-fry in like two minutes. Not a fair deal."

Brooke shrugged. "Okay. There's cereal in the pantry, although I think we're out of milk. You could always make yourself some popcorn."

Julian turned to Walter and said, "You don't know how good you have it, boy. She doesn't make *you* work in exchange for kibble."

"The price just went up to thirty minutes."

"It was already thirty minutes," Julian whined.

"That was thirty minutes total. Now it's thirty minutes feet and another thirty for the back."

Julian pretended to weigh this. "Forty-five minutes and I'll —"

"Any attempts at bargaining only add time onto the total."

He held up his palms. "I'm afraid there's no deal."

"Really?" she asked. "You going to fend for yourself tonight?" she asked, grinning. Julian was an equal partner with the cleaning, bill paying, and dog care, but he was useless in the kitchen and he knew it.

"As a matter of fact, I am. I'm fending for

both of us, actually. I cooked dinner for you tonight."

"You what?"

"You heard me." Somewhere in the kitchen a timer began to beep. "And it's ready as we speak. Please be seated," he said grandly in a faux British accent.

"I am seated," she said, leaning back against the sofa and kicking her feet up on the coffee table.

"Ah, yes," Julian called cheerfully from their miniature kitchen. "I see you've found your way to the formal dining room. Perfect."

"Can I help?"

Julian walked back in holding a Pyrex casserole dish between two oven mitts. "One baked ziti for my love . . ." He was about to set the dish down on the bare wood before Brooke yelped and jumped up to retrieve a trivet. Julian began to spoon the steaming pasta.

Brooke could only stare. "Is this where you tell me you've been having an affair with another woman for the entire duration of our marriage and you want my forgiveness?" she asked.

Julian grinned. "Shut up and eat."

She sat down and helped herself to some salad while Julian continued spooning ziti on her plate. "Baby, this looks incredible. Where did you learn to do this? And why aren't you doing it every night?"

He looked at her with a sheepish smile. "I *may* have picked the ziti up at the store today and just heated it in the oven. That's possible. But it was purchased and heated with love."

Brooke held her wineglass aloft and waited for Julian to clink it. "It's perfect," she said, and meant it. "Absolutely, incredibly perfect."

As they ate, Brooke told him about Randy and Michelle and was pleased to see how happy he was, even going so far as to suggest they drive to Pennsylvania and babysit for their new niece or nephew. Julian brought her up to date on Sony's plans now that the album was nearing completion and told her about the new manager he'd hired on the recommendation of his agent.

"Apparently, he's the best of the best. He does have the reputation of being a little aggressive, but I think that's probably what you want in a manager."

"Well what did he seem like when you interviewed him?"

Julian thought about this. "I'm not sure 'interview' is the right word. It was more like he laid out his entire plan for me. Says we're at a critical junction right now, and it's time to start really 'orchestrating the action.' "

"Well, I can't wait to meet him," Brooke said.

"Yeah, he's definitely got a little of that smarmy Hollywood thing going on — you know, where you feel like they're always working an angle? — but I like how confident he is."

Julian emptied the remainder of the wine bottle evenly between their glasses and sat back in his chair. "How's everything at the hospital going? Was it a crazy day?"

"It was, but guess what? I got the highest ratings in patient evaluations of anyone on staff, and they're going to give me a few more peds shifts." She took another sip from her wineglass; it would be worth the next morning's headache.

Julian broke into a huge smile. "That's great news, Rook. Not the least bit surprising, but absolutely great. I'm so proud of you." He leaned over the table and kissed her.

Brooke did the dishes, then took a bath while Julian finished some work on the new website he was designing for himself, and they met back on the couch, each clad in flannel pajama pants and T-shirts. Julian

67

spread the throw blanket across both their legs and grabbed the clicker.

"Movie?" he asked.

She glanced at the clock on the DVR: ten fifteen. "I think it's too late to start one now, but what about a *Grey's*?"

He looked at her with a horrified expression. "Seriously? Can you, in good conscience, make me watch that after I cooked you dinner?"

She smiled and shook her head. "I'm not quite sure 'cooked' is a fair word, but you're right. Your choice tonight."

Julian scrolled through their DVR list and clicked on a recent *CSI* episode. "Come here, I'll do your feet while we watch."

Brooke flipped herself around so she could rest her legs in his lap. She could've purred with happiness. On television the detectives were examining the mutilated body of a presumed prostitute lying in a landfill outside of Vegas, and Julian watched with rapt attention. She didn't love the gadget-oriented murder mystery stuff as much as he did — he could watch them find killers by scanning and lasering and tracing things all night long — but tonight she didn't mind. She was happy to sit quietly next to her husband and focus on the wonderful sensation of his kneading her feet.

"I love you," she said as she rested her head on the armrest and closed her eyes.

"I love you, too, Brooke. Now be quiet and let me watch."

But she had already drifted off to sleep.

She had just finished getting dressed when Julian walked into their bedroom. Despite the fact that it was Sunday, he looked stressed out.

"We have to go right now, or we're going to be late," he said, grabbing a pair of sneakers from their shared closet. "You know how much my mother loves late."

"I know, I'm almost ready," she said, trying to ignore the fact that she was still sweating from her three-mile run an hour earlier. Brooke trailed Julian out of the bedroom, accepted the wool coat he handed her, and followed him down to the street.

"I'm still unclear why your dad and Cynthia are in the city today," Julian said as they ran-walked from their apartment to the Times Square subway station. The shuttle train appeared the moment they stepped on the platform.

"It's their anniversary," Brooke replied, shrugging. It was unnaturally cold for a March morning, and she desperately wanted a cup of tea from the corner bodega, but they didn't have a second to spare.

"And they decided to come here? On a freezing day in winter?"

Brooke sighed. "I guess it's more exciting than Philly. Apparently Cynthia has never seen *The Lion King* and my dad thought it'd be a good excuse to visit us. I'm just glad you'll get to tell them the news in person. . . ."

She sneaked a look at Julian and saw him smile, just a little. He *should* be proud of himself, she thought. He'd just gotten some of the best news of his career, and he deserved it.

"Yeah, well, I think it's safe to say that my parents are going to be lacking in the enthusiasm department, but maybe your parents will understand," he said.

"My father already tells anyone who will listen that you have the songwriting talent of Bob Dylan and a voice that will make them cry," she said, laughing. "He'll be thrilled, guaranteed."

Julian squeezed her hand. His excitement was palpable.

Brooke managed a weak smile as they transferred to the 6 train.

"What's wrong?" Julian asked.

"Oh, nothing's wrong. I'm so excited for you to tell them all I can barely stand it.

I'm just slightly dreading having to deal with the awkwardness of both sets of parents in one room."

"Do you really think it's going to be that bad? It's not like they haven't all met before."

Brooke sighed. "I know, but they've only really seen each other in big groups: our wedding, holidays. But never one-on-one like this. All my father wants to talk about is how the Eagles will do next season. Cynthia is excited to be seeing *The Lion King,* for chrissake, and thinks no trip to the city is complete without lunch at the Russian Tea Room. Then we have your parents: the most intense, intimidating lifelong New Yorkers I've ever met, who probably think the NFL is a French nonprofit group, who haven't seen a musical since the sixties, and who won't eat anything unless it's prepared by a celebrity chef. You tell me: what are they all going to say to each other?"

Julian squeezed the back of her neck. "It's brunch, baby. Some coffee, a few bagels, and we're out. I really think it's going to be fine."

"Yeah, sure, as my dad and Cynthia blather on nonstop in their manically happy way and your parents sit in stony, silent judgment of them. Sounds like a delightful

Sunday morning."

"Cynthia can talk shop with my parents," Julian offered meekly. He made that face that said, *I don't even believe this myself,* and Brooke started to laugh.

"Tell me you didn't say that," she said, her eyes starting to tear up as she laughed harder. They emerged at Seventy-seventh and Lex and began walking toward Park Avenue.

"Well, it's true!"

"You're so sweet, do you know that?" Brooke asked, leaning over to kiss his cheek. "Cynthia is a high school nurse. She watches out for strep throats and gives out Motrin for cramps. She knows nothing about whether Botox or Restylane is recommended for a particularly deep smile line. I'm not sure where their professional experiences overlap."

Julian feigned offense. "I think you're forgetting that Mom was also named one of the best in the country at varicose vein removal," he said with a grin. "You know how big that was."

"Yes, of course. Big."

"All right, I hear what you're saying. But my dad can talk to anyone. You know how easygoing he is. He'll make Cynthia love him."

"He's a great guy," Brooke agreed. She grabbed his hand as they approached the Alters' building. "But the man *is* a world-renowned breast augmentation specialist. It's only natural that a woman would assume he's sizing up her breasts and finding them inadequate."

"Brooke, that's idiotic. Do you assume that all dentists you encounter in social situations are staring at your teeth?"

"Yes."

"Or any psychologist you meet at a party is analyzing you?"

"Absolutely, one hundred percent, beyond a doubt."

"Well that's just ridiculous."

"Your father examines, handles, and evaluates breasts eight hours a day. I'm not suggesting he's some pervert, but it's his *instinct* to check them out. Women can feel it, that's all I'm saying."

"Well, that begs the obvious question now."

"Yeah?" she asked, glancing at her watch as their awning came into view.

"Do you feel like he's checking out your breasts when he sees you?" Poor Julian looked so crushed at the mere mention of it that Brooke wanted to hug him.

"No, baby, of course not," she whispered

as she leaned in and hugged his arm. "At least, not after all these years. He knows the situation, and he knows he's never getting his hands on them, and I think he's finally over it."

"They're perfect, Brooke. Just perfect," Julian said automatically.

"I know. That's why your dad offered to do them at cost when we got engaged."

"He offered his *partner,* and not because he thought you needed it —"

"Why, because *you* thought I needed it?" Brooke knew that wasn't it at all — they'd talked about it a hundred times and she knew that Dr. Alter had only offered his services the way a tailor would have offered a discounted custom suit — but the whole thing still irked her.

"Brooke . . ."

"Sorry. I'm just hungry. Hungry and nervous."

"It's not going to be nearly as bad as you're anticipating."

The doorman greeted Julian with a high five and a backslap. It wasn't until he ushered them into the elevator and they were whisking up toward the eighteenth floor that Brooke realized she hadn't brought anything.

"I think we should run back out and pick

up some cookies or flowers or something," Brooke said, tugging Julian's arm urgently.

"Come on, Rook, it doesn't matter. They're my *parents.* They really don't care."

"Uh-huh. If you believe your mother isn't going to notice when we show up empty-handed, you're delusional."

"We're bringing ourselves. That's all that matters."

"Okay. You just keep telling yourself that."

Julian knocked and the door swung open. Smiling at them from the doorway was Carmen, the Alters' nanny and housekeeper of thirty years. In a particularly intimate moment early in their relationship, Julian had confided to Brooke that he called Carmen "Mommy" until his fifth birthday because he just hadn't known any better. She immediately flung her arms around Julian.

"How's my baby?" Carmen asked him after smiling at Brooke and pecking her on the cheek. "Your wife here feeding you enough?"

Brooke squeezed Carmen's arm, wondering for the thousandth time why Carmen *couldn't* be Julian's mother, and said, "Does he look like he's starving, Carmen? I have to pry the fork from his hands some nights."

"That's my boy," she said, gazing at him with pride.

A shrill voice came from the formal living room down the hallway. "Carmen, darling, send the children in here, please. And don't forget to snip the stems before you the put the flowers in a vase. The new Michael Aram one, please."

Carmen glanced around for the flowers but Brooke merely held out her empty hands. She turned to Julian and gave him a knowing look.

"Don't say it," Julian muttered.

"Fine. I won't say I told you so because I love you."

Julian led her into the formal living room — Brooke had been hoping they would skip the living room altogether and move straight to the eating part — and found both sets of parents sitting opposite each other on identical, low-profile, ultra-modern couches.

"Brooke, Julian." His mother smiled but didn't stand. "So glad you could join us."

Brooke immediately interpreted this as an attack on their tardiness. "So sorry we're late, Elizabeth. The subways were just so —"

"Well, at least you're here now," Dr. Alter said, both hands cupped rather effeminately around a fat orange juice glass, exactly the way she imagined he cradled all his breasts.

"Brookie! Julian! What's up, guys?"

Brooke's dad jumped up and embraced them both in one bear hug. He was clearly turning up the camp factor for the Alters' benefit, but Brooke couldn't really blame him.

"Hi, Dad," she said, hugging him back. She also walked over to Cynthia, who remained trapped by all of their bodies on the couch and gave her an awkward standing-sitting hug. "Hey, Cynthia. Good to see you."

"Oh, you too, Brooke. We're so excited to be here! Your father and I were just saying that we can barely remember the last time we were in New York."

It was only then that Brooke was able to really absorb Cynthia's appearance. She wore a fire-engine-red pantsuit, probably polyester, with a white blouse, black patent leather flats, and a triple strand of faux pearls wrapped around her neck, and topped off the entire ensemble with a highly curled and lacquered updo. She looked like she was channeling Hillary Clinton at a State of the Union address, determined to stand out in a sea of dark suits. Brooke knew she was only trying to fit in with her notion of how a wealthy Manhattan woman might dress, but her calculations were all wrong, especially in the midst of the Alters' sleek, Asian-inspired apartment. Julian's mother — although twenty years older than Cynthia — looked ten years younger in her fitted, dark jeans and featherweight cashmere wrap over a sleeveless, stretchy tunic. She wore a pair of delicate ballet flats with a discreet Chanel logo and accessorized only with a single gold bangle and her massive diamond ring. Her skin glowed with a healthy tan and light makeup, and her hair swung loosely down her back. Brooke immediately felt guilty: she knew how intimidated Cynthia must feel — after all, Brooke felt that way in her mother-in-law's presence all the time — but she was also embarrassed at how badly she had miscalculated. Even Brooke's dad looked uncomfortably aware that his khakis and tie were out of place next to Dr. Alter's short-sleeve polo shirt.

"Julian, sweetheart, I know you want a Bloody. Brooke, would you like a mimosa?" Elizabeth Alter asked. It was a simple question but, much like everything the woman asked, it felt like a trap.

"Actually, I'd love a Bloody Mary as well."

"Of course." Julian's mom pursed her lips in some sort of indefinable drink disapproval. To this day, Brooke wasn't sure whether her mother-in-law's dislike of her

78

had to do with Julian and the fact that Brooke supported his musical ambitions, or if the woman found Brooke distasteful all on her own.

They were left no choice but to take the two remaining chairs — both straight backed, wooden, and unwelcoming — that sat opposite each other but were wedged between both couches. Feeling vulnerable and awkward, Brooke tried to jumpstart the conversation.

"So, how were your weeks?" she asked the Alters, smiling at Carmen as she accepted a tall, thick Bloody Mary complete with lemon wedge and celery stalk. It was all she could do not to drain the whole thing in one gulp. "Busy as always?"

"Yes, I just cannot even imagine how you both maintain schedules like that!" Cynthia said a bit too loudly. "Brooke's told me how many, uh, procedures you both do in a day, and well, it's enough to exhaust anybody! Me, I get a strep outbreak and I'm ready to collapse, but you two! Geez Louise, it must be madness."

Elizabeth Alter's face broke into a wide, immensely condescending smile. "Yes, well, we do manage to keep busy. But isn't that so boring! I'd love to hear what's going on with the children. Brooke? Julian?"

Cynthia sat back, deflated and properly reprimanded. The poor woman was walking through a minefield she was helpless to navigate. She absentmindedly rubbed her forehead and looked suddenly very tired. "Yes, of course. How are you two doing?"

Brooke knew better than to offer any details about her own job. Although her mother-in-law had been the one to get Brooke the interview at Huntley, she'd done so only after thoroughly satisfying herself that Brooke wouldn't reconsider a career in magazines, fashion, auction houses, or public relations. If Brooke simply *had* to use that graduate degree in nutrition, she couldn't understand why she didn't at least serve in an advisory role to *Vogue* or serve as a private consultant to her legion of Upper East Side friends; anything, really, with a little more glamour than, in her words, "a dingy ER with homeless people and drunks."

Julian knew enough to step in and save her. "Well, I actually have a little announcement," he said with a cough.

Suddenly, although Brooke was so excited for Julian she could barely contain it, a wave of panic washed over her. She found herself *praying* he wouldn't tell them about the showcase, since he'd undoubtedly be disappointed by their reaction and she hated to watch him go through that. No one brought out that protective instinct in her like Julian's parents; the mere thought of what they'd say made Brooke want to bundle him up and take him straight home, where he'd be shielded from their meanness and, worse, their indifference.

They all waited a moment while Carmen brought in a new pitcher of freshly squeezed grapefruit juice and then turned their attention back to Julian.

"I, uh, just heard from my new manager, Leo, that Sony wants to showcase me this week. Thursday, actually."

There was a beat of silence when everyone expected someone else to say something, and Brooke's father was the first one to speak. "Well, I might not know exactly what showcasing is, but it sure sounds like good news. Congratulations, son!" he said, leaning across Cynthia to clap Julian on the back.

Dr. Alter, looking irritated at the use of "son," scowled into his coffee before turning to Julian. "Why don't you explain to we laypeople what that means?" he asked.

"Yes, does that mean someone is finally going to hear your music?" Julian's mother asked, tucking her feet under her like a young girl and smiling at her son. Everyone pointedly ignored the emphasis on "finally" — everyone except Julian, whose face registered the hit, and Brooke, who witnessed it.

After all these years Brooke was certainly accustomed to hearing Julian's parents say awful things, but she never hated them any less for it. When she and Julian were first dating, he had slowly revealed how fundamentally his parents disapproved of him and of the life he'd chosen. During their engagement, she'd seen their objection to the plain gold band Julian insisted on giving Brooke rather than one of the "Alter family estate pieces" his mother had pushed. Even when Brooke and Julian conceded to marrying at the Alters' home in the Hamptons, his parents had been horrified at the couple's insistence that the wedding be small, low-key, and off-season. After they were married and in the years since, when the Alters acted more freely in front of her, she saw at countless dinners and brunches and holidays just how toxic they could be.

"Well, basically it means that they realize the album is close to being finished and they really like it so far. They're going to arrange a showcase of industry people, sort of introduce me to them in a private performance, and then gauge the reaction." Julian, who was usually so modest he wouldn't even tell Brooke when he'd had a good day at the recording studio, couldn't help but beam with pride. She wanted to kiss him on the spot.

"I might not know a whole lot about the music industry, but that sounds like a huge vote of confidence on their part," Brooke's dad said, holding his glass aloft.

Julian couldn't contain his smile. "It is," he said, grinning. "It's probably the best-case scenario right now. And I'm hoping —"

He stopped as the phone began to ring and Julian's mother immediately began to look around for a handset. "Oh, where is that damn phone? That must be L'Olivier calling to confirm a time for tomorrow. Hold that thought, dear. If I don't reserve them now, I'm not going to have flowers for tomorrow night's party." And with that, she unfolded herself from the couch and disappeared into the kitchen.

"You know your mother with her flowers," Dr. Alter said. He sipped his coffee, and it was unclear whether or not he'd even heard Julian's announcement. "We're having the Bennetts and the Kamens over for dinner tomorrow and she's been in a tizzy about the planning. Christ, you'd think the decision between stuffed sole or braised short ribs was a matter of national security. And the flowers! She must have spent half the afternoon with those *fegelas* last weekend, and she's still wavering. I told her a thousand times: no one cares about the flowers; no one will notice. Everyone throws these lavish weddings and spends tens of thousands of dollars on mountains of orchids or whatever the hell is in fashion these days, and who ever even looks at the damn things? Such a colossal waste, if you ask me. Spend the money on great food and booze — that's what people really enjoy." He took another gulp, looked around the room, and squinted. "Now, what were we talking about?"

Cynthia gracefully stepped in and smoothed over the tense moment. "Well isn't that just some of the greatest news we've heard in ages!" she said with excessive enthusiasm. Brooke's dad nodded excitedly. "Where exactly will it be held? How many people are invited? Have you decided yet what you're going to play?" Cynthia peppered him with questions and for once Brooke didn't find the interrogation irritating. They were all the things Julian's own parents should have asked but never would, and Julian was clearly delighted to be on the receiving end of such interest.

"It'll be at a small, really intimate downtown music venue, and my agent said they were inviting about fifty people in the industry — television and radio bookers, music execs, some people from MTV, that sort of thing. Most likely nothing too exciting will come of it, but it's a good sign that the label is happy with the album."

"They rarely do these for their debut artists," Brooke announced with pride. "Julian's actually being too modest — it's a very big deal."

"Well at least *that's* good news," his mother announced, taking her seat on the couch again.

Julian's mouth tightened and his fists clenched by his sides. "Mom, they've been supportive with the way the album's been taking shape for months now. Sure, the senior execs were pushing for more of a guitar focus, but ever since then, they've been great. So I don't know why you have to say it like that."

Elizabeth Alter looked at her son and appeared momentarily confused. "Oh, sweetheart, I was talking about L'Olivier. It's good news that they have enough of the calla lilies I was wanting, and the designer I like the most is available to come over and install them. Don't be so touchy."

Brooke's father glanced at her with a look that said, *Who is this woman?* Brooke shrugged. She, like Julian, had accepted that his parents were never going to change. It was why she stood by him a hundred percent when he rejected their offer to buy the newlyweds an apartment near theirs on the Upper East Side. It was why she chose to work two jobs rather than take the "allowance" they'd once proposed, understanding all the strings that would accompany it.

By the time Carmen announced brunch was ready, Julian had gone completely silent and glazed over — turtled, Brooke always called it — and Cynthia looked rumpled and exhausted in her polyester pantsuit. Even Brooke's dad, who still valiantly searched for neutral conversation ("Do you believe this brutal winter we're having this year?" and "You into baseball, William? Yanks seem like an obvious choice, but I know a man's team isn't always determined by where he's from. . . .") appeared defeated. Under normal circumstances Brooke would have felt responsible for everyone's misery — after all, they were all only there because of her and Julian, right? — but today she let it all go. *Suffer one, suffer all,* she thought, and excused herself to use the powder room, which she bypassed immediately for the kitchen.

"How's it going out there, love?" Carmen asked as she spooned apricot jam into a sterling silver bowl.

Brooke held out her empty Bloody Mary glass and paired it with a pleading look.

"That bad?" Carmen laughed and motioned for Brooke to pull the vodka from the freezer as she prepared the tomato juice and Tabasco sauce. "How are your parents holding up? Cynthia seems like a real nice lady."

"Uh-huh, she's lovely. They're grown-ups and they made their own idiotic choice to come visit. It's Julian I'm worried about."

"Nothing he hasn't seen before, love. No one deals with them better."

Brooke sighed. "I know. But he's depressed for days afterward."

Carmen plunged a celery stalk into the thick Bloody Mary and handed it to Brooke. "Reinforcement," she announced, and kissed Brooke on the forehead. "Now get back out there and protect your man."

The actual eating part of brunch wasn't half as bad as the cocktail hour. Julian's mother threw a minor hissy fit over the crepe filling (although everyone else loved the chocolate ones Carmen whipped up, Elizabeth thought they were far too fattening for an actual meal), and Dr. Alter disappeared for a spell into his study, but as a result, neither of them insulted their son for more than an hour. Good-byes were blessedly painless, but by the time she and Julian put her father and Cynthia into a cab, she could see Julian was withdrawn and unhappy.

"You okay, baby? My dad and Cynthia were so excited. And I can barely —"

"I don't feel like talking about it, okay?"

They walked in silence for a couple minutes.

"Hey, we have the whole rest of the day free. Absolutely nothing to do. Want to go to a museum while we're up here?" Brooke asked, taking his hand and tugging gently on his arm as they walked toward the subway.

"Nah, I don't think I'm up for the Sunday crowds."

She thought for a moment. "You've been wanting to see that 3-D IMAX movie for a while. I wouldn't mind going with you," she lied. Desperate times called for desperate measures.

"I'm fine, Brooke. I really am," Julian said quietly, pulling on his wool scarf. She knew he was the one lying now.

"Can I invite Nola to the showcase? It sounds so fabulous, and you know Nola can't miss any opportunity at fabulousness."

"I guess, but Leo said it's going to be really small, and I already invited Trent. He's only in New York on this rotation another couple weeks and he's been working like crazy. I thought he could use a night out."

They talked more about the showcase, and they discussed what he would wear, which songs he would play, and in what order. She was happy she could draw him out, and by the time they reached their apartment, Julian seemed almost like himself.

"Have I told you how proud I am of you?" Brooke asked when they stepped onto their own elevator, both clearly relieved to be home.

"Yeah," Julian said with a small smile.

"Well, come inside, baby," Brooke said, pulling him down the hallway by the hand. "I think it's about time I showed you."

3

MAKES JOHN MAYER LOOK LIKE AMATEUR HOUR

"Where are we?" Brooke grumbled, stepping out of the cab and looking around the dark and deserted side street in West Chelsea. The tall black pull-on boots she'd found at an end-of-season sale kept sliding down her tights.

"Heart of the gallery district, Brooke. Avenue and 1 OAK are right around the corner."

"I should know what those are, shouldn't I?"

Nola just shook her head. "Well, at least you look good. Julian's going to be proud to have such a hot wife tonight."

Brooke knew her friend was just being kind. It was Nola who, as usual, looked stunning. She'd jammed her suit jacket and her sensible pumps into her oversized LV tote and replaced them with a massive multistrand necklace and a pair of those sky-high Louboutin heels that were somewhere between a bootie and sandal, a style approximately six women on earth could pull off without being mistaken for a professional dominatrix. Things that would look downright trashy on everyone else — scarlet lipstick, flesh-colored fishnets, and the black lace bra that peeked through her sheer tank — on Nola managed to look both edgy and playful. Her pencil skirt, which as one-half of an expensive suit had been appropriate enough for one of the most conservative work environments on Wall Street, now showed off her toned backside and perfect legs. If Nola had been any other female on earth, Brooke would have hated her mightily.

Brooke looked at her BlackBerry. "Between Tenth and Eleventh. That's exactly where we are, isn't it? Where is this place?" She saw a darting shadow out of the corner of her eye and yelped.

"Oh relax, Brooke. It's much more scared of you than you are of it." Nola waved off the rat spotting with a cocktail-ring-adorned hand.

Brooke hurried to cross the street, seeing that the even-numbered addresses they wanted were on the opposite side. "Easy for you to say. You could pierce its heart with one stomp of that heel. My dumpy flat boots put me at heightened risk."

Nola laughed and scampered gracefully behind Brooke. "There, I think that's it," she said, pointing to the only building on the block that didn't look condemned.

The girls followed a small staircase down from the sidewalk to a windowless basement door. Julian had explained that these kinds of showcases were constantly on the move, and music-biz people were always looking for the next hip place to help generate buzz, but still, she had been envisioning a venue somewhere that looked like a smaller version of Joe's Pub. What was this? No line fanning out to the sidewalk. No marquee announcing the night's talent. There wasn't even the requisite sullen girl with a clipboard, petulantly telling everyone to take a step back and wait his turn.

Brooke felt a small wave of anxiety until she heaved open the vaultlike door, stepped inside, and was enveloped in a warm cocoon of semidarkness and low laughter and the subtle but unmistakable scent of marijuana. The entire space was the size of a large living room, and everything — the walls, the sofas, even the paneling on the small corner bar — was swathed in plush burgundy velvet. A single lamp rested atop the piano and cast a soft light onto the empty stool.

Hundreds of tiny votives were magnified by the mirrored tabletops and ceiling, a look that somehow managed to be impossibly sexy without so much as a twinge of eighties-throwback.

The crowd looked like they had been hand-plucked from a poolside cocktail party in Santa Barbara and dropped in New York City. Forty or fifty mostly young and attractive people milled about, sipping from low-ball glasses and exhaling plumes of cigarette smoke in long, languorous wafts. The men were dressed almost uniformly in jeans, and the few who still wore their daytime suits had ditched their ties and loosened their top buttons. Almost none of the women wore stilettos or the short, tight black cocktail dresses that made up the Manhattan uniform; instead, they were all roaming about in beautifully printed tunics and tinkling beaded earrings and jeans so perfectly worn in that Brooke actually yearned to strip out of her black sweater dress then and there. Some had hippie-chic headbands around their foreheads and beautiful hair falling to their waists. No one appeared the least bit self-conscious or stressed out — another Manhattan unlikelihood — which of course made Brooke doubly anxious. This was a far cry from Julian's usual audiences.

Who were all these people and why did each and every one of them look a thousand times better than she did?

"Breathe," Nola whispered in her ear.

"If I'm this nervous, I can't even imagine how Julian feels."

"Come on, let's find ourselves some drinks." Nola flung her blond hair over her shoulder and held out a hand for Brooke, but before they could move through the crowd, Brooke heard a familiar voice.

"Red, white, or stronger?" Trent asked, magically appearing next to them. He was one of the only men in a suit and looked uncomfortable. It was probably his first time away from the hospital in weeks.

"Hey there!" Brooke said, hugging him around the neck. "You remember Nola, right?"

Trent smiled. "Of course I do." He turned to Nola and kissed her on the cheek. There was something in his tone that said *Of course I remember meeting you, because you randomly went home with my friend that night and he was very impressed with both your willingness and your creativity in the bedroom.* But Trent was much too discreet to joke about it, even after all these years.

Not so with Nola. "How is Liam? God, he was fun," she said with a huge smile. "Like,

94

really fun."

Trent and Nola exchanged knowing looks and laughed.

Brooke held up a hand. "Okay then. Trent, congratulations on the engagement! When do we get to meet her?" She couldn't bring herself to say Fern's name, didn't trust herself to say it without laughing. What kind of name was *Fern?*

"Considering we are almost never *not* at the hospital at the same time, possibly not until the wedding."

The bartender motioned to Trent, who turned to the girls.

"Red, please," they said in unison, and all three watched as the bartender poured from a bottle of California cabernet. Trent handed them each a glass and downed his own in two swift swallows.

He turned to Brooke with a sheepish look on his face. "I don't get out much."

Nola excused herself to do a loop of the room.

Brooke smiled at Trent. "So tell me about her. Where's the wedding going to be?"

"Well, Fern's from Tennessee and has a huge family, so we're probably just going to do it at her parents' place. Next February, I think."

"Wow, moving right along. Well, that's

great news."

"Yeah, the only way we can be matched at the same place for our residencies is if we're married."

"So you're both continuing on with gastro?"

"Yeah, that's the plan. My interests are more in the scoping and testing area — they're doing some incredibly high-tech things these days — but Fern is more a Crohn's/celiac kind of person." Trent paused for a moment and appeared to reflect on this before breaking into a wide smile. "She's a great girl. I really think you'll like her."

"Hey, buddy!" Julian said, clapping Trent on the back. "Of course we'll like her. She's going to be your *wife*. How crazy is that?" Julian leaned over and kissed Brooke full on the lips. He tasted delicious, like chocolate mint, and just seeing him was reassuring.

Trent laughed. "Not as crazy as the fact that my socially stunted cousin has had himself a wife for five *years* now, but it's up there."

It was on nights like this that Brooke couldn't be prouder to be Julian's wife. He was wearing his uniform, unchanged even after all these years: white T-shirt, Levi's, and a knit cap. The outfit couldn't have been less exceptional, but it had come to signify pure sexiness to Brooke. The cap was Julian's signature, the closest thing he had to a "look," but only Brooke knew it was more than that. Just last year Julian had been crushed to discover the tiniest bald spot in the history of hair loss. Brooke tried to assure him that it was barely noticeable, but Julian would hear none of it. And truth be told, it *may* have gotten slightly bigger since he'd first pointed it out, although she'd never admit it.

No one who saw all those luscious dark curls peeking out from under the cap would ever guess what Julian was trying to cover up underneath it, and for Brooke, it only added to Julian's appeal, made him more vulnerable and human. She secretly loved that she was the only one who ever got to see Julian without the cap, when he would safely pull it off at home and shake his curls just for her. Had someone told Brooke a few years earlier that she'd find her thirty-two-year-old husband's increasing baldness to be one of his most appealing qualities she would've laughed with disbelief, but that is exactly what had happened.

"How are you feeling? Are you nervous?" Brooke asked, searching his face for a hint as to how he was holding up. He'd been a wreck all week — barely eating, never sleeping, even vomiting earlier that afternoon — but when Brooke tried to talk to him about it, he'd completely turtled. She had wanted to accompany him to the venue that night, but Julian insisted she go with Nola. He said he needed to talk through a few things with Leo, get there early, make sure everything was set up. Something must have worked, because he looked a little more relaxed.

"I'm ready," he said with a determined nod. "I'm feeling good."

Brooke kissed him on the cheek, knowing he was racked with nerves but proud of him for holding it together. "You look good. You look ready. You're going to be fantastic tonight."

"You think so?" He sipped his club soda, and Brooke noticed his knuckles were white. She knew he was dying for something stronger, but he never drank before a performance.

"I know so. When you're sitting at that piano, all you're thinking about is the music. Tonight is no different from doing a gig at Nick's. The crowd always loves you, baby. Remember that. Just be yourself, and they're going to love you here too."

"Listen to her," said an unfamiliar male voice. When Brooke turned around, there stood one of the best-looking guys she had ever laid eyes on. He was at least six inches taller than her, which immediately made Brooke feel girlishly slight and dainty. She wished for the umpteenth time that Julian were as tall as this mystery man but then forced the thought from her head; Julian probably wished Brooke's body was more like Nola's, so what right did she have? The guy wrapped an arm around Brooke's back and squeezed her left shoulder, so close she could smell his cologne. Masculine, subtle, and expensive. She blushed.

"You must be the wife," he said, leaning down to kiss the top of her head, a gesture that felt oddly intimate and impersonal at the same time. His voice was not nearly as deep as Brooke would've expected from someone of his height and obvious level of fitness.

"Leo, I'd like you to meet Brooke," Julian said. "Brooke, this is Leo, new manager extraordinaire."

A gorgeous Asian girl walked by at that exact moment and both Brooke and Julian watched as Leo winked at her. Where the hell was Nola? She needed to warn her early and often that Leo was off-limits. It wasn't going to be easy — Leo was exactly her type. His pink dress shirt was open one button more than most men would dare, and it highlighted his lovely tan — dark enough but without a hint of booth or aerosol. His pants were low-waisted and European slim. He dressed as though his hair should've been slicked back with heavy product, but he smartly let his thick, dark locks wave freely just over his eyes. The only flaw she could make out was a scar that bisected his right eyebrow in a hairless dividing line, but it actually worked to his benefit, taking away any hint of effeminate over-grooming or perfection. He didn't have an ounce of fat on his entire body.

"Pleasure to meet you, Leo," Brooke said. "I've heard so much about you."

He didn't appear to hear. "Okay, listen," he said, turning to Julian. "I just got word that you're scheduled as the final act. One down, one to go, then you." Leo peered intently over Julian's shoulder as he talked.

"Is that good news?" Brooke asked politely. Julian had already told her that none of the other musicians scheduled to perform that night were in any real competition. One was an R&B group who everyone thought sounded like a modern-day Boyz II Men, and the other was a heavily tattooed female country singer who wore frilly dresses and her hair in pigtails.

She looked at Leo and saw that once again, his gaze had wandered. Brooke followed it and saw he was staring directly at Nola. Or, more precisely, Nola's pencil-skirt-swathed bum. She made a mental note to threaten Nola with banishment and worse if she went anywhere near him.

Leo cleared his throat and took a swig of whiskey. "The chick went already, and she was decent. Not mind-blowing, but mildly entertaining. I think —"

He was cut off by the sound of voices harmonizing. There wasn't a stage, exactly, but there was a cleared area in front of the piano where four African-American men in their early twenties stood, each leaning in toward a central microphone. For a moment it sounded like a really good college a capella group, but then three of the guys stepped back and left the main singer alone to croon about his childhood in Haiti. The crowd nodded and grooved appreciatively.

"Listen, Julian," Leo said. "Just forget where you are and why you're here and do your thing. Got it?"

Julian nodded and tapped his foot furiously. "Got it."

Leo motioned toward the area in the back of the room. "Let's get you set up."

Brooke stood on her tiptoes and kissed

Julian on the mouth. She squeezed his hand and said, "I'll be right here the whole time, but forget about all of us. Just close your eyes and play your heart out."

He shot her a grateful look but couldn't bring himself to say anything. Leo led him off, and before she could finish her wine, one of the A&R guys announced Julian over the microphone.

Brooke looked around again for Nola and spotted her talking to a group of people in front of the bar. That girl knew everyone. Happy to have Trent there, Brooke let him lead her to a little sliver of couch space, where he motioned for her to take a seat. She perched herself on the end of a velvet sofa and nervously gathered her hair into a knot. She rooted around in her bag for a hair tie but couldn't find one.

"Here," said the beautiful Asian girl Leo had winked at earlier. She pulled a brown elastic off her wrist and handed it to Brooke. "I have a million."

Brooke paused for a minute, unsure what to do, and the girl smiled. "Really, it's fine. There's nothing more annoying than not being able to get hair off your face. Although if I had your hair, I'd never tie it back."

"Thanks," Brooke said, accepting the tie and immediately twisting it into her ponytail. She was going to say something more, maybe something self-deprecating about how she wouldn't wish being a redhead on anyone, but at that moment Julian took his seat at the piano, and she heard his voice, a little shaky, thanking everyone for coming.

The girl took a swig from the bottle of beer she was holding and asked, "Have you ever heard him before?"

Brooke could only nod and pray the girl would stop talking. She didn't want to miss a single moment, and she was totally preoccupied wondering if anyone else could hear the slight wobble in Julian's voice.

"Because if not, you're really in for something. He is the sexiest singer I've ever seen."

This caught her attention. "What?" she asked, turning to the girl.

"Julian Alter," the girl said, waving toward the piano. "I've heard him a couple times in different venues around the city. He has a few regular gigs. And I'm telling you, he's ridiculously good. Makes John Mayer look like amateur hour."

Julian had begun to play "For the Lost," a soulful song about a young boy who loses his older brother, and she felt Trent glance in her direction — he was probably the only other person in the entire room who knew what truly inspired that song. Julian himself was an only child, but Brooke knew he often thought of the brother who had died of SIDS before Julian was born. To this day the Alters never discussed James, but Julian had gone through a stage where he wondered, sometimes obsessively, what James would've been like today, how different life might have been with an older brother.

His hands moved across the piano keys, producing the first haunting notes that would eventually build to a powerful crescendo, but Brooke couldn't focus on anything but the girl beside her. She wanted to hug her and slap her all at the same time. It was disconcerting to hear this perfectly attractive girl rave about Julian's sexiness — no matter how long they'd been together, she never got used to that aspect — but it was so rare to hear a totally honest and unfiltered opinion.

"You think so?" Brooke asked, suddenly desperate for the girl to agree.

"Oh, definitely. I tried to tell my boss, like, a dozen times, but Sony got him first." The girl's attention to Brooke started to wane as Julian's volume increased, and by the time he tilted his head and sang out the raw, emotional chorus, she was fixated only on him. Brooke wondered if she noticed Julian's wedding band through the haze of worship.

Brooke turned to watch, and it was all she could do not to sing along. She knew every word by heart.

They say Texas is the promised land
In the highway's dust you become a man
Blind and blue, lonely in love
Scars on your hands, broken above

He was a mother's dream, he was a fist
  of sand
My brother, you slipped away with the
  second hand
Like parallel lines that never cross
For the lost, for the lost

The woman sits alone in a room
Alone in a house like a silent tomb
The man counts every jewel in his crown
What can't be saved is measured in
  pounds

He was a father's dream, he was a fist of
  sand
My brother, you slipped away with the
  second hand
Like parallel lines that never cross
For the lost, for the lost

In my dreams the voices from beyond the
    door
I remember them saying you weren't
    coming no more
You wouldn't believe how quiet it's
    become
The heart obscure fills with shame

He was a brother's dream, he was a fist
    of sand
My brother, you slipped away with the
    second hand
Like parallel lines that never cross
For the lost, for the lost

He finished the song to rousing applause
— genuine, enthusiastic applause — and
moved effortlessly into the second. He had
hit his stride, and there wasn't a single sign
of any anxiety. Just that familiar sheen
across his forearms and the furrowed brow
of concentration as he sang the words he
had spent months, sometimes years, perfect-
ing. The second song was over in a flash,
and then the third, and before she realized
what was happening, the crowd was ecstati-
cally cheering and calling for an encore. Julian looked pleased and a little confused —
his instructions to play three songs in under
twelve minutes couldn't have been clearer

— but he must've gotten the green light from someone offstage, because he smiled and nodded and eased right into one of his more upbeat songs. The crowd roared their approval.

By the time he pushed back the piano bench and took a modest bow, the air in the room had changed. More than the loud cheering and clapping and whistles, there was that electrified feeling of having been part of something important. Brooke stood, hemmed in on all sides by her husband's admirers, when Leo approached. He gruffly greeted the hair-tie girl by name — Umi — but she immediately rolled her eyes and walked away. Before Brooke could process that, Leo grabbed her arm a little too tightly and leaned in so close she wondered for the briefest second if he was going to kiss her.

"Get ready, Brooke. Get ready for one fucking crazy ride. Tonight is only the start, and it's going to be insane."

4
A TOAST TO HOT REDHEADS

"Kaylie, sweetheart, I don't know how else to say it: you do not need to lose weight. Look at your statistics; look at this chart. You are absolutely perfect just the way you are."

"No one else here looks like me," Kaylie said, lowering her eyes. The girl absently twisted her limp brown hair in circles around her forefinger, methodically wrapping and turning, wrapping and turning. Her face was filled with anxiety.

"What do you mean?" Brooke asked, although she knew exactly what Kaylie meant.

"I just . . . I never felt fat until I came here. At public school, I was totally normal, maybe even on the skinny side! And then this year rolls around and they stick me in this weird place because it's supposed to be so fancy and special, and suddenly I'm obese." The girl's voice cracked at the last word, and it was all Brooke could do not to hug her.

"Oh, sweetheart, you're no such thing! Come here, look at this chart. One hundred twenty-five pounds at five-one is well within the healthy range." Brooke held out her laminated chart showing the huge range of normal weights, but Kaylie barely glanced at it.

She knew it wasn't particularly comforting in light of all the astonishingly thin girls in Kaylie's ninth-grade class. Kaylie was a scholarship student from the Bronx, the daughter of an air-conditioning repairman who raised her alone after her mother was killed in a car accident. Her father was clearly doing something right, considering the girl's straight-A record in middle school, success on the field hockey team, and, according to what Brooke heard from other teachers, an ability to play the violin that far surpassed that of her peers, and yet here was his lovely, accomplished daughter, and all she could see was that she didn't fit in.

Kaylie tugged at the hem of her plaid skirt, which rested across thighs that were strong and muscular, but nowhere near fat, and said, "I guess I just have bad genes. My mom was really overweight, too."

"Do you miss her?" Brooke asked, and

Kaylie could only nod, the tears welling in her eyes.

"She always told me I was perfect just the way I am, but I wonder what she would've said if she could see the girls here. *They're* perfect. Their hair is perfect and their makeup is perfect and their bodies are perfect, and even though we all have the same exact uniform, even the way they *wear* it is perfect."

It was one aspect of the job she had least expected but had grown to appreciate more than she could express, this crossover between nutritionist and confidante. They'd learned in grad school that anyone who came into regular contact with teenagers and was merely willing to listen could play an important role as a caring, involved adult, but Brooke hadn't known what they meant until she started at Huntley.

Brooke spent a few more minutes explaining that although it might not have felt that way, Kaylie was well within a healthy weight limit. It was a hard argument, especially considering the girl's muscular, athletic body was broader than most of her classmates', but she tried. *If only I could fast-forward her through four years of high school and send her straight to college,* Brooke thought. *She'd realize then that none of this*

110

ninth-grade nonsense means anything in the long run.

But Brooke knew from experience that this was impossible. She, too, had self-consciously been on the larger end of normal all through high school and Cornell, straight up until grad school, when she went on a drastic diet and lost almost twenty pounds. She couldn't keep it off, though, and gained fifteen of it back almost immediately. Now, despite mostly healthful eating and a dedicated running program, Brooke was also on the outer limits of the healthy range for her height and, just like Kaylie, was acutely aware of that fact. She felt hypocritical even trying to tell Kaylie not to worry when she herself thought about it every day.

"You *are* perfect, Kaylie. I know it doesn't always feel that way, especially surrounded by girls with so many advantages, but believe me when I tell you that you're absolutely beautiful. You're going to make friends here, find the girls you connect with, and feel more at home. And then before you know it, you'll kiss the SATs and prom and some dumb boyfriend from Dalton good-bye, and you'll run off to a fantastic college where everyone's perfect in their *own* way, in exactly the way *they* choose. And you'll love it. I can honestly promise you that."

Brooke's phone rang, the special piano-sounding ring that she'd attached only to Julian's number. He never called when she was at work, knowing she wouldn't be able to answer, and even kept his texts to a minimum. She knew in an instant something was wrong.

"Excuse me, Kaylie. This will just be a minute." She swiveled in her chair the best she could to get some privacy in the small office. "Hi. Is everything okay? I'm with a patient right now."

"Brooke, you are not going to believe this, but —" He stopped and breathed in deeply, dramatically.

"Julian, seriously, if this is not an emergency, I need to call you back."

"Leo just called. One of the main bookers from *Leno* was at the showcase last week. They want me to perform on the show!"

"No!"

"It's true! It's a hundred percent guaranteed done deal. Next week, Tuesday night. Taping at five. I'll be the musical performance on the show, probably right after the interviews. Do you believe it?"

"Ohmigod!"

"Brooke, say something else."

She forgot where she was for a moment.

"I can't believe it. I mean, of course I can believe it, but it's just so incredible." She heard Julian laughing and thought how long it'd been. "When are you home tonight? We *must* celebrate. I have something in mind. . . ."

"Does it involve my favorite mesh thingy?"

Brooke smiled into the phone. "I was thinking more along the lines of that Dom Pérignon we got as a gift and can never justify opening."

"Mesh. Tonight deserves champagne *and* mesh. Meet you home at eight? I'll take care of dinner."

"You don't have to deal with dinner. Let me pick something up. Or we can go out! Why don't we go somewhere and really celebrate?"

"Let me handle it," Julian said. "Please? I have something in mind."

Brooke's heart surged. Maybe now he'd be able to ease up on his time at the studio and spend more time at home. She felt the familiar pangs of excitement and anticipation she'd felt earlier in their marriage, before anything had become routine. "Absolutely. I'll see you at eight. And, Julian? I can't wait."

"Me neither." He made a kissing sound into the phone — something he hadn't done in years — and hung up. For the first time in five full minutes, Brooke remembered where she was.

"Wow, sounds like some hot stuff," Kaylie said with a grin. "Big date tonight?"

It never failed to amaze Brooke how young these girls really were, despite all the confident backtalk and a distressing familiarity with everything from extreme dieting to the best blow-job techniques. (Brooke had read a highly detailed how-to list when one of the girls left behind a notebook — so detailed, in fact, she briefly considered making a few notes for herself before realizing that taking sex tips from a high school freshman was horrifying on too many levels.)

"Big date with my *husband.*" Brooke corrected her, trying to salvage at least a little professionalism. "I'm so sorry for the interruption. Now, back to what —"

"Sounded pretty exciting," Kaylie said. She loosened her grip on her hair just long enough to gnaw a hangnail on her right index finger. "What happened?"

Brooke was so relieved to see the girl smile that she said, "Yeah, actually it is really exciting. My husband is a musician. He just got a call from Leno's people inviting him to be on the show." Brooke could hear her voice surge with pride, and although she knew it was both unprofessional and even silly to be sharing the news with her teen-age patient, she was too happy to care.

Kaylie's head snapped to full attention. "He's going to be on *Leno?*"

Brooke nodded and shuffled some papers around on her desk in an unsuccessful attempt to hide her pleasure.

"That is the coolest fucking thing I've ever heard!" the girl exclaimed, her ponytail bobbing as if to underscore her point.

"Kaylie!"

"Sorry, but it is! What's his name and when's he on? I want to make sure I see it."

"Next Tuesday night. His name is Julian Alter."

"That is so fuck — freaking cool. Con-gratulations, Mrs. A. Your husband must be pretty awesome if Leno wants him. You're going to go to L.A. with him, right?"

"What?" Brooke asked. She hadn't had a second to think about the logistics, but Ju-lian hadn't mentioned them either.

"Isn't *Leno* in L.A.? You, like, *have* to go with him."

"Of course I'll go with him," Brooke replied automatically, although she had a nagging, uncomfortable feeling in the pit of her stomach that Julian's omission of an invitation wasn't just a detail that got lost in all the excitement.

Brooke still had another ten minutes with Kaylie, then a full hour afterward with a Huntley gymnast whose coach's weigh-ins were having disastrous effects on the girl's self-esteem, but she knew she wouldn't be able to concentrate for one more second. Figuring she'd already acted inappropriately by oversharing and using their session time to talk about her personal life, Brooke turned back to Kaylie.

"I'm sorry to do this, sweetheart, but I need to cut our session short this afternoon. I'll be back on Friday, and I'll notify your sixth-period teacher that we didn't get a chance to finish so we can reschedule another full session for then. Is that okay?"

Kaylie nodded. "Hell, yeah, Mrs. A. This is big news for you. Say congratulations to your husband for me, okay?"

Brooke smiled at her. "Thanks, I will. And, Kaylie? We're going to continue talking about this. I can't condone you losing weight, but if you want to talk about eating more healthfully, I'm happy to advise you. Does that sound good?"

Kaylie nodded and Brooke thought she may have even detected a small smile before the girl walked out of her office. Although she didn't look the least bit fazed about cutting their session short, Brooke was overcome with guilt. It wasn't easy to get these girls to open up, and she actually felt like she was starting to get somewhere with Kaylie.

Pledging to set things right with everyone on Friday, Brooke sent a quick e-mail to Rhonda, her principal, claiming sudden sickness, threw all her stuff in a canvas tote bag, and jumped directly into the backseat of an idling taxi. Hell, if Leno wasn't sufficient reason to splurge, nothing was.

Despite the fact that it was rush hour, the park crossing at Eighty-sixth Street wasn't unbearable and the West Side Highway was moving at a brisk twenty miles an hour (downright dreamy for that time of night), and Brooke was delighted to find herself standing in her apartment by six thirty. She got down on the floor and let Walter lick her face for a few minutes and then gently replaced herself with a thickly braided, extra-smelly bully stick — Walter's favorite. After pouring herself a glass of pinot grigio from an open bottle in the fridge and taking a long, deep swallow, Brooke toyed with the idea of posting Julian's news as a Facebook status update but quickly dismissed it; she didn't want to announce anything without running it by him first.

The first status update on her homepage was, unpleasantly, from Leo. Apparently, he had linked his Twitter account to his Facebook page, and despite the fact he usually had *not one* redeeming tidbit to share, he was taking full advantage of the constant-update feature.

Leo Walsh . . . PUMPED JULIAN ALTER WILL BE ROCKING THE LENO SHOW NEXT TUESDAY. L.A., HERE WE COME. . . .

The update's mere association with her husband made Brooke feel queasy, as did what it pointed out: that Julian was definitely planning a trip to Los Angeles, Leo was definitely joining him, and it was only Brooke who had not yet received an invitation.

She showered, shaved, brushed, flossed, and toweled dry. Was it weird to assume she'd accompany Julian to Los Angeles for the taping? She had no clue if Julian wanted her there for the support, or if he figured that this was a business trip and he should be traveling with his manager, not his wife.

As she slathered a Julian-approved scent-free moisturizer on her freshly shaved legs — he couldn't stand the smell of scented products — Brooke watched Walter watch her. "Did Daddy make a bad call hiring Leo?" she asked him in a high-pitched voice.

Walter lifted his head from the fluffy bath mat that always made his fur smell like mildew, wagged his tail, and woofed.

"Is that a no?"

Walter woofed again.

"Or a yes?"

Another woof.

"Thank you for that insight, Walter. I will surely treasure it."

He rewarded her with an ankle lick and sank back into the mat.

A quick time check revealed it was ten to eight, so after taking a minute to psych herself up, Brooke pulled a crumpled pile of black fabric from the back of her underwear drawer. The last time she'd worn this getup had been over a year before, when she had accused Julian of not being interested in sex anymore and he had gone straight to that drawer, pulled out the jumpsuit, and said something to the effect of "It's a crime to own this and not wear it." It had immediately broken the tension and Brooke remembered putting it on and dancing exaggerated stripper moves around their bedroom to Julian's loud cheers and cat-calls.

Somewhere along the way, that jumpsuit began to symbolize their sex life. She'd bought it in their first or second year of marriage, after a discussion where Julian confessed, as though it were some scandalous, shameful secret, that he just loved women in tight black lingerie . . . and maybe didn't love all the brightly colored boy shorts and striped racerback tanks that Brooke wore each night to bed and would've sworn were sexy in their teenage girlness. Although she couldn't remotely afford it back then, Brooke immediately set out on a lingerie-buying spree and, within two days, had acquired a super-soft black jersey chemise with spaghetti straps from Bloomingdale's; a babydoll-style, ruffled black nightie from Victoria's Secret; and a short black cotton nightshirt with "Juicy Sleeper" splashed across the bum. Each one, in succession, had been met with barely tepid enthusiasm along the lines of "Mmm, that's cute," before Julian turned back to his magazine each night. When not even the babydoll nightie elicited a modicum of interest, Brooke called Nola the very next morning.

"Clear your Saturday afternoon," Nola had announced. "We're going shopping."

"I already went shopping and spent a fortune," Brooke whined, shuffling through her receipts like they were toxic gin rummy cards.

"Can we backtrack for a minute, please? Your husband says he wants to see you in sexy black lingerie and you come home with a Juicy *nightshirt?* Are you serious?"

"What? He wasn't exactly specific. He said he liked black and not the bright colors. It's all black and short and tight. The 'Juicy' part is even in rhinestones. What's wrong with that?"

"Nothing's wrong with that . . . if you're a sophomore in college and you're super-psyched to look cute at your first sleepover at his fraternity. Like it or not, you're all grown up now. And what Julian is trying to tell you is that he wants you to look like a woman. A hot, sexy *woman.*"

Brooke sighed. "Okay, okay, I'm in your hands. What time Saturday?"

"Noon at the corner of Spring and Mercer. We're hitting Kiki De Montparnasse, La Perla, and Agent Provocateur. The whole thing will take under an hour and you will be equipped with exactly what you need. See you then."

Although she'd looked forward to the shopping expedition all week, it turned out to be a miserable failure. In all her banker-salary-and-massive-bonus glory, Nola had not told Brooke that the less material a piece of lingerie contained, the more expensive it would be. Brooke was dumbfounded to discover that the French maid outfit Nola raved about at Kiki was $650, and a simple black chemise — not all that different from her Bloomie's version — was $375. Where on earth was she — a graduate student! — going when a single black lace thong cost $115 ($135 if she wanted the crotchless version)? After two of the three stores, she told Nola firmly that while she appreciated her help, there would be no purchasing that afternoon. It wasn't until the following week, when Brooke found herself in the curtained-off room at Ricky's to buy paraphernalia for another friend's bachelorette party, that she stumbled on the solution.

There, in a floor-to-ceiling display between the vibrators and the penis-themed paper plates, was a wall of individually wrapped "fantasy outfits." They were in flat, envelope-like packets that reminded her of pantyhose packaging, but the pictures on the front depicted beautiful women in all manner of sexy outfits: French maid, schoolgirl, firefighter, jailbird, cheerleader, and cowgirl, plus a whole bunch of non-themed getups, almost all of which were short, tight, and black. Best of all, the most expensive among them was $39.99, and most of the packets were marked less than $25. She began to examine the pictures, trying to imagine what Julian would like most, when a blue-haired and heavily guylinered employee pushed aside the beaded curtains and walked right up to Brooke.

"Can I help you with anything?" he asked.

Brooke quickly averted her attention to a cluster of penis straws and shook her head.

"I'd be happy to make some recommendations," he lisped. "On the outfits, the sex toys, whatever. Tell you which are bestsellers."

"Thanks, I'm just picking up some of this stupid stuff for a bachelorette party," she said quickly, already mad at herself for being embarrassed.

"Uh-huh. Well, just let me know."

He swished back into the main store area, and Brooke sprang into immediate action. Knowing she'd lose her nerve if he came back — or anyone else walked into the room — she grabbed the first non-themed outfit and tossed it into her shopping basket. She practically sprinted to the cash register, tossing in a bottle of shampoo, a travel-sized packet of Kleenex, and some refill razor blades on the way there, just to throw off the cashier. It wasn't until she was on the subway home, sitting in the far back car, miraculously isolated from other people, that she allowed herself a peek in the bag.

The picture featured a redheaded woman who didn't look drastically different from Brooke — save the forty-two-inch legs — wearing a high-necked, long-sleeved, full-length mesh bodysuit. The woman jutted out her hip provocatively and stared at the camera, but despite all the dramatic posturing, she managed to convey "sexy" and "confident" and not just "sleazy" and "slutty." *I can do this one,* she thought to herself, and that very night, when she walked out of the bathroom wearing that bodysuit and a pair of heels, Julian had nearly fallen off the bed.

Brooke had donned the now-infamous jumpsuit over the years on some of Julian's birthdays, their anniversaries, and the occasional warm-weather vacation, but lately, like all the old remnants of their pre-exhaustion sex life, it had gotten pushed to the back of the drawer. As she unrolled the material over her legs and shimmied first her hips and then her arms into the outfit, she knew it would send the message loud and clear: *I'm so proud of you for this amazing accomplishment, now get over here so I can show you.* No matter that the one-size-fits-all jumpsuit was digging tightly into her thighs and doing a weird thing on her upper arms; she felt sexy anyway. She had just shaken her hair out of her ponytail and reclined on top of the covers when the landline rang. Certain it was Julian calling to say he was on his way home, Brooke answered on the first ring.

"Rook? Honey, can you hear me?" Her mother's voice rang through the receiver.

Brooke took a deep breath and wondered why the woman had an uncanny knack for calling at exactly the worst possible times. "Hey, Mom. I hear you."

"Oh, good. I was hoping I'd catch you. Listen, I need you to grab your calendar and check a date for me. I know you hate planning ahead, but I'm trying to make some arrangements for —"

"Mom! Hey, sorry to interrupt, but it's not a great time right now. Julian's going to be home any second, and I'm late getting ready," she lied.

"Are you going out to celebrate? Such amazing news. You both must be so happy."

Brooke opened her mouth to talk and then remembered she hadn't yet told her mother Julian's good news. "How did you know?" she asked.

"Randy, sweetheart. He saw some update on Julian's fan page — is that what you call it? I wish I could say my daughter had called to tell me on her own, but luckily Randy remembered his dear old mom."

"Mmm, right. Facebook. I almost forgot. So yeah, we're both really excited."

"So how are you two going to celebrate tonight? Going out to dinner?"

Brooke glanced down at her mesh-covered body; as if to emphasize the ludicrousness of talking to one's mother while wearing a crotchless mesh jumpsuit, one of her nipples popped through the fabric. "Um, I think Julian's bringing dinner home. We already have a bottle of good champagne, so we'll probably have that."

"Sounds lovely. Give him a kiss for me. And as soon as you have a second, I'd really like to get a date nailed down —"

"Uh-huh, okay, Mom. I'll call you tomorrow."

"Because it'll only take a second, and —"

"Mom . . ."

"Okay. Call me tomorrow. Love you, Rookie."

"Love you, too, Mom." She heard the door open just as she hung up the phone.

She knew he would take his coat off and greet Walter, which gave her just enough time to peel off the foil wrapper and unscrew the wire basket around the cork. She had remembered to bring two flutes, which she placed on her bedside table before stretching out, catlike, atop the made bed. Her nervousness lasted only a second, just until Julian opened the door.

"Guess who's staying at the Chateau Marmont?" he said, his smile a mile wide.

"Who?" She sat up in bed, momentarily forgetting her outfit.

"I am," he said, and instantly Brooke felt a wave of anxiety.

"No way," she breathed. It was all she could manage.

"Oh yes. In a suite. Where I'll be picked up by limo and taken to the NBC studio for the *Leno* taping."

She forced herself to focus on his good news and remind herself that it had nothing to do with her. "Wow, Julian, that's amazing! They mention that place constantly in *Last Night, US Weekly,* all of them. Kate Hudson just hosted an all-night party in the bungalows. J. Lo and Marc Anthony ran into Ben Affleck by the pool and Marc supposedly made a scene. Belushi *overdosed* there, for chrissake. The place is absolutely legendary."

"And guess what else?" Julian asked, sitting down beside her on the bed and running his hand over her mesh-covered thigh.

"What?"

"My extremely hot wife is going to be joining me, so long as she promises to bring this mesh outfit with her," he said, leaning in to kiss Brooke.

"Stop it!" she shrieked.

"Of course, only if she wants to."

"You're joking!"

"I'm not. I spoke to Samara, my new *publicist*" — his eyebrows shot up and he grinned at her — "and she said it's fine so long as we pay for your plane ticket. Leo thought it'd be better if we went alone, just so I wouldn't be distracted, but I told him I could never do something this big without you. So what do you say?"

She ignored the Leo part. "I think that's freaking incredible!" she said, throwing her arms around his neck. "I think I can't wait to *canoodle* with you by the bar and party all night in the bungalows."

"Is that really what it's like?" Julian asked, pushing her backward against the pillows and arranging himself, still fully dressed, on top of her.

"Hell yes. From everything I've read, we can fully expect Cristal-filled pools, heaping mountains of cocaine, more cheating celebrities than a high-end escort service, and enough gossip on an hourly basis to fill ten tabloids. Oh, and orgies. I've never read that, but I'm sure they happen. Probably right in the restaurant."

Walter jumped up on the bed and, chin to the air, began to howl.

"That does sound pretty awesome, doesn't it, Walter?" Julian asked, kissing Brooke's neck.

Walter howled in response and Brooke laughed.

Julian dipped his finger in his champagne glass, put it up to Brooke's lips, and kissed her again.

"What do you say to some practice?" he asked.

Brooke kissed him back and pulled off his shirt, her heart swelling with the sense of possibility. "I'd say that's the best damn idea I've heard in a long, long time."

"Can I get you another Diet Coke?" the bermuda-clad waiter asked as he sidled up next to Brooke's lounge chair, blocking her sun. In the direct sunlight it felt reasonably warm, and although she thought the low seventies was a bit too chilly for bikini weather, her fellow pool-goers apparently disagreed.

She glanced at the half-dozen or so people sipping delicious-looking cocktails around the pool, reminded herself that although it was only midafternoon on a Tuesday this was still a vacation of sorts, and said, "I'd love a Bloody Mary, please. Extra spicy and two stalks of celery."

A long, lithe girl who, judging from her astonishing figure, was definitely a model lowered herself elegantly into the pool. Brooke watched as she swam a charming sort of doggie paddle to the side, taking great pains to keep her hair dry, and called out to her male companion in Spanish. Without glancing up from his laptop, the man answered her in French. The girl pouted, the man grumbled, and within thirty seconds he was walking toward the pool with her massive Chanel sunglasses in hand. When she thanked him, Brooke could've sworn she did so in Russian.

Her phone rang. "Hello?" she said quietly, although no one seemed to care.

"Rookie? How's it going out there?"

"Hey, Dad. I'm not going to lie, everything's pretty damn great."

"Did Julian play yet?"

"He and Leo just left so I'm guessing they'll be in Burbank soon. I don't think the actual taping starts until five or five thirty. It sounded like it was going to be a pretty long afternoon, so I'm waiting at the hotel for them."

The waiter returned with her drink, the Bloody Mary in a glass every bit as tall and skinny as the women she'd spied so far in Los Angeles. He set it on the table beside her, along with a little three-part tray of snacks: marinated olives, mixed nuts, and baked vegetable chips. Brooke wanted to kiss him.

"What's the place like? Pretty swanky, I'd bet."

Brooke took a small sip at first and then a gulp. *Damn, that was good.* "Yeah, it really is. You should see the people sitting by the pool. Each one is more gorgeous than the next."

"Do you know Jim Morrison tried to jump off the roof there? And that the members of Led Zeppelin rode their motorcycles through the lobby? From what I've heard, it is *the* place to be for badly behaved musicians."

"Where are you getting your information, Dad? Google?" Brooke laughed.

"Brooke, please! Don't insult me by suggesting —"

"Wikipedia?"

A pause. "Maybe."

They chatted for a few more minutes while Brooke watched the gorgeous thing in the pool shriek like a child when her boyfriend jumped in and tried to splash her. Her father wanted to tell her all about the non-surprise surprise birthday party Cynthia was planning for him in a few months, how determined she was to celebrate his sixty-fifth since it was also his retirement year, but Brooke had a hard time focusing. After all, the woman-child had just climbed out of the water, and Brooke clearly wasn't the only one who noticed that her white bikini was entirely transparent when wet. She glanced down at her own terry-cloth sweats and wondered what she would do to look that good in a bikini, even if just for an hour. She sucked in her stomach and continued to watch.

The second Bloody Mary went down just as smoothly as the first, and she was soon so happily tipsy that she almost didn't recognize Benicio Del Toro when he emerged from a poolside bungalow and collapsed into a lounger directly opposite her. Unfortunately he didn't remove either his jeans or his T-shirt, but Brooke was content to stare at him through her sunglasses. The pool area itself wasn't anything special — she'd seen many grander pools in ordinary suburban homes — but it had a discreet, quiet sexiness that was hard to pinpoint. Despite being only a few hundred feet above

Sunset Boulevard, everything felt hidden, like it was carved out of a jungly tangle of towering trees, hemmed in on all sides by plants in huge terra-cotta pots and black-and-white striped umbrellas.

She could've sat by that pool downing Bloodys all afternoon, but as the sun got lower in the sky and the air grew chillier, she packed up her book and iPod and headed to the room. A quick spin through the lobby on her way to the elevator revealed a jeans-clad LeAnn Rimes having a drink with an older, well-dressed woman, and it was all Brooke could do not to whip out her BlackBerry and send a picture to Nola.

When she got back to their room — a one-bedroom suite in the main building, with gorgeous hillside views — she was delighted to discover a massive gift basket with a note that read, "Welcome, Julian! From your friends at Sony." Inside was a bottle each of Veuve Clicquot and Patrón; a box of those tiny, funkily painted chocolate truffles; an assortment of energy bars and snacks; enough Vitaminwaters to stock a grocery; and a dozen Sprinkles cupcakes. She took a picture of the whole thing splayed out on the coffee table and sent it to Julian with the caption, "They love you," and then she tore into it, demolishing a red velvet cupcake in under ten seconds.

It was the room's landline that eventually woke her.

"Brooke? You alive?" Julian's voice rang through the cordless handset.

"I'm alive," she managed to say, looking around to get her bearings, surprised to discover that she was under the covers, wearing only her underwear, and the entire room was dark. Cupcake crumbs were scattered around her pillow.

"I've been calling your cell phone for the last half hour. Where are you? Is everything okay?"

She bolted upright and looked at the clock. Seven thirty. She'd been asleep for nearly three hours. "Must've been that second Bloody Mary," she mumbled to herself, but Julian began to laugh.

"I leave you alone for one afternoon and you get yourself drunk?"

"It wasn't like that! But whatever, how was the taping? How did it go?"

In the brief pause that followed, Brooke had a mental flash of all the potential things that could've gone wrong, but once again, Julian laughed. It was more than a laugh — he sounded downright giddy.

"Rook, it was incredible! I nailed it, just absolutely nailed it, and the backup band was way better than I expected with so little practice." Brooke could hear other voices in the car and Julian lowered his to a whisper. "Jay came over to me as the song ended, put his arm around me, pointed me to the camera, and said how that was awesome, and he'd like for me to come back every night."

"No!"

"He did! The audience was clapping like crazy, and then when the whole taping was over and we were hanging out backstage, Jay even thanked me, said he couldn't wait to hear the whole album!"

"Julian, that's incredible. Congratulations! This is *huge!*"

"I know, I'm just so relieved. Listen, we'll be back at the hotel in twenty minutes or so. Meet me on the patio for a drink?"

The mere thought of alcohol made her head throb a bit more — when was the last time she was hungover at dinnertime? — but she sat straight up. "I've got to change. I'll meet you down there as soon as I'm ready," she said, but the line had already been disconnected.

Climbing out of the warm, soft sheets wasn't easy, but three Advils and a stint under the rainfall shower helped. She quickly pulled on a pair of legging-style skinny jeans, a silky tank top, and a blazer, but a closer inspection revealed that the jeans were doing hideous things to her butt. As hard as it was to pull the damn things on, it was hell trying to get them off, and Brooke nearly kneed herself in the face trying to yank them down her legs, inch by painful inch. Her stomach rolled and her legs flailed and still, they barely budged. Did White Bikini Girl ever have to suffer such indignity? She flung the jeans across the room in disgust. The only thing left in her suitcase was a sundress. It was too cold for it, but paired with the blazer, a cotton scarf, and a pair of flat boots, she'd have to suck it up.

Not terrible, she thought as she checked herself one last time. Her hair was mostly air-dried and — even Brooke had to admit — looked pretty damn good for requiring zero effort. She'd slicked on some mascara and a few dots of this glimmering liquid blush Nola had pressed into her palm a few weeks earlier and politely insisted she use. She grabbed her phone and her bag and ran. The lip gloss went on in the elevator. The blazer sleeves got rolled while walking across the lobby. She gave her hair a final shake and tousle and actually felt fresh and pretty by the time she saw Julian holding court at a prime patio table.

"Brooke!" He stood up and waved.

She could see his smile from fifty feet, and every inch of self-consciousness vanished as she ran toward him. "Congratulations!" she said, throwing her arms around his neck.

"Thanks, baby," he whispered into her ear. And then, more loudly, "Come and say hello. I don't think you've met everyone yet."

"Hi!" she sang, giving the general table area a wave. "I'm Brooke."

The group was gathered around a plain wooden table, tucked amid an almost private awning of flowering trees. Little seating areas were interspersed throughout the lushly planted patio, and most of them were filled with tanned, laughing people, but the entire space still felt calm, unhurried. Small torches flickered in the dark. Small votive candles flattered everyone's features. Highball glasses clinked and music played softly from speakers hidden in the trees, and if you really tried, you could hear the steady, white-noise din of Sunset Boulevard somewhere off in the distance. Although she'd never been to Tuscany, Brooke imagined this was exactly how a countryside restaurant in the middle of Chianti might look.

Brooke felt Julian's hand in the small of

her back, pushing her gently toward the chair he'd pulled out. So lost in the magical sight of the patio all lit up at night, she almost forgot why she was there. A quick glance around and she saw Leo staring back at her with a surprisingly ill-tempered expression; a thirtysomething woman — fortysomething with great Botox? — with gorgeous olive skin and jet-black hair, who must have been Julian's new publicist, Samara; and a familiar-looking guy she couldn't quite place who . . . *Ohmigod, is that, could it be . . .*

"You already know Leo," Julian was saying as Leo smirked. "And this here is the lovely Samara. Everyone's already told me that she's the best, but now I can confirm beyond any shadow of a doubt."

Samara smiled and held her hand out to Brooke across the table. "Pleasure," she said curtly, although her smile seemed warm enough.

"I've heard so much about you," Brooke said, shaking her hand and trying to concentrate on Samara and not on the fourth table mate. "It's true, when Julian found out that you would be representing him, he came home all excited and said, 'Everyone says she's the best.' "

"Oh, that's sweet of you," Samara said

138

with a dismissive wave of her hand. "But he's making this one easy. He was a total pro today."

"Both of you need to stop," Julian said, and Brooke could immediately tell that he was pleased. "Brooke, I'd also like to introduce you to Jon. Jon, this is my wife, Brooke."

Good god. It *was* him. She didn't have a clue why or how it had happened, but sitting right there at her husband's table, holding a glass of beer and looking perfectly relaxed, was Jon Bon Jovi. What was she supposed to say? Do? Where the hell was Nola when she needed her? Brooke racked her brain. So long as it wasn't something horrifying like "I'm a huge fan" or "I really love and respect the way that you've been married to the same woman for all these years," she'd probably be fine, but it wasn't like she sat down to drinks with a superstar *every* day. . . .

"Hey," Jon said, offering a nod in Brooke's direction. "That's some wicked cool hair you have. Is the color real?"

Brooke's hand immediately flew to her wavy locks, and she knew without looking that her complexion currently matched her hair. Her red was so pure, so intensely pigmented, that you either absolutely loved it or unequivocally hated it. She loved it. Julian loved it. And apparently, so did Bon Jovi. *Nola!* she shouted to herself. *I need you to hear this right now!*

"Yeah, it's real," she said, rolling her eyes in mock disgust with it. "Source of many a cruel childhood joke, but I'm getting used to it." She saw Julian smiling at her out of the corner of her eye; hopefully only he knew how false her modesty was right then.

"Well I think it's fucking awesome," Jon declared, and raised his tall, tapered beer glass. "A toast to fire cro—" He stopped short and an adorably sheepish look crossed his face. Brooke wanted to tell him he could call her "fire crotch" anytime.

"A toast to hot redheads and first appearances on *Leno.* Congrats, man. That's big." Jon held his glass aloft and everyone clinked it with his own. Brooke's champagne flute was the last to touch it, and she wondered if there was any way she could smuggle the glass home with her.

"Cheers!" everyone called out. "Congratulations!"

"So how was it?" Brooke asked Julian, happy to give him the opening to shine once again in front of all these people. "Tell me everything."

"He was perfect," Samara announced in

140

her clipped, professional voice. "His performance followed really solid guests." She paused and turned to Julian. "I thought Hugh Jackman was charming. Did you?"

"Yeah, he was good. And so was that chick from *Modern Family*," Julian said, nodding.

"We caught a break with that — two legitimately interesting and famous guests, none of the child performers or the magicians or the animal trainers," Samara said. "Trust me, nothing's worse than getting upstaged by a studio full of chimpanzees."

Everyone laughed. A waiter arrived at the table and Leo ordered for the group without consulting anyone. Brooke normally hated it when people did that, but even she couldn't argue with his choices: another bottle of champagne, a round of tequila gimlets, and a bunch of snack plates, everything from truffled porcini bruschetta to mozzarella di bufala and arugula. By the time the first dish of crab cakes in an avocado puree arrived, Brooke had happily rediscovered her earlier buzz and was feeling almost euphoric from the excitement. Julian — her Julian, the same one who slept in socks every night — had just performed on *The Tonight Show.* They were staying in a gorgeous suite at the infamous Chateau Marmont, eating and drinking like rock royalty. One of the most famous musicians of the twentieth century had announced he loved her hair. Of course her wedding was the best day of her life (weren't you required to say that no matter what?), but this was quickly clocking in as a very close second.

Her cell phone screeched from her bag on the ground, a shrill fire-alarm-like ring she'd chosen post-nap to ensure she didn't over-sleep again.

"Why don't you get it?" Julian asked through a full mouth as Brooke stared at her phone. She didn't want to answer it, but she was worried something was wrong; it was already after midnight back at home.

"Hey, Mom," she said as quietly as she could. "We're all in the middle of dinner right now. Is everything okay?"

"Brooke! Julian's on right now and he's incredible! He looks adorable, and the band is playing perfectly, and my god, you just want to eat him up. I think it's the best he's ever been." Her mother's words tumbled out in a frantic jumble, and it was all Brooke could do to put the pieces together.

She glanced at her watch. Nine twenty California time, which meant *The Tonight Show* was airing that very second up and down the East Coast. "Really? He looks good?" Brooke asked.

This got everyone's attention.

"Of course, it's airing on the East Coast now," Samara said, pulling out her Black-Berry. Sure enough, it was vibrating with the intensity of a washing machine.

"Amazing," her mother was saying through the receiver. "He looks absolutely amazing. And Jay gave him a really nice introduction. Wait — he's just finishing up the song now."

"Mom, I'll call you later, okay? I'm being really rude right now."

"All right, honey. It's late here so call me in the morning. And congratulate Julian for me."

Brooke clicked to disconnect the call, but her phone instantly rang again. Nola. She glanced around the table and noticed that with the exception of Jon, who had wandered over to say hello to another group, everyone else was on the phone, too.

"Hey, can I call you later? We're just eating."

"He's ridiculously good!" Nola screeched.

Brooke smiled. Nola had never before been that enthusiastic about any of Julian's performances, not even close. "I know."

"Holy shit, Brooke, I'm like at the edge of my seat. When he really lets go and sings that last stanza or whatever you call it, with

143

his eyes closed and his head back like that? Good god, it gave me the chills."

"I've told you. He's the real deal."

Brooke overheard Julian thanking someone with an embarrassed but proud smile. Leo was shouting something about Julian being "fucking awesome," and Samara was saying that she'd check on Julian's availability and call back in the morning. Brooke's phone was blowing up with incoming text messages and e-mails, little notifications popping up on her screen even as she talked to Nola.

"Look, I've got to run right now, things are crazy here. Are you up for another hour?" She lowered her voice to a barely discernible whisper. "I'm having dinner at the Chateau with Jon Bon Jovi. And apparently, he loves redheads."

"Shut up. Shut. The. Hell. Up!" Nola hissed into the phone. "First of all, when on earth did my best friend become so fabulous? 'Dinner at the Chateau'? Are you *kidding* me? And second . . . I need to hang up right this second so I have enough time to book a flight to L.A. and then dye my hair red."

Brooke laughed.

"Seriously, Brooke, don't be surprised if I show up there first thing tomorrow morning, ginger hair and all, and crash on your couch. Consider yourself warned."

"I love you, Nol. I'll call you in a little."

She hung up, but it didn't matter. Each of their phones kept ringing, buzzing, and singing, and each of them kept answering, eager to hear the next round of praise and adulation. By far the winning e-mail of the evening came from Julian's mother, addressed to both of them, which simply read: *Your father and I saw you on Leno this evening. While we weren't impressed with the other guests he interviewed, we thought your performance was quite good. Of course, with the kind of opportunities and support you've had since childhood, we knew anything was possible. Congratulations on your accomplishment!* Brooke and Julian read it at the same time on different devices and laughed so hard they couldn't speak for many minutes.

It was only after another hour that things calmed down, and by then, Jon had wandered back to them, Samara had booked Julian on two other shows, and Leo had ordered their third bottle of champagne. Julian just sat back in his chair, looking equal parts stunned and elated.

"Thank you guys so much," he finally said, holding his flute up and nodding to each of them. "I can't even find the words,

145

but this, this is, uh, just the most amazing night *ever.*"

Leo cleared his throat and held up his own glass. "Sorry, buddy, but I think you're wrong there," he said with a wink to the rest of them. "This night is just the beginning."

5
THEY'LL SWOON FOR YOU

It wasn't yet ten thirty on a late May morning and already the Texas heat was crushing. Julian had already sweated through his T-shirt and Brooke was chugging water by the liter, convinced they were both seriously dehydrated. She'd tried to go for her run that morning but had given up after ten minutes when she felt light-headed, starving, and nauseated at the same time. When Julian had suggested for possibly the very first time in five years of marriage that they spend a couple hours shopping, she couldn't climb into the ugly green rental car fast enough. Shopping meant air-conditioning, and she'd take it.

They drove first through the hotel's residential neighborhood, followed by a long stretch of highway, and then, after nearly twenty minutes, a few miles down a winding country road that was paved in some parts and little more than dust and gravel in others. All through the trip Brooke begged to be told where they were going, and each time Julian smiled wider and refused to answer her.

"Would you have ever guessed it looks like this just ten minutes outside of Austin?" Brooke asked as they passed fields of wildflowers and, on the other side of it, a dilapidated barn.

"Never. It's straight out of a movie for how you'd envision a rural Texas ranchers' town, not a suburb of a major cosmopolitan city. But I guess that's exactly why they film here."

"Yeah, no one at work believed they shoot *Friday Night Lights* here."

Julian turned to look at her. "Everything okay at work? You haven't said much about it lately."

"For the most part everything's good. You know the patient at Huntley, the freshman scholarship student? Remember, the one who has a totally different background from most of the other girls? Well, she feels like she doesn't fit in, in a million ways, but the one that's the hardest for her is the weight. She's now convinced she's morbidly obese, even though she's pretty close to normal."

"What can you do for her?"

She sighed. "You know, not that much.

Besides listen to her and reassure her, I just need to keep an eye on her and make sure nothing gets out of hand. I'm absolutely certain I'm not dealing with a serious eating disorder, but it's scary when someone is so preoccupied with weight, especially when that someone is a teenage girl. With school ending for the summer next month, I'm worried about her."

"And everything at the hospital?"

"It's okay. Margaret wasn't thrilled with me for taking off these two days, but what can you do?"

He turned to look at her. "Is two days really such a big deal?"

"Not by itself, but I took three days for L.A. and *Leno,* that half day for your round of follow-up interviews in New York, and a day to go to your album cover shoot. And that was all in the last six weeks. But whatever. I've barely seen you since then — I wouldn't have missed this for anything."

"Rook, I don't think it's fair to say we've barely seen each other. Things have just been hectic. In a good way."

She disagreed — no one could say that catching glimpses of each other for an hour here or there as Julian passed through their apartment every few days was seeing each other — but she really hadn't intended to sound so critical.

"That's not what I meant, I promise," she said in her most soothing tone. "Look, we're together now, so let's just enjoy it, okay?"

They sat in silence for a few minutes until Brooke touched her fingertips to her forehead and said, "I cannot believe I'm going to meet Tim Riggins."

"Which one is he?"

"Oh, please. Just stop."

"Is he the coach? Or the quarterback? I get confused," Julian said, smiling. As if *anyone* didn't know Tim Riggins.

"Uh-huh, whatever. When he walks into the party tonight and every woman in the room faints with lust, you'll know. Trust me."

Julian slapped the steering wheel in mock outrage. "Aren't they supposed to be swooning because of me? I mean, I'll be the rock star."

Brooke leaned across the seat divider and kissed his cheek. "Of course they'll swoon for you, baby. If they can stop staring at Riggins long enough to notice you, they'll swoon like crazy."

"Now I'm really not telling you where we're going," Julian said.

His brow was furrowed in concentration as he worked to avoid the potholes every ten feet or so, most of which were filled with water from the previous night's thunderstorms. Her husband was simply not used to driving. Brooke panicked that they were going for a hike or a nature walk or some sort of rafting or fishing expedition, but she quickly reminded herself that her husband was a born-and-bred New Yorker, and his idea of communing with nature was the weekly watering of a small bonsai tree that sat on his nightstand. His knowledge of wildlife was limited: he could distinguish between a small rat and a large mouse on any subway platform, and he seemed to possess an instinctive sense of which bodega-dwelling cats were friendly and which would hiss and scratch if you got too close. Other than that, he liked to keep his shoes clean and his bed indoors and would venture outside — say, to Central Park for SummerStage or the Boat Basin when friends threw parties there — only when armed with fistfuls of Claritin and a fully charged cell phone. He hated when Brooke called him a city prince, but he could never successfully deny the charge.

The sprawling, ugly complex seemed to rise directly out of a cleared thicket and advertised itself in glaring neon: Lone Star Western Wear. There were two buildings, not quite adjoining but sharing an unpaved parking lot, and a couple of cars idled outside.

"Here we are," Julian said, pulling off one dirt path and onto another.

"You're joking. Tell me you're joking."

"What? Shopping, just like I said."

Brooke looked toward the squat buildings and the cluster of pickup trucks in front of them. Julian got out of the car, came around to the passenger side, and held his hand out to help Brooke step over the mud puddles in her thong sandals.

"When you said shopping, I was thinking something more like Neiman's."

The first thing Brooke noticed after the welcome blast of air-conditioning was a pretty young girl in tight jeans; a fitted, short-sleeved plaid shirt; and a pair of cowboy boots. Immediately she came over and said, "Good mornin'! Y'all just let me know if you need any help now!"

Brooke smiled and nodded. Julian grinned. Brooke punched him on the arm. A twangy guitar sound emanated from speakers in the ceiling.

"Actually, we'd love some help," Julian said to the blonde.

The girl clapped her hands together placed one on Julian's shoulder and the other on Brooke's. "Well alrighty then, let's get started. What are we looking for today?"

"Yes, what *are* we looking for today?" Brooke asked.

"We're looking for a Western-style outfit for my wife to wear to a party," Julian said, refusing to make eye contact with Brooke.

The salesgirl smiled and said, "Well, that's great, I know just the thing!"

"Julian, I have my outfit all picked out for tonight. That black dress I tried on for you? With the cute purse Randy and Michelle got me for my birthday? Remember?"

He twisted his hands. "I know . . . it's just that I was up early this morning, and I was catching up on e-mail. I finally got around to opening that attachment with the invite to the party tonight, and I saw that the dress code is something called 'Cowboy Couture.' "

"Oh my god."

"Don't panic! See, I knew you'd panic, but —"

"I brought a black strapless dress and gold sandals!" Brooke screeched loud enough that a few fellow shoppers turned to look.

"I know, Rook. That's why I immediately e-mailed Samara and asked her if she could elaborate. Which she did. In great detail."

"She did?" Brooke cocked her head,

surprised but slightly mollified.

"Yes." Julian pulled out his iPhone and scrolled for a second before touching the screen and beginning to read. " 'Hey sweetheart' — she calls everyone that — 'the *Friday Night Lights* people planned a costume party to stay true to their Texas roots. Don't be afraid to go all-out — cowboy hats, boots, chaps, and some very tight sexy jeans will all be on display tonight. Tell Brooke she needs a great pair of Daisy Dukes. Coach Taylor himself is going to pick the winner, so do it up right! Can't wait to . . .' " Julian's voice drifted off as he stopped himself from reading aloud. "The rest is boring scheduling stuff. That was the important part. So . . . that's why we're here. Aren't you happy?"

"Well, I'm glad you found out before we got there tonight. . . ." She noticed Julian looked anxious, eager for her to be appreciative. "I'm definitely grateful you saved me from that fate. Thanks for going to all this trouble."

"It's no trouble," Julian said, his relief obvious.

"You were supposed to practice today."

"There's still time, that's why we came early. I'm just happy you're here with me at all." He gave her a sweet peck and held his hand up and gave the salesgirl a little wave. She bounded over, all smiles.

"Are we ready?" the girl asked.

"We're ready," Brooke and Julian said simultaneously.

When they finally left nearly an hour later, Brooke was flushed with excitement. The shopping had been a thousand times better than she imagined, an exhilarating combination of enjoying Julian's approval when she tried on short shorts and tight tops and sexy boots, and the sheer regressive fun of playing dress-up. The salesgirl, Mandy, had expertly guided Brooke to the perfect party outfit: a cut-off jean skirt, when Brooke felt too self-conscious in the shorts; a plaid shirt identical to the one she was wearing, sexily knotted above her navel (but in Brooke's case, paired with a white tank so she wouldn't have to reveal the soft flesh of her belly); a massive brass belt buckle in the shape of a sheriff's star; a cowboy hat with the sides rolled up and a jaunty chin tassel; and a pair of the sassiest stitched cowboy boots Brooke had ever seen. Mandy suggested Brooke wear her hair in low pigtail braids and handed her a red bandana to tie around her neck. "And don't forget to go really, really heavy on the mascara," Mandy said with a finger waggle. "Cowgirls love their smoky eyes." Although Julian wouldn't get in full costume for the performance, Mandy taught him how to roll a pack of cigarettes into his T-shirt sleeves and equipped him with the matching men's version of Brooke's cowgirl hat.

They laughed the whole way back to the hotel. When Julian leaned over to kiss her and told her he'd be back at six to shower, Brooke wanted to beg him to stay, but she gathered her shopping bags and kissed him back. "Good luck," she said. "I had a great time today." And she couldn't keep herself from grinning when Julian said that he had, too.

He was late getting back to the room and had to rush to shower and dress, and she could feel him start to get jittery when they stepped into the waiting Town Car.

"You nervous?" Brooke asked.

"Yeah, a little, I guess."

"Just remember: of all the songs in the universe, they chose *yours*. Every single solitary time someone tunes in to watch an episode, they're going to hear *your* song. It's incredible, baby. It really is."

Julian placed his hand on top of hers. "I think we're going to have a great time. And *you* look like a model. The cameras are going to go crazy."

Brooke had barely gotten the question out of her mouth — "What cameras?" — before the car pulled up to the entrance of the Hula Hut, a famous local dive reputed to have the best queso north of the border, and they were met with a dozen or so paparazzi.

"Omigod, are they going to take our picture?" Brooke asked, suddenly terrified by this possibility she had failed to consider. She looked up and noticed a long runner in a cow print — the Texas version of a red carpet, she guessed. A few feet down, between the street and the door of the restaurant, she glimpsed a couple of the cast members posing for the cameras.

"Wait there, I'll open your door," Julian said, climbing out his side and walking around to hers. He opened it and leaned in, offering his hand. "Don't worry, they don't care much about us."

Brooke was relieved to discover he was absolutely right. The photographers swarmed them at first, eager to see if they were anyone important, and then faded into the background as quickly as they appeared. Only one of the snappers asked if they could pose for a picture in front of the large black step-and-repeat that was emblazoned with *Friday Night Lights* and NBC near the door.

After he'd halfheartedly shot a few frames, he asked them to spell their names into a tape recorder and then wandered off. They made their way to the door, Brooke clutching Julian's hand, when she spotted Samara across the room. Brooke took one look at the girl's elegantly simple silk dress, gladiator sandals, and tinkling chandelier earrings and felt ridiculous. Why was Brooke dressed for a hoedown when this girl looked like she'd just stepped off a runway? What if there had been some horrible mix-up and Brooke was going to be the only person in full costume tonight? She could feel her breath slow and a wave of panic set in.

It was only then Brooke braved a look around the rest of the room. There were Daisy Dukes and ten-gallon hats as far as the eye could see.

She accepted a fruity-looking cocktail from a tray that passed in their direction and floated happily through the next hour of introductions and mingling, drinking and laughing. It was one of those rare parties where everyone seemed genuinely excited to be there — not just the cast and crew, who obviously knew one another well and got along, but all their spouses and friends and the smattering of celebrities that some of the actors were dating or whom their PR people had wrangled into coming for publicity's sake. Brooke spotted Derek Jeter hovering over a heaping plate of nachos and tried to remember which of the *Friday Night Lights* girls he was engaged to, and Julian reported that he'd glimpsed a half-naked Taylor Swift holding court on the terrace. But mostly it was just a boisterously fun crowd in chaps and plaid and cutoffs, drinking beer and eating queso and jamming to the eighties music that played over the speakers. It was the least self-conscious Brooke had ever felt at any of Julian's gigs, and she reveled in it, enjoying that all-too-rare feeling of being buzzed and charming and just generally *on.* By the time Julian and his band took the makeshift stage, Brooke was part of the gang, having gotten pulled into an impromptu margarita taste test by a bunch of the show's writers. It occurred to her only then that aside from watching the taped *Leno* appearance, she hadn't yet seen Julian play with his new backup band.

Brooke studied them as they climbed on-stage to assemble and test their instruments and was somewhat surprised to discover that they looked less like a rock band and more like a group of twentysomethings who'd all been best friends at their elite

New England boarding school. The drummer, Wes, had the requisite long hair, only his didn't hang in greasy strings around his face. Wes's mahogany locks were thick and wavy and lush, hair only a girl deserved. He wore a sporty green polo shirt with clean, pressed jeans and a pair of classic gray New Balance sneakers. He looked like the kind of guy who'd caddied during the summers in high school — not to earn money, but to "build character" — and then didn't work again until it was time to join his father's law firm. The lead guitarist was the oldest of the crew, probably in his early thirties, and although not quite as preppy as Wes, his beat-up old chinos, black Converse sneakers, and just do it! T were hardly rebellious. Unlike his drummer colleague, Nate didn't fit any of the lead-guitarist stereotypes — he was chunky and had a shy smile and downcast eyes. Brooke remembered how shocked Julian had been to hear Nate at the audition after sizing him up when he first walked onstage. "This guy walks up onstage and immediately you just know he's the kid who got the shit kicked out of him his whole life. He's, like, afraid of his own shadow. And then he starts to play, and man, he just rips it. It was out of this world." Their trio was rounded out by Zack, the bassist, who looked more like a musician than his counterparts but whose cool spiky hair and wallet chain and subtle swipe of eyeliner actually made him seem more poseurish. He was the only band member Julian didn't love, but Sony thought his first choice for bassist — a girl — would overshadow him, and Julian didn't feel like arguing. It was an odd grouping, this band of seeming misfits, but no one could say it wasn't an intriguing one. Brooke looked around the room and noticed everyone had quieted down.

Julian didn't introduce himself or the song the way he normally did when performing, just nodded his head toward his bandmates and began to sing his own version of "Achy Breaky Heart." It was a risky decision but a brilliant calculation. He had chosen a trite, corny song, changed it so it sounded serious, almost profound, and ended up with a completely fresh version that was conspiratorially cool and ironic. It said: *You expected us to come up here and sing an earnest rendition of the song you chose as your show's opener, or maybe something off the future album, but we're not here to take ourselves too seriously.* The crowd laughed and cheered and sang along, and when it was over, broke into mad applause.

Brooke clapped along with everyone else and reveled in all the people she could hear around her saying how talented Julian was, how they could listen to him all night. Hearing the others' excitement didn't surprise her in the least; how could they not feel that way? But it never, ever got old. Now, when Julian sidled up next to the microphone stand and flashed a huge, adorable smile, Brooke could feel the entire room smile back at him.

"Hey, y'all," he said, making an exaggerated tip of his cowboy hat. "Thanks for welcoming this Yankee boy to town."

The crowd hollered and clapped. Brooke saw Tim Riggins raise his bottle of beer to Julian, and she tried not to scream. Derek Jeter put both his hands around his mouth and made a "whoo-hoo!" sound. A couple of the writers, the female ones, with whom Brooke had been taste-testing margaritas earlier, formed a line in front of the stage and catcalled to the band. Julian rewarded them all with another killer smile.

"I think I speak for all of us when I say how proud and honored I am that you've made my song your song." More cheers and catcalls ensued, but Julian held up his hand. "And I can't wait to sing that tonight, here with all of you. But I hope you won't mind indulging me for just a few minutes before I play 'For the Lost.' Right now I'd like to sing a little something for my lovely wife, Brooke. She's been a really good sport lately — trust me, a *really* good sport — and it's been a while since I've said thank you. Rookie, this one's for you."

At the sound of her nickname, Brooke could feel herself blush, and for a split second she was taken aback that Julian had called her that in public. But before she even had time to consider it, she heard the opening chords to "Crazy Love" by Van Morrison — the first song they'd danced to at their wedding — and in a second, she was transfixed by his performance. Julian gazed directly at her as he allowed the song to grow and build, and it wasn't until he hit the chorus and threw his head back to wail the words that Brooke snapped out of their private reverie and noticed that every single person in the room was staring at her. Scratch that. The men in the room were shifting their weight from foot to foot, taking pulls of their beers, and watching the band as they worked over their instruments — it was the women who were staring at Brooke with looks of sheer envy and admiration. It was a surreal feeling; she'd certainly witnessed her fair share of Julian-worship at his other gigs, but she'd never before felt the spotlight focused so directly on her. She smiled and danced a little and watched Julian as he serenaded her and somehow, despite the fact that it was witnessed by hundreds, it felt like one of the most intimate moments they'd ever shared. One of the best she could ever remember.

As Julian finally segued into "For the Lost," Brooke was certain the entire room was in love with him. The energy was palpable and intense, but about halfway through the song, she felt an even stronger frisson of excitement. People started moving around, turning, looking, whispering. A few people craned their necks. One even pointed. Something was happening, but Brooke couldn't quite see what over the crowd until . . . *Wait . . . could that actually be . . .*

Layla Lawson? Oh, it sure was, and while Brooke couldn't figure out for the life of her what Layla Lawson was doing at the season-premiere party for *Friday Night Lights,* there she was . . . and she looked great. Judging from the floral bustier sundress and cowboy boots Layla was wearing, Brooke didn't know whether she was in costume or not, but there was no denying the girl looked fit, happy, and very, very famous. The entire room watched her as she greeted Samara with a huge hug and then made her way to the front of the crowd, near where Brooke stood at the foot of the stage.

It happened before anyone — including Julian — could even process it. Just a couple seconds after they finished the song and were soaking in the applause, Layla marched up the stage's side stairs, strode confidently over to Julian, and enveloped him in a bear hug. She smiled and, after kissing his cheek and wrapping both her hands around his upper arm, turned to face the crowd. She looked as though she was literally hanging from him, gazing up at him with a glimmering white smile and a look of sheer adoration. Until this point Julian had been frozen in disbelief, but something must have clicked — within seconds, he was returning the adoring look and then some.

She leaned toward the microphone as if it were her own and shouted, "How hot is he, everyone? Let's hear it for Julian Alter!"

The room went crazy. All the photographers who had ignored them earlier went wild. They jostled for position, firing off picture after picture, the flashbulbs lighting up like it was Oscar night. It was over almost as quickly as it started, with Layla leaning in to whisper something in Julian's ear and then bounding off the stage again. Brooke assumed she'd stay for a drink or two, but the starlet headed directly for the front door.

Ten minutes later Julian was once again by her side, all sweat and smiles, his usual post-performance glow heightened by the excitement. He kissed her and gave her a look that said, *I can't* wait *to talk about this with you,* and tightly clutched her hand as he worked the room, receiving the congratulations and backslaps with a good-natured laugh.

They weren't alone for a single second until almost one in the morning, when Samara and Leo said good night and headed to their hotel rooms (Leo accompanied by a new friend he'd met at the party, of course). The instant the door closed behind them, Julian turned to her and said, "Do you *believe* Layla Lawson jumped onstage with me?"

"If I hadn't seen it with my own eyes, I would never believe it. I'm still not sure I do." Brooke kicked off her boots and collapsed on the bed.

"Layla fucking *Lawson.* It's surreal. What on earth was she doing there?"

"I have no idea, but let me tell you, that

girl can *move*. Did you see the way she was dancing next to you, sort of shimmying and hip-switching? It was mesmerizing. It's like the instant someone puts a microphone in her hands, she just can't help it."

There was a knock at the door.

Julian looked at Brooke, who shrugged. He walked over to answer it, and Leo barreled in without an invite. Brooke almost laughed out loud: his shirt was unbuttoned to his navel, and he had a smear of what looked suspiciously like lipstick on the inside collar.

"Hey, listen," he said to Julian without so much as a hello or an apology for the interruption. "I know this is last-minute, but Samara just told me that she's set up a bunch of stuff for you tomorrow in L.A. That Layla scene was fucking genius, and people are freaking out about it. We'll leave for the airport at nine, okay?"

"Tomorrow?" Julian managed to say, looking as surprised as Brooke felt.

"Nine sharp, in the lobby. We've got the flights all taken care of. Probably get you back to New York in three, four days. Great job tonight, dude. See you in the morning," he said, and hightailed it out. Brooke sent out a silent thank-you to whichever girl was waiting in his bed that night.

"Well," Brooke said when the door slammed behind Leo.

"Well. Guess I'm going to L.A. tomorrow."

"Okay," Brooke said, because she didn't know what else to say. She'd have to cancel the dinner plans they had the following night with college friends of Julian's who were in from out of town. And he wouldn't be able to come with her to the museum party Nola had invited them to, the one where she was on the junior committee and the tickets had cost them a small fortune.

There was another knock on the door.

Brooke groaned. "What now?"

It was Samara this time, and she was as animated as Brooke had ever seen her. She, too, marched right in without a hello, looked down at her leather-bound notebook, and said, "So, the Lawson photo op worked even better than I'd hoped — absolutely everyone has picked it up. Everyone."

Both Julian and Brooke just stared at her.

"I've already gotten a hundred calls asking for interviews and photos. Brooke, I'm considering a story request for a feature on you, something like a 'Who Is Mrs. Julian Alter?' so stay tuned on that one. Julian, we'll keep you pretty much booked solid for the next week. This is great news, just absolutely terrific results, and I'll tell you now: everyone at Sony is thrilled."

"Wow," Julian said.

"Great," Brooke added weakly.

"The paparazzi are actually already staking out the lobby, so be ready to face them in the morning. I can make some recommendations on people you can consult for privacy and security needs, all really terrific."

"Oh, I don't think that will be necessary," Brooke said.

"Uh-huh. You let me know. In the meantime, I suggest you both start checking into hotels under different names and being very careful about what you put in e-mails to *anyone*."

"Um, is that really —"

Samara cut Julian off and clapped her notebook closed. Meeting officially adjourned.

"Brooke, Julian" — she said both their names slowly and with the sort of smile that gave Brooke chills — "welcome to the party."

6

HE COULD HAVE
BEEN A DOCTAH

"You want me to put these behind the exist-
ing shades or take the other ones down
first?" the installation man asked, motioning behind him, toward Brooke and Julian's
bedroom.

It wasn't a particularly important decision, but Brooke resented having to make it
herself. Julian was somewhere in the Pacific
Northwest — she had a hard time keeping
track these days — and wasn't much help
lately with anything domestic.

"I don't know, what do most people do?"

The guy shrugged. His expression said, *I
couldn't care less either way, just pick one so
I can get the hell out of here and enjoy my
Saturday.* Brooke knew exactly how he felt.

"Um, I guess put them behind the other
shades? Those are probably nicer-looking
anyway."

He grunted and disappeared, Walter following disloyally at his heels. Brooke turned

back to her book but was relieved when the phone rang.

"Hey, Dad, what's up?" It felt like they hadn't talked in ages, and when they did, he only wanted to talk about Julian.

"Oh, Brooke? Hi, it's Cynthia."

"Hey, Cynthia! I saw Dad's number on the caller ID. How are you? Any chance you guys are coming to New York?"

Cynthia attempted a laugh. "Probably not so soon. Last time was . . . tiring. You're always welcome here, you know."

"Yeah, I do know." It came out sounding ruder than she'd intended, although it was a little galling to receive an invitation to visit her own father in her own childhood home. Cynthia must have heard this because she quickly apologized, causing Brooke to feel immediate guilt for being unnecessarily bitchy.

"I'm sorry too," Brooke said with a sigh. "Things are just a little crazy around here right now."

"I can't even imagine! Listen, I know it's probably not possible, but I figure I had to ask. It's for a good cause, you know?"

Brooke inhaled and held her breath. Here it came, the wholly unanticipated aspect of being close to someone newly famous — he *was* famous now, wasn't he? — the part no one ever seemed to warn you about.

"I don't know if you know or not, but I'm one of the co-presidents of the Women's Board at Temple Beth Shalom."

Brooke waited but Cynthia didn't continue.

"Uh-huh, I think I knew that," Brooke said, trying to convey as little enthusiasm as possible.

"Well, we have our annual Speaker's Lunch fund-raiser coming up in a few weeks and our scheduled speaker just canceled on us. That woman who writes the kosher cookbooks? Actually, I don't think they're strictly kosher per se, just kosher style. She has one for Passover, one for Hanukkah, another just for kids."

"Mmm."

"Well, anyway, it turns out that she supposedly needs to have some sort of bunion surgery next week and won't be able to walk for a while, although if you ask me it's probably lipo."

Brooke willed herself to be patient. Cynthia was a good woman and she was only trying to raise money for the less fortunate. She took a deep, slow breath, careful not to let Cynthia hear.

"Maybe it really is for a bunion. Or maybe she just doesn't feel like traveling from

Shaker Heights to Philly, I don't know. Besides, who am I to judge? If someone came along and offered me a free tummy tuck right now, I'd probably sacrifice my own mother." Pause. "God, that sounded horrible, didn't it?"

Brooke wanted to rip her own hair out. Instead she forced a laugh. "I'm sure you're not alone there, but you don't need it. You look great."

"Oh, you're too sweet!"

Brooke waited a few seconds for Cynthia to remember why she called. "Oh! So anyway, I know he's probably so insanely busy these days, but if there's any way Julian could make an appearance at our luncheon, it would be so great."

"An appearance?"

"Yeah, well, an appearance or a performance, really whatever he wanted to do. Maybe sing that song he's famous for? The brunch starts at eleven with a silent auction in the auditorium and some light deli appetizers, and then we all move into the main hall where Gladys and I will talk about the work the Women's Board has done so far this year, the general state of membership at Beth Shalom, give some dates of upcoming —"

"Got it, okay. So you'd want him to . . .

173

perform? At a ladies' luncheon? You know the song is about a dead brother, right? Do you, uh, do you think everyone will like that?"

Thankfully Cynthia didn't take offense to this. "Like that? Oh, Brooke, I think they'd just love it."

Two months earlier Brooke wouldn't have believed it if someone told her she'd be having this conversation; now, having already been approached by the principal at Huntley, one of Brooke's old high school classmates, an ex-coworker, and not one but two cousins — all wanting Julian to sing or sign or send something — Brooke wasn't surprised by anything. All that said, this was probably the best one yet. She tried to picture Julian singing an acoustic version of "For the Lost" on the bimah of Temple Beth Shalom to a group of five hundred Jewish mothers and grandmothers, after receiving a kvelling introduction by the rabbi and the president of the board. Afterward, all the women would turn to one another and say things like, "Well, he's no doctor, but at least he makes a living at it," and "I heard he was premed but never pursued it. Such a shame." Then they'd swarm him and, noticing his wedding ring, want to know everything about his wife. Was she a nice Jewish girl too? Did they have children? No, why not? And more important, when do they plan to start trying? They'd cluck that he'd surely be a much better fit with their daughter or niece or friend's daughter. Despite the fact that they lived on the Main Line in Philly and Julian grew up in Manhattan, at least a dozen of the women present would find a connection to Julian's parents or grandparents or both. Julian would return home that evening shell-shocked, a veteran of a war only a few understood, and there would be nothing Brooke could say or do to comfort him.

"Well, let me talk to him. I know he'll be so honored you thought of him and I'm sure he'd just love to do it, but I'm pretty sure he's completely booked the next few weeks."

"Well if you really think he'd love to do it, I could talk to the other board members about possibly moving the date. Maybe we could —"

"Oh, I wouldn't want you to do that," Brooke said as quickly as she could. She'd never seen this side of Cynthia before and wasn't quite sure what to make of it. "He's incredibly unpredictable these days. Always committing and then having to cancel. He hates it, but his time just isn't his own anymore, you know?"

"Of course," Cynthia murmured, and Brooke tried not to think how ironic it was that she was using the same excuse on Cynthia that Julian now used on her.

Somewhere in the background the doorbell rang, Cynthia begged off, and Brooke sent Cynthia's visitor a telepathic thank-you. She read another two chapters of her book, a nonfiction account of the Etan Patz kidnapping that had her convinced every creepy-looking guy on the street was a potential pedophile, and followed the shade-installer-slash-paparazzi-blocker out the door when he was finished.

She was starting to grow more accustomed to being alone. With Julian gone so much, Brooke often joked that it felt like her old single days, just a whole lot less social. Now she weaved down Ninth Avenue, and when she passed the Italian bakery at the corner, with its hand-painted PASTICCERIA sign and its homemade curtains, there was no way to keep herself from walking in. It was an adorable place with a European-style coffee bar, where people ordered cappuccinos in the morning and espressos the rest of the day and drank them standing.

She surveyed the massive case of baked goods and could practically taste the butter cookies and jam-filled croissants and cheese tarts topped with berries. Of course there was no question that, if forced to choose only one, she'd have to go with a deliciously overstuffed cannoli in its sinful fried shell. First she'd lick the cream from the top, and then, following a palate-cleansing sip of coffee, she'd allow herself a full bite from either end, stopping to savor —

"Dimmi!" the Italian mother said, breaking Brooke's food fantasy.

"A large decaf skim latte, please, and one of those," Brooke said with a sigh, pointing to the un-iced, unstuffed, and otherwise unadorned biscotti resting sadly on a tray near the register. She knew the almond biscotti would be fresh and tasty and just the right amount crunchy, but it was a poor substitute for a cannoli. There wasn't much choice, though. She'd gained four pounds after their weekend in Austin and the mere thought of it made her want to scream. Her couple extra pounds of pudge would have been barely noticeable on the average woman, but on her — not just a nutritionist anymore, but a nutritionist married to someone famous — it was downright unacceptable. After returning from Austin, she'd immediately begun a food diary and accompanied it with a strict 1,300-calorie-per-day diet. Neither was having an impressive effect yet, but she was determined.

Brooke paid for her purchase and was hovering near the coffee bar when she heard her name.

"Brooke! Hey, over here."

She turned around and saw Heather, one of the guidance counselors at Huntley. Their offices were just down the hall from each other and although they occasionally met to discuss a student they had in common, lately they'd been seeing each other more than usual due to Kaylie. It was Heather who first noticed Kaylie's obsession with her weight and suggested she see Brooke; now both women were concerned about the girl. Yet as often as they'd been meeting at school the past couple months, they weren't actually friends, and Brooke felt a twinge of awkwardness seeing her colleague at a café on a Saturday.

"Hey!" Brooke said, sliding into a little wooden chair next to Heather. "I didn't even see you here. How are you?"

Heather smiled. "I'm good! Thrilled it's the weekend, I'll tell you that much. Can you believe we only have two more weeks of school before being off for three months?"

"I know," Brooke said, and decided not to mention that she would still be working full-time at the hospital.

Heather remembered anyway. "Yeah, I'll be doing a lot of private tutoring this summer, but at least I can determine those hours. I don't know if it was the horrible winter or I'm just getting burned out, but I can't *wait*."

"I hear you," Brooke said, feeling a little bit awkward that they didn't really have much else to talk about.

Heather seemed to read her mind. "It's weird to see each other outside school, isn't it?"

"It is! I am constantly paranoid I'm going to run into some of the girls on the street or in a restaurant. Remember what it was like when we were kids and you'd run into your teacher at the mall, and there was this stunning realization that they had a life outside your classroom?"

Heather laughed. "It's so true. Luckily we don't tend to travel in the same circles."

Brooke sighed. "It's crazy, isn't it?" And then: "I had a really productive meeting with Kaylie at the end of last week. I still don't feel comfortable allowing her to lose any weight, but I agreed that we could start her on a food journal to see where she could be eating healthier, more wholesome foods. She seemed pleased with that."

"I'm glad to hear it. I think we both know

that weight isn't her problem; it's the very understandable feeling of not fitting in with classmates who are from another socioeconomic universe. We see it frequently with the scholarship students, unfortunately, but they almost always find their niche."

Brooke disagreed to an extent — she'd worked with a fair number of teenage girls at this point, and in her opinion Kaylie was overly preoccupied with her weight — but she didn't want to start that conversation now. Instead, she smiled and said, "Look at us, talking about work on a Saturday. Shame on us!"

Heather sipped her coffee. "I know, it's all I can think about. I'm actually thinking of switching back to the lower schools in the next year or two. Just a better fit for me. What about you? Any thoughts on how long you'll stay?"

Brooke searched Heather's face for any sign that she was indirectly asking about Julian. Was the girl somehow implying that Brooke could quit now that Julian was making money as a musician? Had Brooke ever told her that was why she had accepted the job in the first place? She decided she was being way too paranoid, that if she didn't talk about Julian in a regular, normal way, how could she expect anyone else to?

"I don't know, actually. Things are, uh, kind of up in the air right now."

Heather looked at her sympathetically but was kind enough not to press. Brooke realized this was the very first time in three or four weeks that someone — anyone — had not immediately asked about Julian. She was grateful to Heather and eager to steer the conversation back to something less awkward. She glanced around, her mind searching for something to say, and then settled on, "So what are you up to today?" She quickly took a bite of her biscotti so she wouldn't have to talk for a few more seconds.

"Not much, really. My boyfriend's away with his family this weekend, so I'm on my own. Just hanging out, I guess."

"Nice. Love those weekends," Brooke lied. She managed to keep herself from announcing that she was quickly becoming the resident expert on how to best spend a weekend when your significant other is somewhere else. "What are you reading?"

"Oh, this?" Heather said, motioning toward the facedown magazine near her elbow without picking it up. "It's nothing. Some dumb gossip rag. Nothing interesting."

Brooke knew immediately it was *that* issue of *Last Night*. She wondered if Heather knew she was two weeks behind the ball.

"Ahh," she said with forced cheer that she knew didn't sound remotely believable. "The infamous photo."

Heather clasped her hands together and stared down at her lap as though she'd just been caught in some horrible lie. She opened her mouth to say something, reconsidered, and then said, "Yeah, it's kind of a weird picture."

"Weird? What do you mean?"

"Oh, I didn't, uh, I didn't mean anything by it. Julian looks great!"

"No, I know what you mean. There is something off about it." Brooke wasn't sure why she was grilling this girl she barely knew, but it suddenly felt crucially important to know what Heather thought.

"It's not that. I think it was just taken in a weird split second when he's, like, *gazing* at her in that way."

So that was it. Other people had made similar comments. Words like "enraptured" and "worshipful" had been thrown around. Which was all utterly ridiculous.

"Yeah, my husband thinks Layla Lawson is hot. Which makes him exactly like one hundred percent of other red-blooded American men." Brooke laughed, trying her best to sound casual.

"Totally!" Heather nodded in overenthusiastic agreement. "I bet it's just great for his career in terms of raising his profile."

Brooke smiled. "You could definitely say that. In one single night, that picture changed, well, everything."

Heather seemed sobered by this admission. She looked up at Brooke and said, "I know it's all so exciting, but I can't even imagine how hard it's been for you. I bet it's all anyone can talk about. Every second of every day must be all about Julian."

Brooke was caught off guard. No one — not Randy, or her parents, or even Nola — had assumed that Julian's newfound fame was anything but absolutely wonderful. She looked at Heather gratefully. "Yeah, but I'm sure it'll all blow over. Slow couple news weeks, you know? We'll be onto the next thing soon enough."

"You have to be ruthless about your privacy. My friend from college, Amber? One day she's getting married in a proper church wedding to her high school sweetheart, and less than a year later her brandnew husband wins *American Idol*. Talk about total and complete upheaval."

"Is your friend married to Tommy? From one of the earlier seasons?"

Heather nodded.

Brooke whistled. "Wow, I don't think I ever even knew he was married."

"Yeah, well, you sure wouldn't. It's literally a new girl every week, has been since the day he won. Poor Amber was so young — only twenty-two — and so naive that she wouldn't leave him, no matter how many girls he was linked to. She thought if she could just give it time, he would settle down and everything could go back to the way it was."

"So what happened?"

"Uch, it was horrible. He kept screwing around and was getting more and more blatant about it. Do you remember those pictures of him skinny-dipping with that model, the ones where they blurred out their genitals but you could see everything else?"

Brooke nodded. Even among the constant influx of paparazzi photos, she remembered those as particularly scandalous.

"Well, it went on that way for over a year with no signs of letting up. It got so bad that her father flew to meet Tommy on tour, showed up in his hotel room. He told him he had twenty-four hours to file divorce papers or else. He knew Amber would never do it herself — she was a good girl and still couldn't really wrap her mind around everything that was happening — and Tommy did it. I'm not sure he was a super stand-up guy before he was famous, but he is undoubtedly a colossal asshole now."

Brooke tried to keep a neutral expression, but she wanted to reach over and slap Heather. "Why are you telling me this?" she asked in as calm a voice as she could manage. "Julian is nothing like that."

Heather clamped a hand over her mouth. "I didn't mean to imply that Julian is *anything* like Tommy. Of course he's absolutely not at all. The only reason I started this whole story was that a little while after their divorce, Amber sent out an e-mail to all her friends and family, requesting that they stop e-mailing her pictures or links, snail-mailing clippings, or calling her with updates on what was happening with Tommy. I remember thinking it was a little weird at the time — like, are that many people really sending her interviews they'd read on her ex-husband? — but after she showed me her e-mail inbox one day, I totally got it. No one was trying to hurt her; they were just highly insensitive. They somehow thought she'd want to know. Anyway, since then, she's totally reclaimed her life and probably understands better than anyone out there how, uh, overwhelming all this fame stuff can be."

"Yeah, that part isn't great." Brooke drained the last of her latte and wiped the foam from her lips. "I probably wouldn't have believed it if you told me that a few weeks ago, but my god . . . I just spent the morning getting blackout shades installed. A few nights ago I walked from the bathroom to the fridge wearing a towel, and all of a sudden there were crazy flashbulbs going off. There was a photographer sitting on top of a car right below our window, obviously hoping to catch a picture of Julian. It was the creepiest thing I've ever seen."

"Oh, how awful! What did you do?"

"I called the nonemergency number of the local police station and said there was a man outside trying to take pictures of me undressed. They said something along the lines of 'Welcome to New York' and told me to lower the shades." She deliberately left out the part about first calling Julian, only to have him tell her that she was overreacting and she needed to deal with these kinds of things without "always" calling him in a panic about "everything."

Heather visibly shuddered. "That is so creepy. I hope you have an alarm or something?"

"Yeah, that's coming next." Brooke was

secretly hoping they'd move before that was necessary — just last night on the phone, Julian had obliquely mentioned something about "upgrading" to a new apartment — but she wasn't sure that was really going to happen.

"Excuse me for a second. I'm just going to run to the restroom," Heather said, taking her purse from the back of her chair.

She watched as Heather disappeared behind the ladies' room door. The moment she heard the lock click into place, she grabbed the magazine. It had been an hour, maybe less, since she'd last seen the photo, but she couldn't stop herself from turning directly to page fourteen. Her eyes moved automatically to the lower left of the page, where the picture was wedged innocently between a photo of Ashton grabbing Demi's highly toned backside and another of Suri perched atop Tom's shoulders while Katie and Posh looked on.

Brooke flattened the magazine open on the table and leaned over it to get a better look. It was every bit as disturbing as it had been sixty minutes earlier. If she had just glanced at it quickly, and it didn't happen to feature her husband and a world-famous starlet, she would have found nothing noteworthy about it. You could see the raised arms of the first couple rows in the lower part of the frame. Julian's right arm was thrust victoriously into the air, and his hand clutched the microphone like it was a saber with special powers. Brooke got chills every time she looked at Julian in that pose, could barely believe how much he looked like a real rock star.

Layla wore a shockingly short floral sundress that may have been a romper and a pair of studded white leather cowboy boots. She was tanned, made-up, accessorized, and extensioned to within an inch of her life, and her expression as she gazed up at Julian was one of sheer joy. It was nauseating, but far more upsetting was Julian's expression. The adoration, the worship, the *ohmigod you're the most amazing creature I've ever laid eyes on* look was undeniable, plastered across his face in blazing color thanks to the professional Nikon. It was the kind of look a wife would hope to see a couple times in her life, on her wedding day, maybe the day her first child is born. It was exactly the kind of look you never wanted your husband to give another woman on the pages of a national magazine.

Brooke heard the sink run behind the wooden door. She quickly closed the copy of *Last Night* and placed it facedown in front of Heather's chair. When Heather returned she looked at Brooke and glanced at the magazine; her eyes seemed to say, *I probably shouldn't have left that there.* Brooke wanted to tell her that it was fine, that she was slowly getting used to all of it, but of course she said nothing. Instead, she blurted out the first thing that came to her mind to smooth over the awkwardness.

"It was so great *seeing* you. It's such a shame that we spend so many hours each week at that school and we never see each other outside. We'll have to work on that! Maybe make a plan for brunch on the weekend, or even a dinner. . . ."

"Sounds great. Have fun tonight, okay?" Heather gave a little wave as she walked out. "See you next week at Huntley."

Brooke waved back, but Heather had already stepped onto the sidewalk. She was getting ready to leave herself, trying not to wonder if she'd overshared or not shared enough or done something else to freak out Heather, when her phone rang. The caller ID showed it was her friend from grad school, Neha.

"Hey!" Brooke said as she tossed a couple dollars on the counter and walked outside. "How are you?"

"Brooke! I'm just calling to say hello. It

seems like forever since we've talked."

"Yeah, it really has been. How's Boston? Are you liking the clinic you're working for? And when the hell are you coming to visit?"

It had probably been six months since the girls had last seen each other when Neha and her husband, Rohan, were in New York over Christmas. They'd been close friends in graduate school, living only a few blocks from each other in Brooklyn, but it had been harder to keep in touch since Neha and Rohan had moved to Boston two years earlier.

"Yeah, I like the clinic just fine — it's actually way better than I expected — but I'm so ready to move back to New York. Boston's nice, but it's just not the same."

"Are you really thinking of coming back? When? Oh, tell me everything!"

Neha laughed. "Not for a little while. We'd both need to find jobs, and it'll probably be easier for me than Rohan. But we're coming to visit over Thanksgiving since we both have off. Will you and Julian be around?"

"We usually go to my father's in Pennsylvania, but he's been saying they may go to my stepmother's family's this year. So there's a chance we'll just suck it up and host in New York. If we do, will you guys come? Please?" Brooke knew both their families lived in India and neither one especially celebrated Thanksgiving, but they would be such a welcome distraction from all the intense family time.

"Of course we'll come! But can we just backtrack for a second, please? Can you even believe what's going on in your life right now? Are you pinching yourself every day? It's just the craziest thing ever. What does it feel like to have a famous husband?"

Brooke took a deep breath. She thought about being honest with Neha, telling her how much the picture had turned their world upside down, how ambivalent she felt about everything that was happening, but suddenly it all seemed too exhausting. Not really knowing how to handle it, she just laughed a little and lied.

"It's amazing, Neha. It's just the coolest thing in the world."

There was nothing worse than being at work on a Sunday. As one of the more senior nutritionists on staff, Brooke hadn't endured regularly scheduled Sunday shifts in years, and she'd all but forgotten how lousy they were. It was a perfect late June morning; everyone she knew was having brunch outside or picnicking in Central Park or jogging along Hudson River Park. A group of teenage girls in jean shorts and flip-flops sat gabbing and sipping smoothies at a café a block from the hospital, and it was all Brooke could do not to tear off her lab coat and hideous clogs and join them for pancakes. She was just about to walk into the hospital when her cell phone rang.

She stared at the screen and debated whether or not to pick up the unfamiliar 718 area code that indicated an outer borough, but she must have thought about it too long, because it went to voice mail. When the caller didn't leave a message and called back a second time, Brooke got worried.

"Hello, this is Brooke," she said, instantly certain she'd made a mistake and the mystery caller was going to be a reporter.

"Mrs. Alter?" a timid voice squeaked through the line. "It's Kaylie Douglas. From Huntley."

"Kaylie! How are you? Is everything okay?"

Just a couple weeks earlier, at their last session before school broke for the summer, Kaylie seemed to take a turn for the worse. She'd abandoned her food diary, which until then she had been diligent with, and had announced her determination to spend the summer on a punishing workout regimen and various quick-loss diets. No attempt at trying to talk her out of it seemed to work; Brooke had only succeeded in bringing the girl to tears and an announcement that "no one understood what it felt like to be poor and fat in a place where everyone else is rich and beautiful." Brooke was so worried that she had given Kaylie her cell phone number and insisted the girl call her anytime over the summer, whether anything was wrong or not. She had certainly meant it, but she was still surprised to hear her young patient on the other end.

"Yeah, I'm okay. . . ."

"What's been going on? How have your couple weeks off been?"

The girl started to cry. Big, gulping breaths interspersed with the occasional "I'm sorry."

"Kaylie? Talk to me. Tell me what's wrong."

"Oh, Mrs. A, everything is such a disaster! I'm working at Taco Bell and I get a free meal every shift and my father says I have to eat the free food, so I do. But then I come home and my grandmother's made all this fattening food and I go to my friends' apartments, from my old school, and it's, like, buckets of fried chicken and burritos and cookies and I eat all of it because I'm just so hungry. I've only been out of school for a few weeks, and I already gained eight pounds!"

Eight pounds in three weeks did sound alarming, but Brooke kept her voice soothing and calm. "I'm sure you haven't, sweetheart. You just need to remember what we talked about: meat portions the size of your palm, as much leafy green salads and vegetables as you want so long as you're careful with the dressing, cookies in moderation. I'm not at home right now, but I can check out the Taco Bell menu and give you some healthier alternatives if you want. The important thing is not to panic. You're young and healthy — go for a walk with your friends, or kick around a ball in the park. It's not the end of the world, Kaylie, I promise."

"I can't come back to school next year if I look like this. I'm over the limit now! Before I was just at the high end of normal, and that was bad enough, but now I'm officially obese!" She sounded almost hysterical.

"Kaylie, you are nowhere *near* obese," Brooke said. "And you're going to have a wonderful year at school this fall. Listen, I'm going to do a little research later tonight, and I'll call you back with the info, okay? Please don't worry so much, sweetheart."

Kaylie sniffled. "I'm sorry to bother you," she said quietly.

"You didn't bother me at all! I gave you my number so you would use it, and I'm happy you did. Makes me feel popular." Brooke smiled.

They hung up and Brooke sent herself an e-mail reminder to look up the nutritional information for fast-food restaurants and pass it along to Kaylie. She was a few minutes late getting upstairs to the hospital break room, and only her colleague Rebecca was there when she arrived.

"What are you doing here today?" she asked.

"Oh, I'm making up a few missed shifts. Unfortunately, the trade was three shifts for a double on Sunday."

"Ouch. Tough terms. But worth it?"

Brooke laughed ruefully. "Yeah, I think I got killed, but seeing Julian perform at Bonnaroo was really cool." She placed her purse and her packed lunch in her locker and followed Rebecca into the hallway. "Any idea if Margaret's in today?"

"I'm right here!" A cheerful voice trilled out behind them. Brooke's boss was wearing a pair of black dress slacks, a light blue blouse, and black loafers, all topped by a perfectly starched and pressed lab coat that was embroidered with her name and credentials.

"Hello, Margaret," Rebecca and Brooke said in unison before Rebecca peeled out, claiming she was late for her first patient.

"Brooke, why don't you join me in my office for a minute? We can talk there."

Nightmare. She should've remembered that Margaret almost always put in an appearance on Sunday mornings just to make sure things were running smoothly.

"O-oh, everything's fine," she stammered. "I, uh, I was just wondering if I was going to get to say hello to you."

Her boss had already begun walking down the long hallway toward her office. "Come now," she called to Brooke, who had no choice but to follow her. The woman must have sensed Brooke was about to ask for more time off.

Margaret's office was located down a dark hallway, next to the supply closet and on the same floor as the maternity ward, which meant there was a pretty good chance the conversation would be punctuated by an errant scream or a groan. The only upside was getting to glance in the nursery as they walked by. Maybe she'd have a free second a little later to go in there and hold a baby or two. . . .

"Come right in," Margaret said as she swung open the door and turned on the lights. "You caught me at the perfect time."

Brooke tentatively walked in behind her and waited for her boss to clear a pile of papers off the guest seat before lowering herself into the chair.

"To what do I owe this honor?" Margaret smiled, but Brooke read between the lines. They'd always enjoyed an easy, natural relationship, but lately Brooke had begun to sense tension between them.

She forced herself to smile and prayed this wasn't an inauspicious start to a conversation she really needed to go well. "Oh, hardly an honor, I'm sure, I just wanted to talk to you about —"

Margaret smiled. "It is a bit of an honor considering I haven't seen much of you lately. I'm glad you're here, because there's something I need to discuss with you."

Brooke took a deep breath and reminded herself to keep calm.

"Brooke, you know how fond I am of you, and it goes without saying that I've been extremely pleased with your performance in all the years you've worked here. And of course, so have your patients, as evidenced by those terrific evaluations a few months ago."

"Thank you," Brooke said, unsure how to respond but certain this wasn't going somewhere good.

"Which is why it's upsetting to me that you've gone from having the second-best attendance record to having the second-worst in the entire program. Only Perry's is worse than yours."

She didn't need to finish. They'd finally been briefed on what was happening with Perry, and everyone had been relieved it wasn't something worse. Apparently she'd suffered a late miscarriage six months earlier, which accounted for some of her absences. Now, pregnant again, she'd been put on mandatory bed rest in her second trimester. It meant that the remaining five full-time RDs on staff needed to work extra hours to cover for Perry, which, considering the circumstances, no one minded. Brooke was doing her best to cover her extra workday each week and her extra on-call weekend, now bumped from once every six weeks to once every five, but trying to keep up with Julian's travel schedule — to share in the excitement with him — was making it almost unbearable.

Don't explain yourself; don't apologize; just reassure her you'll do better, Brooke told herself. A psychologist friend had once told her that women felt compelled to offer long explanations and excuses whenever they needed to deliver negative news, and that it was much more powerful to state it without an apology or an excuse. Brooke worked on this often, to little success.

"I'm so sorry!" she blurted before she could stop herself. "I've been having, um, a lot of family issues recently, and I'm doing my best to handle them. I'm really hopeful that things should calm down soon."

Margaret raised a single eyebrow and peered intently at Brooke. "Do you think I'm not aware of what's been happening?" she asked.

"Why, no, of course not. It's just that there is so much —"

"One would have to live in a cave." She smiled, and Brooke felt a little better. "But I do have a staff to run and I'm getting concerned. You've taken seven days off in the last six weeks — which isn't even counting your three sick days from the first part of the year — and I'm assuming you're here to request even more time. Am I correct?"

Brooke quickly debated her options. Deciding she had none, she merely nodded.

"When and for how long?"

"In three weeks, just the Saturday. I know I'm scheduled to work all weekend, but Rebecca is going to switch with me and I'll take her weekend in three weeks. So it's, uh, technically just one day."

"Just one day."

"Yes. It's an important, um, family event, or I wouldn't even ask." She made a mental note to be even more diligent than usual about avoiding the cameras at Kristen Stewart's birthday party in Miami, where Julian had been invited to perform four songs. When he'd balked at appearing at a young starlet's birthday party, Leo had pleaded with him. Brooke couldn't help but feel a little queasy for Julian; the least she could do was be there to support him.

Margaret opened her mouth to say something and then changed her mind. She tapped her pencil against her chapped lower lip and stared at Brooke. "You do realize you're already closing in on your total number of vacation days this year and it's only June?"

Brooke nodded.

Margaret tapped her pencil against her desk. *Tap-tap-tap,* it went in unison with Brooke's pounding headache.

"And I don't need to remind you that calling in sick to attend parties with your husband cannot happen anymore, right? I'm sorry, Brooke, but I can't give you special treatment."

Ouch. Brooke had done that only once so far and was certain Margaret didn't know, but she'd definitely been planning to dip into her ten remaining sick days once her vacation ran out. Now that was clearly not an option. Brooke did her best to look unruffled and said, "Of course not."

"Well, all right then. Saturday is yours. Is there anything else?"

"Nothing else. Thank you for understanding." Brooke stuck her feet back into her clogs underneath Margaret's desk and stood up. She gave a little wave and disappeared through the office door before Margaret could say another word.

7

BETRAYED BY A
BUNCH OF TWEENS

Brooke walked into Lucky's Nail Design on Ninth Avenue and found her mother already seated and reading a copy of *Last Night*. With Julian gone so often, her mother had volunteered to come into the city, take Brooke for a post-work mani and pedi, get some sushi for dinner, and spend the night before heading back to Philly in the morning.

"Hi," Brooke said, leaning over to kiss her. "Sorry I'm late. The train was weirdly slow today."

"Oh, you're fine, dear. I just got here and was catching up on my celebrity gossip." She held out the copy of *Last Night*. "Nothing about Julian or you, so don't worry."

"Thanks, but I've already read it," she said, plunging her feet into the warm soapy water. "Comes in the mail a day earlier than it hits the newsstands. I think you can officially call me an authority on the subject."

Brooke's mom laughed. "Maybe if you're such an expert, you can explain these reality TV stars. I have a lot of trouble keeping them straight."

Mrs. Greene sighed and turned the page, revealing a double-page spread of the teenage actors from the latest vampire movie. "I miss the old days when Paris Hilton could be depended on to flash her panties and George Clooney would pull through with yet another cocktail waitress. I feel like I've been betrayed by a bunch of tweens."

Brooke's phone rang. She thought about letting it go to voice mail, but on the off chance it was Julian, she dug it out from her bag.

"Hey! I hoped it might be you. What time is it there?" She checked her own watch. "What on earth are you doing calling now? Aren't you setting up for tonight?"

Although this was Julian's fifth or sixth solo trip to Los Angeles since the *Friday Night Lights* party, Brooke still felt out of sorts with the time difference. By the time Julian woke up in the morning on the West Coast, Brooke had finished her lunch hour and was back at work for the rest of the afternoon. She'd call him the moment she got home in the evening, which usually put him right in the middle of meetings, and then he was always out to some dinner when she was going to bed and could never utter more than a whispered "good night" against the backdrop of glasses clinking and people laughing. It was only a three-hour difference, but to people working such opposite schedules, they may as well have been communicating across the international date line. She tried to be patient, but just last week, three nights had passed with little more than a bunch of texts and a quickie "Call you later."

"Brooke, it's crazy, all kinds of things are happening here." He sounded wired, like he'd been up for days.

"Good things, I hope?"

"Beyond good things! I wanted to call you last night but by the time I got back to the hotel, it was already four in the morning your time."

The pedicurist finished cutting the cuticles and yanked Brooke's right foot into her lap. She squirted a bright green soap onto a pumice stone and raked it roughly over the sensitive middle of the foot. Brooke yelped.

"Ow! Well, I could use some good news. What's up?"

"It's official: I'm going on tour."

"What? No! I thought you said the chances of that happening before the album came out were slim to none. That record companies don't really sponsor them anymore."

There was a moment's pause. Julian sounded irritated when he said, "I know I said that, but this is different. I'll be linking up with Maroon 5 in the middle of their tour. The lead singer of their first opener had some sort of breakdown, so Leo got in touch with some of his people at Live Nation, and guess who got the slot? Supposedly there's a chance to become the second opener if that band goes on tour separately, but even if that doesn't happen, the exposure is ridiculous."

"Oh, Julian, congratulations!" Brooke tried to gauge her own voice to make sure she sounded excited and not devastated. With the odd way her mother was staring at her it was difficult to tell if she was succeeding.

"Yeah, it's pretty insane. We're going to spend this week in rehearsals, and then we'll hit the road. The album will drop in the first few weeks, which is awesome timing. And, Rook? They're talking real money."

"Yeah?" she asked.

"Real money. A percentage of all ticket sales. Which would jump even higher if we ever make second opener. Considering

Maroon 5 is selling out places like MSG . . . it's an insane amount of cash. And it's weird" — his voice got lower — "it's like people are always looking at me. Recognizing me."

The pedicurist slathered on warm cream and began to knead Brooke's calves. Brooke wanted nothing more at that moment than to press End on her cell phone, recline her massage chair, and enjoy the foot rub. She felt nothing but anxiety. She knew she should've asked about the fans and the press, but all she could manage was, "So rehearsals start this week? Aren't you coming home on the red-eye tonight? I thought I was going to see you tomorrow morning before work."

"Brooke."

"What?"

"Please don't."

"Please don't what? Ask when you're coming home?"

"Please don't ruin this for me. I'm really, really excited — this is probably the biggest thing since the album deal last year. Bigger, maybe. In the grand scheme of my entire career, does another six or seven days really matter?"

Six or seven days until he came home, maybe, but what about being on tour? The mere thought of it made her panicky with dread. How would they deal with that? Could they? But in the very same moment she remembered the night, years earlier in Sheepshead Bay, when only four people showed up and Julian could barely contain his tears. Not to mention all the hours they'd already logged apart during their hectic work schedules, all the stressing about money and time and the what-ifs they threw out when one of them was feeling particularly negative. That sacrifice, it was all for this, for right now.

The old Julian would've asked about Kaylie. When she'd told him all about the girl's hysterical phone call the month before and how she had researched fast-food alternatives and e-mailed them to her young patient, Julian had hugged her and told her how proud he was. Just last week Brooke had e-mailed Kaylie to check in with her and had been concerned to receive no reply. She followed up again a day later and Kaylie wrote back that she was starting on some sort of cleanse she'd read about in a magazine, and that she was certain this was the answer she'd been looking for. Brooke almost jumped through the computer screen.

Those goddamn cleanses! They were a

health risk for normal adults, but they were an all-out disaster for the still-growing teen-age population who seemed forever drawn to their celeb testimonials and promises of quick and miraculous results. Brooke had immediately called Kaylie to read her the riot act — she had it memorized by now, since cleanses, fasts, and juice diets were such favored Huntley methods — and was relieved to discover that Kaylie, unlike most of her classmates, was actually receptive to what she had to say. She pledged to check in with her once a week throughout the summer, and she was hopeful that as long as she got back to their regular sessions once school resumed, she could really help this girl.

But Julian didn't ask about Kaylie, or her work at the hospital, or Randy, or even Walter, and Brooke held her tongue. She chose not to remind Julian that he'd only been home a handful of nights the past few weeks, and that most of those he'd spent either on the phone or at the studio in seem-ingly never-ending conversations with Leo or Samara. And, most challenging of all, she forced herself not to inquire about his tour dates or ask how long he might be on the road.

Almost choking from the effort of it all,

she simply said, "No, Julian, it only matters that you get this right. This is truly great news."

"Thanks, baby. I'll call you later today when I have more details, okay? Love you, Rookie," he said with more tenderness than she'd heard from him in a while. Julian had started calling Brooke "Rook" when they'd first started dating, which had naturally segued to "Rookie." Her friends and family began using it themselves after they overheard Julian call her that, and although she often rolled her eyes or feigned some sort of displeasure, she felt an inexplicable gratitude to Julian for giving her this affectionate nickname. She tried to focus on that and not the fact that he'd hung up without so much as asking how she was doing.

The manicurist slicked on the first coat of polish, and Brooke thought the color looked too garish. She thought about saying something but decided it wasn't worth the effort. Her mother's toenails were painted a perfect shade of pinkish-white, a color that looked both chic and natural.

"Sounds like Julian got some good news?" Mrs. Greene asked, placing the magazine facedown in her lap.

"He sure did," Brooke said, hoping her voice sounded brighter than she felt. "Sony's sending him on a warm-up tour of sorts. They're rehearsing in Los Angeles this week and then they'll be opening for Maroon 5, so it'll give them a chance to practice in front of audiences before they go on tour themselves. It's a huge vote of confidence on their part."

"But it means he'll be around even less."

"Yep. He's staying out there the rest of this week to rehearse. Then maybe he'll come home for a few days and then he's off again."

"How do you feel about that?"

"It's pretty much the best news he could've gotten."

Her mom smiled as she slid her finished feet into the salon-provided paper flip-flops. "You didn't answer my question."

Brooke's phone pinged. "Saved by the bell," she said cheerily.

It was a text from Julian. It read: "Forgot to tell u: they want me to get new clothes! They say my look doesn't work. Total nightmare!"

Brooke laughed out loud.

"What is it?" her mom asked.

"Maybe there is justice after all. I guess the publicist or the marketing people or someone is saying that Julian's 'look' doesn't work. They want him to get new clothes."

"What do they want him in? I can't exactly see Julian in Michael Jackson military jackets or MC Hammer pants." She looked proud of her pop culture references.

"Are you kidding? I have been married to him for five years and can count on two hands the number of times I've seen him in anything besides jeans and a white T-shirt. He's going to struggle with this. Big-time."

"So let's help him!" her mom said. She handed her credit card to the woman who presented her with the bill. Brooke tried to grab her own wallet, but her mother waved her away.

"Trust me, there is no way on earth Julian is going to agree to a new 'look.' He'd rather die than go shopping, and he's more attached to his jeans-and-white-T-shirt uniform than some men are to their children. I don't think Sony knows what they're up against, but they are definitely *not* going to convince him to start dressing like Justin Timberlake."

"Brooke, sweetie, this one can be fun. Since Julian's never going to buy anything himself, let's go shopping *for* him." Brooke followed her mother out the door and directly into the subway stairs. "We'll buy him stuff he already has, just nicer. I have a brilliant idea."

Two trains and two stops later, the women exited at Fifty-ninth Street and entered Bloomingdale's from the basement level. Brooke's mother confidently led the way to the men's department.

Her mom held up a pair of classic boot-cut jeans in a vintage wash. Not too dark, not too light, perfectly faded, and without any annoying patches, zippers, holes, rips, or weird pockets. Brooke felt the fabric. It was surprisingly lightweight and soft, possibly even softer than Julian's beloved Levi's.

"Wow," Brooke said, taking them from her mother. "I think he'd actually love these. How did you do that?"

Her mother smiled. "I dressed you kids pretty well when you were younger. I guess I've still got it."

It was only then Brooke noticed the price tag. "Two hundred fifty dollars? Julian's Levi's are forty bucks. I can't get him these."

Her mother snatched them out of her hand. "Oh yes you can. And you will. You're going to get him these and a couple other pairs. Then we're going to march right over to the clothing section and get him the softest, best-fitting white T-shirts we can find, and they're probably going to cost seventy dollars each, and that's okay. I'll help you cover the cost."

Brooke stared at her mother, dumb-founded, but Mrs. Greene only nodded. "This is important. For all sorts of reasons, but especially because I think it's crucial right now that you're there to help and support him."

The bored salesman finally sauntered over. Brooke's mother waved him away.

"Are you suggesting I'm not supportive of him? That I don't help him? Why have I been working two jobs for four years now if I'm not completely and totally behind him? What do a few pairs of jeans have to do with it?" Brooke could hear her voice growing almost hysterical, but she couldn't help it.

"Come here," her mother said, holding open her arms. "Come here and let me hug you."

Whether it was her sympathetic look or just the unfamiliar feeling of being embraced, the moment she felt her mother's arms close around her, Brooke started to sob. She wasn't sure why she was crying. Aside from Julian announcing he wasn't coming home for another week, nothing was really that tragic — everything was actually really great — but once she began, she couldn't stop. Her mother hugged her tighter and smoothed her hair, murmuring comforting nothings the way she had when

Brooke was little.

"There's a lot of change happening right now," she said.

"But all of it's good."

"That doesn't mean it's not scary. Brooke, sweetheart, I know you don't need me to point this out, but Julian is on the cusp of becoming a nationally known musician. When that album comes out, your entire lives are going to be turned upside down. Everything up until now is just the warm-up."

"But it's what we've worked toward for so many years."

"Of course it is." Mrs. Greene first patted Brooke's arm and then cupped her face with one hand. "But that doesn't mean it isn't really overwhelming. He's already away from home a lot, your schedules have been thrown into chaos, and there are all sorts of new people on the scene, weighing in, giving opinions, intervening in your business. It's probably only going to intensify, both the good stuff and the bad stuff, so I want you to be prepared."

Brooke smiled and held up the jeans. "And I'm preparing by buying him more expensive jeans than I wear? Really?" Her mother had always been more into clothes than her, but even she didn't spend recklessly or to excess.

"That's exactly right. There's a lot you're not going to be a part of in the next couple months, due only to the fact that he's going to be traveling and you'll be working here. He's probably not going to have a tremendous amount of control over his own life, and you aren't either. It's going to be tough. But I know you, Rook, and I know Julian too. You guys are going to get through this, and once everything settles into more of a groove, you're going to be great. And please forgive me for meddling in your marriage — I am hardly an expert here, as we all know — but until this crazy time has passed, you can make it easier by getting involved in any way you possibly can. Help him brainstorm marketing ideas. Wake up in the middle of the night when he calls, regardless of how tired you are — he'll call more if he knows you want to hear from him. Buy him fancy new clothes when he's told he needs them but doesn't know where to start. Screw the cost! If this album sells half as well as everyone's predicting, this little shopping spree won't even be a blip on the radar screen."

"You should've heard him talk about how much he's going to rake in on this tour. I'm not great at math, but I think he's talking high six figures."

Her mother smiled. "You two deserve it, you know that? You've both worked so hard for so long now. You'll go on some totally ridiculous spending binge, buying all sorts of luxuries you never even knew existed, and you're going to love every minute of it. I, for one, am hereby officially volunteering to accompany you on all cash-blowing expeditions as the official credit card and shopping bag holder. There's a lot of crap to put up with between now and then, no doubt. But you're up for it, sweetheart. I know you are."

When they finally left the store an hour and a half later, it took both of them to lug home all the new clothes. Together they'd selected four pairs of blue jeans and one pair of faded black ones, plus a pair of tight, denim-like corduroys that Mrs. Greene convinced Brooke were close enough to jeans to pass muster with Julian. They ran their fingers through heaping piles of white designer T-shirts, comparing the softness of jersey to Egyptian cotton, debating whether one might be too see-through or another too boxy, before selecting a dozen of them in various styles and fabrics. They'd split up when they hit the main floor and her mother went off to buy Julian some Kiehl's men's products, swearing that she'd never met a man who didn't worship their shaving cream and aftershave. Brooke had her doubts that he would use anything besides the old-school Gillette foam in an aerosol can they sold for two bucks at Duane Reade, but she appreciated her mother's enthusiasm. She made her way to the accessories department, where she carefully chose five knit caps, all in muted colors — one in a subtle black-on-black stripe — rubbing each one against her face to ensure it wasn't hot or itchy.

The grand total of their shopping expedition came to a staggering $2,260, the largest single sum she had ever charged — furniture purchases included — in her entire life. It took her breath away to think about writing the check for that credit card bill, but she forced herself to stay focused on what was important: he was on the verge of a major career breakthrough, and she owed it to both of them to be behind him one hundred percent. Plus she was also pleased that she'd stayed true to his personal look, had respected his timeless jeans, white tee, and knit cap aesthetic and hadn't tried to push some new image on him. It was one of the headiest afternoons she'd had in a long, long time. Even if the clothes weren't for her, it didn't make choosing and buying them any less fun.

By the time Julian called the following Sunday to say he was in the cab on his way home from the airport, she was beside herself with excitement. At first she laid out all the new purchases in the living room, draping the couch with jeans and the dining room chairs with T-shirts and hanging the knit caps from lamps and bookshelves around the room like ornaments on a tree, but just moments before he was due to arrive, she changed her mind and gathered everything back up again. She quickly folded the goods and returned them to their rightful shopping bags, which she tucked into the back corner of their shared closet, imagining how much more fun it would be for them to go through the pieces one by one. When she heard the front door open and Walter begin to bark, she ran out of the bedroom and flung her arms around Julian.

"Baby," he murmured, burying his face in her neck and inhaling deeply. "My god, I missed you."

He looked thinner, even more gaunt than usual. Julian outweighed Brooke by a good twenty pounds, but she was never really sure how. They were the exact same height, and she always felt like she was enveloping him, crushing him. She looked him up and down, leaned over, and pressed her lips against his. "I missed *you* so much. How was your flight? And the cab? Are you hungry? I have some pasta I can heat up."

Walter was barking so loudly it was almost impossible for them to hear each other. He wasn't going to quiet down until he'd been properly greeted, so Julian collapsed onto the couch and tapped the spot next to him, but Walter had already jumped onto his chest and begun bathing Julian's face with his tongue.

"Whoa, ease up there, good boy," Julian said with a laugh. "Wow, that is some wicked doggy breath. Doesn't anyone brush your teeth, Walter Alter?"

"He's been waiting for his daddy," Brooke called merrily from the kitchen, where she was pouring them wine.

When she returned to the living room, Julian was in the bathroom. The door was slightly open and she could see him standing in front of the toilet. Walter stood at his feet and watched with fascination as Julian peed.

"I've got a surprise for you," Brooke sang out. "Something you are just going to loooove."

Julian zipped up, made a halfhearted attempt at running his hands under the faucet, and joined her on the couch. "I have a surprise for you, too," he said. "And I think *you're* going to love it."

"Really? You got me a present!" Brooke knew she sounded like a child, but who didn't love gifts?

Julian smiled. "Well, yeah, I guess you could call it a present. It's sort of for both of us, but I think you'll like it even more than me. You go first. What's your surprise?"

"No, you first." Brooke wasn't going to take any chances of having her clothing presentation overshadowed; she wanted his full attention for that one.

Julian looked at her and grinned. He stood up, walked back to the foyer, and returned with a rolling suitcase she didn't recognize. It was black, Tumi, and absolutely gigantic. He rolled it right in front of her and waved his hand.

"You got me a suitcase?" she asked with a bit of confusion. There was no denying it was gorgeous, but it wasn't exactly what she was expecting. Plus this one looked packed to the point where it was ready to pop right open.

"Open it," Julian said.

Brooke hesitantly leaned down and gave the zipper a little tug. It didn't budge. She pulled a little harder, but still nothing.

"Here," Julian said, hefting the massive thing onto its side and yanking open the zipper. He flipped the top open to reveal . . . piles of neatly stacked clothing. Brooke was more confused than ever.

"Looks like, uh, clothes," Brooke said, wondering why Julian appeared so happy.

"Yeah, they're clothes, but not just any clothes. You, my dear Rookie, are looking at your husband's new and improved image, care of his brand-new, label-provided stylist. How cool is that?"

Julian looked at Brooke expectantly, but it was taking time for her to process what he meant. "Are you saying that a *stylist* bought you a new wardrobe?"

Julian nodded. "Completely and totally new — a 'fresh and totally unique look' was how the chick described it. And, Rook, let me tell you, this girl knew what she was doing. It only took a few hours and I didn't have to do anything but sit in a huge private dressing room at Barneys, and all these girls and gay guys kept bringing in hangers full of clothes. They put together, like, outfits and showed me what to wear with what. We had a couple beers and I tried on all these crazy things and everyone was weighing in on what they thought worked and what didn't, and when all was said and done, I walked out with all this stuff." He motioned toward the suitcase. "Just look at some of this stuff, it's outrageous."

He plunged his hands into the piles, yanked out an armful of clothing, and tossed it on the couch between them. Brooke wanted to scream at him to take better care of it, to mind the folds and the piles, but even she realized how ridiculous this was. She leaned over and held up a moss green cashmere hoodie. It had a waffle knit to it and felt as soft as a baby blanket. The tag read $495.

"How sweet is that one?" Julian asked with the kind of excitement he normally reserved only for musical instruments or new electronic gadgets.

"You never wear hoodies," was all Brooke could manage.

"Yeah, but what better time to start than now?" Julian said with another grin. "I think I could get used to a five-hundred-dollar hoodie. Did you feel how soft it is? Here, check these out." He tossed her a buttery leather jacket and a pair of John Varvatos black leather boots that were a cross between motorcycle and cowboy boots. Brooke wasn't quite sure what they were, but even she knew they were cool. "How much do those rock?"

Again, she nodded. Scared she would start to cry if she didn't do *something,* Brooke leaned over into the suitcase and pulled another pile of clothes onto her lap. There were heaps of designer and vintage T-shirts in every imaginable color. She spotted a pair of Gucci loafers — the ones with the sleek dress sole and without the telltale logo — and a pair of white Prada sneakers. There were hats, so many hats, chunky knit caps like the ones he always wore, but also cashmere ones and Panama Jacks and white fedoras. Probably ten or twelve hats in different styles and colors, each one different but stylish in its own unique way. Handfuls of whisper-thin cashmere V-necks, slim-cut Italian blazers that screamed casual cool, and jeans. So many jeans in every imaginable cut, color, and wash that Julian could probably wear a new pair every day for a fortnight and not have to repeat. Brooke forced herself to unfold and look at each of them until she found — as she knew she would — the same pair her mother had first selected at Bloomingdale's that day, the ones Brooke had deemed perfect from the start.

She tried to murmur, "Wow," but only a choked sound came out.

"Isn't it incredible?" Julian asked, his voice growing more excited as she rifled through the clothes. "I'm finally going to look like a grown-up. A really expensively dressed grown-up. Do you have any idea how much all this stuff cost them? Just guess."

She didn't have to guess; she could tell by looking at the quality and sheer quantity of merchandise that Sony had laid out no less than ten thousand dollars. Still, she didn't want to ruin it for Julian.

"I don't know, two thousand? Maybe three? It's craziness!" she said with as much enthusiasm as she could muster.

He laughed. "I know, that's probably what I would've guessed too. Eighteen grand. Can you even believe it? Eighteen fucking grand on clothes."

She rubbed one of the cashmere sweaters between her palms. "Are you okay with them changing your look, though? Do you mind that you'll be wearing completely different stuff?"

She held her breath while he seemed to think about this for a moment.

"Nah, I can't be like that," he said. "Time to move on, you know? The old uniform worked for a while, but I'm starting fresh. I've got to embrace the new look, and hopefully with it the new career will come. I have to say, I'm kinda surprised myself, but I'm totally on board with it." He smiled devilishly. "Besides, if you've gotta do it, better do it right, you know? So, how happy are you?"

She forced another smile. "So happy. It's just awesome that they're willing to invest in you like this."

He yanked off his old, pilled cap and put on the white fedora with a chambray band. He jumped up to look in the hallway mirror and turned a few times, admiring himself from different angles. "So what's your news?" he called out. "If I remember correctly, I'm not the only one around here with a surprise tonight."

She smiled to herself, a sad smile despite the fact that no one could see her. "It's nothing," she called back, hoping her voice sounded cheerier than she felt.

"Oh come on, there was something you wanted to show me, wasn't there?"

She folded her hands in her lap and stared at the overflowing suitcase. "Nothing quite as exciting as this, sweetie. Let's enjoy this now and I'll keep my surprise for another night."

He walked over to her, fedora and all, and kissed her on the cheek. "Sounds good, Rookie. I'm going to unpack all my new loot. Wanna help?" He began dragging everything toward the bedroom.

"I'll be there in a minute," she called, praying he wouldn't notice the shopping bags in the closet.

He came back to the living room a moment later and sat next to her on the couch. "Are you sure everything's okay, baby? Is anything wrong?"

She smiled again and shook her head, willing the lump in her throat to go away. "Everything's great," she lied, squeezing his hand. "Nothing's wrong at all."

8
MY WEAK HEART
CAN'T HANDLE
ANOTHER THREESOME

"Is it wrong I'm dreading this?" Brooke asked as she turned onto Randy and Michelle's street.

"We really haven't seen them in a while," Julian mumbled, furiously typing on his phone.

"No, the party. I'm dreading the party. All those people from my childhood, each of them interrogating us about our lives and telling me all about their children's lives, every one of which I used to be friends with but who have now gone on to out-accomplish me in every imaginable way."

"I guarantee none of their kids married as well as you did."

Out of the corner of her eye, she saw him smiling.

"Hah! I might have agreed with you before I ran into Sasha Phillips's mother in the city six months ago. Sasha was the queen bee of sixth grade, the one who could

227

get everyone to gang up on you with a single flick of her snap bracelet and who, incidentally, had *the* scrunchiest socks and the whitest-ever leather Keds."

"Is this going somewhere?"

"So before I can take cover, I see Sasha's mother at Century 21, in the housewares department."

"Brooke . . ."

"And she corners me right between the shower curtains and the towels and starts bragging that Sasha is now married to a guy who's being 'groomed' to be someone 'very influential' in a well-known Italian 'business family,' wink, wink. How this guy — this real catch — could have any woman on earth, and he was just smitten with her gorgeous Sasha. Who, by the way, is now the stepmother to his four children. She's bragging! The woman was so skilled, I actually left there feeling badly that you weren't in the mob and didn't have a handful of children from a previous wife."

He laughed. "You never told me that."

"I didn't want to put your life at risk."

"We'll get through this together. Some appetizers, some dinner, a toast, and then we're out. Okay?"

"If you say so." She pulled into the driveway of Randy's condo, number 88, and immediately noticed that his highly worshipped two-seater Nissan 350Z was nowhere to be seen. She was about to say something to Julian about it, but his phone rang for the thousandth time in the last two hours, and he had already climbed out of the car.

"I'll come back for our bags, okay?" she called out to him, but he was at the end of the driveway, the handset pressed to his ear, nodding furiously. "Okay, great then," she mumbled to herself and headed to the front door. She was about to walk up the stairs when Randy flung it open, rushed out, and enveloped her in a hug. "Hey, Rookie! So good to see you guys. Michelle's coming out now. Where's Julian?"

"On the phone. Let me tell you, T-Mobile is not going to be happy they offered an unlimited plan when they see his bill."

They both watched as Julian smiled, pocketed his phone, and walked back to their open trunk.

"You need some help with those bags?" Randy called out.

"Nah, I'm fine," Julian called, swinging both over his shoulder with ease. "You're looking good, man. Lost weight?"

Randy patted his ample-but-maybe-slightly-less-ample belly. "The old lady's got me on a strict diet," he said with unmistakable pride. Brooke wouldn't have believed it a year ago, but Randy was obviously thrilled to have an adult relationship, a supposedly furnished home, and a baby on the way.

"Might want to go stricter," Brooke said, simultaneously sidestepping him so he couldn't swat her.

"Big talker over here. I admit, I've got a few pounds to lose, but you're a nutritionist — what's your excuse? Aren't you supposed to be, like, totally anorexic?" Randy reached her across the sidewalk and mussed up her hair.

"Wow, a weight comment and an insult to my profession all in the same breath. You're on fire today."

"Oh come on, you know I'm just kidding. You look great."

"Uh-huh. Maybe I should lose five pounds, but Michelle's got her work cut out for her," she said with a grin.

"Trust me, I'm working on him," Michelle called out as she gingerly stepped down the stairs. Her belly looked like it extended six feet in front of her despite the fact that she still had seven weeks to go, and her face broke into an instant sweat in the crushing August heat. Despite all of it, she looked happy, almost exhilarated. Brooke had always thought the whole pregnancy glow thing was a myth, but there was no denying something agreed with Michelle.

"I'm working on Brooke, too," Julian said as he kissed Michelle on the cheek.

"Brooke's gorgeous just the way she is," Michelle immediately replied, her expression registering the hit.

Brooke turned to face Julian, forgetting that Michelle and Randy were watching the whole thing.

"What did you just say?"

Julian shrugged. "Nothing, Rook. It was a joke. Just a joke."

"You're 'working on me'? Was that it? What, you're trying to keep my morbid obesity in check?"

"Brooke, can we talk about this another time? You know I was just kidding around."

"No, I'd like to talk about this right now. What *exactly* did you mean by that?"

Julian was beside her in a second, instantly contrite. "Rookie, it was totally just a joke. You know I love the way you look and wouldn't change a thing. I just, uh, don't want *you* to be uncomfortable."

Randy reached out for Michelle's hand and announced, "We're going to get everything set up inside. Here, let me take these bags. Come in whenever you're ready."

Brooke waited until they'd shut the screen door. "Why, exactly, would I be *uncomfortable?* I'm not a supermodel, I know, but who is?"

"No, I know, it's just that . . ." He kicked at the stoop with his Converse sneaker and then sat down.

"It's just what?"

"Nothing. You know I think you're gorgeous. It's just that Leo thought you might feel uncomfortable in terms of publicity, and, you know, stuff like that."

He looked at her, waiting, but she was too stunned to speak.

"Brooke —"

She pulled a piece of gum from her purse and stared at the ground.

"Rookie, come here. Christ, I shouldn't have said that. It's not at all what I meant."

She paused and waited for him to explain what he had really meant, but there was only silence.

"Come on, let's go inside," she said, trying to keep from tearing up. In a way, it'd be easier not knowing what he really meant.

"No, wait a minute. Come here," he said, pulling her down next to him on the stoop and taking both her hands in his.

"Baby, I'm sorry I said that. Leo and I do not sit around and talk about you, and I know all this horseshit about my 'image' is nothing more than that, but I'm *freaking out* about all of this, and I need to listen to him right now. The album just dropped, and I'm trying not to let all this go to my head, but whichever way I think about it, I'm terrified: If it works and the album's a hit — terrifying. If, more likely, this has all just been a lot of very lucky smoke and mirrors and nothing is really going to come of it — even more terrifying. Yesterday I was sitting in my safe little recording studio playing the music I love, totally able to pretend it was just me and a piano and no one else, and all of a sudden there's this other stuff: TV appearances, dinners with executives, interviews. I'm just . . . not prepared. And if it means I've been kind of an asshole lately, I'm really, *really* sorry."

There were a million things Brooke wanted to say — how much she missed him now that he was gone so often; how nervous she was about all their recent fighting, the constant roller coaster of up and down; how thrilled she was that he had actually opened up a little and let her in — but instead of pushing him even more, of asking all her questions or airing all her feelings, she forced herself to appreciate the tiny step he'd just taken.

She squeezed his hands and kissed his cheek. "Thank you," she said quietly, meeting his eyes for the first time all day.

"Thank *you*," he replied, and kissed her cheek right back.

With much still left unsaid and a lingering uneasy feeling, Brooke clasped her husband's hand and allowed herself to be pulled up and escorted inside. She would do her best to forget the weight comment.

Randy and Michelle were waiting for them in the kitchen, where Michelle was preparing a platter of food for make-your-own-sandwiches: sliced turkey, roast beef, rye bread, Russian dressing, tomatoes, lettuce, and pickles. There were cans of Dr. Brown's black cherry soda and a liter of lime seltzer. Michelle handed them each a paper plate and motioned for them to get started.

"So, what time do the festivities begin?" Brooke asked, helping herself to a few slices of turkey, no bread. She hoped both Randy and Julian would notice and feel guilty.

"The party starts at seven, but Cynthia wants us there at six to help set up." Michelle moved around with surprising grace considering her size.

"Do you think he's going to be surprised?" Brooke asked.

"I can't believe your father is turning

sixty-five." Julian spread Russian dressing on a piece of bread.

"I can't believe he finally retired," Randy said. "It's weird, but this September is going to be the first year in almost fifteen that we won't be starting a school year together."

Brooke followed everyone else into the dining room and set her plate and a can of Dr. Brown's next to her brother. "Aw, you're going to miss him, aren't you? Who are you going to eat lunch with?"

Julian's phone rang, and he excused himself to answer it.

"He seems relatively calm considering the album only just dropped," Randy said, taking a huge bite of an even bigger sandwich.

"He might seem it, but he isn't. His phone's ringing off the hook, and he's constantly talking to people, but no one's really sure of anything yet. I think we'll know something later today, or maybe tomorrow? He says everyone's hopeful that it'll debut in the top twenty, but I guess you can never be sure," Brooke said.

"It's incredible," Michelle said, nibbling a piece of rye bread. "I mean, did you ever think you'd be saying that Julian's album is going to debut in the top *twenty*? People try their whole lives for that, and this is only his first. . . ."

Brooke swallowed her soda and wiped her mouth. "It hasn't happened yet. . . . I just don't want to jinx it. But yes, it's just about the craziest thing ever."

"It's actually not the craziest thing ever," Julian said, walking back into the room with one of his signature grins. His smile was so enormous, it made Brooke forget their earlier tension.

Michelle held up her hand. "Don't be so modest, Julian. Objectively speaking, having your first album debut in the top twenty is the craziest thing ever."

"Actually, having your album debut at number four is the craziest thing ever," he said quietly before breaking into yet another killer smile.

"What?" Brooke asked, her mouth falling.

"That was Leo. He said it's not official, but it's on track to hit at number four. Four! I can't even process it."

Brooke leapt out of her chair and into Julian's arms. "Ohmigod, ohmigod, ohmigod," she kept saying over and over. Michelle let out a little shriek and after giving both Brooke and Julian hugs, she went to retrieve a special bottle of whiskey to toast Julian.

Randy returned with three highball glasses of brown liquid and one with orange juice for Michelle. "To Julian," he said, holding his glass up. They all clinked and sipped. Brooke grimaced and set hers down on the table, but Randy and Julian downed both of theirs in single gulps.

Randy clapped Julian on the back. "You know, I'm happy for you and all the success and blah, blah, blah, but man, I have to say — it's pretty fucking cool having a *rock star* in the family."

"Oh, come on, guys, it's not —"

Brooke swatted Julian's shoulder. "They're right, baby. You're a star. How many people can say they debuted at number four on the charts? Five? Ten? I mean, like, the Beatles and Madonna and Beyoncé and . . . Julian Alter? It's total insanity!"

They celebrated and talked and peppered Julian with questions for another forty-five minutes before Michelle announced that it was time to get ready, that they'd be leaving for the restaurant in an hour. The moment Michelle handed them a pile of towels and closed the guest room door behind her, Brooke tackled Julian in a hug so hard they both ended up falling onto the bed together.

"Baby, it's happening. It's really, undeniably happening," she said, kissing his forehead and then his eyelids, cheeks, and lips.

Julian kissed her back and then propped

himself up on his elbows. "You know what else it means?"

"That you are now an official celebrity?" She kissed his neck.

"It means you can finally quit Huntley. Hell, you can quit both jobs if you want."

She pulled back and looked at him. "Why would I do that?"

"Well, for starters, you've been working like crazy the last couple of years and I think you deserve a break. And things are starting to fall together financially. Between the percentage I get from the Maroon 5 tour, the private parties Leo books, and now the proceeds from this album — well, I just think you should relax and enjoy it a little."

Everything he said was perfectly logical, but for reasons she couldn't quite articulate, Brooke felt herself bristle. "I don't do it only for the money, you know. The girls need me."

"It's perfect timing, Brooke. The school year doesn't start for another two weeks, so I'm sure they could find someone to replace you. Then even if you decide to stay at the hospital, you'll hopefully have some free time."

" 'If' I decide to stay at the hospital? Julian, this is my career. It's what I went to grad school for, and even though it might not be as important as debuting at number four, I happen to love it."

"I know you love it. I just thought maybe you'd want to love it from afar for a little." He nudged her and smiled.

She peered at him. "What are you suggesting?"

He tried to pull her back down on top of him, but Brooke squirmed away.

He sighed. "I'm not suggesting anything horrible, Brooke. Maybe if you weren't so stressed about your hours and your schedule, you'd enjoy being able to take a little time off. Maybe travel with me more, come to the events?"

She was silent.

"Are you upset?" he asked, reaching out for her hand.

"I'm not upset," she lied. "I feel like I've been making a huge effort to find a balance between my work and everything that's going on with you. We went to *Leno* together, and the *Friday Night Lights* party, and Kristen Stewart's birthday party in Miami and Bonnaroo. I stop by the studio on nights when you work late. I don't know what else I can do, but I'm pretty sure the answer isn't to quit on my career and follow you around. I don't think you'd be happy with that no matter how much fun it might be in the beginning, and honestly, I don't think I'd respect myself for doing it."

"Just think about it," he said as he pulled off his shirt and walked toward the bathroom. "Promise me that."

The sound of the running shower drowned out her answer. Brooke resolved to put the issue out of her mind for the night; they didn't need to decide anything, and just because they weren't on exactly the same page didn't mean anything was wrong.

Brooke took off her clothes, pushed back the shower curtain, and climbed in.

"To what do I owe this honor?" Julian asked through squinted eyes. His entire face was covered in soap.

"To the fact that we have less than a half hour to get ready," Brooke said as she twisted the hot water handle a full turn.

Julian yelped. "Show a little mercy!"

She slid past him, enjoying the feel of his soapy chest against hers, and immediately hogged the stream of piping hot water. "Aaah. That feels great."

Julian feigned a sulk and retreated to the far end of the tub. Brooke laughed. "Come on over," she said, even though she knew he couldn't tolerate anything hotter than lukewarm water. "There's more than enough for both of us."

She squeezed some shampoo into her palm, changed the water temperature back to tepid, and kissed his cheek. "There you go, baby." She slid past him again and smiled as he tentatively stepped under the stream. She lathered her hair and watched Julian enjoy the barely warm water.

It was one of the hundreds, maybe thousands of tiny little details they knew about each other, and this knowledge never failed to make Brooke happy. She loved thinking that she was probably the only person on earth who knew that Julian hated submerging himself in very hot water — baths, showers, Jacuzzis, hot springs, he scrupulously avoided them all — but could withstand muggy, humid temperatures without complaint; that he was also a self-proclaimed "hot drink gulper" (put a cup of scorching hot coffee or a bowl of steaming soup in front of him, and Julian could pour the contents down his gullet without so much as a testing sip); that he had an impressive tolerance for pain, as evidenced by the time he'd broken his ankle and hadn't reacted with more than a quick "Dammit!" but would squeal and squirm like a little girl whenever Brooke tried to pluck an errant eyebrow hair. Even now, as he lathered up, she knew he was grateful to have bar soap instead of a liquid body wash, and that as long as it didn't smell like lavender or, worse, grapefruit, he would use anything handed to him.

She leaned over to kiss his unshaven cheek and got a spray of water right in the eyes.

"Serves you right," Julian said, and patted her butt. "That'll teach you to mess with a number-four artist."

"What does Mr. Number Four think about a quickie?"

Julian kissed her back but then stepped out of the shower. "I'm not explaining to your father that we're late for his party because his daughter jumped me in the shower."

Brooke laughed. "You're such a wuss."

Cynthia was already at the restaurant when they arrived, bustling around the private room in a frantic whirlwind of energy and orders. They were at Ponzu, which, according to Cynthia, was the new hippest restaurant in southeastern Pennsylvania. According to Randy, the place used "Asian fusion" to describe their overambitious attempt to tackle sushi and teriyaki dishes from Japan, Vietnamese-inspired spring rolls, a pad thai that few Thai people would recognize, and a "signature" chicken and broccoli dish that was no different from his cheapie Chinese delivery joint. No one seemed to mind the lack of any actual fusion dishes, so the four of them kept their mouths shut and immediately set to work.

The guys hung two massive, matching foil signs that read, HAPPY 65TH! and CONGRATULATIONS ON YOUR RETIREMENT, while Brooke and Michelle arranged the flowers Cynthia had brought in the glass vases provided by the restaurant, enough for two arrangements per table. They'd only finished the first batch when Michelle said, "Have you thought about what you're going to do with all that *money?*"

Brooke almost dropped her scissors she was so surprised. She and Michelle had never talked about anything personal before, and a conversation about Julian's financial potential seemed totally inappropriate.

"Oh, you know, we've still got tons of student loans and all sorts of bills to pay. Not as sexy as it seems." She shrugged.

Michelle switched out a rose for a peony and cocked her head to the side, examining her work. "Come on, Brooke, don't kid yourself. You two are going to be rolling in it!"

Brooke had no idea what to say to this, so she just laughed awkwardly.

All of her dad and Cynthia's friends

showed up at exactly six and milled around munching passed hors d'oeuvres and sipping wine. By the time Brooke's father arrived for what he fully knew was his "surprise" party, the crowd appeared appropriately festive. They proved it when Mr. Greene was escorted to the back room by the maître d' and everyone shouted "Surprise!" and "Congratulations!" and her father cycled through the usual reactions of people pretending to be surprised by their non-surprise surprise parties. He took the glass of red wine that Cynthia handed him and downed it in a determined effort to enjoy the party, although Brooke knew he'd rather have been home preparing himself for Sunday's preseason game schedule.

Thankfully Cynthia planned to do the toasts during the cocktail hour; Brooke was a nervous public speaker and didn't want to spend the entire evening dreading her two minutes. One and a half vodka tonics made it a bit easier, and she was able to deliver her preplanned speech without a hitch. The audience seemed to especially like the story Brooke told about the first time she and Randy visited their father after the divorce and found him in the kitchen one morning, packing his oven with piles of old magazines and paid bills since he didn't have a ton of storage space and didn't want the oven to "go to waste." Randy and Cynthia followed suit, and despite an awkward mention on Cynthia's part regarding "the instant connection they felt the very first time they met" — which, incidentally, was when Brooke's father was still married to Brooke's mother — everything went off without a hitch.

"Hey, everyone, can I have your attention for just one more minute?" Mr. Greene asked, rising from his place in the middle of a long, banquet-style table.

The room grew quiet.

"I want to thank you all so much for coming. I'd especially like to thank my lovely wife for scheduling this party on a Saturday instead of a Sunday — she finally knows the difference between college and professional football — and thanks to all four of my lovely children for being here tonight; you guys make it all worthwhile."

Everyone clapped. Brooke blushed and Randy rolled his eyes. When she glanced over at Julian, he was busily typing under the table.

"And one last thing. Some of you may already know that we have a rising star in the family. . . ."

This got Julian's attention.

"Well, I'm just thrilled to announce that Julian's album will be debuting at number four on the *Billboard* chart next week!" The room cheered and clapped. "Please raise your glass to my son-in-law, Julian Alter, for accomplishing the near-impossible. I know I speak for everyone when I say how incredibly proud we are of you."

Brooke watched as her dad walked over and embraced her surprised but clearly delighted husband, and she felt a surge of gratitude to her father. It was exactly the sort of thing Julian had waited a lifetime for his own father to say, and if it wasn't going to come from him, she was happy he'd get to hear it from her family. Julian thanked her dad and quickly took his seat again, and although he was obviously embarrassed to be the center of attention, Brooke could see how pleased he was. She reached over and squeezed his hand and he squeezed it back twice as hard.

The waiters had just begun bringing out the appetizers when Julian leaned over to Brooke and asked if they could go to the restaurant's main room for a moment to talk privately.

"Is this your way of getting me into the bathroom?" she whispered as she followed Julian. "Can you imagine the scandal? I just hope if we're caught, it's Sasha's mother who catches us. . . ."

Julian led her into the hallway where the restrooms were, and Brooke yanked on his arm. "I really was just kidding," she said.

"Rook, I just got a call from Leo," he said, leaning against a bench.

"Oh yeah?"

"He's out in L.A. now, and I guess he's been having a bunch of meetings on my behalf." Julian looked like he wanted to say more, but he stopped.

"And? Anything exciting?"

With this, Julian couldn't contain himself anymore. A huge smile broke out on his face, and although Brooke had an immediate gut feeling that the something exciting was going to be something she didn't like, she mirrored him and smiled right back.

"What? What is it?" she asked.

"Well, actually . . ." Julian's voice trailed off and his eyes grew wide. "He said that *Vanity Fair* wants to include me with a group of up-and-coming young artists for the October or November cover. A *cover,* can you believe it?"

Brooke wrapped her arms around his neck.

Julian brushed his lips quickly against her and pulled away first. "And guess what? Annie Leibovitz is shooting it."

"You're joking!"

He grinned. "I'm not. It's going to be me and four other artists. Mixed mediums, I think. Leo thought they'd probably do a musician, a painter, an author, that sort of thing. And guess where they're going to shoot it? At the Chateau."

"Of course they are. We're going to be regulars!" She was already mentally calculating how she could miss the least amount of work and still accompany him. There was also the issue of what to pack. . . .

"Brooke." Julian's voice betrayed nothing but his expression was pained.

"What's wrong?"

"I'm sorry to do this to you, but I've got to leave right now. Leo booked me on a six o'clock flight out of JFK tomorrow morning, and I still need to get back to New York and grab some things from the studio."

"You're leaving *now?*" she sputtered, realizing Julian's ticket for one was already booked, and although he was doing his best to appear solemn faced, he couldn't contain his excitement.

Instead, he hugged her and scratched the spot between her shoulders. "I know it sucks, baby. I'm sorry this is so last-minute, and I'm sorry I have to leave in the middle of your dad's party, but —"

"Before."

"What?"

"You're not leaving in the middle of the party, you're leaving before we even eat."

He was silent. For a moment she wondered if he was going to tell her the entire thing was a big joke, that he didn't have to go anywhere.

"How are you getting home?" she finally asked, her voice tinged with resignation.

He pulled her into a hug. "I called a taxi to the train station so no one has to leave. That way you'll have the car to get back tomorrow. Does that work?"

"Sure."

"Brooke? I love you, baby. And I'm going to take you out to celebrate everything as soon as I'm back. It's all good stuff, you know?"

Brooke forced a smile for his sake. "I know it is. And I'm excited for you."

"I think I'm back on Tuesday, but I'm not totally sure," he said, kissing her softly on the lips. "Leave all the planning to me, okay? I'd like for us to do something special."

"I'd like that too."

"Will you wait for me here?" he asked. "I'm just going to run back in and quickly say good-bye to your dad. I don't want to draw all sorts of attention to myself. . . ."

"Honestly, I think it'd be better if you just went," Brooke said, and she could see his relief. "I'll explain what happened. They'll understand."

"Thank you."

She nodded. "Come on, I'll walk you out."

They walked hand-in-hand together down the stairs and managed to escape to the parking lot without running into any of the party guests or her family. Brooke once again assured Julian that it was better this way, that she would explain everything to her father and Cynthia and thank Randy and Michelle for their hospitality, and that all of it was preferable to making a big good-bye scene where he'd need to explain himself a hundred times over. He tried to look solemn when he kissed her good-bye and whispered his love, but the moment the taxi came into view, he bounded toward it like an excited golden retriever going after a tennis ball. Brooke reminded herself to give him a big smile and a happy wave, but the taxi pulled away before Julian could turn around and wave back. She headed back inside, alone.

She glanced at her watch and wondered if

250

she had time for a run after her last appointment and before going to Nola's. She committed to making it happen just as she remembered that it was ninety-three degrees outside and only an insane person would run anywhere in that kind of heat.

There was a knock on her door. It was her first session with Kaylie since the new school year had begun, and she was eager to see the girl. Her e-mails had been sounding more and more positive, and Brooke was confident that she was well on her way to adjusting to school. But when the door opened, it was Heather who walked in.

"Hey, what's up? Thanks again for the coffee this morning."

"Oh, my pleasure. Listen, I just wanted to let you know that Kaylie won't be making her appointment today. She's home with some sort of stomach flu."

Brooke glanced at the day's absentee sheet on her desk. "Really? Because she's not on the list today."

"Yeah, I know. She was in my office earlier today and she looked horrible, so I sent her to the nurse and the nurse sent her home. I'm sure it's nothing serious, but I just wanted to let you know."

"Thanks, I appreciate it."

Heather turned to leave, but Brooke called

out, "How did she seem to you? Other than feeling ill."

Heather appeared to think about this. "You know, it's hard to say. It was only our first meeting since last year, and she didn't really open up. I've heard some rumblings from the other girls that Kaylie befriended Whitney Weiss, which gives me pause for obvious reasons, but Kaylie didn't bring it up. I will say that it definitely looks like she lost a significant amount of weight."

Brooke's head snapped up. "How much would you say is significant?"

"I don't know . . . twenty, maybe twenty-five pounds? She looked terrific, actually. She seemed really pleased with herself." Heather noticed that Brooke looked worried. "Why? Is that bad?"

"Not necessarily, but that's an awful lot of weight to lose in a short amount of time. And the whole Whitney friendship? Let's just say that together, I think there's a red flag there."

Heather nodded. "Well, I think at this point you'll see her before I do, but keep me in the loop, okay?"

Brooke said good-bye to Heather and leaned back in her chair. Twenty-five pounds was actually an enormous weight loss over two and a half months, and the Whitney connection wasn't comforting. Whitney was an extremely slim girl who had put on five or seven pounds after she quit playing field hockey the previous year, and her underweight mother had immediately shown up in Brooke's office demanding the name of a reputable "fat camp," as the woman so crudely put it. All of Brooke's vehement protestations that it was a completely normal, even welcome, amount of weight gain for a growing fourteen-year-old girl made no difference, and Whitney was sent to a posh camp upstate to "work it off." Predictably, the girl had begun to show signs of bingeing and purging since then, something to which Kaylie certainly didn't need any exposure. She made a mental note to call Kaylie's father after their first meeting and see if he'd noticed anything unusual about her behavior.

She made a few notes about her earlier sessions and then left, the suffocating blanket of early September humidity hitting her like a wall as all thoughts of taking the subway went straight to hell. As though an angel above had read her mind or, more likely, a Bangladeshi taxi driver had seen her frantic arm-waving, a cab pulled directly up to the school's entrance to dispatch a customer and Brooke fell into the air-conditioned backseat.

"Corner of Duane and Hudson, please," she said as she moved her legs closer to the cold air pouring from the vent. She spent the entire duration of the ride with her head back and her eyes closed. Just before the taxi pulled up to Nola's building, a text came in from Julian.

Just got an e-mail from John Travolta!!! Says he "loves" the new album and congratulated me on it, it read.

Brooke could feel Julian's excitement through the screen. *John Travolta?!* she texted back. *No way! So awesome.*

He wrote it to his agent and agent forwarded it to Leo, Julian responded.

Congrats! Very cool. That's a keeper, she wrote, and then followed it up with, *At Nola's now. Call when you can. Xoxo.*

Nola's one-bedroom was at the very end of a long hallway, and it overlooked a trendy café with outdoor tables. Brooke walked straight through the propped-open door, dumped her bag while simultaneously kicking off her shoes, and beelined for the kitchen.

"I'm here!" she shouted as she helped herself to a can of Diet Coke from the fridge. Her favorite guilty pleasure, and one she allowed herself only at Nola's apartment.

"There's Diet Coke in the fridge. Grab me one, too!" Nola screamed out from the bedroom. "I'm almost finished packing. I'll be right out."

Brooke cracked open both their cans and walked back to hand one to Nola, who was sitting in a massive pile of clothing, shoes, cosmetics, electronics, and guidebooks.

"How the *fuck* do they expect me to get all this stuff into a backpack?" she snapped, trying to cram a round brush into the pack's front pocket and, when she failed, flinging it across the room. "What was I thinking, signing up for this?"

"I have no idea," Brooke said, surveying the chaos. "I've actually been asking myself that for about two weeks now."

"This is what happens when your vacation time doesn't roll over and you don't have a boyfriend — you make decisions like this. Sixteen days with eleven strangers in Southeast Asia? Seriously, Brooke, I blame you for this."

Brooke laughed. "Nice try. I told you it was the worst idea I'd *ever* heard the moment you floated it, but you were very determined."

Nola pulled herself up, took a sip of Diet

Coke, and walked to the living room. "I should be a cautionary tale for single women everywhere. No impulsive, last-minute group tours. Vietnam is not freaking going anywhere — what was my big rush?"

"Oh come on, it'll be fun. Besides, maybe there'll even be a cute guy in your group."

"Uh-huh. Sure there will be. Definitely not a bunch of middle-aged German couples or wannabe Buddhist hippies or, possibly, all lesbians. No! It'll be chock-full of adorable, eligible men aged thirty to thirty-five."

"I like your positive attitude!" Brooke said with a grin.

Something caught Nola's eye and she moved toward the living room window. Brooke glanced out and saw nothing out of the ordinary.

"At that first table all the way on the left? Natalie Portman? Wearing that little page-boy cap and sunglasses as a disguise, as though her essential Natalie Portman-ness doesn't shine right through?" Nola said.

Brooke looked again, this time noticing the girl in the cap as she sipped from her wineglass and laughed at something her dinner partner said. "Mmm, yeah, I think that probably is her."

"Of course it is! And she looks freaking

fantastic. I can't figure out why I don't hate her. I should, but I don't." Nola cocked her head to the side but never took her eyes off the window.

"Why should you hate her?" Brooke asked. "She actually seems like one of the more normal ones."

"Even more of a reason you should hate her. Not only is she insanely attractive — including when she's completely bald — but she's also a Harvard graduate, she speaks like fifteen languages, she's traveled all over the world encouraging people to support microfinance, and she's so in love with the environment that she won't wear leather shoes. And on top of all that, everyone who's ever worked with her or so much as sat next to her on a plane swears she's the coolest, most down-to-earth person they've ever met. Now, tell me, please, how can you possibly not hate someone like that?"

Nola finally left her window perch and Brooke followed her. They both flopped down on opposite slipcovered love seats and each turned on her side to face the other.

Brooke took a gulp and shrugged, thinking about the photographer outside their apartment. "Good for Natalie Portman, I guess?"

Nola shook her head slowly from side to

side. "My god, you're a piece of work."

"What did I say? I don't understand. Am I supposed to be obsessed with her? Jealous of her? She's not even real."

"Of course she's real! She's sitting right across the street, and she looks amazing."

Brooke draped an arm across her forehead and moaned. "And now we're stalking her, which I'm not feeling great about. Leave her be."

"Feeling a little sensitive about Natalie's privacy?" Nola asked more gently.

"Yeah, I guess. It's weird; the part of me that's been reading these magazines for years and has seen every movie she's ever been in and can name every dress she's worn to the awards show makes me want to sit at that window and stare at her all night. Then there's the part of me . . ."

Nola pointed the remote control to the TV and scrolled through the channels until she found the alternative rock station. She propped herself up on her elbow. "I hear you. What else is going on? Why are you in such a shitty mood?"

Brooke sighed. "I had to ask for another day off for next weekend in Miami, and let's just say that Margaret was less than thrilled."

"She can't expect her staff not to have

personal lives."

Brooke snorted. "It's probably not unfair for her to expect us to show up every now and then."

"You're being too hard on yourself. Can I change the topic to something a little more fun? No offense."

"What, the party this weekend?"

"Am I invited?" Nola grinned. "I could be your date."

"Are you kidding? I'd love it, but I didn't think it was an option."

"What, would I rather be in New York having drinks with some loser when I could be nibbling caviar with a fledgling rock star's wife?"

"Done. I'm sure Julian will be thrilled he won't have to babysit me all night." Brooke's phone vibrated on the coffee table. "Speak of the devil . . ."

"Hey!" Brooke said into the receiver. "Nola and I were just talking about the party this weekend."

"Brooke? Guess what? I just spoke to Leo who heard from the VP at Sony. They said that the album's initial numbers are far exceeding their expectations."

Brooke could hear music and some general clattering in the background, but she couldn't remember where Julian was that afternoon. Maybe Atlanta? Or were they playing in Charleston that night? Yes, that was definitely it. Atlanta was last night — she remembered speaking to Julian when he called around one in the morning, and he sounded drunk but in generally good spirits. He'd been calling from the Ritz in Buckhead.

"No one wants to commit to anything yet since the airplay-tracking week still has three days to go, but the sales-tracking week ended today and supposedly it's on pace."

Brooke had spent two hours the night before reading up on all the other singers and groups who had released albums in the last couple weeks, but she still didn't understand how the tracking worked. Should she ask? Or would he just get annoyed at her ignorance?

"For at *least* a move from number four to number three. Possibly even higher!"

"I'm so proud of you! Are you guys having fun in Charleston?" she asked brightly.

There was silence. She panicked for a second. Were they not in Charleston? But then he said, "Believe it or not, we're all busting our asses down here. Practicing, performing, breaking down, setting up, staying in a different hotel every night. Everyone's *working* here."

Brooke was quiet for a moment. "I wasn't suggesting that all you're doing is partying." Brooke somehow managed to refrain from reminding him about his drunken, very late call last night.

Nola caught Brooke's eye and motioned that she'd be in the other room, but Brooke waved and gave her a look that said, *Don't be ridiculous.*

"Is this about leaving in the middle of your dad's party? How many times have I apologized about that? I can't believe you're still punishing me."

"No, it's not about that, although for the record you walked out with about six seconds' warning and you haven't been home since and that was almost two weeks ago." She softened her voice. "I guess I thought you'd be back for a day or two after the shoot, before you resumed the tour."

"What's with the attitude?"

It felt like a slap. "The *attitude?* Is it really so horrible that I said I hoped you were having fun? Or asked when we might see each other? Gee, I'm an awful person."

"Brooke, I don't have time for a tantrum right now."

The way he said her full name gave her a chill.

"A 'tantrum,' Julian? *Really?*" She almost

never told him how she really felt — he was too stressed, too busy, too distracted, or too far away — so she tried hard not to complain. To be upbeat and understanding, just like her mother said, but it wasn't easy.

"Well then what exactly are you so worked up about? I'm sorry I can't get home this week. How many times do you want me to apologize? I'm doing this for us, you know. You might want to remember that sometimes."

Brooke felt that all-too-anxious feeling. "I don't think you understand," she said quietly.

He sighed. "I'll try and take a night and get home before Miami this weekend, okay? Would that make things better? It's just not so easy two weeks after your album drops."

She wanted to tell him to go screw himself, but instead she took a deep breath, counted to three, and said, "That would be great if you could manage it. I'd love to see you."

"I'm going to try, Rook. Look, I've got to run, but please know I love you. And I miss you. I'll call you tomorrow, okay?" Before she could say another word, he hung up.

"He hung up on me!" she yelled, before slamming her cell phone into the cushiony couch, where it bounced off a pillow before landing on the floor.

"You okay?" Nola's voice was soft and soothing. She stood in the doorway of the living room, holding a handful of takeout menus and a bottle of wine. "For the Lost" began playing from the TV's radio station, and both Nola and Brooke turned toward the set.

He was a brother's dream, he was a fist
   of sand
He slipped away with the second
   hand . . .

"Can you turn that off, please?" Brooke collapsed onto the couch and covered her eyes, although she wasn't crying. "What am I going to do?" she moaned.

Nola swiftly changed the channel. "First, you're going to decide whether you want lemongrass chicken or jumbo prawn curry from the Vietnamese place, and then you're going to tell me what's going on with you guys." Nola seemed to remember the bottle in her hand. "Scratch that. First, we're going to have a drink."

She quickly cut the foil wrapper with the tip of the wine opener and was about to plunge it into the cork when she said, "Are you still upset about that stupid Layla picture?"

Brooke snorted and accepted a glass of red from Nola that, in more polite company, would've been considered overfilled but for tonight looked exactly right. "What, you mean the one where my husband has his arm wrapped around her twenty-six-inch waist with a smile so massive, so positively beatific, that he looks like he's in the throes of an orgasm?"

Nola sipped her wine and put her feet up on the table. "Some dumb starlet was looking to take advantage of a little press time with the next big thing. She couldn't care less about Julian."

"I know that. And it's not the picture so much as . . . He went from Nick's and a part-time internship to this? It all changed overnight, Nola. I wasn't ready."

There was no point in denying it anymore: Julian Alter, her husband, was officially and undeniably famous. Intellectually, Brooke was aware that it had been an impossibly long and difficult road; so many years of daily practice and gigs and songwriting (not including the countless gigs and hours Julian had logged before they'd even met). There'd been demo tapes, promo tracks, singles that almost worked but never did.

Even once he'd scored the long-shot record deal that was never supposed to go anywhere, there had been weeks and months of poring over contract books, hiring and working with entertainment lawyers, contacting more experienced artists for their advice and possible mentoring. There were the many months that followed spent in a Midtown recording studio, tweaking the keyboard and the vocals hundreds, maybe thousands of times to get the sound just right. The endless meetings with producers and A&R guys and intimidating executives that knew — and acted like — they held the golden keys to his future. There was the Sony casting call for new band members and then the interviewing and auditioning that followed; the nonstop travel between Los Angeles and New York to make sure everything was proceeding smoothly; the consultations with PR people who could guide the public's perception; and the instructions from the media trainers on how to behave in front of the cameras. And of course the stylist in charge of Julian's image.

For years Brooke had willingly worked two jobs to support them despite the confusing twinges of resentment she sometimes felt when she was exhausted and alone, a studio widow in the apartment. There were her own dreams — sidelined for now by choice — the wish to really carve out a niche for herself at work, travel more, have a baby. There was the financial strain from having to invest and reinvest every last dollar into different areas of Julian's career. The hideously long hours in the studio. All the late nights away from home, when both of them were in loud, smoky bars for Julian's gigs instead of curled up on the couch or away for the weekend with other couples. And now the travel! The constant, unrelenting, endless travel for Julian, moving from city to city, coast to coast. They both tried, they really did, but it seemed to be getting harder and harder. An uninterrupted phone conversation these days felt like a luxury.

Nola refilled both their glasses and picked up her phone. "What do you want?"

"I'm not really hungry," Brooke said, and was surprised herself that she actually meant it.

"I'm ordering us a shrimp and a chicken to share and a bunch of spring rolls. That okay?"

Brooke waved her glass, nearly spilling her wine. The first one had gone down so quickly. "Fine, that's fine." She thought for a moment and remembered she was doing to Nola exactly what Julian always did to her. "So what's going on with you? Anything new with . . ."

"Drew? He's done. I had a little . . . distraction this past weekend, and it reminded me that there are a lot more exciting men out there than Drew McNeil."

Brooke once again covered her eyes. "Oh no. Here we go."

"What? It was just a little fun."

"When did you find the time?"

Nola feigned looking hurt. "Remember after dinner on Saturday, you wanted to go home and Drew and I were going out?"

"Oh, god. Please don't tell me this was another threesome. My weak heart can't handle another threesome."

"Brooke! Drew left right after you did, but I wanted to stay for a little. I had another drink and then left all by my lonesome around one thirty and went outside to hail a cab."

"Aren't we a little too old for late-night booty calls? Do the kids even still call them that these days?"

Nola covered her eyes. "My god, you're such a prude. I was about to get into the first open cab in twenty minutes when this guy tries to steal it from me. He just jumped into the other side."

"Oh?"

"Yeah, well, he was pretty cute and I told him he could share with me as long as I got dropped off first, and before I even knew what was happening, we were making out."

"And then?" Brooke asked, even though she knew.

"It was amazing."

"Do you even know his name?"

"Save it," Nola said, rolling her eyes.

She stared at her friend, trying to remember back to her single days. She'd dated plenty of guys and hooked up with her fair share, but never had she been so, so . . . free in her willingness to fall into bed with one of them. Sometimes, when she wasn't terrified for Nola, she was envious of her confidence and the assertive way she approached her sexuality. The one time Brooke had had a one-night stand, she had to force herself to do it by repeatedly telling herself that it would be fun and exciting and empowering. One broken condom, twenty-four hours of nausea from the morning-after pill, six weeks until the HIV test could be assuredly negative, and exactly zero calls from her so-called lover later, she knew she wasn't cut out for that lifestyle.

She took a deep breath and was relieved to hear the buzzer sound to let them know the food had arrived. "Nola, do you realize you could've been —"

"Could you just spare me the 'he could've been a serial killer' lecture, please?"

She held her hands up in surrender. "Okay, okay. Look, I'm glad you had fun. Maybe it's just my own jealousy talking."

Nola made a little shrieking sound at this. She pulled her knees up on the couch and reached over to take Brooke's hand, which she promptly slapped.

"What was that for?" Brooke asked with a wounded look.

"Don't ever say you're jealous again!" Nola said with an intensity Brooke rarely saw from her. "You're beautiful and talented and you can't even imagine how wonderful it is, as your friend, to see the way Julian looks at you. I know I haven't always been his number one fan, but he loves you, there's no denying it. Whether you realize it or not, you guys are inspiring to me. I know it took a lot of hard work for both of you, but it's all paying off."

There was a knock at the door. She leaned over and hugged Nola. "I love you. Thanks for that — I needed to hear it."

Nola smiled, grabbed her wallet, and headed into the hallway.

The girls ate quickly and Brooke, exhausted from the day and a half bottle of wine, ducked out as soon as they finished. Out of habit she purposefully walked to the 1 train and claimed her favorite end seat, not remembering until she was halfway home that she could afford to take taxis. She screened her mother's call during the three-block walk home and began to fantasize about her single-girl evening ritual: herbal tea, hot bath, freezing cold room, sleeping pill, and a blacked-out sleep under her massively puffy comforter. Perhaps she'd even shut off her phone so Julian wouldn't wake her with his sporadic calls, unpredictable in every way except for the certainty that she would hear music, girls, or both in the background.

Lost in a reverie and desperate to get inside and strip off her clothes, Brooke didn't see the flowers on her doormat until she tripped over them. The cylindrical glass vase was as tall as a toddler and lined with vibrantly green banana leaves. It brimmed over with calla lilies, rich purple and creamy white in color, a single towering stalk of bamboo the only accent.

There had been the occasional floral arrangement, the kinds that all women received at one time or another — the sunflowers from her parents when she had her wisdom teeth removed her freshman year, the requisite dozen roses from various uncreative boyfriends on Valentine's Days, the bodega-bought bunches friends brought over as hostess gifts — but never in her life had she gotten something like this. A sculpture. An object of art. Brooke heaved it inside and yanked the tiny envelope from the discreet spot where it was taped to the base. Walter bounded over to sniff this new fragrant acquisition.

Dear Brooke,
I miss you so much. Counting the days until I can see you this weekend.

                                    Love, J

She smiled and leaned forward to smell the gorgeous lilies, a joy that lasted exactly ten seconds until all her doubts rushed forward. Why had he written *Brooke* when he almost always called her Rookie, especially when he was trying to be romantic or intimate? Was this his way of apologizing for being an inconsiderate jerk the last few weeks, and if so, why hadn't he actually said he was sorry? Could someone who prides himself on having a way with words — a songwriter, for chrissake — have possibly written something so generic? And most of all, why would he choose now of all times to send his very first flower arrangement when Brooke knew how much he hated the very idea of retail flowers? According to Julian, they were a clichéd, overpriced, commercialized crutch for people who couldn't adequately express their emotions creatively or verbally, not to mention the fact that they died quickly, and what kind of symbol was that? Brooke had never cared much either way, but she understood where Julian was coming from, and she always treasured the letters and the songs and the poems he so carefully took the time to make for her before. So what was up with this "counting the days" crap?

Walter nudged her knee and let out a mournful howl.

"Why can't your daddy walk you?" Brooke asked as she leashed him and went right back outside. "Oh, I know why. Because he's never here!" Despite feeling tremendous guilt for leaving Walter alone so long, she dragged him back inside the moment he finished and bribed him with extra kibble for dinner and a particularly fat carrot for dessert. She picked up the card again, reread it twice more, and then gently placed it on top of the pile in the garbage can before walking right back over and retrieving it. It may not have been the loveliest thing Julian had ever written, but still, it was a gesture.

She dialed Julian's cell, already working out what she would say, but the call went straight to voice mail.

"Hey, it's me. I just got home and got the flowers. My god, they're . . . incredible. I barely know what to say." *At least you're being honest,* she thought. She thought about asking him to call her so they could talk, but it suddenly seemed too exhausting. "All right, then. Um, have a good night. Love you."

Brooke filled the tub with the hottest water she could stand, grabbed the latest copy of *Last Night* that had just arrived, and gently eased her way in, taking almost five full minutes until she could tolerate having her entire body submerged. As soon as the water washed over her shoulders, she breathed a huge sigh of relief. *Thank god this day is about to end.*

In the days Before the Picture, nothing was better than settling into a bath with a fresh-off-the-presses *Last Night.* Now she was always vaguely terrified of what she might stumble across, but old habits were tough to break. She worked her way through the first few pages, pausing for a moment to reflect on how so many married celebs were willing to dish on their sex lives with gems like, "Our secret to keeping things sexy? He brings me breakfast in bed on Sundays and then I *really* show him my appreciation," and "What can I say? I'm a lucky guy. My wife is seriously hot stuff in the bedroom." The page where they showed stars doing "normal people" things was unusually boring: Dakota Fanning shopping at a mall in Sherman Oaks, Kate Hudson hanging on her guy du jour, a shot of Cameron Diaz picking a bikini wedgie, Tori Spelling clutching a blond child and exiting a salon. There was a mildly interesting spread on what had become of eighties childhood stars (who knew Winnie Cooper was a math genius!), but it wasn't until she turned to the so-called features section that she forgot to breathe. There she found a multipage spread titled "Soulful Songwriters Who Rock Our World," and it featured write-ups and pictures on probably a half dozen artists. Her eyes flew across the page, searching intently. John Mayer, Gavin DeGraw, Colbie Caillat, Jack Johnson. Nothing. She flipped the page. Bon Iver, Ben Harper, Wilco. Nothing again. But wait! *Oh my god.* There, at the bottom of the fourth page was a yellow box. WHO IS JULIAN ALTER? the purple headline screamed. That hideous

picture of Julian and Layla Lawson oc-
cupied the top half of the box and the bottom was filled with text. *Ohmigod,* Brooke
thought, and noticed in an oddly out-of-
body way that her heart was pounding and
she was holding her breath. She was simultaneously desperate to read it and desperate
for it to evaporate, vanish, completely disappear from her consciousness forever. Had
anyone read this yet? Had *Julian* read this
yet? As a subscriber, she knew she received
the magazine a day before it hit the newsstands, but was it really possible no one had
managed to tell her about this beforehand?
She grabbed a towel to blot the sweat from
her forehead and dry her hands, took a deep
breath, and began to read.

Not only did Julian Alter make a splash
earlier this summer with a rocking Leno
performance and a super-steamy photo,
but he's got the goods to back it up: his
first album debuted at #4 on the *Billboard*
charts last week. Now everyone can't help
but wonder . . . who is this singer?

Brooke used her feet to push herself into
more of a sitting position. She was aware of
a growing queasiness and she quickly
blamed it on the combination of too much

wine and steaming hot water. *And if you believe that . . .* she thought to herself. Deep breath. It was natural to feel a little strange reading a surprise article about your own husband in a national magazine. She willed herself to keep going.

EARLY YEARS: Born on Manhattan's Upper East Side in 1977, he attended the prestigious Dalton School and spent summers in the south of France. Positioned to be the perfect prepster, Alter's interest in music didn't jibe well with his society parents.

CAREER: After graduating from Amherst in 1999, Alter turned down med school to pursue his musical ambitions. He signed with Sony in 2008 after a two-year stint as an A&R intern. Alter's first album is projected to be one of the most successful debuts of the year.

PASSIONS: When he's not in the studio, Alter likes to spend quality time with his pooch, Walter Alter, and hang out with friends. High school classmates claim he was quite the tennis star at Dalton but doesn't play anymore because tennis doesn't "gel with his image."

LOVE LIFE: Don't get your hopes up for a hookup with Layla Lawson any time soon! Alter has been married to longtime love Brooke for five years, despite whispers of trouble in paradise due to Julian's new scheduling demands. "Brooke was incredibly supportive when he was a nobody, but she's having a really hard time with all the attention," said a source who knows both Julian and Brooke. The couple live in a modest one-bedroom near Times Square, although friends say they're looking to upgrade.

At the very bottom of the box was a photo of herself and Julian, taken by one of the professional photographers at the *Friday Night Lights* party, one that she hadn't seen yet. Her eyes hungrily devoured it, and she breathed an enormous sigh of relief: somehow, miraculously, they both looked good. Julian was leaning down and kissing her shoulder, and you could see the hint of a smile on his face. Brooke had one arm draped across the back of his neck and the other was holding a brightly colored margarita; her head was thrown back a bit and she was laughing. Despite the cocktail, the two cowboy hats, and the pack of cigarettes rolled up in Julian's shirtsleeve as part of his costume, Brooke was thrilled they looked happy and carefree, not drunk or sloppy. Were she forced to find something wrong with the picture, she probably would've pointed to her midsection, where, due to a perfect storm of her body contorting in an unusual angle, the shadows cast off from the dark room, and a bit of a breeze from the back patio, her plaid shirt puffed out like she had a potbelly. Nothing egregious, just the suggestion of a little spare tire that in reality didn't exist. But the truth was, she could live with a bad camera angle. All things considered — and there were myriad other ways each could've looked horrifically bad — she was pretty pleased.

But then there was that article. Where to even begin? Julian sure wasn't going to be happy about all the prep school stuff. No matter how many times Brooke tried to reassure him that no one cared where anyone went to high school, he couldn't stand even the mildest suggestion that his accomplishments were somehow the result of his extremely privileged upbringing. There was that bit about Julian's passions including spending time with his dog — a little humiliating for all involved, considering they didn't mention how much he loved hanging with her or his family, nor were

there any real hobbies listed. The suggestion that girls across America were upset
that Julian and Layla wouldn't be getting
together soon was alternately flattering and
disconcerting. And that quote about her being supportive but stressed by the attention? It was certainly true, so why was it
worded like a nasty accusation? Did one of
their friends really give that quote, or do
these magazines just make things up and
credit them to anonymous sources whenever
it suits them? Of everything written in the
entire article, the single line that really got
her heart pounding was the part about how
she and Julian were supposedly looking to
upgrade their apartment. *What?* Julian knew
full well that Brooke was desperate to get
back to Brooklyn, but they certainly hadn't
started looking.

Brooke tossed the magazine on the floor,
stood up slowly to avoid the hot-water head
rush, and climbed out of the tub. She hadn't
washed her body or her hair, but that didn't
matter now. The only thing that counted
was reaching Nola before she turned off her
phone for the night and went to sleep. With
a towel wrapped around her chest and Walter licking the excess water from her ankles,
Brooke grabbed the portable and dialed
Nola's number from memory.

She answered after four rings, just before the voice mail usually picked up. "What? Didn't we talk enough earlier tonight?"

"Did I wake you?"

"No, but I'm in bed. What's up? Are you filled with regret at implying that I'm the world's biggest whore tonight?"

Brooke snorted. "Not in the least. Did you see *Last Night?*"

"Oh no. What?"

"You subscribe, don't you?"

"Tell me what it says."

"Can you please go get it?"

"Brooke, don't be ridiculous! I am literally under the covers, night cream applied, Lunesta swallowed. Nothing on earth can convince me to go down to the *mailroom* right now."

"There's a huge box called 'Who Is Julian Alter?' and a picture of the two of us on page twelve."

"Call you back in two minutes."

Despite her anxiety, Brooke smiled to herself. She only had time to hang up her towel and climb naked under the covers before the phone rang.

"Did you get it?" Brooke asked.

"Did I ever."

"Now you're freaking me out. Is it really that bad?"

Silence.

"Nola! Say something! I'm panicking here. It's worse than I even thought, isn't it? Am I going to get fired for being an embarrassment to the hospital? Margaret is not going to love this. . . ."

"This has got to be the coolest thing I've ever seen."

"Are we reading the same page?"

" 'Who is this sexy singer?' Yeah, we're reading the same thing. And it's awesome!"

"Awesome?" Brooke nearly shouted. "What's awesome about the line that says Julian's and my marriage is on the rocks? Or the part where we're supposedly already looking at apartments and I don't know the first thing about it?"

"Shhh," Nola said. "Take a deep breath and calm down. I won't let you twist this into something negative like you always do. Take just a second and remember the fact that your husband — *your husband* — is famous enough to warrant an entire box in *Last Night,* and one that in my opinion is extremely flattering. It basically states that the entire country wants him, but he's *yours.* Think about it for a second."

Brooke was quiet while she considered this. She hadn't really thought about it like that.

"Look at the big picture here. Julian's the real deal now, and you're not shallow or evil if you're pretty fucking psyched about that."

"I guess . . ."

"I know! He got to where he is right now in large part because of *you*. Just like we talked about earlier. *Your* support, *your* hard work, *your* love. So go ahead and be proud of him. Be excited about the fact that your husband is famous and young girls all across the country are jealous of you right now. It's okay, it really is. Enjoy it!"

Brooke was silent as she took it all in.

"Because all the other stuff is bullshit. It doesn't really matter what they're writing, just that they're writing it at all. If you think this is crazy, what's going to happen when he's on the cover of *Vanity Fair* next month? Huh? Now, what does Julian think about it? I bet he's euphoric."

It only occurred to her then.

"I haven't even spoken to him yet."

"Well in that case, let me give you a word of advice. Call him up and *congratulate* him. This is *exciting*. It's a milestone! The clearest indication that he's made it. Don't get caught up in the small stuff, okay?"

"I'll try."

"Take that magazine, get in bed, and think about the fact that girls across America are wishing they could trade places with you right now."

Brooke laughed. "I don't know about that."

"It's true. Okay, I've got to go to sleep. Stop stressing and just enjoy, okay?"

"Thanks, I will. Love you."

"Love you too."

Brooke picked up the magazine and examined the picture again, only this time she focused on Julian. It was true, there was no denying that in the moment this photo was snapped, he looked like he was filled with love for her, doting and happy and sweet. What more could she ask for? And although she'd never admit it to anyone, it was pretty heady stuff to see yourself in a magazine like that and know your husband was a heartthrob. Nola was right — she should just let herself enjoy it for a little. No harm in that.

She picked up her cell phone and typed a quick text to Julian:

Just saw Last Night *— so awesome, I'm so proud of you. Thanks for the ridic flowers, love them, love you. xoxo*

There. That's what Julian needed right now — some love and support, not more criticism and freaking out. Proud of herself for fighting through her initial panic, Brooke set her phone aside and picked up her book. There were ups and downs in every marriage, she told herself as she began to read. Theirs were heightened a bit by extraordinary circumstances, no doubt, but with some dedication and effort on both their parts, it was nothing they couldn't get through.

9

A Bun in the Oven and a Drink in Hand

Walter Alter rested his chin on Brooke's ankle and let out a contented sigh. "This is cozy, isn't it?" she asked him, and he blinked. When she handed him a fat piece of popcorn, he sniffed it and then gently plucked it from her fingertips with his mouth.

It felt so good to be curled up on the couch, looking forward to Julian's arrival and a chance to spend some real time together, but her mind kept drifting back to Kaylie. She'd been shocked when she first laid eyes on her patient at the start of the new school year. It turned out Heather had been right: Kaylie had lost too much weight, enough that it nearly took Brooke's breath away when the girl had first walked in her office. They'd immediately had a long conversation about the difference between healthful food choices and dangerous crash dieting — talks that had continued over the past few weeks — and Brooke was starting to feel hopeful that she was making progress.

Her cell phone buzzed and snapped her back to reality. It was a text from Julian saying he was twenty minutes away. She raced into the bathroom, tearing off her clothes as she ran, intent on at least rinsing away the lingering Windex smell from her hair and hands after a particularly intense, slightly OCD housecleaning fit. She had just stepped under the water when she heard Walter begin to bark with a franticness that could only mean one thing.

"Julian? I'll be out in two minutes!" she called in vain, knowing from experience he wouldn't be able to hear a thing from the living room.

A moment later, she felt the rush of cold air before she even saw the door open. He materialized out of the steam almost immediately, and despite the fact that he'd seen her naked thousands upon thousands of times before, Brooke had an intense, almost desperate desire to cover herself. The clear plastic curtain made her feel as exposed as she would have been showering in the middle of Union Square.

"Hey, Rook," he said, raising his voice to make himself heard over the running water and Walter's frenzied barks.

She first turned her back to him and then berated herself for being so ridiculous. "Hey," she said. "I'm almost done here. Why don't you wait for me . . . uh, grab a Coke and I'll be right out."

She was met with silence before he said okay, and Brooke knew he was probably hurt. Again, she reminded herself that she was entitled to her feelings and she didn't have to apologize for them or explain herself.

"I'm sorry," she called while keeping her back to the door, although she could sense he'd already left. *Don't apologize!* She berated herself again.

She rinsed as quickly as possible and toweled off even faster. Julian was not in the bedroom, thankfully, and she furtively — as though there were company over who might accidentally walk in at any moment — threw on a pair of jeans and a long-sleeved T-shirt. There was no choice but to quickly comb out her wet hair and gather it into a ponytail. She glanced in the mirror and hoped that the ruddiness of her makeup-free face would look like some sort of healthy, happy glow to Julian, although she suspected this was unlikely. It wasn't until she stepped into the living room and saw her husband settled on the sofa, reading last Sunday's real estate section of the *Times* with Walter by his side, that the excitement hit her.

"Welcome home," she said, hoping it didn't sound as fraught as it felt. She sat next to him on the couch. He looked at her, smiled, and gave her what felt like a rather lukewarm hug.

"Hey, baby. I'm so happy to be here, you can't even imagine. If I never see another hotel room . . ."

After leaving in the middle of her dad's party, Julian had come home for two nights in late September, one of which was spent at the studio. He'd left to promote the new album, hitting the road for another three weeks, and although they'd both been good about e-mail, Skype, and phone calls, the distance was beginning to feel insurmountable.

"Finding anything good?" she asked, sitting next to him on the couch. She wanted to kiss him but couldn't get past the lingering awkwardness.

He pointed to a listing titled "Tribeca Luxury Loft." It boasted three bedrooms, two bathrooms, a home office, a shared roof deck, a gas fireplace, a full-time doorman, and a tax abatement for the "Best Downtown Value" price of $2.6 million. "Look at this one. Prices are falling like crazy."

Brooke tried to ascertain whether or not he was kidding. Like every New York couple, they often participated in Sunday-morning real estate porn by circling listings that were astronomically out of their price range and wondering aloud what it would be like to actually own them. But something about this felt different.

"Yeah, it's a total bargain. We should buy two and combine them. Maybe three," she laughed.

"Seriously, Brooke, two point six is very reasonable for a full-service three-bedroom in Tribeca."

She stared at the person sitting next to her and wondered where on earth her husband had gone. Was this the same man who ten months earlier had fought vigorously to re-sign the lease on the Times Square apartment they both loathed because he didn't want to spend the extra thousand dollars it would cost to pay a moving company?

"You know, Rook," he said, continuing despite the fact that she'd said nothing, "I know it must feel surreal when you really think about it, but we can afford a place like this. With everything that's starting to come in, we could easily put twenty percent down. And with all the paid performances I have lined up, plus the record royalties, the monthly payments would be more than manageable."

Once again she didn't know what to say.

"Wouldn't you love to live in a place like this?" he asked, pointing to the picture of an ultramodern loft with exposed-pipe ceilings and an overall industrial-chic feel. "It's freaking awesome."

Every fiber of her wanted to scream no. *No,* she didn't want to live in a converted warehouse. *No,* she didn't want to live in faraway, hyper-trendy Tribeca with its world-class galleries and fancy restaurants and nowhere to get a cup of bodega coffee or a basic burger. *No,* if she had two million dollars to spend on an apartment, that was absolutely, positively *not* what she would choose. It almost felt like she was having this conversation with a complete stranger, considering the number of times they'd dreamed together of owning a town house in Brooklyn or, if that was out of reach — and it always had been — then maybe a floor-through in a town house on a quiet, tree-lined street, perhaps with a little garden out back and lots of great molding. Something warm and cozy, prewar preferably, with high ceilings and charm and character. A home for a family in a real neighborhood with independent bookstores and cute coffee shops and a couple of cheap but good restaurants where they could be regulars. The exact opposite, actually, of that steely cold Tribeca loft in the picture. She couldn't help but wonder when Julian's ideal had shifted so drastically and, more to the point, why.

"Leo just moved into a new building on Duane Street with a hot tub on the roof deck," he continued. "He said he's never seen more attractive people in one place in his entire life. And he eats at Nobu Next Door like three times a week. Can you imagine?"

"Do you want some coffee?" she blurted out, desperate to change the subject. Every word he uttered managed to upset her even more.

He glanced up at her and appeared to study her face. "You okay?"

She turned her back and headed to the kitchen, where she spooned coffee into the filter basket. "I'm fine," she called.

Julian's iPhone whooshed as he sent texts or IMs from the next room. Overcome with an inexplicable sadness, she leaned against the counter and watched the coffee drip into the pot, bit by bit. She prepared their mugs as she always did. Julian took the coffee, but he didn't look up from his phone.

"Hello?" she said, trying unsuccessfully to mask her irritation.

"Sorry, just a text from Leo. He asked me to call him right away."

"By all means . . ." She knew her tone made it clear she meant the exact opposite.

He peered at her and, for the first time since arriving, put the phone in his pocket. "No, I'm here right now. Leo can wait. I want us to talk."

He paused for a moment, as though waiting for her to say something. It felt like a strange flashback to their early dating days, although she didn't *ever* remember feeling this kind of awkwardness or distance before, not even in the beginning when they were practically strangers.

"I'm all ears," she said, wanting nothing more than for him to envelop her in a bear hug, announce his undying love for her, and swear that life would immediately go back to normal. Back to boring and poor and predictable. Back to happy. And while that was unlikely — and she really didn't want that anyway, since it would mean the end of Julian's career — she would have loved for him to initiate a real conversation about the challenges they'd been facing and a strategy for dealing with them.

"Come here, Rook," he said with such tenderness that her heart surged.

Oh, thank god. He got it, he also felt the strain of their never seeing each other, and he wanted to figure out how to make it better. She felt a glimmer of hope.

"Tell me what you're thinking," she said softly, hoping she conveyed an open, receptive feel. "It's been a hard few weeks, hasn't it?"

"It has," Julian said in agreement. He got that familiar look in his eye. "Which is why I think we deserve a vacation."

"A vacation?"

"Let's go to Italy! We've been talking about going forever, and October is the perfect time of year. I think I can manage six or seven days off starting the end of next week. I just have to be back before the *Today* show. We'll hit Rome, Florence, Venice . . . take a gondola ride and pig out on pasta and wine. Just you and me. What do you say?"

"That sounds amazing," she said, before she remembered that Randy and Michelle's baby was due next month.

"I know how much you love cured meats and cheeses." He teased her, giving Brooke a poke. "Salted meats and hunks of Parmesan to your heart's content."

"Julian —"

"If we're going to do it, let's just freaking go for it. I'm thinking we should fly first-class. White tablecloths, endless champagne, flat-bed seats. Really treat ourselves."

"It sounds incredible."

"Then why are you looking at me like that?" He pulled his knit cap off and ran his fingers through his hair.

"Because I don't have any vacation days left, and it's right in the middle of the semester for the Huntley girls. Do you think we could go over Christmas instead? If we left on the twenty-third, it would give us almost —"

Julian released her hand and collapsed back into the couch with a loud, frustrated exhalation. "I have no idea what will be happening in December, Brooke. I know I can go now. I just can't believe you'd let something like that get in the way of an opportunity like this."

Now it was her turn to stare at him. " *'That'* happens to be my job. Julian, I've taken off more days this year than anyone. There is no way I can just march in there and ask for another *week* off. I would be fired immediately."

His eyes were steely when they met hers. "Would that really be so bad?"

"I'm going to pretend you didn't say that."

"No, I'm serious, Brooke. Would that be the worst thing in the world? Between Huntley and the hospital, you've been killing yourself. Is it so horrible to suggest that you take some time off?"

Everything was spinning out of control. No one knew better than Julian that Brooke needed to get through one more year before she'd hopefully be opening her own practice. Not to mention how close she'd grown to a couple of the girls, especially Kaylie.

She took a deep breath. "It's not horrible, Julian, but it's not happening. You know I only need one more year and then —"

"So what if it's just a temporary break?" he interrupted, waving his hands. "My mom thought they'd probably even hold your job for you if that's what you wanted, but I don't think it's necessary. It's not like you'd never find another —"

"Your mom? Since when do you talk to your mother about anything?"

He looked at her. "I don't know, I was just telling them how tough it is being away from each other all the time, and I thought she had some good ideas."

"That I should quit my job?"

"Not necessarily quit, Brooke, although if you wanted to do that, I'd totally support you. But maybe time off is the answer."

She couldn't imagine it. Of course, the idea of being entirely unencumbered with schedules and shifts and cramming in as many extra hours as possible sounded heavenly — who wouldn't want that? But she genuinely loved her work, and she was excited to be her own boss one day. She'd already thought of a name — Healthy Mom & Baby — and could perfectly envision how she wanted the website to look. Brooke even had the logo figured out: it was going to be two sets of feet, standing side by side, one obviously a mother's with just a hand reaching down to hold the hand of a toddler.

"I can't, Julian," she said, reaching over to take his hand despite the anger she felt toward him for not understanding. "I'm doing my best to be a part of everything that's happening to your career, to share in all the excitement and craziness, but I have a career, too."

He appeared to be thinking about this, but then he leaned over and kissed her. "Have a sit and a think, Rook. Italy! For a week."

"Julian, I really —"

"No more talking," he said, pressing his fingers to her lips. "We won't go if you don't want to" — he corrected himself when he saw Brooke's expression — "if you're not able to. I'll wait until we can see it together, I swear. But promise you'll think about it?"

Not trusting her voice, Brooke just nodded.

"Okay, then. How about we go out tonight? Somewhere low-key but great. No press. No friends. Just us. What do you say?"

She had figured they would spend their first night together at home, but the more she thought about it, she couldn't remember the last time the two of them went out alone. There was still so much to talk about, but they could do it over a bottle of good wine. Maybe she was just being too hard on him and it would do them both some good if she could just relax. "Okay, let's do it. I just want to dry my hair a little so it doesn't frizz."

Julian beamed and kissed her. "Excellent. Walter and I will call around and find the perfect spot." He turned to Walter and kissed him, too. "Walty, boy, where should I take the wife?"

Brooke quickly ran the blow-dryer over her damp hair and picked out her cutest pair of ballet flats. She slicked on some lip gloss, added a double-chain gold necklace, and after a bit of a debate, decided in favor of a long, soft cardigan rather than a boxier blazer. The look wasn't going to win her any awards, but it was the best she could do without completely stripping down and starting from scratch.

Julian was on the phone when she walked back into the living room, but he immediately hung up and walked over to her.

"Come here, beautiful girl," he murmured, kissing her.

"Mmm, you taste good."

"You look even better. We'll get some dinner, drink some wine, and then what do you say we come directly back here and get reacquainted?"

"I say yes," Brooke said, kissing him back. The uneasy feeling she'd had since the moment Julian walked in — the sense that so much was happening, so quickly, and they hadn't resolved anything — was still nudging her, but she tried her best to ignore it.

Julian had chosen a great little Spanish restaurant on Ninth Avenue and the weather was still warm enough to sit outside. After they kicked the first half bottle of wine they ordered, both of them relaxed, and the conversation grew easy again, more comfortable. Randy and Michelle's baby was due soon, Julian's parents were going away over New Year's and had offered up their Hamptons home, Brooke's mother had just seen an incredible play off-Broadway and was insisting they go see it as well.

It wasn't until they got home and undressed that the awkwardness came rushing back. Brooke had expected Julian to make good on his offer of makeup sex the instant they walked into the apartment — after all, it had been three weeks — but he was distracted first by his phone and then his laptop. When he finally joined her in the bathroom to brush his teeth, it was already after midnight.

"What time are you up tomorrow?" Julian asked as he plucked out his contact lenses and squirted them with cleaning solution.

"I have to be at the hospital by seven thirty for a staff meeting. What about you?"

"I'm meeting Samara at some hotel in SoHo for a photo shoot."

"Got it. So, should I put my face moisturizer on now or later?" she asked Julian as he flossed. Since Julian hated the smell of her intensive night cream and refused to come near her when she was wearing it, this was code for "Are we going to have sex tonight?"

"I'm beat, baby. The schedule is pretty intense now. So close to the new single." He set the little plastic box of floss on the sink and kissed her cheek.

She couldn't help but be insulted. Yes, she

could understand how absolutely exhausted he must be after all that time on the road. She was pretty tired, too, after her daily six o'clock wake-ups to walk Walter, but he was a man and it had been *three weeks*.

"Got it," she said, and immediately slathered on her thick, yellow face cream — the same one every reviewer on beauty.com opined was 100 percent fragrance free but which her husband swore he could smell from across the living room.

Okay, fine, she'd admit it: she was also relieved. Which is not to say she didn't love sex with her husband, because she did — from the very first time, it had been one of the best features of their relationship, and certainly one of the most constant. Of course, having sex every day (sometimes twice) when you're twenty-four and it still feels vaguely scandalous just to sleep over at someone else's apartment isn't such a rarity, but things hadn't slowed much as they dated or even married. For years she'd listened as her friends would joke about their different methods for avoiding husbands and boyfriends each night and Brooke would laugh right along with them, but she didn't understand. Why would they *want* to? Crawling into bed with her husband and making love before they fell asleep had been her favorite part of the day; hell, it was the *good* part about being an adult in a committed relationship.

Well, she got it now. Nothing between them had changed — the sex was still every bit as great as it had always been — but the two of them were just so *exhausted* all the time. (The night before he'd left, he'd fallen asleep on top of her, halfway through, and Brooke only managed to be insulted for about ninety seconds before she passed out, too.) They were both constantly in motion, often separated, and overwhelmed. She hoped it was only temporary and that once Julian was home more often and she could more easily determine her own hours, they'd rediscover each other.

She turned off the bathroom light and followed him to their bed, where Julian had settled in with a copy of *Guitar Player* in hand, Walter snuggled in the crook of his elbow. "Look, baby. There's a mention of my new song." He showed her the magazine.

She nodded, but she was already thinking about sleep. Her routine was military efficient, designed to bring on unconsciousness in the shortest amount of time possible. She turned the air conditioner colder despite the fact that it was a pleasantly cool sixty degrees outside, stripped naked, and climbed under their hugely puffy down comforter. After washing her birth control pill down with a swig of water, she arranged a pair of blue foam earplugs and her favorite satin eye mask right next to the alarm clock and, satisfied, began to read.

When she shivered, Julian leaned over and rested his head on her shoulder. "My crazy girl," he murmured with pretend exasperation. "Never seems to realize that she could be warmer any time she'd like. Just has to turn on the heat a little, or — god forbid — turn the AC off. Or maybe wear a T-shirt to bed . . ."

"Not a chance." Everyone knew that good sleeping conditions were cool, dark, and quiet; therefore, it stood to reason that the best sleeping conditions were freezing cold, pitch-black, and completely silent. She'd slept naked from the time she was old enough to take her pajamas off and could never sleep really well when situations (summer camp, freshman-year dorm, early-twenties sleepovers with guys she hadn't had sex with yet) demanded she wear a nightshirt.

Brooke tried to read for a while, but her mind kept drifting to a series of anxious thoughts. She knew she should have just snuggled up beside Julian and asked for a back rub or a head scratch, but before she knew it, she was saying something completely different.

"Do you think we have enough sex?" she asked while adjusting the band on her eye mask.

"*Enough* sex?" Julian asked. "According to whose standards?"

"Julian, I'm serious."

"So am I. Against whom are we judging ourselves?"

"No one in particular," she said, a hint of exasperation becoming apparent. "Just, you know, the norm."

"The norm? I don't know, Brooke, I think we feel pretty normal. Don't you?"

"Mmm."

"Is this because of tonight? Because we are both really tired? Seriously, don't be so hard on us."

"It's been three weeks, Julian. The longest we've ever gone before was maybe five days, and that was when I had walking pneumonia."

Julian sighed and kept reading. "Rook, can you please stop worrying about us? We're fine. I promise."

She was quiet for a few moments as she thought about this, knowing she didn't actually want to have more sex — not now, not being this tired — but that she wanted *him* to want to.

"Did you lock the front door when you came home tonight?" she asked.

"I think so," he murmured without looking up. He was reading an article on the best guitar techs in America. She knew he had zero recollection of whether he'd locked the front door or not.

"Well did you or didn't you?"

"Yes, I definitely did."

"Because if you're not sure, I'll get up and check. I'd rather be inconvenienced for thirty seconds than dead," she said with a deep, dramatic sigh.

"Really?" He snuggled deeper under the covers. "I couldn't disagree more."

"Julian, seriously. That guy on our floor died just last week. Don't you think we should try to be a little bit more careful?"

"Brooke, sweetheart, he drank himself to death. I'm not sure that could've been prevented if he'd locked his door."

She knew this, of course — knew every single thing that happened in the building because the super was a constant talker — but would it kill Julian to give her a little attention?

"I think I might be pregnant," she announced.

"You are not," he replied automatically and continued to read.

"Yeah, well what if I was?"

"But you're not."

"But how do you know? Mistakes happen all the time. I could be. Then what would we do?" She managed a faux sniffle.

He smiled and finally — finally! — put down the magazine. "Oh, sweetheart, come here. I'm sorry, I should've realized earlier. You want to cuddle."

She nodded. Beyond immature, but she was desperate.

He shimmied over to her side of the bed and enveloped her in a hug. "And did it ever occur to you to say, 'Julian, oh loving husband, I want to cuddle. Will you pay attention to me?' rather than picking fights?"

She shook her head no.

"Of course it didn't," he said with a sigh. "Are you really concerned about our sex life or was that all part of the plan to get a reaction?"

"Yeah, just going for the reaction," she lied.

"And you're not pregnant?"

"No!" she said, a little louder than she intended. "Absolutely, definitely not." She resisted asking him if it would be the worst thing in the world if she actually *were* pregnant. They'd been married five years, after all. . . .

They kissed good night (he suffered the spackled-on moisturizer, but not without a nose wrinkle and a highly exaggerated gagging sound), and she waited the requisite ten minutes until his breathing steadied before pulling on her robe and padding out to the kitchen. After checking that the front door was locked (it was), she headed over to the computer for a quick surf.

In the early days of Facebook, she'd been content to confine her online time to the all-encompassing world of Ex-Boyfriend Stalking. First she searched out her handful of longer-term boyfriends from high school and college, plus that Venezuelan guy she dated for a couple months in graduate school who fell somewhere between a fling and a relationship (had his English been just a touch better . . .) and brought herself up to date on their lives. She'd been pleased to see that each and every one of them looked worse than when she'd known them, and she repeatedly wondered the same thing that was on the minds of so many twenty-something women: why was it, exactly, that nearly every girl she knew looked far better than she had in college when every guy looked fatter, balder, and much, much older?

A couple months had passed like this until she became interested in anything beyond pictures of her senior prom date's twin boys, and before long she began accumulating friends from every era of her life: kindergarten in Boston, while her own parents were still doing their graduate work; sleepaway camp in the Poconos; high school in suburban Philadelphia; dozens and dozens of friends and acquaintances from undergrad at Cornell and her master's program at NYU; and now, colleagues from both jobs at the hospital and the Huntley School. And although she'd forgotten the existence of many of the early friends until their names resurfaced in her Notifications folder, she was always eager to reconnect and see what the last ten or even twenty years had brought.

Tonight was no different: she accepted a friend request from a childhood playmate whose family had moved away in middle school and then hungrily scanned the new profile, registering all the details (single, graduated from UC Boulder, currently living in Denver, appears to love mountain biking and guys with long hair), and sent the girl a quick, cheerily bland message that she knew would likely be the beginning and the end of their "reunion."

She clicked the Home button and was transported back to the addictive Live News Feed, where she quickly scanned her friends' status updates on the Cowboys game, their babies' daily milestones, their Halloween costume ideas, their happiness that "TGIF!" and the photos they'd posted from various vacations they'd taken all over the world. It wasn't until she'd scrolled to the bottom of the second page that she saw Leo's update, in all caps, of course, as though he were screaming directly at her.

Leo Walsh . . . GETTING PUMPED FOR JULIAN ALTER'S PHOTO SHOOT TO-MORROW!! SOHO. HOT MODELS. MES-SAGE ME IF YOU WANT TO STOP BY. . . .

Yuck. Yuck, yuck, yuck. Thankfully, her regular e-mail inbox pinged with a welcome distraction before she could dwell on the grossness of Leo's update.

The new e-mail was from Nola. It was the first (well, really the second: the very first had merely read: "SAVE ME FROM THIS HELL!!!") Brooke had heard from her since she'd left, and she opened it eagerly. Maybe there was a *chance* she was having fun? No, it was impossible. Nola's vacations trended more toward the skiing in the Swiss Alps/sunning in St. Tropez/partying in Cabo types. They were generally frequent, expensive, and almost always included a man extremely fond of sex whom she had only just met and most likely wouldn't see again once they returned home. Brooke literally hadn't believed Nola when she announced that she'd signed up for a group tour of Vietnam, Cambodia, Thailand, and Laos . . . alone. Staying in two-star hotels and guesthouses and traveling by bus. A single backpack for over two weeks. A comprehensive lack of Michelin-starred restaurants, Town Car services, or hundred-dollar pedicures. Zero chance of partying on a new friend's yacht or wearing a single pair of Louboutins. Brooke had tried to talk her out of it by showing Nola her own honeymoon pictures to Southeast Asia, which were replete with close-ups of exotic insects, house pets as dinner, and a collage of all the squat toilets they'd encountered, but Nola insisted it would be fine right until the very end. Brooke wouldn't say I told you so, but judging from the e-mail, things were going exactly as expected.

Greetings from Hanoi, a city so crowded

it makes the NYC subway at rush hour feel like a golf vacation. I'm only on day five and I'm not sure I'll make it to the end. The actual sightseeing has been great, but the group is killing me. They wake up every day with a brand-new lease on life — no bus trip is too long, no market too crowded, no lack of air-conditioning is too unbearable for this crew. Yesterday I broke down and told the group leader I'd be willing to pay the single supplement for my own room after five mornings of my roommate waking up an hour and a half early to jog six miles before breakfast. One of those "I just don't feel like myself if I don't exercise" types. It was sickening. Demoralizing. All-around toxic to my self-esteem, as you can well imagine. So she's been eliminated, which I think is the wisest way I have ever spent five hundred dollars. Otherwise, not too much to report. The country is beautiful, of course, and endlessly interesting, but for the record, the only single man under forty in my group is here with his mother (who, incidentally, I like a lot — maybe I should reconsider???). I'd ask you what's going on there, but since you haven't cared enough to write me once since I've been gone, I don't imagine this time will be any different. Regardless, I miss you and hope that at least in some small, insignificant way, you're having a worse time than I am. xoxo, me

It took mere seconds for Brooke to respond.

Dearest Nola,
I won't say I told you so. Actually, scratch that — I totally will. I TOLD YOU SO! Wtf were you thinking? Did my eight-by-ten of the clear-colored scorpion have no effect on you? Sorry for being the worst keeper-in-toucher in the world. I don't even have a good excuse. Not too much to report here. Work's been crazy for me — I'm covering a bunch of shifts for people on vacation, hoping I can collect at a later date when we can actually go away. Julian's been traveling all week, although I guess it's working because the album is doing incredibly well. Things are a little weird. He seems distant. I'm chalking it up to . . . hell, I don't know. Where's my best friend when I need a good backstory? Help a girl out here!
Okay, I'm signing off and putting us

both out of our misery. Already counting the days until you're home and we can go out for Vietnamese food. I'll bring a flask of murky mystery water and you'll feel like you're still on vacation. It'll be a blast. Stay safe and have some rice for me. Xoxo me

P.S. Have you found a use yet for those gross hand-me-down sarongs I insisted you bring just so you'd get them out of my apartment?

P.P.S. For the record, I strongly encourage you to go for the/any guy who travels with his mother.

She hit Send and heard Julian padding toward her.

"Baby, what are you doing out here?" he asked sleepily as he poured himself some water. "Facebook will be here in the morning."

"I'm not on Facebook!" she said indignantly. "I couldn't sleep so I came out here to write Nola. I don't think she's loving her travel partners."

"Come back to bed." He began to drink his water as he walked back to the bedroom.

"Okay, I'll be right in," she called out, but he was already gone.

■ ■ ■ ■

Brooke awoke instantly from the noise in the apartment, bolted straight up in bed on full alert, terrified until she remembered that Julian was actually home that night. They hadn't gone to Italy; instead, Julian had been on a city-hopping tour of major radio stations, meeting DJs, doing brief in-studio performances, and answering callers' questions. Once again, he'd been gone for two straight weeks.

She leaned over to read the bedside clock, a task made harder by Walter's hot tongue on her face and her inability to find her glasses. Three nineteen A.M. What on earth was he doing awake when they had to be up so early?

"All right, come along," she crooned to Walter, who was wagging and jumping at this unexpected nighttime excitement. Brooke wrapped herself in a robe and padded to the living room, where Julian sat in the dark, clad only in boxers and a pair of headphones, playing his keyboard. He didn't appear to be practicing anything so much as zoning out — his gaze was fixed on the wall opposite the couch and his hands moved across the keys without a hint of awareness. If she hadn't known better, she might have thought he was sleepwalking or on drugs. She was able to sit down next to him before he was even aware of her presence.

"Hey," he said, pulling his headphones down around his neck like a scarf. "Did I wake you?"

Brooke nodded. "It's muted, though," she said, pointing to the keyboard, which was hooked up to the headphones, "so I'm not sure what I heard."

"These," Julian said, holding up a handful of CDs. "I knocked them over just a minute ago. Sorry."

"It's okay." Brooke snuggled close. "You okay? What's going on?"

Julian wrapped his arms around her shoulders but seemed no less distracted. His eyebrows knit together. "I guess I'm just really nervous. I've done a lot of interviews by now, but none as big as the *Today* show."

Brooke grabbed his hand, squeezed it, and said, "You're going to be great, baby. Seriously, you're a natural at this media stuff." Maybe that wasn't exactly true — the few television interviews she'd seen Julian do so far had been a little on the awkward side — but if there was ever a time to lie . . .

"You have to say that. You're my wife."

"You're absolutely right, I do have to say it. But I also happen to mean it. You're going to be amazing."

"It's live and it's *national.* Millions of people watch every single morning. How terrifying is that?"

Brooke nuzzled into his chest so he couldn't see her expression. "You're just going to go out there and do your thing. They'll have that stage set up outside and all the screaming tourists, and it won't feel any different than a tour performance. Far less people than that, actually."

"Fewer."

"What?"

"Fewer. It's 'far fewer' people, not 'less.' " Julian smiled weakly.

Brooke punched him. "So that's what I get for trying to comfort you, huh? Grammar correction? Come on, let's go back to bed."

"What's the point? Don't we have to be there any minute?"

Brooke glanced at the clock on the DVD player. Three thirty-five. "We can sleep for another, oh, let's say fifty minutes before we have to start getting ready. They're sending a car at five fifteen."

"Jesus Christ. This is inhumane."

"Scratch that. I think we can only do

forty-five minutes. Don't think because you're some celebrity now you don't have to walk your own dog."

Julian groaned. Walter woofed.

"Come on, you'll be better off if you lie down, even if you can't sleep," Brooke said, standing and tugging on his arm.

Julian stood and kissed her on the cheek. "Go ahead, I'll be right in."

"Julian . . ."

He flashed another smile, this one real. "Don't be a tyrant, woman. Do I need permission to go to the bathroom? I'll be right in."

Brooke feigned irritation. " 'Tyrant'? Come on, Walter, let's go back to bed and leave Daddy in peace to sit on the toilet and download iPhone apps." She pecked Julian on the lips and made a kissing noise so Walter would follow her.

The next thing Brooke knew, the clock radio was blaring "All the Single Ladies," and she bolted upright in bed, convinced they'd somehow missed the whole thing. She was relieved when the clock read four fifteen A.M. and leaned over to shake Julian, but on his side of the bed she found only a tangle of blanket and a sprawled-out spaniel. Walter was stretched out on his back, all four paws straight in the air, head on Julian's pillow like a human. He looked at her with one eye that seemed to say, *I could get used to this,* before closing it again and letting out a contented sigh. Brooke buried her face in his neck and then tiptoed into the living room, certain she'd find Julian right where she'd left him. Instead, she saw a crack of light under the door of the guest half bathroom, and when she moved closer to ask if he was all right, she heard the unmistakable sound of retching. *Poor thing's a wreck,* she thought with a combination of sympathy for Julian and relief that she wasn't the one who had to give this interview right now. If the situation were reversed, she had no doubt she'd be right there in that bathroom, puking and praying for some divine intervention.

She heard the water run for a moment and then the door opened, revealing a pale, sweaty version of her husband. He ran the back of his hand along his mouth and offered her an expression that toed the line between nauseated and mildly amused.

"How are you feeling, baby? Can I get you anything? Some ginger ale maybe?"

Julian slumped into a seat at their two-person kitchenette table and raked his fingers through his hair. Brooke noticed that his hair was looking fuller lately, almost like he wasn't thinning on top as much as he had been in the last year. It was probably the great haircuts he'd been getting from the hair and makeup people, who must have discovered a way to somehow conceal or camouflage it. Whatever they were doing, it was working. Without the distraction of the small bald spot, your eyes were immediately drawn to those ridiculous dimples.

"I feel like shit," he announced. "I don't think I can do this."

Brooke knelt beside him, kissed him on the cheek, and took both his hands in hers. "You're going to be great, baby. This is going to help you and your album so tremendously."

For a second Brooke thought he might cry. Thankfully, he plucked a banana from the centerpiece bowl, peeled it, and began taking long, slow chews.

"And I really think the interview part is going to be a breeze. Everyone knows you're there to *perform*. You'll do 'For the Lost,' the crowd will go crazy, you'll forget the cameras are even there, and then they'll come up to you on the stage and ask how it feels to be a sudden star or something like that. You'll give your bit about how much you love and adore all your fans, and then straight to Al for the weather. It'll be a cakewalk, I promise!"

"You think?"

His imploring eyes reminded Brooke how long it had been since she had to soothe him like this, how much she missed doing it. Her husband the rock star could still be her husband the nervous guy.

"I know! Come on, let's get you in the shower and I'll make you some eggs and toast. The car will be here in a half hour and we can't be late. Okay?"

Julian nodded. He rumpled her hair as he stood and took off for their bathroom without another word. He got nervous before every performance, regardless of whether it was a routine gig at a college bar or a small showcase in an intimate venue or a huge crowd in a Midwestern stadium, but Brooke couldn't remember ever seeing him like this.

She jumped in the shower as he was climbing out, and she thought about offering a few more words of encouragement but decided maybe a little silence would be better. By the time she finished, Julian had left with Walter for a walk, and she raced to pull on the easiest outfit she could find that was guaranteed comfortable without being hideous: a tunic-style sweater over black leggings paired with low-heel ankle boots. She had been a late adopter of the legging, but once she caved and bought her first gloriously stretchy and forgiving pair, Brooke had never looked back. After so many years of fighting to pour herself into skintight, low-rise jeans and binding pencil skirts and slacks that always felt like a vise around her waist, she found leggings were God's apology to women everywhere. For the first time, something that was in style actually flattered her figure perfectly by hiding her less-than-stellar mid- and rear section while accentuating her reasonably shapely legs. Every day she pulled a pair on she offered a silent thank-you to their inventor and a quiet prayer that they'd remain in fashion just a little bit longer.

The drive from their apartment to Rockefeller Center went quickly. There was no traffic that early in the morning, and the only sound came from Julian's fingers tap-tap-tapping against the wood grain of the armrest. Leo called to say he was waiting for them at the studio, but otherwise no one spoke. It wasn't until the car pulled up alongside the talent entrance that Julian gripped Brooke's hand so tightly she had to clamp her mouth shut to keep from calling out.

"You're going to be great," she whispered

to him as a young man in a page uniform and a headset led them to the greenroom.

"It's live and it's national," Julian replied, his eyes fixed straight ahead. He looked even paler than he had this morning, and Brooke prayed he wouldn't throw up again.

She pulled a packet of chewable Pepto tablets from her purse, discreetly removed two from the wrapper, and pressed them into Julian's palm. "Chew those," she said quietly.

They passed a couple of studios, each emanating the telltale freezing cold air that kept the anchors cool under the blazing stage lights, and Julian tightened his grip. They rounded a corner, walked past a space that looked like a makeshift salon where three women were setting up hair and makeup supplies, and were deposited in a room with a few armchairs, two love seats, and a small breakfast buffet. Brooke had never been in an official greenroom of any kind before, and although this one said as much on the door, everything was done in shades of beige and mauve. Only Julian was tinted green.

"There he is!" Leo boomed, his voice sounding at least thirty decibels louder than necessary.

"I'll, uh, be back to take you into hair and

makeup as soon as the rest of the band is here," the page said, looking uncomfortable. "Just, um, have some coffee or something." He quickly ducked out.

"Julian! How we doing this morning? You ready? You're not looking ready, man. You okay?"

Julian nodded, looking every bit as unhappy to see Leo as Brooke felt. "Fine," he murmured.

Leo clapped Julian's back and then pulled him into the hallway for some sort of pep talk. Brooke fixed herself a cup of coffee and took a seat in the corner farthest from everyone. She surveyed the room and took her best guess on the other guests that morning: a little girl who, judging from both the violin she clutched and her snotty attitude, was most likely a musical prodigy; the editor of a men's magazine who was rehearsing with his publicist the ten weight-loss tips he planned to discuss; a well-known chick-lit author holding her most recent novel in one hand and her cell phone in the other, looking supremely bored as she scrolled through her call list.

The other band members straggled in over the next fifteen minutes, each managing to appear exhausted and excited at the same time. They slurped coffee and took turns in the hair and makeup room, and before Brooke had another opportunity to gauge how Julian was holding up, they were whisked out to the promenade to greet the fans and do a final sound check. It was a crisp fall morning and the crowd was huge. By the time they began their performance, right around eight, the audience had swelled to hundreds of people, almost all female between the ages of twelve and fifty, and it seemed like nearly every one of them was screaming Julian's name. Brooke stared at the monitor in the greenroom, trying to remind herself that Julian was — at that very moment — on televisions across America, when the page came by and asked if she'd like to watch the interview portion from inside the studio itself.

Brooke jumped up and followed the boy down a flight of stairs and onto the familiar set she recognized from years of watching the show. The icy air hit her immediately.

"Wow, it's a beautiful set. For some reason I just figured they'd interview him outside in front of the crowd."

The page held a couple fingertips up to his earpiece, listened, and nodded. He turned back to Brooke but didn't seem to really see her. "Normally they would, but the wind today is wreaking havoc with the mics."

"Got it," Brooke said.

"You can sit right here," he said, motioning to a folding chair between two of the massive cameras. "They'll be coming inside any second and will be on air" — he checked a stopwatch hanging from a lanyard around his neck — "in just under two minutes. Your cell phone's off, right?"

"Yeah, I left it upstairs. Oh, this is just so cool!" Brooke said. She'd never been on a television set before, never mind one so famous. It was almost overwhelming just to sit there and watch all the camera guys and sound technicians and producers in headsets scurry around in preparation. She was watching as a man swapped out overstuffed couch cushions for smaller, tighter ones when there was a rush of outside air and a lot of commotion. About a dozen people walked through the studio door and Brooke saw Julian was flanked on either side by Matt Lauer and Meredith Vieira. He looked a bit dazed and had a thin bead of sweat on his upper lip, but he was laughing at something and shaking his head.

"One minute thirty seconds!" a female voice boomed over the loudspeaker.

The group walked right in front of her,

and for a moment Brooke could only stare at the anchors' familiar faces. But then Julian caught her eye and gave her a nervous smile. He mouthed something to her, although Brooke couldn't tell what. She sat in the chair the page had pointed out. Immediately two more people descended on him, one showing him how to weave the microphone up the back of his shirt and clip it onto his collar, and the other applying pressed powder to his shiny face. Matt Lauer leaned in to whisper something to Julian, who laughed, and then walked off the stage. Meredith took the seat opposite Julian and although Brooke couldn't hear what they were saying, it looked like Julian was quite comfortable with her. She tried to imagine how nervous he must be right then, how utterly terrifying and surreal the whole thing must feel, and just the thought of it was enough to make her queasy. She dug her fingernails into her palms and prayed it would go well.

"Forty-five seconds to live!"

It only felt like ten seconds had passed, but a deep quiet settled over the set and Brooke saw a Tylenol commercial on the monitors in front of her. It was probably on for about thirty seconds when the opening chords of the *Today* show song began to play, and the voice over the loudspeaker began to count down. Immediately, the entire room stood still, except for Meredith, who scanned her notes and ran her tongue over her front teeth to check for lipstick.

"Five. Four. Three. Two. And live!" At the exact moment the voice called out the word "and," someone flipped on the massive overhead studio lights and immediately the entire set was bathed in intense, hot light. At that same moment, Meredith smiled broadly, turned toward the camera with the blinking green light, and read from the teleprompter.

"Welcome back, everyone! For those of you who are just joining us, we are lucky to have one of the hottest young stars on the musical scene today, singer-songwriter Julian Alter. He has already toured with Maroon 5 before embarking on his very own tour, and his first album debuted at number four on the *Billboard* chart." She turned to Julian and her smile grew. "And he just gave us a terrific performance of his song 'For the Lost.' You were great, Julian! Thanks for joining us today."

He grinned, but Brooke could see the tightness in the lips and the way his left hand death-gripped the arm of the chair.

"Thanks for having me. I'm thrilled to be here."

"I have to say, I really enjoyed that song," Meredith said with lots of enthusiasm. Brooke was fascinated by the way the anchor's makeup looked spackled and fake in person but flawless and beautiful on the monitor. "Can you tell us a little bit about how you came to write it?"

Julian's face instantly came alive and he leaned forward in his chair. His entire body seemed to relax as he described his inspiration for "For the Lost."

The next four minutes elapsed in a flash. Julian sailed through questions about how he got discovered, how long it took him to record the album, if he could believe all the incredible feedback and attention. The media training had definitely paid off: his answers were funny and charmingly self-deprecating without sounding like each had been scripted by a team of people (which they absolutely had). He maintained good eye contact, looked relaxed without being disrespectful, and at one point smiled so winningly for Meredith Vieira that she herself nearly giggled and said, "I can see why you're such a big hit with your younger female fans." It wasn't until Meredith picked up a copy of an unidentifiable celeb magazine that must have been facedown on the table between them, and flipped to a bookmarked page, that Julian stopped smiling.

Brooke remembered the night Julian had come home from media training and told her it was the most important thing he'd learned. "You are not required to answer the question they ask you, and if you don't like the question, you go ahead and answer any question you feel like answering. It does not need to be related whatsoever to the asked question. The only requirement is that you convey information *you* want to share. Take back control of the interview. Don't let them bully you into answering anything unpleasant or uncomfortable. Just smile and change the subject. The onus is on the anchor to keep the interview moving forward, to make it appear smooth and seamless, and they're not going to call you out on refusing to answer a question. This is morning television, not the presidential debates, so as long as you're smiling and relaxed, you've succeeded. You'll never get cornered or pinned down if you only answer questions you like."

That night felt like a year ago, and Brooke just prayed Julian could muster the same confidence right now. *Stick to the script,* she willed him, *and don't let her see you sweat.*

Meredith folded over the magazine, which Brooke could now see was *US Weekly,* and held a page toward Julian. She pointed to a photo in the upper-right-hand corner, which was Brooke's first indication this wasn't about the infamous Layla picture. Julian was smiling, but he looked confused.

"Ah yes," he said in response to nothing, since Meredith had not asked a question yet. "My beautiful wife."

Oh no, Brooke thought. Meredith was pointing to a picture of Brooke and Julian with their arms around each other, smiling happily for the cameras. The camera zoomed in on the picture and Brooke could make out the details now: her standby black sweater dress, Julian looking uncomfortable in a pair of dress slacks and a button-down shirt, both of them holding wineglasses aloft . . . where were they? She leaned forward in her chair and stared at the nearest monitor and it hit her all at once. Her father's sixty-fifth birthday party. The picture must have been taken just after Brooke gave her toast, since she and Julian were standing in front of an otherwise seated table. Who on earth had taken that and, more to the point, why did *US Weekly* care?

Then the camera moved down just a touch and she was able to see that the photo had a caption that read, "A Bun in the Oven and a Drink in Hand?" She felt a horrible, anxious jolt in the middle of her stomach when she realized that the new issue of *US Weekly* had probably come out that very day, and no one on Julian's team had seen it yet.

"Yes, I've read that you and your wife, Brooke, have been married for what, five years now?" Meredith asked, looking to Julian. He just nodded, clearly nervous about where this line of questioning was going.

Meredith leaned in close to Julian and, with a huge smile, said, "So can you confirm it here first?"

Julian peered back at her, meeting her eyes, but he looked just as confused as Brooke felt. Confirm what? Brooke knew he hadn't processed the whole "bun in the oven" thing and most likely thought he was being questioned about the state of his marriage.

"Sorry?" It wasn't exactly articulate, but Brooke could hardly blame him. What, exactly, *was* she asking?

"Well, we just couldn't help but wonder if that was a baby bump your wife is sporting." Meredith smiled broadly, as though an answer in the affirmative was a mere formality, not really a question at all.

Brooke inhaled sharply. Definitely not what she was expecting, and poor Julian was about as likely to use the phrase "baby bump" as he was to answer the question in Russian. Not to mention that while she might not be in the absolute best shape of her life, she sure as hell didn't think she looked pregnant. It was just another awkward picture angle, taken from below and exposing the weird puffiness of fabric around the waist where the dress was cinched closed. So what?

He squirmed in his seat; his distress only seemed to confirm the truth of her question.

"Oh come on, you can tell us here. That would be quite a big year for you — debut album and a new baby! I'm sure the fans would love to know for sure. . . ."

It took Brooke a second to realize she wasn't breathing. Was this actually *happening?* Who the hell did she think they were? Brangelina? Did anyone actually care if they were pregnant? Was it anyone's business? Did she really look so huge in that picture that the only assumption could be she was with child? And most of all, if the whole goddamn world was going to assume she was pregnant, that picture made her look like a pregnant woman with a drinking problem. It was almost too much to believe.

Julian opened his mouth to say something, appeared to remember his instructions to smile and answer whatever he wanted, and said, "I love my wife very much. None of this would have ever happened without her incredible support."

None of what? Brooke wanted to scream. *The horrible timing of the pregnancy that didn't exist? The fact that his wife was drinking straight through her faux pregnancy?*

There was an awkward silence that probably only lasted a couple seconds but felt endless, and then Meredith thanked Julian, looked directly at the camera, ordered everyone to buy his new album, and cut to commercial. Brooke was vaguely aware that the intense lights had been lowered and Meredith had unhooked her microphone and stood up. She extended a hand to Julian, who looked shell-shocked, offered a few words Brooke couldn't hear, and quickly walked off the set. A dozen people began scurrying around the studio, checking wires and pushing cameras and exchanging clipboards. Julian continued to sit there, looking like he'd just been whacked over the head with a shovel.

Brooke stood up and was about to make her way to Julian when Leo materialized in front of her.

"Our boy did pretty well, dontcha think, Brooke? Little weird on the last question, but nothing major."

"Mmm." Brooke was intent on getting to Julian, but out of the corner of her eye, she watched as Samara, the media trainer, and two PAs escorted Julian back outside to prepare for his next set. He still had two more songs to sing, one at eight forty-five and one at nine thirty, before this hellish morning would finally end.

"You wanna come outside or watch from the greenroom? Might want to take it easy, you know, put your legs up?" Leo leered, which felt grosser than usual right then.

"You think I'm pregnant?" she asked in disbelief.

Leo threw his hands in the air. "I'm not asking. That's your deal, you know? Granted, it wouldn't be the *best* timing in terms of Julian's career, but hey, I guess babies come when they're ready. . . ."

"Leo, I would really appreciate —"

Leo's cell phone rang and he yanked it from his pocket and cradled it like it was the Bible. "Gotta take this," he said, and turned to walk outside.

Brooke stood rooted to her spot. She couldn't even begin to process what had happened. Julian had all but confirmed an imaginary pregnancy on live, national television. The page who had greeted them this morning appeared by Brooke's side.

"Hi! Can I show you back to the green-room? They're getting set up for the next segment, so things are kind of crazy here," he said, checking his clipboard.

"Sure, that'd be great. Thanks," Brooke said gratefully.

She followed him in silence back up the stairs and down the long hallway. He opened the greenroom door for her and Brooke thought he may have said "congratulations" before he left, but she wasn't sure. Her seat had been claimed by a man in full chef whites, so she took the only empty chair left.

The child prodigy with the violin looked up at her. "Do you know what it is?" she asked, her voice so high-pitched it sounded like she had just inhaled a helium balloon.

"Pardon me?" Brooke glanced at the child, uncertain she had heard her correctly.

"I asked," the girl said excitedly, "if you know what you're having yet. A boy or a girl?"

Brooke's mouth dropped in shock.

The girl's mother leaned over and whispered something in her ear, probably something about her question being rude or inappropriate, but the girl only glared back. "I just asked what she was having!" she screeched.

Brooke tried to relax. Might as well have a little fun — god knows her family and friends weren't going to be quite as amused. She scanned the room to make sure no one else was listening and leaned over. "I'm having a girl," she whispered, only feeling slightly evil for lying to a child. "And I can only hope she is every bit as lovely as you."

The phone calls from friends and family began pouring in during the car ride home and continued nonstop for days. Her mother announced that while she was hurt she had to find out on television, she was nonetheless ecstatic that her only daughter would finally be a mother herself. Her father was delighted that the picture from his party had been posted on national television and wondered how he and Cynthia hadn't figured it out earlier. Julian's mother weighed in with the expected "Oh, well! We sure don't feel old enough to be grandparents!" Randy kindly offered to include Brooke's future son on the small football team of Greene children he was mentally drafting, and Michelle volunteered her services to decorate the little one's nursery. Nola was livid that Brooke hadn't confided in her first, although she admitted that she'd be more apt to forgive were the little girl named after her. And every single one of them — some more gently than others — commented on the wine.

That she had to convince her entire family, Julian's entire family, all her coworkers and all their friends that first, she was not pregnant, and second, she would *never* drink during her purely hypothetical pregnancy, felt to Brooke like more than an insult. An affront. And she could still sense skepticism. The only thing that worked — that actually made people back off for half a second — was the following week's *US Weekly,* which showed a paparazzi picture of Brooke grocery shopping at her neighborhood Gristedes. Her belly looked flatter, no doubt, but that wasn't what did the trick. In the photo she held a basket with bananas, a four-pack of yogurt, a liter of Poland Spring, a bottle of Windex, and, apparently, a box of Tampax. The Pearl version, super absorbency, should the world be interested, and it was circled with a thick black marker and a caption that screamed "No Baby for the Alters!" as though the magazine, through some sort of savvy detective work, had really gotten to the bottom of the issue.

Thanks to that stellar journalism, the entire world knew she was *not* pregnant but she *did* have heavier-than-average periods. Nola found the entire thing hysterically funny; Brooke couldn't stop thinking that everyone from her tenth-grade boyfriend to her ninety-one-year-old grandfather — not to mention every single teenager, housewife, frequent flyer, grocery shopper, salon visitor, manicure seeker, and subscriber in North America — was privy to the details of her menstrual cycle. She hadn't even *seen* the photographer! From that day on, she ordered all products that were sex, period, or digestion related online.

Thankfully, Randy and Michelle's baby, Ella, proved to be the ultimate distraction. She arrived, like a blessing from above, two weeks after the *Today* show drama, and she had the courtesy to arrive right on Halloween, thereby giving them a perfect excuse to bail on Leo's costume party. Brooke couldn't help but feel immense gratitude toward her new niece. Between all the retellings of the birthing story (Michelle's water breaking while they were out at an Italian restaurant, the race to the hospital only to wait another twelve hours, the offer of free lifetime meals for Ella from the owner of Campanelli's), the swaddling lessons, and the counting of fingers and toes, the focus had shifted away from Brooke and Julian. At least, within their own family.

They were the model aunt and uncle, making it to the hospital with time to spare before the baby was born, remembering to bring with them two dozen New York bagels and enough lox to feed the entire maternity ward. Even Julian had seemed pleased by the whole event, cooing in Ella's ear that her tiny hands looked like they were made to play the piano. She would forever think of baby Ella as the last delicious calm before the hell storm to come.

10
BOY-NEXT-DOOR
DIMPLES

Brooke's cell phone rang just as she'd lugged the twenty-two-pound turkey into the apartment and managed to heave it on top of the counter.

"Hello?" she said as she began clearing her fridge of every nonessential item to make room for the gigantic bird.

"Brooke? It's Samara."

She was caught off guard. Samara had never, ever called her before. Did she want to check in and see what they thought of the *Vanity Fair* cover? It had just hit the stands and Brooke couldn't stop staring at it. She thought of it as vintage Julian, in jeans and a tight white T-shirt, wearing one of his favorite knit caps and smiling in just that way that showed off his astonishingly endearing dimples. He was by far the cutest of the gang.

"Oh, hi! Doesn't he just look amazing on the *Vanity Fair* cover? I mean, I'm not surprised, but he just looks so —"

"Brooke, do you have a minute?"

Obviously, this wasn't a social call about a magazine cover, and if that woman was even going to try to tell Julian that he couldn't make it home for the very first Thanksgiving *they* were hosting, well, she'd kill her.

"Um, yeah, just hold on one sec." She closed the fridge and sat down at their tiny table, which reminded her that she needed to call and check on the status of the table and chair rental. "Okay, I'm settled now. What's going on?"

"Brooke, there's been an article written, and it's not pleasant," Samara announced in that clipped, curt way she always had, although with news like this there was something comforting about it.

Brooke tried to laugh it off. "Well, seems like these days there's always an article written. Hey, I'm the hard-drinking pregnant lady, remember? What did Julian say?"

Samara cleared her throat. "I haven't told him yet. I suspect he'll be very upset, and I wanted to talk to you first."

"Oh, Christ. What do they say about him? Do they make fun of his hair? Or his family? Or did some creepy attention whore from his past surface with claims that —"

340

"It's not about Julian, Brooke. It's about you."

Silence. Brooke felt her fingernails digging into her palms, but she couldn't consciously stop it from happening.

"What about me?" she finally asked, her voice a near whisper.

"It's a collection of offensive lies," Samara said coolly. "I wanted you to hear it from me first. And I also want you to know that we have our legal team on it, refuting the entirety of it. We're taking this very seriously."

Brooke couldn't bring herself to speak. No question it must be pretty horrible if Samara was going to such lengths over some tabloid piece. Finally she said, "Where is it? I need to see it."

"It will be in tomorrow's issue of *Last Night,* but you can read it online right now. Brooke, please understand that everyone here is behind you, and we promise —"

For possibly the first time since she was a teenager — and certainly for the first time involving anyone but her mother — Brooke hung up midsentence and moved to the computer. She found the page within seconds and did a double take when a huge picture on the homepage showed her and Julian having dinner at an outdoor table.

She racked her brain, trying to figure out where they were, before she noticed a street sign in the background. Of course, the Spanish meal they'd shared the night Julian came home shortly after leaving in the middle of her father's birthday party. Then she began to read.

The couple sharing an order of paella at an outdoor table in Hell's Kitchen might look like anyone else, but those in the know recognized them as America's favorite new singer-songwriter Julian Alter and his longtime wife, Brooke. Alter's debut album has crushed the charts, and his boy-next-door dimples have wowed female fans from coast to coast. But just who is the woman by his side? And how are they weathering Julian's newfound fame?

Not well, according to a source close to the couple. "They married very, very young, and, yes, they've made it five years so far, but they are on the verge of collapse," the source said. "His schedule is demanding, and Brooke hasn't been very accommodating."

The two met shortly after the terrorist attacks of September 11 and clung to each other in the aftermath that rocked New York. "Brooke practically stalked Julian for months, following him all over Manhattan and sitting alone at all his gigs until he had no choice but to notice her. They were both just lonely," the source explained. A close family friend of the Alters' agrees. "Julian's parents were devastated when he announced his engagement to Brooke after less than two years of dating. What was the rush?" However, the couple tied the knot in a small, no-frills ceremony at the Alter family home in the Hamptons despite the fact that the Drs. Alter "always suspected that Brooke, a girl from some nowhere town in Pennsylvania, was trying to hitch her wagon to Julian's star."

Over the last few years, Brooke worked two jobs to help support her husband's musical aspirations, but one of her friends explains that "Brooke would've done anything necessary to help Julian seek the fame she's always so desired. Two jobs, ten jobs — none of it mattered, so long as she was married to a celebrity." The mother of a student enrolled at the elite Upper East Side private school where Brooke offers nutritional counseling reports, "She seems like a perfectly nice person, although my daughter did tell me that she often leaves early or cancels appointments." The work problems don't stop there. A colleague at NYU Medical Center explains that "Brooke used to be the number one performer in our entire program, but she's really slipped lately. Whether she's distracted by her husband's career or just bored of her own, it's been sad to watch."

As for those pregnancy rumors that were started on the *Today* show and quickly quashed by *US Weekly* the following week with photographic evidence that the Alters are not expecting? Well, don't expect that to change any time soon. An old friend of Julian's claims that Brooke has been "pushing for a baby since the day they met, but Julian keeps putting her off because he's still not positive she's the One."

And with trouble brewing like that, who can blame him?

"I have complete faith that Julian will do the right thing," a source close to Julian said recently. "He's an amazing kid with such a solid head on his shoulders. He'll find the right path."

She didn't know when the tears began, but by the time she finished reading, they had puddled near the keyboard and dampened her cheeks, chin, and lips. There were no words to describe how it felt to read something like that about yourself, to know that it was patently untrue but to wonder — because how couldn't you? — if there weren't tiny kernels of truth. Of course all that stuff about how she and Julian met, and why, was ridiculous, but *did* his parents really hate her? *Was* her reputation at both her jobs being compromised by how much work she'd missed? Could there be *any* sliver of truth to the story's supposed reason why Julian didn't want a baby right now? It was horrifying beyond comprehension.

Brooke read it a second time and then a third. She may have sat there reading and rereading it all day long, but her phone rang again. It was Julian this time.

"Rook, I can't even tell you how pissed I am! It's one thing if they want to write a bunch of trash about me, but when they start in on you . . ."

"I don't want to talk about it," she lied. She wanted nothing more than to talk about it, to ask Julian point by point if he agreed with any of the twisted claims the article made, but she didn't have the energy.

"I've already spoken to Samara, and she promised me that the legal team at Sony was preparing to —"

"Julian, I really don't want to talk about

345

it," she repeated. "It's horrible and hateful and universally untrue — I hope — and there's not a damn thing I can do about it. We are hosting nine people including ourselves for Thanksgiving tomorrow, and I need to start preparing."

"Brooke, I don't want you to think for a single second that —"

"Okay, I know. You're still coming home tomorrow, right?" She held her breath.

"Of course! I'm on the first flight out, so I'll land around eight and come directly from LaGuardia. Do you need me to pick up anything?"

Brooke clicked the hateful article closed and opened her Thanksgiving shopping list. "I think I've got everything . . . actually, a couple more bottles of wine. Maybe one more red and one more white."

"Of course, baby. I'll be home in just a little bit and we can work through this, okay? Call you later."

"Mmm. Okay." Her voice sounded cold and distant, and even though it wasn't Julian's fault, she couldn't help feeling resentful.

They hung up and she thought first about phoning Nola and then her mother, but decided the only way to deal with this was not to deal with it. She called to check on the table rentals, brined the turkey, washed the potatoes for mashing the next day, made the cranberry sauce, and trimmed the asparagus. After that, it was time for a massive apartment clean and reorganization, which she tackled to the blasting sounds of an old hip-hop CD from high school. She'd planned to go for a manicure around five, but when she peeked out the window, at least two and maybe four men with Escalades and cameras were lurking on the street below. Brooke glanced at her cuticles and back at the men: so not worth it.

By the time she crawled into bed that night with Walter, she had managed to delude herself into believing that the whole thing would just go away. Even though it was the very first thing that popped into her mind when she woke up on Thanksgiving morning, she managed to force the thought back. There was so much to do to get ready, and people would be there in five hours. When Julian arrived home a little after nine, she insisted they change the subject.

"But, Rook, I just don't think it's healthy not to discuss this," he said as he helped push all their living room furniture against the walls to make room for the rented table.

"I just don't know what there is to say. It's all a massive bunch of lies, and yes, it's upsetting — mortifying — to read stuff like that about myself and my marriage, but unless any of it's actually true, I just don't see what hashing and rehashing this is going to do. . . ." She looked at him questioningly.

"Not a single word of it is true. Not that crap about my parents, or me not thinking you're 'the one' — none of it."

"So let's focus on today, okay? What time did your parents say they're leaving? I won't have Neha and Rohan come over until they're gone. I just don't think we'll be able to fit everyone at the same time."

"They're coming at one for a drink, and I told them they had to be gone by two. Does that work?"

Brooke picked up a stack of magazines and hid them in the hallway closet. "That's perfect. Everyone else is arriving at two. Tell me again I shouldn't feel guilty that we're kicking them out."

Julian snorted. "We're hardly kicking them out. They're going to the Kamens'. Trust me, they won't want to stay a minute longer."

She shouldn't have been worried. The Alters arrived exactly on time, agreed only to drink the wine they'd brought ("Oh, dears, save your bottles for your other guests — why don't we drink the good stuff now?"), made only one disparaging comment about the apartment ("It certainly is *charming,* isn't it? It's just a wonder you two have been able to live here for as long as you have"), and left fifteen minutes ahead of schedule. Thirty seconds after they left, their buzzer rang again.

"Come on up," she called into the intercom.

Julian squeezed her hand. "It's going to be great."

Brooke opened the hallway door and her mother swooped in with barely a hello. "The baby's sleeping," she declared, as though she were announcing the arrival of the president and first lady. "Where should we put her?"

"Well, let's see. Being that we're all eating in the living room, and I'm guessing you don't want her in the bathroom, that only leaves one option. Can you just put her on our bed?" Brooke asked.

Randy and Michelle materialized holding baby Ella in a portable carry seat. "She's still way too young to roll so it's probably fine," Michelle said, leaning over to kiss Julian hello.

"No way!" Randy said, dragging what looked like a folded-up tent. "That's exactly why I brought the Pack 'n Play. You are not putting her on a bed."

Michelle gave Brooke a look that said, *Well, who can argue with the overprotective daddy?* and they both laughed. Randy and Mrs. Greene took Ella back to the bedroom and Julian began to pour glasses of wine.

"So . . . are you doing okay?" Michelle asked.

Brooke closed the oven, set the baster down, and turned to Michelle. "Yeah, I'm fine. Why?"

Her sister-in-law looked instantly contrite. "Oh, sorry, I probably shouldn't have brought it up, but that article was just so . . . so vicious."

Brooke inhaled sharply. "Oh, yeah, I guess I figured no one else had read it yet. Since it's not even out, you know?"

"Oh, I'm sure no one else has!" Michelle said. "A friend of mine forwarded it to me online, but she's a total freak about the gossip websites. No one reads as much as she does."

"Got it. Hey, would you mind bringing this to the living room?" Brooke asked, handing Michelle a cheese platter with miniature bowls of fig jam and assorted crackers.

"Of course," Michelle said. Brooke figured she got the message, but Michelle took two steps out of the kitchen, turned around, and said, "You know, someone keeps calling and asking me questions about you guys, but we don't say a word."

"Who?" Brooke asked, her voice filled with the panic she'd successfully suppressed until now. "Remember, I've asked you guys not to talk to any reporters about us. Not on the phone, in person, not *ever.*"

"Oh, we know that. And we never would. I just thought you should know that there are people out there hunting around."

"Yeah, well, judging from their accuracy, they haven't done a terrific job with sources," Brooke said, pouring herself another glass of white wine.

Her mother's voice broke the awkward silence and Michelle scurried out with the cheese. "What's going on in here?" she asked, kissing Brooke's hair. "I'm so relieved you've taken over the hosting! It was getting lonely year after year when all you kids went to your father's."

Brooke didn't tell her that the only reason she'd volunteered to make Thanksgiving dinner this year was because her father and Cynthia were going to Cynthia's family's place in Arizona. Besides, it was nice to feel like a proper grown-up, even if it was only for an afternoon.

"Yeah, well, let's see if you're still saying that when you try the turkey," Brooke said.

The doorbell rang, and Ella began to wail from the bedroom.

Everyone dispersed: Randy and Michelle to tend to Ella, Julian to open another bottle of wine, and Mrs. Greene to trail Brooke to the door.

"Remind me who these friends are again?" she asked. "I know you've told me before, but I can't remember."

"Neha and I went to grad school together and she now does prenatal nutrition at a gynecologist's office in Brookline. Her husband, Rohan, is an accountant, and they've been living in Boston for about three years now. Both of their families are still in India, so they don't really celebrate Thanksgiving, but I thought it'd be nice to include them," Brooke whispered as they stood in the foyer.

Her mother nodded. Brooke knew she wouldn't remember half of it and would end up asking Neha and Rohan for the whole story again.

Brooke opened the door and Neha immediately leaned in for a hug. "I can't believe how long it's been! Why don't we see each other more often?"

Brooke hugged her back and then stood

on her tiptoes to kiss Rohan on the cheek. "Come in, you guys. Neha, Rohan, this is my mom. Mom, these are friends from way back."

Neha laughed. "Like, back when we were in our twenties and still hot?"

"Yeah, we do lab coats and clogs better than anyone. Here, let me take your coats," Brooke said as she ushered them inside.

Julian emerged from the tiny galley kitchen. "Hey, man," he said, shaking Rohan's hand and clapping him on the shoulder. "Great to see you. How is everything?" Julian looked especially adorable in a pair of black jeans, a cashmere gray waffle sweater, and a pair of vintage sneakers. His skin glowed with a subtle L.A.-acquired tan and despite being exhausted, his eyes were bright and he moved with a relaxed confidence Brooke had only recently noticed.

Rohan glanced at his own navy chino pants, dress shirt, and tie and actually blushed. He and Julian had never been close friends — Julian found Rohan way too quiet and conservative — but they'd always managed to make small talk in the presence of their wives. Now Rohan could barely meet Julian's eyes, and he mumbled, "Oh, same old for us. Not nearly as exciting as you. We actually saw your face on a billboard the other day."

There was an awkward pause until Ella, no longer crying and sporting the cutest little cow onesie Brooke had ever seen, made an appearance, and everyone could ooh and aah over her for a bit.

"So, Neha, how do you like Boston?" Brooke's mother asked. She smeared a small hunk of blue cheese on a cracker and popped it in her mouth.

Neha smiled. "Well, we love our neighborhood and we've met some nice people. I like our apartment a lot. The city really does have a great quality of life."

"What she wants to say is that it's boring beyond description," Brooke said, spearing an olive with a toothpick.

Neha nodded. "She's right. It's spirit crushing."

Mrs. Greene laughed and Brooke could tell her mother was charmed. "So why don't you two move back to New York? I know Brooke would be thrilled."

"Rohan will be done with his MBA next year, and if I have any say at all, we'll sell our car — I hate the driving — give up our perfectly lovely apartment, say good-bye to our extremely polite neighbors, and hightail it right back here where we can only afford a walk-up in a sketchy neighborhood surrounded by rude, aggressive people. And I will love every minute of it."

"Neha . . ." Rohan overheard this last part and gave his wife a look.

"What? You can't expect me to live there forever." She turned to Brooke and Mrs. Greene and lowered her voice. "He hates it, too, but he feels guilty about hating it. Who ever hates Boston, you know?"

By the time everyone had gathered around the cloth-draped card table to start the meal, Brooke had all but forgotten about the hideous article. There was plenty of wine, and the turkey was moist and perfectly cooked, and although the mashed potatoes were a little bland, her guests protested that they were the best damn mashed potatoes they'd ever eaten. They chatted easily about the new Hugh Grant movie and the upcoming trip to Mumbai and Goa that Neha and Rohan were planning over the holidays to visit their families. Things were so relaxed, in fact, that when Brooke's mother leaned over and quietly asked her how she was holding up, she almost dropped her fork.

"*You've* read it?" Brooke spat, staring at her mother.

"Oh, honey, of course I read it. Four different women forwarded it to me this morning. Gossip hounds, each and every one of them. I can't even imagine how devastating it is to read —"

"Mom, I don't want to talk about it."

"— something like that about yourself, but anyone who's ever met you two will know it's complete — pardon my French — bullshit."

Neha must have caught the tail end of this, because she too leaned over and said, "Seriously, Brooke, it was all so obviously fictional. I mean, not one word of it was true. Don't think about it for a second."

She felt like she'd been slapped again. Why did she think no one would read this? How had she managed to delude herself into believing that the whole thing would just go away?

"I'm trying not to think about it," she said.

Neha nodded, and Brooke knew she understood. If only she could say the same for her mother.

"Did you see those photographers out there when you came in?" Mrs. Greene asked Neha and Rohan. "They're like vultures."

Julian must have seen her face tighten, because he cleared his throat, but Brooke wanted to explain once and for all so they could move along. "It's not that bad," she said, passing the platter of grilled asparagus to Randy. "They're not there all the time, and we had a bunch of blackout shades put in, so they really can't get any shots. Unlisting our number helped. I'm sure it's the initial excitement over the album. They'll be totally bored of us by New Year's."

"I hope not," Julian said with a dimpled smile. "Leo just told me he's pushing for a Grammy appearance. He thinks there's a pretty good chance I could get picked to perform."

"Congratulations!" Michelle said with more enthusiasm than she'd displayed the entire day. "Is it a secret?"

Julian glanced at Brooke, who met his gaze and gave him a look back.

He coughed. "Well, I don't know if it's a secret, but they won't announce performers until after the New Year, so it probably doesn't make sense to say anything."

"Awesome, man," Randy said, grinning. "We're all going if you go. You know that, right? This family's a package deal."

Julian had told her of the possibility when they were on the phone before, but hearing him tell everyone else somehow made it more real. She could barely even wrap her mind around it: her husband performing at the Grammys for the entire world.

Ella squawked from her portable swing

next to the table and broke the spell. Brooke took the time to put all the homemade goodies on cake plates and platters: two homemade pies from her mother, one pumpkin and one rhubarb; a dozen mint brownies from Michelle; and a plate of Neha's specialty, coconut *burfi,* which looked a little like Rice Krispie treats but tasted more like mini cheesecakes.

"So, Brooke, how's work going for you?" Rohan asked through a mouthful of brownie.

Brooke sipped her coffee and said, "It's going well. I love the hospital, but I'm hoping to go into business for myself in the next couple years."

"You and Neha should think about doing it together. It's all she's been talking about lately."

Brooke looked at Neha. "Really? You're thinking of opening a private practice?"

Neha nodded so hard her black ponytail swung up and down. "Sure am. My parents have offered to loan me part of the start-up money, but I'd still need a partner to be able to make it work. Of course, I wasn't even thinking about it until we got back to the city. . . ."

"I had no idea!" Brooke said, her excitement growing by the second.

"I can't work in an OB office forever. Hopefully one day we'll have a family" — something about the way Neha glanced at Rohan, who immediately blushed and looked away, made Brooke think they were newly pregnant — "and I'll need some more flexible hours. Ideally, a small private practice that focuses exclusively on pre- and postnatal nutrition for moms and babies. Maybe bring in a lactation consultant as well, I'm not sure."

"That is exactly what I've been thinking!" Brooke said. "I need another nine months to a year in hands-on clinical experience, but after that . . ."

Neha delicately bit off a piece of *burfi* and smiled. She turned to the other side of the table. "Hey, Julian, you think you can cough up some cash to get your wife started here?" she asked, and everyone laughed.

Later, after everyone had gone home and they'd done all the dishes and folded the chairs, Brooke curled up next to Julian on the couch.

"Pretty crazy that Neha's been planning the exact same thing, isn't it?" she asked excitedly. Although the conversation had naturally drifted to other subjects over dessert, Brooke hadn't stopped thinking about it.

"It sounds absolutely perfect," Julian said, kissing the top of her head. His phone had been ringing all night, and although he kept silencing it and pretending everything was fine, he was clearly distracted.

"Even more perfect, because as soon as I can get out there on my own, I'll have so much more free time to travel with you, so much more flexibility than I do now. Won't that be great?"

"Mmm. Definitely."

"I mean, the time and effort that would go into doing something like that on your own — never mind the money — is so overwhelming, but it would be perfect for the two of us to do it together. We'd be able to cover for each other and still see double the patients. It is literally the *ideal* scenario," Brooke said happily.

It was just the good news she'd needed. Julian's absences, the snoopy reporters, the horrible article still stung, but something to look forward to helped turn the volume down on everything else.

His phone rang yet again. "Just answer it already," she said, sounding more irritated than she'd intended.

Julian stared at the caller ID, which read "Leo," and clicked Talk. "Hey, man, happy Thanksgiving." He nodded a few times, laughed, and then said, "Sure, okay. Yeah, I'll check with her, but I'm sure she can make it. Yep. Count us in. Later."

He turned and faced her with a huge grin. "Guess where we're going?"

"Where?"

"We, my dear, were invited to the ultra-exclusive Sony VIP holiday lunch and cocktails. Leo said the whole world goes to the party at night in the city, but only their top artists are invited to join all the top record execs at some crazy, trillion-dollar house in the Hamptons during the day. Performances by surprise guests. We'll travel back and forth by *helicopter*. Nothing has ever been written about this party before because it's so secret and so exclusive. And *we* are going!"

"Wow, that sounds incredible. When is it?" Brooke asked, her mind already cycling through outfit options.

Julian jumped up and headed to the kitchen. "Friday before Christmas. I don't know what the date is."

She grabbed his phone and scrolled through to the calendar. "December twentieth? Julian, it's my last day at Huntley before school closes for the holidays."

"So?" He pulled a beer from the refrigerator.

"So, that's *our* holiday party. At Huntley. They asked me to plan their first-ever healthy menu of fun party foods for the girls. I also promised Kaylie that I'd meet her father and her grandmother. Parents are invited to the party and she's been very excited about introducing all of us."

Brooke was proud of her tremendous progress with the girl over the last couple months. By increasing the frequency of their sessions and asking a lot of pointed questions about Whitney Weiss, Brooke was able to determine that Kaylie was flirting with purging, but she was also now certain that she didn't fit any of the criteria of someone suffering from a full-blown eating disorder. With lots of talking and listening and an abundance of extra attention, Kaylie had put back on a healthful portion of the weight she'd lost so rapidly, and she seemed to have developed more self-confidence to go with it. Probably most important of all, she'd joined the theater club and scored a coveted supporting role in this year's production of *West Side Story*. She finally had friends.

Julian rejoined her on the couch and clicked on the television. Noise filled the room.

"Can you turn that down?" she asked, trying to mask the irritation in her voice.

He obliged, but only after giving her a strange look. "I don't mean to sound insensitive here," he said, "but can't you just call in sick? We're talking helicopters and meeting the head of Sony Music. Don't you think someone else can figure out the cupcakes?"

At no point in the last five years of marriage could she remember him being so patronizing, so incredibly condescending. What made it worse was the way he was peering at her, oblivious to how obnoxious and self-centered he sounded.

"You know what? I'm positive someone else could 'figure out the cupcakes,' as you so asininely put it. What's my silly, frivolous job compared to the worldwide importance of yours, right? But you're forgetting one thing. I actually like what I do. I help these girls. I've invested a ton of time and energy in Kaylie, and guess what? It's paying off. She's happier and healthier than she's been in a year. She's not hurting herself anymore or crying every day. I know that can't compare to a number four *Billboard* hit in your world, but in mine, it's pretty freaking great. So no, Julian, I won't be joining you at your super-fancy VIP holiday party. Because I've got my own party to attend."

She stood up and glared at him, waiting for an apology, an attack, anything but what he was doing: staring blankly at the muted TV, shaking his head in disbelief, a look on his face that seemed to say, *I'm married to a lunatic.*

"Well, I'm glad we worked that out," she said quietly as she walked back toward the bedroom.

She waited for him to come in and talk about it, hug her, remind her that they never went to sleep angry, but when she crept back to the living room over an hour later, he was curled up on the couch, under the purple afghan, snoring softly. She turned and went back to bed alone.

11
KNEE-DEEP IN TEQUILA AND EIGHTEEN-YEAR-OLD GIRLS

Julian laughed as the fatter lobster pulled ahead. "One and a half pounds has taken the lead. They're just about to round the corner, folks," he said in his best imitation of a sports announcer. "I think I've got this one."

Its rival, a smaller lobster with a shiny black shell and what Brooke would swear were soulful eyes, scuttled forward to close the gap. "Not so fast," she said.

They were sitting on the kitchen floor, their backs against the island, cheering on their respective competitors. Brooke felt vaguely guilty for trying to race her lobster before tossing him in a pot of boiling water, but they didn't seem to mind. It was only when Walter nosed one of them and it refused to move another inch that Brooke swooped in and rescued hers from further torture.

"Victory by surrender! I'll take it," Julian

shouted with a fist pump. He then pro-
ceeded to high-five his lobster's rubber-
banded claw. Walter woofed.

"Winner gets to put them in the water,"
she said, motioning to the lobster pot they'd
unearthed in the Alters' pantry. "I don't
think I can handle it."

Julian stood up and extended a hand to
help Brooke. "Go check the fire, and I'll
deal with these guys."

She took him up on his offer and headed
toward the living room, where a couple
hours earlier Julian had taught her how to
build a fire. It was something her father or
Randy had always handled, and she was
delighted to discover how satisfying it was
to stack the logs strategically and use the
poker to shuffle them around just so. She
grabbed a medium-sized log from the
hearthside basket and gently placed it
diagonally across the top; she sat back on
the couch, watching the flames, transfixed.
She could hear Julian's cell phone ring from
the other room.

He came in from the kitchen with two
glasses of red wine and joined her on the
couch. "They should be done in fifteen
minutes. They didn't feel a thing, I promise."

"Uh-huh. I'm sure they loved it. Who was

that calling?" she asked.

"Calling? Oh, I don't know, doesn't matter."

"Cheers," Brooke said, and clinked his glass.

Julian sighed, a deep, satisfied sigh that seemed to say everything was right with the world. "How nice is this?" he asked. It was the right sigh, the right sentiment, but something about it struck Brooke as strange. He was almost being *too* sweet.

Things between them had been noticeably strained in the weeks leading up to the Sony party; Julian kept expecting Brooke to bail on her responsibilities at Huntley, and when she didn't — when he actually did fly to the Hamptons dateless — he had seemed downright shocked by it. In the ten days since the party, they'd discussed it as best they could, but Brooke couldn't get rid of the feeling that Julian still didn't understand her perspective, and despite a heroic effort on both their parts to move past it and act like everything was normal, things still didn't feel right.

She took a sip of the wine and felt that familiar warming sensation as it first hit her stomach. "Nice is an understatement. This is lovely," she said with an almost awkward formality.

"I can't understand why my parents never come out here in the winter. It's gorgeous when it's snowing, they have this awesome fireplace, and there's no one else around."

Brooke smiled. "There's no one else around — that's what they can't stand. What's the point of going to eat at Nick & Toni's if there's no one to witness you get the best table?"

"Yeah, well, Anguilla should be perfect for that. I'm sure they're very happy fighting the holiday crowds. Plus everything will cost two to three times as much now, which they adore. Makes them feel special. I bet they're happy as can be."

Although neither of them liked to admit it, they were both so grateful that the Alters owned the East Hampton house. Not that they ever spent a weekend out there with Julian's parents or dared visit during the summer — even their wedding had been in early March, when there was still snow on the ground — but it gave them a free, luxurious escape from the city a full six months a year. They'd taken advantage of it often for the first couple years, going out to see the first spring bloom or visit a local vineyard or walk the beach in October when the weather was starting to turn, but with the craziness of both their schedules, they hadn't been there in over a year. It had been Julian's idea to spend New Year's out there, just the two of them, and while she suspected it was a peace offering more than a genuine desire to hole up together, Brooke had readily accepted.

"I'm going to make the salad," she said, standing up. "Do you want anything?"

"I'll help."

"What'd you do with my husband?"

His phone rang again. He glanced at it and shoved it back in his pocket.

"Who was it?"

"I don't know. Private number. I don't know who would be calling now," he said, following her into the kitchen, and, without being asked, he drained the boiled potatoes and began mashing them.

Their conversation over dinner was easier and more relaxed, probably thanks to the wine. There seemed to be some sort of tacit understanding that they wouldn't talk about work at all, not hers or his; instead, they chatted about Nola and the promotion she'd just received, how happy Randy was around baby Ella, and whether or not they might be able to sneak in a weekend trip together somewhere warm before Julian's tour schedule really heated up in the new year.

The brownies Brooke had made for dessert were gooier than she would've liked, and topped with whipped cream, vanilla ice cream, and chocolate chips, they looked more like a hot brownie stew, but they were delicious. Julian suited up in full snow gear to take Walter out for his final walk while Brooke cleaned up and made coffee. They met back in front of the fire. His cell phone rang, but he silenced it once again without glancing at the screen.

"How are you feeling about not playing tonight? It must have been pretty strange to turn it down," Brooke asked, resting her head in his lap.

Julian had been invited to perform on MTV's New Year's Eve countdown show in Times Square and then host a celeb-heavy party at the Hotel on Rivington from midnight on. He'd been thrilled when Leo told him about it in the early fall, but as the night got closer, Julian grew less and less enthused. When he finally instructed Leo to cancel the whole thing last week, no one was more shocked — or delighted — than Brooke. Especially when he'd turned to Brooke and asked if she'd join him in the Hamptons for a stay-at-home date night.

"We don't have to talk about all that stuff tonight," Julian said. She could tell he was trying to be sensitive to her, but it was clear something was bugging him.

"I know," Brooke said. "I just want to make sure you're not regretting it."

Julian stroked her hair. "Are you crazy, woman? Between that whole *Today* show drama and all the travel, and looking ahead at how much crazier it's going to get next year, I just needed a break. *We* needed a break."

"We really did," she murmured, feeling more contented than she had in months. "I'm guessing Leo isn't thrilled, but I sure am."

"Leo jumped the first flight to Punta del Este. He is no doubt knee-deep in tequila and eighteen-year-old girls. Do *not* feel badly for Leo."

They finished their wine. Julian carefully drew first the screen and then the glass doors over the dwindling fire, and they walked upstairs hand in hand. This time it was the landline ringing, and before Julian could say a word, Brooke picked up an extension in the guest room she and Julian always stayed in.

"Brooke? It's Samara. Look, sorry to call tonight, but I've been trying to reach Julian for hours. He said he was going to be out

371

there, but he hasn't been answering his phone."

"Oh, hi, Samara. Yeah, he's right here. Hold on a sec."

"Wait, Brooke? Look, I know you can't be at the Grammys because of work, and I just wanted to reassure you that there will be some great after-parties in New York that I'll get the two of you into."

Brooke thought she heard wrong. "What?"

"The Grammys. For Julian's performance."

"Samara? Can you hold for just a minute?" She clicked the Mute button and walked into the bathroom, where Julian was filling the bathtub.

"When were you going to tell me about the Grammys?" she asked, trying to keep the hysteria out of her voice.

He looked up at her. "I was going to wait until tomorrow. I didn't want it to dominate our entire night together."

"Oh come on, Julian! You don't want me to go, that's why you didn't say anything."

At this, Julian looked truly alarmed. "Why would you think that? Of course I want you to!"

"Well, it doesn't sound like Samara thinks so. She just told me she totally understands why I'm too busy with work to make it. Are you kidding? My husband is going to be performing at the Grammys and she thinks I can't get off *work* for it?"

"Brooke, I'm guessing she only thinks that because you couldn't, uh, get off work for the Sony holiday party, you know? But I swear the only reason I didn't tell you yet is because I thought we could use a night without talking shop. I'll tell her you're coming."

Brooke turned and headed back into the bedroom. "I'll tell her myself."

She unmuted the phone and said, "Samara? There must have been some misunderstanding, because I'm definitely planning to accompany Julian."

There was a long pause before Samara said, "You know it's a performance and not a nomination, right?"

"I understand."

Another pause. "And you're sure your own commitments won't interfere this time?"

Brooke wanted to scream at the girl that she didn't understand anything, but she forced herself to remain silent.

"Well, okay then. We'll make that happen," Samara said.

Brooke tried to ignore the hesitation — disappointment? — in her voice. Why should she care what Samara thought? "Okay, great. So, what should I wear? I mean, I definitely don't have anything that fancy. Do you think I should rent something?"

"No! Let us handle everything, okay? We'll just need you to show up six hours before and we'll have a dress, shoes, undergarments, bag, jewelry, hair, and makeup. Don't wash your own hair for twenty-four hours beforehand, no fake-baking unless our stylist specifically recommends an aesthetician, get a good manicure and use either Allure by Essie or Bubble Bath by OPI, get a full leg and arm wax five to seven days ahead of time, and get a deep-conditioning hair treatment seventy-two hours before. As for color, I'll send you a recommendation for the salon we work with in New York. You'll start a highlighting regimen next week."

"Oh, wow. Okay, do you —"

"Don't worry, I'll put this all in an e-mail and we'll review it. Listen, you know the cameras will be all over Julian, and I know Leo mentioned a trainer for you both — have you had time to think about that? — so let me make you an appointment at the place we got Julian's teeth done. The man's a genius, you can never tell they're caps, they really look so natural. You'll be amazed what a difference it makes."

"Um, okay. You'll just tell me what —"

"We've got it covered. I'll touch base soon, Brooke. We'll work it all out. Can I talk to Julian? I promise it's just a quick question."

Brooke nodded dumbly, completely unaware that Samara couldn't see her, and handed the phone to Julian, who'd come into the bedroom to get undressed. He said, "yes," "no," and "Sounds good, I'll call you tomorrow," and then he turned to her.

"Can you come get in the bath? Please?"

His eyes were pleading, and she forced herself to put the Grammys out of her mind. They had been having such a lovely night; she decided she shouldn't let any lingering weirdness ruin it. She followed him into the bathroom and stripped down. They wouldn't ever sleep in Julian's parents' bed — way too creepy — but they did love using the master bathroom. It was heaven on earth, pure luxury. Heated floors, a massive soaking tub with a separate steam shower, and best of all, a small gas fireplace. Although he couldn't bring himself to climb into the piping hot water, Julian always drew Brooke a bath and, after his own shower, turned on the fire and climbed onto the tub platform, clad only in a towel, to keep her company.

Brooke spooned some more lavender salts into the water and lay back against the terry-cloth bath pillow. Julian was reminiscing about the first bath they'd taken together, on a weekend trip early in their relationship. He was recounting his misery over the scalding water, which he'd silently endured in an effort to impress, and Brooke could only gaze at him as he spoke, so overcome with that intense relaxation and utter exhaustion that comes from a piping-hot bath.

Afterward, wrapped in a huge plush bath sheet, Brooke walked with Julian back to their bedroom, where he'd lit a candle on either night table and turned on some relaxing music. They made love softly, slowly, like two people who have been together for years and know everything about each other, and for the first time in ages, they fell asleep entwined.

They slept until almost noon and woke to six inches of snow, a sure sign they'd be spending another night in the Hamptons. Delighted, Brooke gathered her mussed hair into a bun, pulled on her Uggs and her puffy winter coat, and climbed in the passenger side of the Jeep the Alters kept there year-round. Julian looked adorably dorky in one of his father's winter hats he'd found in the closet; it was topped with a yarn ball, and extending from the earflaps were strings that could be tied under the chin. He pulled up to the East Hampton Starbucks so Brooke could run in for a *Times,* but then they headed to the Golden Pear Café, for breakfast.

Ensconced in a booth with her hands wrapped around a cup of hot coffee, Brooke sighed in happy contentment. If she could've scripted the most perfect New Year's Eve ever, it would've looked exactly like their last twenty-four hours. Julian was reading aloud to her from the paper, an article about a man imprisoned for twenty-eight years before being exonerated by DNA evidence, when her phone rang.

He looked up.

"It's Nola," Brooke said, staring at the screen.

"Aren't you going to answer it?"

"You don't mind? She's going to want to tell me all about her night, I'm guessing."

Julian shook his head. "I'm happy to just sit here and read. I really don't mind."

"Hey, Nol," Brooke said as quietly as possible. She couldn't stand people shouting into cell phones.

"Brooke? Where are you?"

"What do you mean, where are we? We're

in the Hamptons, you know that. I actually think with all this snow, we're going to have to stay until —"

"Have you seen the online edition of *Last Night* yet?" Nola interrupted.

"*Last Night*? No, the Wi-Fi at the house was down. I have the *Times* right here. . . ."

"Look, I'm only telling you this because I don't want you to hear it somewhere else. *Last Night* wrote this whole horrible column this morning, theorizing on all the possible reasons Julian canceled his New Year's gig last night."

"They *what*?"

Julian looked at her and raised his eyes questioningly.

"Of course they're all ridiculous. But I remember you said Leo was in South America somewhere, and, well, I just thought you guys might want to know if you didn't already."

Brooke took a deep breath. "Great. That's just great. Can you tell me what it said?"

"Just pull it up on Julian's phone, okay? I'm really sorry to ruin your morning, but it also says that you two are probably 'hiding out' in the Hamptons, so I wanted to give you the heads-up that you might get some company."

"Oh no," Brooke moaned.

"I'm sorry, sweetheart. Let me know if I can do anything, okay?"

They said good-bye and Brooke only realized after they'd hung up that she hadn't so much as asked about Nola's night.

Before she was even finished briefing Julian, he began searching for the *Last Night* article on his phone. "Here, I got it."

"Read it out loud."

Julian's eyes skimmed back and forth. "Wow," he murmured, flicking the screen with his pointer finger. "Where do they get this stuff?"

"Julian! Start reading or hand it over!"

A timid young girl not a day over sixteen appeared at their table holding two plates. She looked at Julian, but Brooke wasn't totally positive she recognized him. "Veggie egg white omelet with wheat?" she asked in a near-whisper.

"Right here," Brooke said, holding up a hand.

"I guess that means you're having the breakfast combo?" she said to Julian with a smile so huge there was no longer any doubt. "French toast with powdered sugar, two eggs sunny-side up, and well-done bacon. Can I get you guys anything else?"

"Thanks, we're good," Julian said, immediately plunging his fork into the fluffy

French toast. She had completely lost her appetite.

He washed everything down with a swig of coffee and picked up his phone again. "You ready?"

Brooke nodded.

"Okay. The headline is 'Where Is Julian Alter?' and right next to it is a picture taken from god knows where of me looking sweaty and wasted." He showed her the screen.

Brooke chewed her dry toast, wishing she'd opted for the rye. "I recognize that one. It was taken thirty seconds after you walked offstage after your performance at Kristen Stewart's party in Miami. It was ninety-five degrees that day and you'd been singing for nearly an hour."

Julian began reading. " 'Although sources tell us the famous singer is hiding out in his parents' house in East Hampton after canceling a New Year's Eve MTV performance last night, what no one seems able to agree on is *why*. Many suspect trouble in paradise for the sexy crooner who shot to fame with his debut album, *For the Lost*. One source with knowledge of the music industry claims that now is "temptation time" when so many quick-rising stars give in to the lure of drugs. Although there have been no *specific* reports of drug abuse, "rehab is one of the first places I look when a new artist goes off the radar," said the music industry source.' "

Julian looked up at her, his mouth agape, the phone hanging limply in his hand. "They're suggesting I'm in *rehab?*" he asked.

"I don't think they're suggesting *you're* in rehab per se," Brooke said, drawing out her words. "Actually, I'm not sure what they're saying. Keep reading."

" 'A source with knowledge of the music industry'?" Julian read again. "Are they kidding?"

"Keep reading." Brooke ate a forkful of omelet and tried to look unworried.

" 'Others claim Julian and his long-term love, nutritionist wife Brooke, have been feeling the strain of fame. "I can't imagine any couple thriving under such trying circumstances," said noted Beverly Hills psychiatrist Ira Melnick, who has not treated the Alters personally but has broad experience with such "inter-fame couples" (where one person is famous and the other is unknown). "If they are in fact receiving couples' counseling right now," Dr. Melnick continued, "they'll at least have a fighting chance." ' "

" 'A fighting chance'?" Brooke screeched.

"Who the hell is Dr. Melnick and why is he commenting on our relationship when we've never met him?"

Julian just shook his head. "And who said we're 'feeling the strain of fame'?" he asked.

"I don't know. Maybe they're referring to the whole *Today* show/pregnancy thing? Keep reading."

"Wow," Julian said, clearly reading ahead. "I always knew these gossip rags were bullshit, but this just keeps getting better and better. 'While rehab or couples' counseling is the most likely cause of Julian's disappearance' " — Julian spat out this last word dripping with sarcasm — " 'there is a third option. According to a close family source, the singer was being courted by famous Scientologists, most notably John Travolta. "I don't know if it was just a friendly gesture or a recruiting reach-out, but I can say without doubt that they have been in touch," the family source said. Which leads us all to wonder: will JBro go the way of TomKat and keep the faith? Stay tuned. . . .' "

"Did I hear you correctly? Did you just say 'JBro'?" Brooke asked, convinced he'd made that part up.

"Scientology!" Julian nearly shouted before Brooke shushed him. "They think we're Scientologists!"

Brooke's mind was racing to take it all in. Rehab? Couples' counseling? Scientology? *JBro?* That all those thing were lies wasn't so upsetting, but what about the small kernels of truth? What "family source" had mentioned anything about John Travolta, a person Julian had actually heard from, although not in relation to Scientology? And who was implying — for the second time in this very publication — that she and Julian were having relationship problems? Brooke almost asked just that, but seeing the look of devastation on Julian's face, she forced herself to keep it light.

"Look, I don't know about you, but between Scientology, the world-renowned shrink who's never met us, and JBro, you have totally made it. I mean, if those aren't fame indicators, I don't know what is." She smiled widely but Julian still looked despondent.

Out of the corner of her eye, Brooke saw a flash of light and had a split-second thought of how strange it was to see lightning in the middle of a snowstorm. Before she could comment on it, the young waitress reappeared at their table.

"I, uh, wow," she mumbled, managing to appear both embarrassed and excited at the same time. "I'm sorry about the photographers out there. . . ." Her voice trailed off in time for Brooke to turn and see four men with cameras pressed against the café windows. Julian must have spotted them before she did, because he reached over, took her hand, and said, "We need to go now."

"The, uh, the manager told them they couldn't come inside, but we can't force them to leave the sidewalk," the waitress said. She had that *I'm two seconds from asking for your autograph* look about her, and Brooke knew they had to leave immediately.

She yanked two twenties from her wallet, thrust them at the girl, and said, "Is there a back door?" When the girl nodded, Brooke squeezed Julian's hand and said, "Let's go."

They grabbed their coats and gloves and scarves and beelined toward the back of the café. Brooke tried not to think about how gross she looked, how desperately she didn't want the entire world to see pictures of her in her sweatpants and ponytail, but even more than that, she wanted to protect Julian. By some lucky miracle, their Jeep was parked in the back lot, and they had managed to climb in, start the engine, and make a right turn out of the parking lot before the paparazzi spotted them.

"What do we do?" Julian asked with more

than a hint of panic. "We can't go back to the house or they'll follow us. They'll stake it out."

"Don't you think they probably know where it is already? Isn't that why they're here?"

"I don't know. We were in the middle of East Hampton Village. If you're looking for someone you know is in the Hamptons in the middle of winter, it's a damn good place to start. I think they were just lucky." Julian drove east on Route 27, away from his parents' house. At least two cars were following them.

"We could drive straight back to the city. . . ."

Julian smacked the steering wheel with his palm. "All our stuff is at the house. Besides, it's too treacherous out — we'd kill ourselves."

They were silent for a moment before Julian said, "Dial the nonemergency number of the local police and put it on speaker."

Brooke didn't quite know what his plan was, but she didn't want to argue. She dialed and Julian began talking when a female dispatcher answered the phone.

"Hello, my name is Julian Alter and I'm currently driving east on Route 27, just past East Hampton Village. There are a number of cars — photographers — chasing my car at unsafe speeds. I'm afraid if I go home, they'll try to force their way into my house. Is there any way an officer could meet me at the house and remind them they would be trespassing?"

The woman agreed to dispatch someone within twenty minutes and after giving her the address of his parents' home, he hung up.

"That was smart," Brooke said. "What made you think of that?"

"I didn't. It's what Leo told me to do if we were anywhere outside of Manhattan and we started getting followed. Let's see if it actually works."

They continued driving in circles for the full twenty minutes before Julian checked his watch and made a right onto the smaller country road that led out to the open pasture land where the Alters' home sat on an acre and a half. The front yard was large and prettily landscaped, but the house was simply not set far enough back to evade a telescopic lens. They were both relieved to see a police car sitting at the intersection of the farm road and the driveway. Julian pulled up next to it and lowered his window; the two cars following them had now become four, and all rolled to a stop following

386

them. They could instantly make out the sound of cameras clicking as the officer made his way over to the Jeep.

"Hello, sir. I'm Julian Alter and this is my wife, Brooke. We're just trying to get home in peace. Can you please help us?"

The officer was young, probably in his late twenties, and he didn't look particularly annoyed at having his New Year's Day morning interrupted. Brooke offered a silent prayer of thanks and found herself actually hoping the cop would recognize Julian.

He didn't disappoint.

"Julian Alter, hey? My girlfriend's a huge fan. Couple of us had heard a rumor your folks live out here, but we weren't real sure. This their place?"

Julian squinted at the man's name tag. "It is, Officer O'Malley," he said. "I'm happy to hear your girlfriend's a fan. Do you think she'd like an autographed album?"

The clicking from the cameras continued, and Brooke wondered how these pictures would be captioned. "Julian Alter Arrested in Drug-Fueled Drag Race"? Or "Officer to Alter: We Don't Want Your Kind Out Here." Or maybe everyone's favorite, "Alter Tries to Convert Police Officer to Scientology."

O'Malley's face lit up at the suggestion. "I'm sure she would," he said, blowing on his hands, which looked red and chapped. "I think she'd love that."

Before Julian could even utter a word, Brooke opened the glove compartment and handed Julian a copy of *For the Lost*. They had stashed a brand-new copy in there to see if Julian's parents would actually listen to it before next summer, but she realized this was a far better use. She dug in her purse and unearthed a pen.

"Her name is Kristy," the officer said, carefully spelling it twice.

Julian tore the plastic wrap off the CD, removed the liner notes, and scrawled, "To Kristy, with love, Julian Alter."

"Hey, thanks. She's going to freak out," O'Malley said, carefully placing the CD in his side jacket pocket. "Now, what can I do for you?"

"Arrest those guys?" Julian said with a half smile.

" 'Fraid I can't do that, but I can definitely tell them to back off and remind them of private property rules. You two go on ahead. I'll brief your friends back here. Give a call if there are any other problems."

"Thank you!" both Brooke and Julian said at once. They said their good-byes to O'Malley and without looking back, pulled into the garage and closed the door.

"He was nice," Brooke said as they walked into the mudroom and kicked off their boots.

"I'm calling Leo right now," Julian said, already halfway to his father's study in the back of the house. "We're under siege and he's stretched out on some beach."

Brooke watched him go and then walked from room to room, closing all the blinds. The early afternoon had grown dark gray already, and she could see the flashbulbs firing directly at her as she moved from window to window. From behind one of the guest room shades on the second floor, she peeked out front and nearly shrieked when she saw a man with a zoom lens the size of a football pointed directly at her. There was only one room with no window coverings — a small powder room no one ever used on the third floor — but Brooke wasn't taking any chances. She duct-taped an industrial-strength garbage bag over it and then headed back downstairs to check on Julian.

"You okay?" she asked, pushing the study door open after receiving no response to her knock.

Julian glanced up from his laptop. "Yeah, fine. You? Sorry about all this," he said, although Brooke couldn't quite identify the tone in his voice. "I know it's ruining every-thing."

"It's not ruining anything," she lied.

Again, no response. He continued to stare at the screen.

"Why don't I go build us a fire and we can watch a movie. How does that sound?"

"Fine. Good. I'll be out in a few minutes, okay?"

"Perfect," she said with forced cheerful-ness. She gently closed the door behind her and silently cursed those goddamn photog-raphers, that miserable *Last Night* column, and — only partially — her husband for be-ing famous in the first place. She would do her best to be strong for Julian, but he was right about one thing: their blissfully quiet, much-needed retreat was over. No one dared drive down the driveway or walk across the lawn, but the crowd on the street only continued to grow. They slept that night to the distant sounds of men talking and laughing, engines turning on and off, and although they tried their best to ignore it, neither of them succeeded. By the time the snow melted enough the next day to leave, they'd only dozed an hour or two and felt like they'd run two marathons, and they barely spoke at all on the drive back to the

city. They were followed the whole way
home.

12
BETTER OR WORSE
THAN THE SIENNA
PICTURES?

"Hello?" Brooke said into her phone.

"It's me. Are you dressed yet? Which one did you choose?" Nola's voice sounded breathy, eager.

Brooke sneaked a look at the thirtysomething woman standing next to her and saw the woman sneaking a look right back. The security guards at the Beverly Wilshire were doing their best to keep out the paparazzi, but plenty of reporters and photographers had circumvented the rules by booking rooms at the hotel. She'd caught this same woman watching her in the lobby before when she'd run down to see if the gift shop had Altoids, and sure enough, she'd slid onto the elevator with Brooke just before the doors closed. Judging from her appearance — silk tank top tucked into well-tailored pants, expensive pumps, and elegantly understated jewelry — Brooke deduced she wasn't a blogger, gossip columnist, or secret paparazzo à la the guy who sat outside their building and the supermarket stalker. Which made her something even scarier: a real, live, thinking, observant reporter.

"I'll be in my room in one minute. I'll call you back then." Brooke clicked the phone off before Nola had a chance to utter another word.

The woman smiled at her and revealed a beautiful set of pearly white teeth. It was a gentle smile, one that said, *I understand what it's like! I too get pestering phone calls from my friend,* but Brooke had honed her instincts the past few months to perfection: despite her unthreatening appearance and her sympathetic expression, this woman was a predator, a scoop-seeking, always-on-the-record vampire. Stay and you'll get bitten. Brooke was desperate to escape.

"You here for the Grammys?" the woman asked kindly, as though she was all too familiar with the rigors of preparing for such an event.

"Mmm," Brooke murmured, unwilling to commit to anything more. She knew, just knew, this woman was about to spring a series of rapid-fire questions on her — she'd seen this disarm-and-attack routine before with a particularly aggressive blogger who'd approached her after Julian's *Today* show performance pretending to be an innocent fan — but she still couldn't bring herself to be preemptively rude.

The elevator stopped on the tenth floor and Brooke had to endure an "Oh, is this going up? Well, I'm going down" conversation between the woman and a couple who had that telltale European look (both the man and the woman were wearing capris, his tighter than hers, and each had a different version of the same neon-colored Invicta backpack). She held her breath and willed the elevator to move.

"Must be exciting going to your first Grammys, especially considering your husband's performance is so highly anticipated."

There. Brooke exhaled and felt, oddly, momentarily better. It was a relief having her suspicions confirmed; now neither of them had to fake it. She silently cursed herself for not letting Leo's assistant run the errand, but at least now she knew what was expected of her. She fixed her eyes on the button panel above the doors and did her best to pretend she hadn't heard a word the woman said.

"I was just wondering, Brooke" — at the sound of her name, Brooke's head reflexively snapped up — "if you had any comment on the recent photographs?"

Recent photographs. What was she talking about? Brooke once again stared at the elevator doors and reminded herself that these people would say anything to elicit a single sentence from you — a sentence they'd then twist and turn to fit whatever garbage they'd just dreamed up. She pledged she wouldn't fall into the trap.

"It must be so difficult to endure all those awful rumors about your husband and other women — I can't even imagine it. Do you think it will keep you from enjoying tonight's festivities?"

The elevator doors finally whooshed open on the penthouse floor. Brooke stepped out into the foyer that led to their three-bedroom suite, currently ground zero of Grammy Preparation Madness. She wanted nothing more than to roll her eyes and say that if Julian was actually sleeping with the number of women the tabs suggested, he would not only have Tiger beat by a mile, but he wouldn't have a second left to perform a single song. She wanted to say that after you'd read countless detailed accounts from unnamed sources about how your husband has fetishes for everything from tattooed strippers to overweight men, claims of regular old infidelity barely even registered. Most of all, she wanted to tell this woman what she knew beyond all doubt to be true: that her husband, while superbly talented and now undeniably famous, still puked before every performance, visibly sweated when teenage girls shrieked in his presence, and had an inexplicable affinity for clipping his toenails on the toilet. He just wasn't the cheating type, and it was obvious to anyone who really knew him.

But of course she couldn't say any of this, so, as usual, she said nothing at all and merely watched as the elevator doors closed.

I'm not thinking about any of that tonight, Brooke instructed herself as she unlocked the door with her key card. *Tonight is all about Julian. Nothing more, nothing less.* It was the night that would make all the invasions of privacy and the scheduling horrors and the carnival aspect of their lives worth it. No matter what happened — a new, vile rumor about Julian and other women, a humiliating paparazzo shot, a nasty comment made by someone on Julian's staff trying to be "helpful" — she was determined to enjoy every second of such a momentous evening. Only a couple hours earlier her mother had waxed poetic about how a night like this was "once-in-a-lifetime stuff," and it was her obligation to experience it as fully as she could. Brooke vowed to do just that.

She strode into the suite and smiled at one of the assistants — who could keep them straight these days? — who ushered her directly into a makeup chair without so much as a hello. The anxiety that hung over the room like a wet blanket didn't mean the night itself wasn't going to be fabulous. She wouldn't let the preparations get her down.

"Time check!" one of the assistants called out in an irritatingly screechy voice, made even worse by a thick New York accent.

"Ten after one!" "A little after one!" "One ten!" Three other people answered simultaneously, all with hints of panic.

"Okay, people, let's *step it up!* We are T-minus one hour and fifty minutes, which means, judging from the look of things" — she paused and surveyed the room with an exaggerated swivel and locked eyes with Brooke, maintaining full eye contact as she finished — "we are not even *close* to presentable here."

Brooke gingerly raised her hand, careful not to disturb the pair of people working on her eyes, and motioned for the assistant to come over.

"Yes?" Natalya asked, making no effort to hide her irritation.

"When do you expect Julian back? There's something I need to —"

Natalya jutted her barely there hip out and consulted a Lucite clipboard. "Let's see, he's just finishing up with his relaxation massage and is en route to his hot shave. He's due back here at exactly two o'clock, but he'll need to meet with the tailor to make sure we finally have the lapel situation under control."

Brooke smiled sweetly at the harried girl and decided to take a different tack. "You must be so looking forward to having this day be over. From the looks of it, you haven't stopped running for a second."

"Is that your way of saying I look like shit?" Natalya snapped back, her hand automatically flying to her hair. "Because if it is, you should just say it."

Brooke sighed. Why was it impossible to say anything right around these people? Just fifteen minutes earlier, when she'd gamely asked Leo if the Beverly Hills hotel they were staying in was the same one where they filmed *Pretty Woman,* he'd snapped back that she should sightsee on her own time.

"I wasn't saying that at all. Just that I know it's super-crazy today, and I think you're doing an amazing job handling it all."

"Well someone has to," Natalya said, and

walked away.

Brooke was tempted to call her back and have a little conversation about common courtesy, but she reconsidered when she remembered the reporter observing everything from eight feet away. This one, unfortunately, had been approved to follow them for the hours leading up to the Grammys, as research for a long feature piece the magazine was doing on Julian. Leo had negotiated some sort of deal whereby he would grant unfettered access to Julian over the course of a week if *New York* magazine would guarantee the cover, and so now, four days into the week, Julian's entire entourage was working hard to maintain an all-smiles-we-love-our-job facade — and failing miserably. Every time Brooke caught a glimpse of the reporter — a nice enough guy, it seemed — she fantasized about killing him.

She was impressed by how skillfully a good reporter could blend into the background. Back in her civilian days, it always seemed ridiculous that a couple would fight or reprimand an employee or even answer their cell phone in the presence of a scoop-hunting journalist; now she had nothing but sympathy for the subjects. The man from *New York* magazine had been shadowing them for the last four days, but by acting blind, deaf, and mute, he felt as threatening as wallpaper. Which, Brooke knew, was exactly when he was most dangerous.

She heard the sound of the doorbell but couldn't turn around without risking curling iron mutilation. "Any chance that's lunch?" Brooke asked.

One of the makeup artists snorted. "Not likely. Doesn't really look like the Schedule Nazi thinks food is a priority. Now, no more talking while I work on hiding your laugh lines."

Comments like that barely even registered anymore; Brooke was happy the girl hadn't yet asked if she'd considered lightening treatments to eradicate her freckles, something that seemed to be a go-to topic of discussion these days. She tried to distract herself with the *Los Angeles Times,* but she couldn't concentrate with the surrounding excitement. Brooke surveyed the 2,100-square-foot duplex penthouse suite and identified two makeup artists, two hairstylists, a nail artist, a stylist, a publicist, an agent, a business manager, the *New York* reporter, a fitter from Valentino, and enough assistants to staff the White House.

It was undeniably ridiculous, but Brooke couldn't help being excited by the whole thing. She was at the Grammys — the

Grammys! — about to escort her husband down the red carpet in front of the entire world. To say it felt surreal was an understatement; would an event like this ever feel real? From the first time she'd heard Julian sing at the divey Rue B's nearly nine years earlier, she'd told anyone who would listen he was going to be a star. What she never envisioned was the reality of that word — "star." Rock star. Superstar. Her husband, the same guy who still bought only Hanes boxers by the three-pack and loved the bread sticks at Olive Garden and picked his nose when he thought she wasn't looking was an internationally acclaimed rock star with *millions* of screaming, adoring, devoted fans. She couldn't imagine a time, now or in the future, when she'd be able to wrap her mind around that fact.

The doorbell rang a second time before one of the impossibly young assistants scampered over to open it — and promptly squealed.

"Who is it?" Brooke asked, unable to open her eyes while they were being lined.

"The security guard from Neil Lane," she heard Natalya answer. "He's got your jewelry."

"My jewelry?" Brooke asked. She didn't trust herself not to squeal as well, so she clamped her mouth shut and tried not to smile.

When it was finally time to put on her dress, Brooke thought she might faint from excitement (and lack of nourishment, but even with the army of helpers in that hotel suite, not one seemed concerned about food). Two assistants held open the magnificent Valentino gown and another held her hand as she stepped into it. It zipped smoothly up the back and hugged her recently slimmed hips and expertly pushed-up chest as though it had been custom fitted — which, of course, it had. The mermaid shape highlighted her somewhat trim waist while completely masking her "curvy" bum, and its scalloped sweetheart neckline accentuated her cleavage in exactly the right way. Aside from its color (a deep gold hue, not metallic, but like she was wearing a perfect, shimmering tan), it was a lesson in how gorgeous fabric and a flawless fit went miles farther than ruffles, beads, sleeves, sashes, sequins, crinoline, or crystals ever could in taking a dress from beautiful to absolutely spectacular. Both the Valentino fitter and Brooke's own stylist nodded their approval, and Brooke was ecstatic that she'd redoubled her workout efforts over the past couple months. It had finally paid off.

The jewels came next, and it was almost too much to handle. The security guard, a shorter-than-average man with shoulders the size of a linebacker, handed three velvet boxes to the stylist, who opened them immediately.

"Perfect," she declared as she plucked the pieces from their velvet boxes.

"Ohmigod," Brooke said, catching a first glimpse at the earrings. They were pear-shaped diamond drops outlined in a delicate pavé, and they had a look of very Old Hollywood glamour.

"Turn around," the stylist commanded. She expertly clipped the earrings to Brooke's lobes and clasped a similarly styled bracelet to her right wrist.

"They're gorgeous," Brooke breathed, staring at the glittering pile of diamonds on her arm. She turned to the security guard. "You better follow me into the bathroom tonight. I have a habit of 'losing' jewelry all the time!" She laughed to show she was kidding but the guard didn't even crack a smile.

"Left hand," the stylist barked.

Brooke extended her left arm, and before she realized what was happening, the woman removed her plain gold wedding band, the one Julian had engraved with their wedding date, and replaced it with a diamond ring the size of a macaroon.

Brooke snatched her hand back as soon as she realized. "No, that's not going to work, because you know, uh, that's, um —"

"Julian will understand," the girl said, and underscored her decision by snapping the ring box closed. "I'm going to get the Polaroid so we can take a few test shots and make sure everything looks good on film. Don't move."

Finally left alone, Brooke spun around in front of the full-length mirror that had been brought in especially for the occasion. In her entire life, she couldn't remember ever feeling close to this beautiful. Her makeup made her feel like a prettier but still real version of herself, and her skin was glowing with health and color. Diamonds sparkled everywhere, her hair looked chic yet natural gathered and twisted low at her nape, and her dress was complete, utter perfection. She beamed at her reflection and grabbed the bedside phone, excited to share this moment.

It rang before she could dial her mother's number, and Brooke felt a familiar anxious jolt deep in her stomach when the number for NYU Medical Center came up on the caller ID. Why on earth would they be calling her? Another nutritionist, Rebecca, had agreed to cover Brooke's two missed shifts in exchange for two regular shifts, one holiday, and one weekend. They were brutal concessions, but what choice did she have? It was the *Grammys*. Another thought flashed in her mind before she could push it away: was Margaret calling to tell her that the entire peds rotation was all hers?

Brooke allowed herself a moment of hopeful excitement before deciding that it was probably only Rebecca asking for clarification on a chart. She cleared her throat and said hello.

"Brooke? Can you hear me?" Margaret's voice boomed through the line.

"Hello, Margaret. Is everything all right?" Brooke asked, trying to make her voice as calm and assured as possible.

"Oh, hi there. I can hear you now. Listen, Brooke, I was just wondering if everything is okay. I was starting to get a little worried."

"Worried? Why? Everything's great here." Could Margaret have read whatever trash the reporter from the elevator had been referring to? She prayed that wasn't it.

Margaret sighed heavily, almost sadly. "Look, Brooke. I know this is a huge weekend for you, for Julian. There's nowhere else you should be, and I hate having to call you right now. But I still have a staff to run, and I can't do it when I'm short on people."

"Short on people?"

"I know this is probably the last thing you were thinking about in light of everything that's going on, but if you're going to miss work, it's imperative that you find someone to cover for you. Your shift began at nine this morning and it's already after ten."

"Ohmigod. I'm so sorry, Margaret. I know I can clear this all up. Please just give me five minutes. I'll call you right back."

Brooke didn't wait for an answer. She disconnected the call and scrolled through her phone to find Rebecca's number. She prayed as the phone rang and felt a surge of relief when she heard Rebecca answer.

"Rebecca? Hi. It's Brooke Alter."

There was a second's hesitation. "Oh, hi! How are you?"

"I'm fine, but Margaret just called wondering where I was, and since we switched shifts today . . ." Brooke let her words trail off, fearful that she'd say something irreparably unkind if she continued.

"Oh yes, we were *supposed* to," Rebecca said brightly, her voice all sugar and cheer, "but I left you a message saying I wasn't able to after all."

Brooke felt like she'd been slapped. She heard a young man screech in glee from the suite's living room and she wanted to kill him, whoever he was. "You left me a message?"

"Sure did. Let's see, today is Sunday . . . hmm, I would have left you a message early Friday afternoon."

"Friday afternoon?" Brooke had left for the airport around two. Rebecca must have called her home phone and left a message on her answering machine. She could feel herself grow more nauseated.

"Yes, now I remember exactly. It would have been about two fifteen, two thirty, because I'd just picked up Brayden at kindergarten, and Bill called to see if we could make it to my in-laws' on Sunday for a family reunion of sorts. His sister and her husband were flying in with their new baby, a little girl they adopted from Korea, and well —"

"Got it," Brooke interrupted, again exerting every ounce of willpower to keep from snapping at Rebecca. "Okay, well, thanks for clearing that up. Sorry to hang up, but I've got to call Margaret back this minute."

Brooke pulled the phone away from her ear, but not before hearing "I'm really sorry" from the receiver before she clicked it off.

Fuck. This was even worse than she thought. She forced herself to dial the number, not wanting to waste another second of such a great night.

Margaret picked up on the first ring. "Hello?"

"Margaret, I really can't apologize enough, but it seems there's been a huge misunderstanding. I had arranged for Rebecca to cover me today — I hope you know I would never just leave you in a bind like this — but it sounds like she had some sort of last-minute emergency and couldn't make it. I suppose she left me a message, but I didn't —"

"Brooke." The sadness in her voice was unmissable.

"Margaret, I know this is a terrible inconvenience for you, and I'm so sorry for that, but you must believe me when —"

"Brooke, I'm sorry. I know I've told you before, but with all the budget cuts, they are breathing down my neck about performance and attendance. They examine each and every person's time card and record."

Brooke wasn't at all unclear on what was happening. She knew she was being fired, and she was absolutely terrified by it, but the only thing going through her mind was, *Please don't say it! So long as you don't say it, it's not really happening. Please don't do this now. Please! Please! Please!*

Instead she said, "I'm not sure I understand."

"Brooke, I'm asking for your resignation. I think your frequent absences and emphasis on your private life have gotten in the way of your commitment to the program, and I feel you're no longer a good fit."

The knot in her throat was almost choking her, and she could feel a single, hot tear slide down her cheek. The makeup girl would surely ream her for this transgression.

"You think I'm no longer a good fit?" she said, her voice revealing that she was crying. "I scored the highest of the whole team in the randomized patient evaluations. I had the second-highest graduating GPA at NYU for my year. Margaret, I *love* my job and I think I'm good at it. What do I do?"

Margaret exhaled, and for a moment Brooke was aware that this was almost as hard for her boss as it was for her. "Brooke, I'm sorry. Due to your . . . extenuating circumstances . . . I will be willing to accept your resignation and confirm with any future employers that you left, uh, voluntarily. I know that's hardly comforting, but it's the best I can do."

Brooke struggled to think of something to say next. There's not a script for how to end a phone call after you've been fired, especially when you're not letting yourself scream "Screw you!" a half-dozen times. There was an awkwardly long moment of silence.

Margaret recovered first. "Brooke, are you still there? Why don't we talk more when you come in to clean out your locker?"

The tears were really flowing now, and all Brooke could think about was the imminent temper tantrum of the makeup artist. "Okay. I guess I'll come by next week?" She didn't know what else to say. "Uh, thanks for everything." Why was she thanking the woman who'd just fired her?

"Take care, Brooke."

She disconnected the phone and stared at it for almost a full minute until the reality of the situation set in.

Fired. For the first time in her entire life, including the countless children she'd babysat in middle school, her stint as a TCBY yogurt scooper in high school, a summer waitressing job at TGI Friday's, three semesters as a campus tour guide at Cornell, and what felt like a thousand hours' worth of internship as a graduate student. Now she was finally a full-time, salaried professional, and she was unceremoniously fired. Brooke noticed her hands were trembling and she reached gratefully for the nearby glass of water.

Resentful, uncharitable thoughts popped into her head, making her feel even worse. None of this would have ever happened if it weren't for Julian. She always had to follow him, accompany him, support him. The alternative being they'd never see each other. It was an impossible situation. She felt a lump in her throat.

Brooke drained her glass of water, set it down, and took as full an inhalation as the dress would allow. Next week she would show up at the hospital and plead, beg, and grovel until she convinced them that she was serious about her job — but for now, she had to try her best to put it out of her head. She dabbed at the melted mascara with a warm washcloth and vowed that she wouldn't even *hint* to Julian that anything was wrong. Tonight was about honoring his success, sharing his excitement and anticipation, reveling in all the attention. It was about remembering to soak in every single moment.

She didn't have to wait long. The suite's

bedroom door opened moments later and Julian appeared. He looked supremely stressed out and uncomfortable, probably due to nerves and the fact that he was wearing an extraordinarily shiny suit coupled with a tight, half-buttoned shirt that showed an alarming expanse of chest. Brooke forced herself to smile. "Hi!" She grinned, doing a little spin for him. "What do you think?"

Julian managed a tight, distracted smile. "Wow. You look great."

Brooke was about to remind him that such effort on her part required far more enthusiasm on his when she looked closely at his face. He actually grimaced as though in pain and sat down on a velvet armchair.

"Oh, you must be so anxious!" she said, walking over to him. She tried to kneel beside him but her dress wouldn't allow it, so she stood next to his chair. "You look hot."

Julian was silent.

"Come here, love," she crooned, taking his hand in hers. She felt a little bit fake pretending everything was fine, but she reminded herself it was the right thing to do. "It's natural to be nervous, but tonight is going to be —"

The look in his eyes stopped her midsentence.

"Julian, what is it? What's wrong?"

He raked his fingers through his hair and took a deep breath. When he finally spoke, his deep, even voice gave her chills.

"I have something to tell you," he said, his gaze directed at the floor.

"Okay. So tell me. What is it?"

He inhaled and exhaled slowly and at that moment Brooke knew this had nothing to do with his nerves. Her mind began to cycle through every horrible possibility. He was sick, with cancer or a brain tumor. One of his parents was sick. There'd been a horrific car accident. Maybe it was her family? Baby Ella? Her mother?

"Julian? What is it? I'm terrified. You have to tell me. Just say it."

Finally, he met her gaze with what looked like new resolve. For a split second she thought the moment had passed and they could continue their preparations. But just as quickly that look returned and he motioned toward the bed.

"Brooke, I think you should sit down for this," he said, somehow making her name sound ominous. "This is going to be very hard to hear."

"Are you okay? Are our parents? Julian!" She was panicked, absolutely certain that something too horrible to fathom had happened.

He held his hand up and shook his head. "No, it's nothing like that. It's about us."

What? "About us? What about *us?*" Was he really choosing *now* to talk about their relationship?

Julian stared at the floor. Brooke pulled her hand away and jabbed him in the shoulder. "Julian, what the hell are you talking about? Enough qualifying. Just say it already, whatever it is."

"Apparently some pictures have surfaced." He stated this in the exact same tone he would have used to announce that he had three months to live.

"What kind of pictures?" Brooke asked, but she immediately knew what he meant. Her mind flashed to the reporter in the elevator earlier that afternoon. She'd seen how quickly the news about her nonexistent pregnancy had spread. She'd read about the "affair" with Layla Lawson for months. But there had never before been actual pictures.

"Pictures that don't look good, but also don't tell the true story."

"Julian."

He sighed. "They're not good."

"Better or worse than the Sienna pictures?" It had only been a couple weeks earlier that they'd discussed those infamous pictures. Ironically, Julian was the one who couldn't understand how a married father of four could get photographed on the balcony of a hotel room with a topless actress hanging around his neck. Brooke had offered a number of perfectly logical explanations for how everything may not have been how it appeared, but eventually she agreed that there was no legit reason why Balthazar Getty was cradling Sienna's breast in one shot and shoving his tongue down her throat in another. Why couldn't he have stayed inside the hotel while half-naked, making out, and cheating on his wife?

"About the same. But, Brooke, I swear to you, it wasn't as bad as it looks."

"About the *same?* And *what* wasn't as bad if nothing supposedly happened?" Brooke stared at Julian until he met her gaze. His expression was sheepish.

"Show me," she said, holding her hand out for him to turn over the magazine that he was holding, rolled, in a tight fist.

He unrolled the magazine and she saw it was a copy of *Spin*. "No, this isn't it. I was, uh, reading this before. Can you let me explain first, Brooke? They were taken at the Chateau Marmont, and you know how ridiculous —"

"When were you at the Chateau Marmont?" Brooke snapped, hating the sound of her own voice.

Julian looked like he'd been slapped: his eyes were wide with disbelief (or panic?) and the color drained from his cheeks. "When was I . . . I was there, let's see, four, five . . . last Monday night. You remember? We played in Salt Lake that day and then all of us took a flight to L.A. together since we weren't playing again until Wednesday? I told you that."

"That's not at all how it was presented last week," she said quietly, her hands starting to tremble once again. "I distinctly remember you saying you were going to L.A. to meet with someone — I can't remember who now — but you never said anything about having a night off."

"Huh?"

"Well, only because you swear up and down that you always do everything in your power to get home whenever you can — even if it's only for a night — but apparently *that* night was an exception."

Julian jumped off the chair and walked over to Brooke. He tried to put his arms around her, but she backed away like a skittish deer. "Brooke, come here. I didn't . . .

have sex with her. It's not the way it seems."

"You didn't have *sex* with her? Am I supposed to sit here now and guess what did actually happen?"

He raked his fingers through his hair. "It's not like that."

"Not like what? What the hell happened, Julian? Clearly *something,* because we've never had a conversation like this before."

"It's just that . . . it's complicated."

She felt her breath catch in her throat. "Tell me *nothing* happened. Say, 'Brooke, they're a total scam, a complete distortion,' and I'll believe you."

She looked at him, and he looked away. It was all she needed to know.

For a reason she didn't understand herself, Brooke felt all the rage disappear in an instant. She didn't feel better or at all comforted, but it was like someone had drained her of all her anger and replaced it with a deep, cold hurt. She couldn't bring herself to speak.

They sat in silence, neither one of them daring to say a word. Brooke was shaking now, her hands, her shoulders, everything, and Julian was staring at his lap. She thought she might puke.

Finally, she said, "I got fired."

His head snapped up. "What?"

"Yeah, just now. Margaret said the higher-ups question my 'commitment to the program.' Because I'm never there. Because I've taken more days off and switched more shifts in the last six months than people do in ten years. Because I'm too busy following you all over the country, staying in gorgeous hotel suites and wearing diamonds."

Julian dropped his head in his hands. "I had no idea."

There was a knock at the door. When neither of them said anything, Natalya stuck her head in. "We need to do a final run-through with both of you and then start moving out. You're due on the red carpet in twenty-five minutes."

Julian nodded and she closed the door again. He looked at Brooke. "I'm so sorry, Rook. I can't believe they actually, uh, laid you off. They were lucky to have you, and they know it."

There was another knock at the door.

"We'll be right out!" she shouted, louder than she'd planned.

The door opened anyway, and Leo appeared. Brooke watched as he carefully arranged his expression to one of peacemaker, consensus builder, understanding confidant during hard times, and she immediately wanted to puke.

"Leo, can you give us a minute?" She didn't bother hiding her dislike.

He walked in and closed the door behind him as though he hadn't heard her. "Brooke, I know this can't be easy right now, trust me, but you two have to be on that red carpet in less than thirty minutes, and it's my job to make sure you're prepared."

Julian nodded. Brooke could do nothing but stare.

"Now, of course we all know those pictures are a load of crap, but until I can get to the bottom of it and force a retraction" — he paused here to give everyone a chance to process his power and influence — "I would like you both to be ready."

"Okay," Julian said, and looked at Brooke. "I guess we should probably work out our official response to any questions as a couple. Show a united front."

Brooke realized the anger she'd been feeling at the beginning of their conversation had slowly become a deep sadness. *What happens when you barely recognize your husband anymore?* she wondered. Julian, who used to complete her thoughts, now seemed incapable of understanding her at all.

She took a deep breath. "You two can decide on your own 'official response,' and I don't particularly care what it is. I'm going to finish getting dressed right now." She turned to Julian and looked him straight in the eye. "I'll go with you tonight, and I'll smile for the cameras and hold your hand on the red carpet, but the moment that ceremony is over, I'm going home."

Julian stood up and came to sit next to her on the bed. He pulled her hands into his and said, "Brooke, I beg you, please don't let —"

She pulled her hands back and moved a few inches away. "Don't you *dare* try to put this on me. I'm not the reason we need a huddle and an official statement to the press. You two work it out."

"Brooke, really, can we just —"

"Let her do her thing, Julian," Leo announced in a voice rich with wisdom and experience, accompanied by a look that said, *At least she agreed to go — can you imagine the PR nightmare if she bailed? Take it easy, give the crazy wife a little space, and you'll be on your way to the stage in no time.* . . . "Do what you need to do, Brooke. Julian and I will get everything straightened out here."

Brooke stared at them both before walking back into the living room. Natalya pounced on her immediately. "Jesus Christ,

Brooke! What the hell happened to your makeup? Someone fucking find Lionel!" she screamed as she raced toward the back bedroom. Brooke took the opportunity to slip into the third, blessedly empty bedroom, lock the door, and dial Nola.

"Hello?" The sound of her friend's voice almost made her cry all over again.

"Hey, it's me."

"Are you in the dress yet? Can you have Julian take a picture with your BlackBerry and send it? I'm dying to see you!"

"Listen, I only have two seconds before they find me, so —"

"Find you? Are you being stalked by some sort of awards show killer?" she laughed.

"Nola, please just listen to me. Everything turned into a horror show. Pictures of Julian and some girl. I haven't seen them yet so I don't really know, but they sound bad. And I got fired for missing so much work. Look, I can't explain it all now, but I just wanted to tell you that I'm going to get on a red-eye right after the ceremony, and I was hoping I could come to your place? I have a feeling our apartment is going to be completely staked out."

"Pictures of Julian and some girl? Oh, Brooke, I'm sure it's nothing. Those magazines will print any trash that floats by their desk, true or not. . . ."

"Can I stay with you, Nola? I have to get out of here. But I'll totally understand if you don't want the drama right now."

"Brooke! Shut up this minute. I'll call and book your flight myself. I remember from a project I did in L.A. that the last red-eye to New York is at eleven on American. Do you want that one? Is it enough time? I'll also book you cars to and from the airport."

The mere sound of concern in her friend's voice started the tears flowing again. "Thanks. I'd appreciate that. I'll call you when it's over."

"Remember to find out if Fergie looks as old in person as she does in all the photos. . . ."

"I hate you."

"I know. I love you, too. Don't be afraid to sneak some pics and send them. I'd especially like to see a couple of Josh Groban. . . ."

Despite herself, Brooke smiled and hung up. She checked her reflection in the bathroom mirror and worked up enough nerve to open the door. Natalya looked ready to faint with stress; she physically launched herself at Brooke.

"Do you realize we only have twenty minutes and they need to *completely* redo you? Who fucking *cries* after their makeup is applied?" She mumbled the last part, but it was loud enough for Brooke to hear.

"You know what I need right now, Natalya?" she asked, reaching out to touch the girl's forearm, her voice low but barely concealing a steely rage.

Natalya peered back at her with wide eyes.

"I need you to get my makeup fixed, find my shoes, and order me a vodka martini and a bottle of Advil from room service. And I need you to do those three things without speaking. Not one single, solitary word. Do you think you can do that?"

Natalya stared at her.

"Excellent. I just knew we could work it out! Thanks so much for your help."

And with that, feeling just the tiniest bit of satisfaction, Brooke walked back into the bedroom. She was going to get through this.

13
GODS AND NURSES
DON'T MIX

"Remember, you two: hold hands, smile, and relax. You're happy and in love and you're clearly not worrying about some two-bit, fame-seeking slut. She is not on your radar. Are we ready?" Leo all but shouted at them from his seat three feet away in the back of the limousine.

"We're ready . . ." Julian mumbled.

"Are we psyched? We need to be psyched! Are you two feeling it?" He peered out the window to see if they were being motioned for yet by the woman with the clipboard who was timing artist arrivals. Julian was scheduled to begin his red carpet walk at exactly 4:25 P.M., which according to Brooke's cell phone was in one terrifying minute.

Feeling what, exactly? Brooke wanted to ask. *Like shit? Like I'm about to make a voluntary death march, and if I knew what was good for me I'd immediately turn around, but*

I'm way too conflict-averse to make waves like that, so instead I'll just go quietly to the executioner's? So yes, you jerk, I suppose I am "feeling it."

"I'm not going to lie, guys — they're going to be piranhas." Leo held up his hands, palms out. "I'm just sayin', so you'll be prepared. But ignore 'em, smile, and soak in the moment. You two'll be great." His phone buzzed and after glancing at it for half a second, he clicked Unlock on the doors and turned to Brooke and Julian.

"It's time. Let's do this!" Leo shouted, and threw open the limo door, and before Brooke could even process what was happening, she was blinded by the flashbulbs. And while the flashes of light were piercing and painful, they were nothing compared to the questions.

"Julian! How does it feel to be attending your first Grammy ceremony?"

"Brooke! Do you have any comment on the pictures in the latest issue of *Last Night?*"

"Julian! Look over here! Here! Are you having an affair?"

"Brooke! Turn this way! Here, this camera! Who are you wearing?"

"Brooke! If you could say one thing to the Chateau bimbo, what would it be?"

"Julian! To your left! Yes, just like that!

Will you stay in your marriage?"

"Julian! Is it surreal to be walking the red carpet when no one knew your name a year ago?"

"Brooke! Do you think it's your fault because you don't physically fit the Hollywood norm?"

"What would you say to all the young women watching right now?"

"Julian! Do you wish your wife traveled with you more?"

It was like having stadium lights suddenly turned on in your bedroom at three in the morning: her eyes wouldn't — couldn't — adjust, and every effort only resulted in more discomfort.

She briefly turned her back toward the camera-free zone behind them and caught a glimpse of Nicole Kidman and Keith Urban climbing out of a stretch black Escalade. *Why are you talking to us when there are* real *celebrities here?* she wanted to scream. It was only when she turned back around again, her eyes finally able to handle the stunning flashes of light, that she saw an endless sea of red before them. Was it a mile long? Two? Ten? The people who had progressed farther up the carpet appeared casual, even relaxed. They were standing around in groups of three or five, idly chatting to reporters or one another, posing expertly for the cameras, offering megawatt, professionally engineered smiles at every turn. Was it possible to be like them? Could she do that too? More to the point, did she even stand a chance of surviving the next interminable stretch of carpet?

And then they were moving. She kept one sandaled foot directly in front of the other, chin held high, cheeks most likely flaming, and Julian ushered her through the throngs. When they'd traversed half of the distance to the entrance, Leo placed a hot, sweaty hand on each of their shoulders, leaned his head between theirs, and said, "E! entertainment news, upcoming on your right. If they approach you for an interview, stop and talk to them."

Brooke looked to her right and saw the back of a short blond guy's head. He was holding a microphone out to a trio of black-suited boys, none of whom looked older than fifteen. She had to rack her brain trying to think of their names, and when she finally remembered they were the Jonas Brothers, she felt very, very old. They were kind of cute, she thought, in a koala-bear-type way, but sexy? Seductive? Capable of bringing millions of tween girls to the brink of unconsciousness by merely smiling?

Ridiculous. She thought all those screaming girls should look back at the old *Tiger Beat* photos of Kirk Cameron and Ricky Schroeder if they wanted to see some real teen heartthrobs. She shook her head to herself. Did she just think the word "heart-throb"? She added this to a mental list of things to tell Nola.

"Julian Alter? Can we have a word with you?" The short blond guy had finally bid good-bye to the Jonas children and turned toward Brooke and Julian. Seacrest! Looking every bit as tan as he always did on *Idol*, his smile warm and welcoming. Brooke wanted to kiss him.

"Hey," Julian said, the recognition dawning on his face at the exact same time. "Uh, sure. We'd love to."

Seacrest motioned to the cameraman behind him and positioned himself slightly to the left of Brooke and Julian. He nodded and the cameraman switched on a powerfully bright light, which instantly cast off a surprising amount of heat. He then spoke into the microphone while looking at the camera.

"Joining me now, Julian Alter and his beautiful wife, Brooke." He turned toward them and waved his free hand expansively. "Thanks for taking a moment to say hello to us, you two. I have to say, you're both looking great tonight."

They each reflexively fake-smiled. Brooke had a brief, panic-inducing moment where she remembered that millions of people were watching this right now, all across the country and possibly the world.

"Thanks, Ryan," Julian said, and Brooke was relieved he'd remembered to use his first name. "We're both so excited to be here."

"So tell me, Julian. Your very first album goes platinum in less than eight weeks. As of today" — he paused and glanced at a small square of paper tucked into his palm — "four million copies sold worldwide. Now you're performing at the Grammys. Tell me, what's going through your mind?"

He thrust the microphone under Julian's mouth and smiled. Julian, cooler than she'd ever seen him, smiled back and said, "Well, Ryan, I have to say, it's been one hell of an incredible ride. I've been blown away by the response to the album, and now this? What an honor. What a truly *phenomenal* honor."

Seacrest appeared to like this and rewarded them with another smile and an attentive nod. "Julian, you write a lot about love in your music. Even 'For the Lost,' which at first seems like a nod to your lost brother, is really a song about the redemptive power of love. What's your inspiration?"

A layup if there ever was one. Brooke concentrated on keeping her gaze fixed on Julian, hoping she projected the look of a loving, supportive, attentive wife who hung on his every word instead of the shell-shocked mess she really was.

Julian went right up for the ball and dunked it easily. "You know, it's funny, Sea — Ryan. When I first started out, so much of my music was dark, pretty heavy. I was going through a lot in my own life, and of course I think the music always mirrors what the artist is dealing with. But now?" With this, he turned to face Brooke, gazed directly into her eyes, and said, "Now it's a completely different story. Thanks to my beautiful wife, both my life and my music are infinitely better. She's more than my inspiration — she's my motivation, my influence, my . . . my everything."

Despite all that had happened back at the hotel, despite the lost job and the supposedly horrible pictures, despite the tiny little voice in the back of her head that wondered if he was merely playing it up for his audience, Brooke felt a surge of love for her husband. At that moment, in front of the cameras and wearing ridiculous clothes and getting quoted and photographed and feted, she felt the exact same way toward Julian as she did the day they met.

Seacrest made an *awww* sound and then thanked them both for chatting and wished Julian good luck. The moment he turned toward his next guest — someone who looked exactly like Shakira, although Brooke couldn't be sure it was her — Julian turned toward her and said, "See? Seacrest didn't even bother asking about those dumb pictures. Any responsible journalist knows they're complete bullshit."

Just the mere mention of those pictures brought her right back to the hotel room, negating all her loving feelings. Not knowing what else to do, and acutely aware there were cameras and microphones spread out over every square inch of red carpet, she merely smiled at nothing and nodded. It didn't take long for Leo to jam his face between theirs again — Brooke almost jumped when she felt his hand on the back of her neck.

"Julian, Layla Lawson is right up ahead. I want you to greet her with a kiss on the cheek and then introduce her to Brooke. Brooke, it would be a big help if you could look pleased to meet her."

Brooke glanced up and caught sight of

Layla in a surprisingly elegant short black dress, hanging on the arm of Kid Rock. According to the tabs she read, Kid was just a friend, as Layla hadn't been dating much since her messy breakup with her famous quarterback boyfriend a year earlier. Before she had a chance to say anything snotty to Leo, they had reached the couple. Flashbulbs went off with the intensity of a firefight.

"Julian Alter!" Layla squealed and flung her arms around Julian's neck. "I can't wait for your performance!"

Brooke thought she would've felt something more upon meeting this girl she'd disliked for so long, but she had to admit that Layla exuded a certain kind of charm in person that didn't come across so well on television or in the pages of the gossip magazines. Even with her body pressed tightly against Julian's, there was something appealing about her, something sweeter and more vulnerable — perhaps even a little dumber, which didn't hurt either — that instantly put Brooke at ease.

Julian did his best to extract himself from Layla's embrace and looked sheepish when he introduced her to Brooke.

"Hi there!" she said in her rich, honeyed Southern accent. "It is such a pleasure to finally meet you."

Brooke smiled and offered her hand, but Layla had already come in for the hug.

"Oh, come here, darling, I feel like I've known you for ages! Your husband is one lucky guy!"

"Thanks," Brooke said, instantly feeling ridiculous for ever feeling threatened. "I love your dress."

"Oh, you're a doll-baby. Hey, y'all, I'd like you to meet my friend Kid." With that, she grabbed his hand and tried to direct his attention to Brooke and Julian, but he seemed distracted by a small army of models (backup singers? dancers? plus-ones?) who were parading past. After an awkwardly long moment, his face flashed a glimmer of recognition and he clapped Julian on the back.

"Dude, sweet album," he said, clamping both his hands around Julian's like all the politicians did. "Congrats! Listen, I was wondering if I could ask who you use to . . ."

Brooke didn't get a chance to hear what Kid Rock was asking of her husband because Layla was nudging her to the side and leaning in so close Brooke could smell her citrusy perfume.

"Start spending that money immediately," Layla said directly into Brooke's ear. "It's every bit as much yours as it is his — hell, he probably wouldn't have a dime of it if it weren't for you, am I right? — so don't cut off your nose to spite your face."

"Money?" was all Brooke could manage.

"Brooke, love, that's what I most regret about the whole Patrick situation. I sat through, what, hundreds of college and professional games, flew to every godforsaken, freezing stadium in this country, supported him through all the crap until he finally landed that eighty-million-dollar contract? Then when *he* cheats on *me* with that, that *porn star,* I was the one who thought it was too crass to buy myself a decent house. Well, learn from my mistakes, sweetheart. Buy the damn house. You earned it."

Before Brooke could even respond, Julian and Kid Rock sauntered back over to her and Layla; all four of them automatically stood shoulder to shoulder, smiled, and waved to the cameras.

Brooke didn't even have a chance to address Layla again before Leo hustled them closer to the entrance of the Staples Center. She was just about to congratulate herself on surviving the red carpet when a woman in a sequined tank dress and death-defyingly high heels thrust a microphone under her chin and practically screamed, "Brooke Alter, how does it feel to see pictures of your husband with another woman after you've supported him for so long?"

A hush fell over the area. In the two seconds it took the woman to ask that question, every single other artist, handler, journalist, anchor, cameraman, and fan seemed to go dead quiet. For just a moment, Brooke wondered if the deafening silence was a sign that she was going to faint, but she immediately realized she wasn't that lucky. She saw dozens — hundreds? — of heads turn to watch at the exact same time she felt Julian squeezing her hand so hard that she was certain multiple bones were breaking under the pressure. She had the odd sensation of wanting to scream and laugh at the same time. She wondered what everyone's reaction would be if she merely smiled and said, *Well you know, it's funny you asked. Because it really does feel wonderful. I mean, what girl wouldn't love being told about her husband supposedly having an affair with another woman and having the whole thing play out on national television thanks to people like you? Are there any other brilliant questions you'd like to ask before we make our way inside? No? Well then, it was a pleasure making your acquaintance.* That thought was followed by a single-second fantasy of taking scissors to the woman's sequins and then clobbering her with her own spiked heels. She could barely breathe.

But of course she didn't scream or puke or laugh or assault anyone. She inhaled through her nose, did her best to pretend that no one else was watching, and calmly said, "I'm extremely proud of my husband for his accomplishments, and I'm so excited to be here tonight to watch him perform. Wish him luck!" She squeezed Julian's hand right back and, not having any clue where she'd found such composure, she turned to him and said, "Shall we?"

Julian kissed her and gallantly offered her his arm, and before anyone else could materialize in front of them, she, Julian, and Leo were through the front doors.

"Brooke, you were brilliant!" Leo crowed triumphantly, clamping his still-sweaty palm around the back of her neck.

"Seriously, Rook, that was first-rate media wrangling," Julian said in agreement. "You handled that bitch like a pro."

She dropped Julian's arm. The way he congratulated her made her sick. "I'm going to the ladies' room."

"Wait! Brooke, we need to get seated right away so Julian can get backstage to warm up with —"

"Rook? Can you wait just —"

She left them both behind without so much as a second glance and made her way through the throngs of the gorgeous and gorgeously dressed. She reassured herself that no one knew who she was, that no matter how nauseated she felt, no one was staring at her or talking about her. She beelined toward the restroom sign, desperate to hide and compose herself for just a couple minutes. The ladies' room was surprisingly basic — what one would expect from the Staples Center but hardly befitting the *Grammys* ceremony — and Brooke tried hard not to touch anything as she closed the stall door behind her. She concentrated on taking deep breaths as the other women in the bathroom chitchatted.

One woman was going on and on about how she'd spotted Taylor Swift and Kanye West talking to each other off to the side of the red carpet, and she just couldn't understand why cute little Taylor would be giving Kanye — "that total douchebag!" — the time of day. Her friend weighed in on whether Taylor or Miley looked better in their near-matching black dresses (the vote was split), and each of them named their pick of hottest guy in attendance (one chose

Jay-Z; the other insisted on Josh Duhamel). One of them wondered who was watching Jennifer Hudson's son that evening. Another wanted to know why, exactly, Kate Beckinsale was in attendance when neither she nor her husband had anything to do with the music industry. It was precisely the kind of idle chatter she and Nola would've made if they'd been standing in that bathroom, and she found it oddly comforting. Right up until they started in on their next topic.

"So have you seen the Julian Alter pictures yet?" the one with the annoying voice asked her friend.

"No, are they really that bad?"

"Christ, are they *ever.* The girl is, like, grinding all over him. They could be having actual sex under her skirt in one of them."

"Who is she? Have they found out?"

"Some nobody. A civilian. Just some party girl out looking for a good time at the Chateau."

For what felt like the thousandth time that night, Brooke stopped breathing. The bathroom was busy — women constantly rotated in and out, washing their hands and adjusting imaginary flyaways and refreshing their already-perfect lipstick — but she only had ears for those two voices. It was a bad idea, but her curiosity was getting the better of her. Double-checking the stall door to make sure it was locked, she lined her eyes up with the crack along the hinges and peeked outside. Standing at the sink were two women, both probably in their mid- to late twenties, probably starlets, though neither of them looked familiar.

"What was he thinking, doing that at the Chateau? I mean, if you're going to cheat on your wife, shouldn't you at least *try* to be discreet?"

The other one scoffed. "Oh, *whatever.* Like it matters where they do it! They always get caught. Look at Tiger! Men are just *that* stupid."

This caused the other one to laugh. "Julian Alter is no Tiger Woods, and trust me, his wife is no Swedish supermodel."

She knew full well she wasn't a Swedish supermodel, but she didn't need to hear other people say it. She desperately wanted to leave but she dreaded going back to Julian and Leo every bit as much as she dreaded continuing her bathroom eavesdropping. The woman pulled out a cigarette.

"Do you think she'll actually leave him?" the girl with the too-short trendy bangs asked her friend Screech Voice.

There was a snort. "I don't think she's going anywhere . . . unless he says so."

"What is she, a teacher or something?"

"A nurse, I think."

"Can you imagine? You're just a regular civilian one day and then your husband is a superstar the next."

Screech laughed particularly hard at this. "I don't see Martin at risk of being super-anything. I guess that puts it all on me, huh?"

Bangs exhaled a final smoke ring and stamped her cigarette out in the sink. "They're dead in the water," she announced with the confidence of someone who's seen everything, been everywhere, met everyone. "She's sweet and mousy, and he's a god. Gods and nurses don't mix."

Nutritionist! she wanted to scream. *At least get it fucking right when you're dissecting my marriage and assassinating my character!*

They each gingerly deposited gum past their freshly glossed lips, closed their purses, and left without another word. Brooke's relief was palpable, so much that when she finally left the stall, she didn't even notice the woman who was leaning against the far end of the sink, her back to the mirror, typing something into her phone.

"Forgive me for intruding, but are you Brooke Alter?"

Brooke inhaled sharply at the sound of

her name. At this point she would've chosen a firing squad over another conversation.

The woman turned to face her and extend her hand and Brooke recognized her immediately as a well-respected and hugely famous movie and television actress. Brooke tried to mask the fact that she knew everything on earth about this woman — from all the characters she played in romantic comedies over the years to the horrible fact that her husband left her when she was six months pregnant for a barely legal professional tennis player — but it was useless trying to pretend she didn't recognize Carter Price. Did people ever not recognize Jennifer Aniston or Reese Witherspoon? Please.

"I'm Brooke," she said so quietly and with such softness that she sounded sad even to herself.

"I'm Carter Price. Oh, my . . . I didn't even realize . . . Oh, I'm so sorry. . . ."

Brooke's hands immediately flew to her face. Carter was staring at her with a look of such intense sympathy, she was certain something was very wrong.

"You heard everything those cows said, didn't you?"

"I, uh, I don't really . . ."

"You can't listen to them, to anyone even like them! They're petty, silly, ridiculous

441

people, and they think they understand, think they have the tiniest notion of what it's like to have your marriage play out in public, but they don't know a damn thing. About anything."

Huh. Not what she was expecting, but very welcome.

"Thanks," Brooke said, reaching out to accept a tissue from Carter. She told herself to remember to tell Nola that Carter Price had given her a tissue, and then she immediately felt stupid thinking it.

"Look, you don't know me at all," Carter said, her long, graceful fingers gesticulating through the air, "but I wish someone would've told me that it really does get better. Every story, no matter how juicy or horrible it is, eventually goes away. The vultures always need fresh misery to feed on, so if you just keep your cool and refuse to comment, it *will* get better."

Brooke was so focused on the fact that Carter Price was standing next to her and confiding in her about her ex — conceivably the most gorgeous, talented, revered actor of their generation — that she forgot to speak.

She must have been quiet for longer than she realized, because Carter turned back to the mirror, concealer stick in hand, and said, "God, that was none of my business, was it?" while dabbing at an imaginary circle under her left eye.

"No! That was so, *so* helpful, and *so* appreciated," Brooke said, quite aware that she sounded like an illiterate teenager.

"Here," Carter said, handing over her still-full glass of champagne. "You need this more than I do."

Under any other circumstances, Brooke would have politely refused, but tonight she agreed with Carter, movie star extraordinaire, and drained it in one easy swallow. She couldn't say what she would've paid for another — it was within new-car territory.

Carter gave her an approving look and nodded. "It feels like the entire world has been invited into your home and every one of them has something to say about it."

She was so nice! So normal! Brooke felt guilty for all the times she'd speculated with Nola about whether it was Carter's shrewishness or her botched boob job that had driven her ex into the arms of that tennis player. Never again would she be such a judgmental bitch about someone she didn't know.

"Yes, exactly," Brooke said, smacking her palm against the sink to underscore her point. "And the worst part is, they think it's all true. To just automatically assume that whatever gets printed in those things is accurate, well, it's ridiculous."

With this last sentence, Carter stopped nodding and cocked her head. A moment later, her face registered recognition. "Oh, I didn't realize."

"Didn't realize what?"

"That you think he didn't do it. Sweetheart, those photos . . ." She trailed off. "Look, I know it's heartbreaking — trust me, I've been through all of it before — but it doesn't help anything to live in denial."

It felt like Carter Price had punched her in the gut. "Look, I haven't even seen the pictures yet, but I know my husband, and I —"

The bathroom door swung open and a young woman materialized. She was wearing a sleek skirt suit, a Bluetooth earpiece, and a badge on a lanyard around her neck. "Carter? We need to get you seated right away." She turned and looked at Brooke. "Are you Brooke Alter?"

Brooke merely nodded, praying this woman wasn't going to add in her two cents about Julian. She couldn't handle another opinion.

"Julian's manager asked me to tell you that they had to get Julian backstage, but to proceed to your seat in the audience and he'll send someone to get you right before Julian goes on."

"Thanks," she said. She was relieved she wouldn't be seeing Leo or Julian but nervous about entering the theater area by herself.

She didn't need to worry. "I'll escort you both now if you're ready."

Carter shot Brooke a quick look and a huge smile. "We're ready," she said, linking her arm with Brooke's. "Aren't we?"

It was surreal. In the space of a single minute, one of the most famous actresses on earth had announced she thought Brooke's husband was cheating and then linked arms with her to stroll through the crowd together as though they'd been friends for twenty years. Brooke's face must have revealed her confusion and nausea and all-around discomfort; as the badge lady pointed to Brooke's seat in the fourth row from the stage, Carter leaned in and whispered, "It was real nice meeting you. And you'll survive this, I promise. If I can, anyone can. As for the show right now, remember to smile, smile, smile. Those cameras are going to be *all over* you tonight, just praying for a breakdown, so don't give it to them, okay?"

Brooke nodded, wishing more than anything that she could press a magic button and be transported back to Nola and Walter and her favorite fleece sweatpants. Instead, she took her seat. And she smiled.

She grinned maniacally through Jimmy Kimmel's opening monologue, Carrie Underwood's performance, a song-and-dance duet with Justin Timberlake and Beyoncé, a prerecorded video montage, and a quirky little number by Katy Perry. Her cheek muscles were starting to throb when the girl sitting beside her, a Kardashian, she thought, although she didn't know one from the next or why they were famous, leaned in and said, "You look hot tonight, FYI. Don't let those pictures get you down."

It had seemed impossible enough when it was just her and Julian in a hotel room together, but this? This was unbearable.

She heard the master of ceremonies announce that they'd gone to commercial, and before she could respond to the girl's comment, Leo materialized at the end of her aisle, crouching down so as not to block anyone's view, and motioned for her to follow him. *You know things are grim when you're happy to see* him, she thought to herself. Smiling, smiling, smiling all the way despite feeling a strange light-headedness,

Brooke ignored Potential Kardashian and politely excused herself as she climbed over people's legs (was that just Seal she'd almost straddled?) and followed Leo backstage.

"How's he doing?" She desperately wanted not to care, but knowing Julian and his stage fright, she couldn't help but feel for him. Instantly, despite everything that had happened, she was transported back to the countless times she'd held his hand and rubbed his back and reassured him that he'd be great.

"He only puked, like, seventeen times, so I think we're good to go."

She glared at Leo, who stared at the ass of an extremely young girl as he walked Brooke to the viewing area at stage left. "Really?"

"He's fine. A little nervous, but fine. He's going to rock it tonight."

She caught a split-second view of Julian before a PA, who was listening intently to an earpiece, nodded and gave Julian's shoulder a little shove. He and his bandmates quickly took their positions at their instruments. They were still behind the curtain, and Brooke could hear Jimmy Kimmel joking with the audience, keeping them warm during the commercial break. The monitor in the viewing area was counting down from twenty seconds, and the hand that Julian had wrapped around the microphone was clearly shaking.

Just when she thought she couldn't stand it anymore, Jimmy Kimmel announced Julian's name and the curtain rose on all sides, revealing a crowd of people so huge and so loud, Brooke wondered if Julian would even be able to make himself heard. But then the drummer began with a soft *tap-tap-tap*, the guitarist played a few mournful notes, and Julian pressed the microphone to his lips and began to sing the words that had made him famous. The sound of his baritone voice reverberated around the stadium, causing the audience to quiet almost immediately; to Brooke, it felt like nothing short of an electric jolt.

She flashed back to the first time she'd heard Julian perform "For the Lost," on that balmy Tuesday night at Nick's. He'd already played Brooke's favorite cover material plus two or three of his original songs, but when he played his brand-new song for the very first time, Brooke got chills. Since then, she had witnessed countless performances, but nothing could have prepared her for the experience of watching her husband sing his heart out for millions of people.

What felt like only seconds later, the

crowd had erupted into ecstatic, frantic cheers. Julian was bowing and gesturing a thank-you toward his bandmates, and the very next minute he was walking offstage, the microphone still clutched in his hand. Brooke could see he was exultant, trembling with the excitement and pride of a man who brought down a house of his peers and his heroes. His eyes shone and he moved to pull Brooke into a hug.

She pulled away and he looked like someone had slapped him.

"Come with me," he said, taking her by the hand. People backstage were swarming around, offering their congratulations and admiration, but Julian clasped Brooke's hand and led her into his dressing room. He closed the door behind them and smiled widely.

Brooke looked directly into his eyes. "We need to talk about those pictures. It's not a good time, I know, but I can't stand wondering anymore. If you could hear what people are saying . . . what they've been saying to me . . ."

"Shh," he said, putting a finger across her lips. "We'll talk about everything, we'll figure it all out. Let's enjoy this here now. Let's pop some champagne! Leo said he got us into Usher's post-party at Geisha House, and I'm telling you, it's going to be incredible."

A million images flashed through her mind at the same time, and they all included reporters, flashbulbs, and a rotating retinue of scorned women offering unsolicited advice on how to survive the devastation and humiliation. Before she could tell Julian that she needed the truth and she needed it now, there was a knock on the door.

Neither of them said it was okay to come in, but Leo entered anyway. Samara stood by his side. Both peered at Brooke.

"Hey, Brooke, you okay?" Samara asked without the least bit of concern in her voice.

Brooke flashed a phony smile.

"Listen, guys, CBS wants to do a post-performance interview."

"Samara —" Julian started but Leo cut him off.

"With *both* of you," he said as though he'd just announced their execution date.

"Oh, come on, you guys."

"I know, Julian, and I apologize, but I'm afraid I have to insist you go out there. It's up to Brooke if she joins you" — Samara paused pointedly and looked at Brooke — "but let me go on the record as saying that everyone at Sony would *really* appreciate it if she could do this. There is obviously a lot of interest in those pictures. You two need to get out there and show the world that nothing's wrong."

Everyone was quiet for a moment until Brooke realized they were all looking at her.

"You've got to be kidding me. Julian, tell them that . . ."

Julian didn't respond. When she worked up the nerve to look at him, he was staring at his hands.

"No," Brooke said.

"Five more minutes of solidarity? We'll go out there, we'll smile, we'll tell them everything's great, and then we'll be free."

Leo and Samara were nodding at Julian's wisdom and common sense.

Brooke noticed her dress was badly wrinkled. Her head ached powerfully. She stood, but still, she didn't cry.

"Brooke, come here, let's talk about this," Julian said in his managing-my-crazy-wife voice.

She walked past Samara and stood face-to-face with Leo at the dressing room door. "Excuse me," she said. When he didn't step aside, she turned her body and slid past him to pull open the door. For the final time that day, she felt his sweaty hand touch her skin. "Brooke, wait a minute, okay?" His irritation was unmistakable. "You can't leave like this. There are ten thousand cameras right outside the center. They'll eat you alive."

She turned and faced Leo, holding her breath as her face came within inches of his. "Considering what it's like in *here*, I think I'll take my chances. Now take your disgusting hand off my neck and get out of my way."

And without another word to anyone, she left.

14
THE REMOVAL OF
CLOTHES

Nola had arranged for the car to wait at a specific cross street behind the Staples Center, and through some miracle — or the fact that people didn't generally leave mid-ceremony — Brooke managed to slip out the back and into the waiting car undetected by any paparazzi. Her suitcase was open on the backseat, and everything was neatly folded, thanks to a helpful staffer at the Beverly Wilshire. The driver announced he would give her some privacy while she changed out of her dress and back into her street clothes.

She quickly changed and dialed Nola. "How did you make all this happen?" she asked without saying hello. "You've got a very bright future as an assistant." It was easier to joke than even try to explain what the evening had really been like.

"Look, don't think you're getting off the hook — I want to hear everything — but there's been a change of plan."

"A change of plan? Please don't tell me I have to stay here tonight."

"You don't have to stay there, but you can't come here. The paparazzi have completely staked out my house. There must be eight, maybe ten of them. I already unplugged my landline. If this is my apartment, I can't even imagine what yours looks like. I definitely don't think you want to deal with this."

"Nola, I'm so sorry."

"Oh, please! This is by far the most exciting thing that's ever happened to me, so just shut up. I'm only sorry I won't get to see you. I booked you on a US Airways flight straight to Philadelphia, and I called your mom to tell her. You leave at ten tonight and arrive a little before six A.M. She'll meet you at the airport. I hope that's okay?"

"Thank you. I can't thank you enough. That's more than okay."

The driver was still standing outside the car, talking on his cell phone, and Brooke wanted to get moving before anyone spotted them.

"Remember to wear cute socks for when you take your shoes off at security, because I guarantee there will be someone taking pictures. Smile as much as you possibly can and then get yourself to the business-class lounge — chances are they won't be in there."

"Okay."

"Oh, and leave all your borrowed stuff in the backseat of the car. The driver will return everything to the hotel, and they'll make sure to get it back to the stylist."

"I don't know how I can thank you."

"Save it, Brooke. You would do the exact same thing for me if my husband became a megastar overnight and I was being hounded by the paparazzi. Of course, that would mean I actually had a husband, which we both know is highly unlikely, and that my hypothetical husband would have a modicum of talent, which is even more un-likely. . . ."

"I'm too tired to argue, but for the record, your current chances for happiness and relationship success outweigh mine by, like, a factor of ten thousand, so quit your bitch-ing. I love you."

"I love you, too. Remember — cute socks and call me."

She spent the ride from the Staples Center to LAX carefully packing her dress into the provided garment bag, tucking her shoes into their dust bag, and arranging her jewelry and clutch neatly into the velvet-lined boxes stacked on the seat next to her. It was only when she pulled the giant rock off her left ring finger that she realized the stylist still had her plain wedding band, and she made a note to herself to remind Julian to get it back from the girl. She resisted the impulse to think of it as any kind of sign.

Two in-flight Bloodys and one Ambien guaranteed a much-needed five-hour black-out, but as her mother's reaction at baggage claim revealed, it did not do wonders for her appearance. Brooke smiled and waved when she spotted her mom at the end of the escalator and nearly knocked over the man standing in front of her.

Her mother hugged her hard, then pushed her away and held her at arm's length. She took in Brooke's terry-cloth sweatsuit, sneakers, and ponytail and declared, "You look horrible."

"Thanks, Mom. I feel pretty lousy, too."

"Let's get you home. Did you check a bag?"

"Nope, just this," Brooke said, motioning to her wheel-aboard. "When you have to give back your dress, shoes, bag, jewelry, and underwear, there's not much left to pack."

Her mother began weaving through people

toward the elevator. "I promised myself I wouldn't ask a single question until you're ready to talk about it."

"Thanks, I appreciate that."

"So . . ."

"So what?" Brooke asked. They stepped off the elevator. The cold Philly air hit her hard, as though she needed a reminder that she was no longer in California.

"So . . . I'll be there, waiting, should you want to talk. About anything."

"Great, thanks."

Her mother threw her hands in the air before pulling open the car door. "Brooke! You're torturing me."

"Torturing you?" Brooke feigned incredulousness. "I'm taking you up on your very kind offer of a little breathing room."

"You know perfectly well that offer wasn't genuine!"

Brooke hoisted her suitcase into the trunk and settled into the passenger seat. "Can I just have the car ride to relax before the interrogation begins? Trust me, once you get me started, you're not going to be able to shut me up."

She was relieved when her mother chatted the entire car ride to her Center City apartment, telling Brooke all about the people she'd met in her new jogging club. Even once they parked the car in the building's underground garage and took the elevator to her mother's two-bedroom on the fifth floor, Mrs. Greene maintained a steady, upbeat soliloquy. It was only once they stepped inside and shut the door that she turned to Brooke, who braced herself.

Her mother, in a rare moment of intimacy, cupped Brooke's cheek in her palm.

"First, you shower. There are clean towels in the bathroom and I put out some of this new lavender shampoo I'm in love with. After that, you eat. I'm going to make you an omelet — whites only, I know — and some toast. And then you sleep. Red-eyes are hell, and I'm guessing you didn't sleep all that much on the plane. The second bedroom is all made up and I've already got the AC jacked up as high as it will go." She took her hand away and began walking toward the kitchen.

Brooke exhaled, rolled her suitcase to the bedroom, and collapsed on the bed. She was asleep before she could take off her shoes.

When she finally woke with a need to pee so strong she couldn't ignore it any longer, the sun had moved to its late afternoon position behind the building. The clock read four forty-five and she could hear her mother emptying the dishwasher. It took only about ten seconds for the night to come rushing back. She grabbed her cell phone and was both dismayed and satisfied to see twelve missed calls and as many text messages, each and every one from Julian, beginning at about eleven last night California time and continuing straight through the night and next morning.

She pulled herself off the bed and headed first to the bathroom and then to the kitchen, where her mother was standing in front of the dishwasher, staring at the small television mounted underneath a cabinet. Oprah was hugging an unidentifiable guest as Brooke's mother shook her head.

"Hey," Brooke said, wondering for the umpteenth time what her mother would do when *Oprah* finally went off the air. "Who's on?"

Mrs. Greene didn't even turn around. "It's Mackenzie Phillips," she said. "*Again.* Can you believe it? Oprah's checking in with her to see how she's faring after the initial announcement."

"And how's she faring?"

"She's a recovering heroin addict who had a ten-year sexual relationship with her father. You know, I'm not a shrink, but I wouldn't say her prognosis for long-term happiness is terrific."

"Fair enough." Brooke grabbed a hundred-calorie pack of Oreos from the pantry and ripped it open. She popped a couple pieces in her mouth. "My god, these are good. How can they only be a hundred calories?"

Her mother snorted. "Because they only give you a few lousy crumbs. You have to eat five packs to feel even remotely satisfied. The whole thing is such a scam."

Brooke smiled.

Her mother clicked the television off. She turned to face Brooke. "Let me make you those eggs and toast now, what do you say?"

"Sure. Sounds good. I'm actually starving," she said as she emptied the remainder of the Oreos directly into her mouth.

"Remember when you kids were little and I'd make breakfast for dinner a couple times a month? You both loved it." She pulled a frying pan from a sliding drawer and sprayed it so heavily with Pam that it looked like it had been dunked in water.

"Mmm, I sure do. Only I'm pretty sure you made it two or three times a week, not a month, and I'm positive I was the only one who liked it. Randy and Dad used to order a pizza every time you made eggs at night."

"Oh come on, Brooke, it wasn't that often.

I cooked all the time!"

"Uh-huh."

"I made a huge pot of turkey chili every week. You all loved *that.*" She cracked a half-dozen eggs into a bowl and began to whisk them. Brooke opened her mouth to object when her mother added her self-proclaimed "special sauce" into the mix — a splash of vanilla soy milk that gave the eggs a nauseatingly sweet taste — but thought better of it. She would just drown them in ketchup and choke them down, as usual.

"It was from a mix!" Brooke said, cracking open another packet of Oreos. "All you did was add turkey and a jar of tomato sauce."

"It was delicious and you know it."

Brooke smiled. Her mother knew she was an atrocious cook, never claimed to be anything but horrible, and they both enjoyed this little back-and-forth.

Mrs. Greene scraped the vanilla soy eggs from the nonstick pan using a metal fork and divided them up between two plates. She pulled four slices of bread from the toaster and divided those up too, failing to notice that she'd never pressed the Toast button. She handed a plate to Brooke and motioned toward the little table right outside the kitchen.

They took their plates to the table and claimed their usual seats. Her mom darted back to the kitchen and returned with two cans of Diet Coke, two forks, one knife, an ancient jar of grape Smucker's, and a spray bottle of butter flavoring, all of which she unceremoniously dumped on the table. "Bon appétit!" she trilled.

"Yum!" Brooke said, pushing her vanilla-scented eggs around the plate. She spritzed her untoasted bread with the butter spray and held her can up high. "Cheers!"

"Cheers! To —" Brooke could see her mother stop herself, probably from saying something about being together, or new beginnings, or some other none-too-subtle reference to Julian. Instead she said, "To gourmet meals and good company!"

They ate quickly, and Brooke was pleasantly surprised that her mother still didn't ask her any questions. Of course, it had the desired effect of making Brooke desperate to discuss the situation, something her mom must have known. Regardless, Brooke couldn't get the electric kettle plugged in fast enough. By the time they both settled into the couch with mugs of Lipton and a plan to watch the last three episodes of *Brothers & Sisters* off the DVR, Brooke thought she might explode.

"So, you're probably dying to know what happened last night," she said after taking a sip.

Mrs. Greene pulled out the tea bag and let it drip for a second and then rested it on a napkin on the table. Brooke could tell she was taking great care not to look directly at her. *Things must be bad,* she thought to herself. Her mother was definitely not the no-pressure type. "Whenever you're ready," she said vaguely, waving her hand in a totally nonbelievable *I'm laid back* gesture.

"Well, I guess . . . my god, I don't even know where to start. The whole thing is such a mess."

"Start at the beginning. Last I spoke to you was around noon your time and you were getting ready to put on the dress. It sounded like everything was great then. So what happened?"

Brooke sat back on the couch and rested a foot on the edge of the glass coffee table. "Yeah, that's about when everything went to hell. I had just put on the dress and the jewelry and everything when Margaret called."

"Okay . . ."

"Well, there was some huge screwup that's not worth getting into right now, but the long and the short of it is that she fired me."

"She *what?*" Her mother snapped to attention. She had the same expression that she used to get when Brooke would come home from elementary school and explain how the mean girls had made fun of her at recess.

"She fired me. Told me they couldn't count on me anymore. That the hospital wasn't confident in my commitment to my career."

"What?"

Brooke smiled and sighed. "It's true."

"That woman must be out of her mind," her mother said, slamming her hand down on the table.

"Well, I appreciate that vote of confidence, Mom, but I have to admit that she's got a point. I haven't exactly been giving an A-plus performance these last few months."

Her mother was quiet for a moment as if she were trying to figure out what to say. When she spoke, her voice was low and measured. "You know I've always liked Julian. But I'm not going to lie — seeing those pictures made me want to kill him with my bare hands."

"What did you say?" Brooke whispered, feeling ambushed. She hadn't exactly forgotten about the pictures — the ones her own husband had described as similar to the

464

Sienna/Balthazar spread — but she had managed to push the idea of them to the far back recesses of her mind.

"I'm sorry, sweetheart. I know it's none of my business, and I swore to myself that I wouldn't say anything, but you can't just pretend nothing happened. You need to get some real answers."

Brooke was irritated. "I think it's pretty clear that he and I have a whole lot of things to figure out. I don't recognize this Julian anymore, and it's not just because of some horrible paparazzi pictures."

Brooke looked to her mother and waited for a response, but she was quiet.

"What?" Brooke asked. "What are you thinking?"

"You haven't seen them yet, have you?"

Brooke was quiet for a moment before she said, "I want to, but I can't. It'll all be so real as soon as I see them. . . ."

Mrs. Greene folded her legs up under her and reached across the sofa to take Brooke's hand. "Sweetheart, I hear what you're saying. I do. You must feel like you're on the ledge of a tall building. And it kills me to have to say this, but . . . I think you need to take a look."

She turned and stared at her mother. "Really, Mom? Aren't you always the one advising me to ignore all that crap? Haven't you been reminding me all along, pretty much every time I get upset with something I read, that ninety-nine percent of what's written in the tabloids is lies and distortions?"

"There's a copy on my bedside table."

"On your bedside table?" Brooke screeched, hating the sound of her own voice, a combination of shock and panic. "Since when do you subscribe to *Last Night?* I thought this was strictly an *O* magazine and *Newsweek* household."

"I started subscribing when you and Julian began appearing in it regularly," her mother said quietly. "It was exciting, and I wanted to know what everyone meant when they were talking about it."

Brooke laughed mirthlessly. "Oh well, aren't you glad you did? Isn't it just a fount of fascinating information?"

"It kills me to do this, but I'd rather you see them here for the first time. I'll be right here waiting for you. Go."

Brooke looked at her mother and could see the pain on her face. She pushed herself up from the couch and tried to ignore the overwhelming feelings of fear and dread. The walk from the living room to her mother's bedroom felt like an eternity, but before she could even process what was happening, Brooke sat on the edge of the bed. The cover featured the smiling faces of Justin Timberlake and Jessica Biehl with a long, jagged crack down the center. The words "It's Over!" were splashed in bright red across the top.

Comforted by the fact that Julian wasn't big enough yet to warrant the cover, Brooke turned to the table of contents, planning to scan the headlines. It was unnecessary. At the very top of the page, occupying more than its fair share of space, was a photo of Julian at an outside table in the courtyard of the Chateau Marmont. The girl sitting next to him was mostly shielded by a huge potted plant, but you could make out her profile as she leaned in toward Julian, her head tilted and her mouth open, as though they were just about to kiss. He was holding a beer in one hand and flashing the girl his dimples. Brooke felt a wave of nausea, followed quickly by the sick realization that these magazines never squander their juiciest pictures on the contents page. The worst was yet to come.

She took a deep breath and turned to page eighteen. Whoever claimed that horrible things took a while to process had obviously never faced a double-sided spread of her husband seducing another woman. Brooke's mind took it all in seamlessly. Without the least bit of effort, she saw another version of the first photo, only in this one, Julian appeared to be listening intently as the girl whispered something into his ear. It was time-stamped 11:38 P.M. The next one, stamped with a neon-red 12:22 A.M., showed him throwing his head back in laughter; the girl laughed, too, and now she had her palm planted firmly against his chest. Was she playfully pushing him away? Just looking for an excuse to touch him? The third and final picture on the left-hand side of the page was the worst: it showed the girl pressed right up against Julian, sipping what looked like rosé champagne. Julian was still holding his beer bottle in one hand, but his other hand appeared to be up the girl's dress. You could tell from his arm's angle that he wasn't doing anything more X-rated than touching her upper thigh, but there was no denying that both hand and wrist were completely obscured by fabric. Julian was winking at the girl, giving her that mischievous smile Brooke loved so much, as she gazed at him adoringly through big brown eyes. It was 1:03 A.M.

And then the whammy, no doubt *Last Night*'s crowning glory. On the right-hand side of the page was a full-bleed photo that may as well have been the size of a billboard. The time read 6:18 A.M. And it featured the girl, wearing the exact same drab blue dress from a few hours earlier, walking out of a poolside bungalow room. Her hair was disastrously mussed and she looked every bit the part of a morning-after cliché. She clutched her bag to her chest as though protecting herself from the surprise of the flashbulb, and her eyes were wide, shocked, but there was something else there, too. Pride? Accomplishment? Whatever it was, it clearly wasn't shame.

Brooke couldn't keep from examining each photo with the care of a scientist studying a specimen, looking for clues and signs and patterns. It took a few more sickening minutes, but after staring intently at the last photo, Brooke knew what bothered her the most. The girl wasn't a famous actress or supermodel or pop star, at least not as far as Brooke could tell. She looked ordinary. She had limp, slightly too-long reddish-brown hair, a nondescript blue dress, and a figure so unmemorable — so stunningly average — that it almost took Brooke's breath away when she realized: the girl sort of looked like *her*. From the extra five pounds to the inexpertly applied eye makeup to not-quite-right sandals (the heels just a little too clunky for a night out and the leather just slightly too worn), Julian's Chateau fling and Brooke could have been sisters. And, almost most distressing of all, Brooke was fairly certain *she* would be considered the more attractive one.

It was all too weird. If your husband was going to cheat on you with some stranger he met at a Hollywood hotel, couldn't he at least have the self-respect to choose someone hot? Or, at the very least, someone plastic and cheesy? Where were the huge fake boobs and the skintight skinny jeans? The airbrushed spray tan and the five-hundred-dollar highlights? *How'd she even get* into *the Chateau?* Brooke wondered. Maybe a famous musician couldn't always score a Giselle-level model, but couldn't he at least have found someone who looked better than his own *wife?* Brooke tossed the magazine aside in disgust. It was easier to focus on the absurdity of your husband cheating on you with a less attractive version of yourself than it was to acknowledge the actual *cheating* part.

"You okay?" Her mother's voice surprised her. Mrs. Greene was leaning in the doorway, her face wearing the same pained expression as before.

"You were right," Brooke said. "Those would not have been fun to see on the Amtrak train home tomorrow."

"I'm so sorry, honey. I know it must seem impossible right now, but I think you have to hear Julian out."

Brooke snorted. "You mean listen to something like, 'Honey, I technically could've come home and spent that night with you, but instead I got wasted and hooked up with your less attractive twin sister? Oh, and I just happened to get photographed doing it?" Brooke could hear the anger in her voice, the dripping sarcasm, and was surprised she didn't feel like crying.

Mrs. Greene sighed and joined her on the bed. "I don't know, sweetheart. He certainly needs to do better than that. But let's be clear on one thing: that tramp is no twin of yours. She's just some pathetic girl who threw herself at your husband. You outshine her in *every* imaginable way."

The sound of Julian's single, "For the Lost," rang out from the other room. Brooke's mother looked at her questioningly.

"It's my ringtone," Brooke said, pulling herself up. "I downloaded it a few weeks ago. Now I can spend the night trying to figure out how to make it go away."

She located her phone in the guest bedroom and saw it was Julian calling. She wanted to screen him but couldn't.

"Hey," she said, assuming the same position on this bed.

"Brooke! My god, I've been panicked. Why weren't you answering my calls? I didn't even know if you made it home or not."

"I'm not at home, I'm at my mom's."

She thought she heard a muffled curse and then he said, "Your mom's? I thought you said you were going home?"

"Yeah, well, that was my plan until Nola informed me that our apartment was under siege."

"Brooke?" She heard a horn honking in the background. "*Goddammit,* we almost just got rear-ended. Dude, what's up with that guy behind us?"

Then, to her: "Brooke? Sorry. I almost died there."

She didn't say anything.

"Brooke . . ."

"Yes?"

There was a pause before he said, "Please hear me out."

There was another moment of silence. She knew he was waiting for her to say something about the pictures, but she couldn't give him the satisfaction. Which, incidentally, was upsetting in its own way. How sad was it to be playing such juvenile don't-show-your-feelings games with your own husband.

"Brooke, I —" He stopped and coughed. "I, uh, I can't even imagine how hard it was to look at those pictures. How absolutely, utterly horrible it must have been . . ."

Her hand gripped the phone so tightly she was afraid she might break it, but she couldn't make herself say anything. All of a sudden, her throat had seized shut and the tears began streaming down her face.

"And when all those vile media people asked all those questions last night on the red carpet . . ." He coughed again and Brooke wondered if he was choked up or just getting a cold. "It was brutal for me, and I can only imagine how hellish it was for you, and —"

He stopped talking, clearly waiting for her to say something, to save him from himself, but she couldn't formulate a sentence through the silent tears.

They sat there for an entire minute, maybe two, before he said, "Baby, are you crying? Oh, Rook, I'm so, so sorry."

"I've seen the pictures," she whispered,

and then paused. She knew she had to ask, but a part of her kept thinking it was better not to know.

"Brooke, they look so much worse than the reality."

"Did you spend the night with that woman?" she asked. Her mouth felt like it was coated in wool.

"It wasn't like that."

Silence. The quiet on the phone almost felt alive. She waited and prayed for him to say that it was all a huge misunderstanding, a setup, a media manipulation. Instead, he said nothing.

"Well, okay then," she heard herself say. "That pretty much explains it." Her last two words were choked, muffled.

"No! Brooke, I . . . I did not have sex with that girl. I *swear* to you."

"She was leaving your room at six in the morning."

"I'm telling you, Brooke, we did not have sex." He sounded miserable, his voice pleading.

And then she finally understood. "So you didn't actually have sex with her, but something else happened, right?"

"Brooke . . ."

"I need to know what happened, Julian." She wanted to throw up at the horror of having this conversation with her husband, this weirdly horrible version of "what base did you get to?"

"There was the removal of clothes, but after that, we just passed out. Nothing happened, I swear to you, Brooke."

The removal of clothes. It was such an odd way to phrase it. So distant. She felt the bile rise in her throat at the mental picture of Julian lying naked in bed with someone else.

"Brooke? Are you still there?"

She knew he was talking, but she couldn't hear what he was saying. She moved the phone away from her ear and looked at the screen; a picture of Julian with his face pressed against Walter's stared back at her.

She sat on the bed for another ten seconds, maybe twenty, looking at Julian's picture and listening to the rise and fall of his voice. She took a deep breath, brought the microphone panel to her lips, and said, "Julian, I'm hanging up. Please don't call me back. I want to be alone." Before she could lose her nerve, she turned off the phone, pulled the battery out, and stashed them both separately in the night table drawer. There would be no more talking that night.

15
NOT A SHOWER
SOBBER

"Are you sure you don't want us to come in, even for a few minutes?" Michelle asked, eyeing the row of SUVs with tinted windows that lined the block outside Brooke's building entrance.

"I'm positive," Brooke answered, trying to sound definitive. The two-hour car ride from her mother's place to New York with her brother and Michelle had given her more than enough time to bring them up to date on the Julian situation, and they'd arrived in Manhattan just as they started asking the sorts of questions about Julian that she wasn't prepared to answer.

"Why don't we just help you get in the front door?" Randy asked. "I've always wanted to punch a paparazzo."

She gritted her teeth and smiled. "Thanks, guys, but I can handle this. They've probably been sitting here since the Grammys and I don't think they're leaving any time soon."

Randy and Michelle exchanged a skeptical look so Brooke pressed on. "I'm serious, you two. You have another three hours minimum and it's getting late, so you better get going. I'll walk down the block, ignore them when they jump out of the cars, and keep my head high. I won't even say 'no comment.' "

Randy and Michelle were on their way to a wedding in the Berkshires and planned to arrive a day or two early for their first trip without the baby. Brooke sneaked another look at Michelle's impressively tight belly and shook her head in wonderment. It was nothing short of a miracle, especially since pregnancy had replaced her formerly trim, compact body with a short, stocky figure with zero delineation between her chest and waist or waist and thighs. Brooke thought it would be years before Michelle would regain her figure, but only four months after Ella's birth she looked better than ever.

"Well, all right . . ." Randy said, raising his eyebrows. He asked Michelle if she wanted to run into Brooke's apartment and use the bathroom.

Brooke slumped. She was dying for a few minutes to herself before Nola arrived and round two of the inquisition began.

"No, I'm good," Michelle answered, and Brooke exhaled. "If traffic's going to be that bad, we should probably get going. You sure you're going to be okay?"

Brooke smiled widely and leaned into the passenger seat to hug Michelle. "I promise. I'm more than fine. Please just focus on sleeping and drinking as much as possible, okay?"

"We are at risk of sleeping straight through this wedding," Randy mumbled, leaning out through the driver's window to accept Brooke's kiss.

There was an explosion of flashbulbs close by. The man taking pictures from across the street had obviously spotted them before anyone else, despite Randy parking nearly an entire block from the entrance. He was wearing a navy hoodie and khakis and didn't appear to be making the least bit of effort to disguise his intentions.

"Wow, he was all over that, wasn't he? Didn't waste a second," her brother said, leaning out the window to get a better look at the guy.

"I've actually seen him before. Guaranteed you'll see a pic online in the next four hours of us kissing with some sort of caption like 'Jilted Wife Wastes No Time Taking New

Lover,' " she said.

"Will they mention I'm your brother?"

"Most definitely not. Or the fact that your wife is sitting next to you in the car. There's actually a distinct possibility they'll call it a threesome."

Randy smiled, a sad one. "Sucks, Brooke. I'm sorry. About everything."

Brooke squeezed his arm. "Stop worrying about me. Go enjoy your trip!"

"Call if you need anything, okay?"

"Will do," she said with more fake cheer than she would have thought possible. "Drive safely!" She stood and waved until they turned the corner, then beelined for the front door. She barely made it ten feet when the other photographers — no doubt tipped off by the earlier flashbulbs — seemed to fly right out of the various SUVs and convene in a loud, flapping group directly outside the door of her building.

"Brooke! Why didn't you go to any after-parties with Julian?"

"Brooke! Did you throw Julian out?"

"Did you know your husband was having an affair?"

"Why hasn't your husband come home yet?"

Good question, Brooke thought to herself. *That makes two of us wondering the exact same thing.* They shouted and shoved cameras in her face, but she refused to make eye contact with any of them. Feigning a calmness she didn't feel at all, she first unlocked the outer door, pulled it closed behind her, and then unlocked the door to the lobby. The flashbulbs continued until the elevator closed behind her.

The apartment was eerily quiet. To be honest, she had allowed herself to hope against hope that Julian would drop everything and fly home to talk things through. She knew his days were jam-packed and nonnegotiable — as an approved member of the "cc" list, she received his daily schedules, contact info, and travel plans by e-mail every morning — and she *knew* he couldn't very well cancel any of the post-Grammy press opportunities to come home a couple days early. But it didn't change the fact that she desperately *wanted* him to do it anyway. As it stood now, he was scheduled to land at JFK in two more days, on Thursday morning, to do another round of New York media and talk shows, and she was trying not to think about what would happen then.

She only managed a quick shower and a bag of microwave popcorn before the buzzer rang. Nola and Walter burst through into the tiny foyer in a happy entanglement of leashes and coats, and Brooke laughed for the first time in days when Walter jumped vertically four feet in the air and tried to lick her face. When she finally caught him in her arms, he squealed like a piglet and covered her mouth in kisses.

"Don't expect the same greeting from me," Nola said, scrunching her face in disgust. Then she relented and hugged Brooke hard, and together with Walter, the three of them made a funny little tepee. Nola kissed Brooke on the cheek and Walter on the nose and then headed straight for the kitchen to pour vodka over ice with some olive juice.

"If what's going on outside your apartment right now is any indication of how it was in Los Angeles, I think you might need this," Nola said, handing a glass of cloudy vodka to Brooke. She sat opposite Brooke on the sofa. "So . . . you ready to tell me what happened?" she asked.

Brooke sighed and sipped her drink. The liquid was sharp, but it warmed her throat and hit her stomach in a surprisingly pleasant way. She couldn't bring herself to relive the whole thing again, point by miserable point, and she knew that although Nola would be sympathetic, she could never really understand what the night had been like.

So she told Nola about all the assistants swarming, the gorgeous hotel suite, the gold Valentino. She made her laugh with the story of the Neil Lane security guard and bragged about how perfect her hair and nails had been. She glossed over the call from Margaret, saying only that the hospital higher-ups were crazy and she really had missed a lot of work, and waved off the look of shock on Nola's face with a laugh and a sip of her drink. She dutifully provided details on what the red carpet was like ("so much hotter than I thought — you don't realize until you're there how many lights are beating down") and what the stars looked like in person ("thinner, for the most part, than in their photos, and almost universally older"). She answered Nola's questions about Ryan Seacrest ("charming and adorable, but you know I'm a Seacrest lover and apologist"), whether or not John Mayer was cute enough in real life to warrant all the women he cycled through ("I honestly think Julian is cuter, which, now that I think of it, really doesn't bode well"), and offered a highly unhelpful opinion on whether Taylor Swift looked better or worse than Miley Cyrus ("I'm still not positive I can tell them apart"). Not really knowing why, she deliberately omitted the Layla Lawson meeting, the women in the bathroom, and the lecture from Carter Price.

What she didn't tell Nola was how thoroughly devastated she'd been when she hung up the phone after being fired. She didn't describe how icy Julian had been when he told her about the pictures, how it was Julian's focus on "managing their impact" and "staying on message" that upset her the most. She left out the part where, as they strolled the red carpet, the paparazzi hounded them with humiliating questions about the pictures and screamed insults, hoping to make them turn toward the camera. How could she explain to anyone the way she felt listening to Carrie Underwood perform "Before He Cheats," wondering if every single person in the auditorium was staring at them and chuckling to themselves — then trying not to remain stony-faced when Carrie delivered the song's refrain, "Cause the next time that he cheats / Oh, you know it won't be on me."

She omitted the parts about sobbing in the car on the way to the airport and praying Julian would beg her to stay, absolutely *forbid* her from leaving, how his tepid, halfhearted protestations were devastating. Brooke couldn't admit that she was the last to board the flight in the pathetic hope that Julian would come sprinting to the gate, like in every movie, and plead with her to stay, or how, when she finally walked the jetway and watched the door close behind her, she hated him more for letting her go than whatever idiotic crime he'd committed in the first place.

When she finally finished, she turned to Nola and looked at her expectantly. "Was that a good summary?"

Nola just shook her head. "Come on, Brooke. What's the *real* story?"

"The real story?" Brooke laughed, but it sounded hollow, miserable. "You can read the real story on page eighteen of this week's *Last Night*." Walter jumped up on the couch and rested his chin on Brooke's thigh.

"Brooke, have you even considered that there's a logical explanation?"

"It gets harder and harder to blame it on the tabloids when your husband actually confirms it."

The expression on Nola's face was one of disbelief. "Julian admitted . . ."

"He did."

Nola set her drink down and stared at Brooke.

"I think the exact quote was 'there was the removal of clothes.' Like, he has no idea how *that* happened, but 'removal' took place."

"Oh my."

"He claims he didn't sleep with her. As if I'm supposed to believe that." Her cell phone rang but she immediately silenced it. "Oh, Nola, I just can't get the picture of the two of them *naked* together out of my mind! And you want to know the weirdest part? The fact that she is ordinary looking makes me feel even worse. Like, he can't even claim he was sooo wasted and this hot model just fell into his bed." She held up a copy of *Last Night* and shook it. "I mean, she's average. At best! And let's not lose sight of the fact that he spent the entire evening *courting* her. Seducing her. You expect me to believe he didn't actually sleep with her?"

Nola looked down at her lap.

"Even if he didn't, he was obviously trying." Brooke stood up and paced the room. She felt exhausted and keyed up and nauseated at the same time. "He's having an affair, or wants to be. I'd be an idiot not to accept that."

Nola remained silent.

"We hardly see each other, and when we

do, we fight. We barely ever have sex anymore. While he's traveling, he's always out somewhere, with girls and music in the background, and I never even know where. There have been *so many rumors*. I know every jilted wife on the planet wants to believe her situation is different, but I'd be a fool to think this couldn't happen to me." She exhaled and shook her head. "My god, we're just like my parents. I always thought we'd be different, and here we are. . . ."

"Brooke, you need to talk to him."

Brooke threw her hands up. "I couldn't agree more, but where is he? Grabbing sushi in West Hollywood before his late-night-talk-show circuit? Isn't it hard to ignore the small, simple fact that if he really *wanted* to be, he would be here right now?"

Nola swirled the contents of her glass and appeared to think about that. "*Could* he be?"

"Of course he could! He's not the president, he's not performing life-saving surgery, and he's not guiding the shuttle through the atmosphere to a safe landing. He's a *singer,* for chrissake, and I think he could figure it out."

"Well, when *will* he be back?"

Brooke shrugged and scratched Walter's neck. "The day after tomorrow. Not for me, mind you. New York is already on the schedule. Apparently the dissolution of your marriage doesn't warrant a line on the itinerary."

Nola set her drink down and turned to Brooke. "*The dissolution of your marriage?* Is that really what's happening here?"

That phrase hung in the air. "I don't know, Nola. I really hope not. But I don't know how we're going to get over this."

Brooke tried to suppress the nausea that washed over her. For all her talk the last couple days of "taking time" and "needing space" and "figuring things out," she'd never allowed herself to really consider the possibility that she and Julian wouldn't make it through this.

"Look, Nol, I hate to do this, but I'm kicking you out now. I need to sleep."

"Why? You're unemployed. What in the world do you have to do tomorrow?"

Brooke laughed. "Thanks for the sensitivity. I'll have you know, I'm not unemployed, just *under*employed. I still have the twenty hours a week at Huntley."

Nola poured herself another inch of vodka and didn't bother with the olives this time. "You don't have to be there until tomorrow afternoon. You really need to go to sleep this minute?"

"No, but I need a couple hours to sob in

the shower, try not to Google the Chateau girl, and then cry myself to sleep when I do it anyway," Brooke answered. She was mostly joking, of course, but it didn't end up sounding that way.

"Brooke . . ."

"I'm kidding. I'm not really a shower sobber. Besides, I'll probably take a bath."

"I'm not leaving you like this."

"Well then you're sleeping on my couch, because I'm headed to bed. Seriously, Nola, I really am fine. I think I could use a little time alone. My mother was shockingly nonintrusive, but I haven't had a second to myself yet. Not that there won't be plenty of time for that . . ."

It took another ten minutes to convince Nola to leave, and when she finally did, Brooke wasn't as relieved as she'd predicted. She took a bath and put on her coziest cotton pajamas and her rattiest robe and climbed on top of the covers, yanking her laptop into bed with her. They'd agreed early on in their marriage never to have a television in the bedroom — which they carried over to computers as well — but considering Julian was nowhere to be found, it felt almost right for her to download *27 Dresses* or something equally chick-flickish and zone out. She briefly entertained the idea of bringing in some ice cream but decided it was just too Bridget Jones. The movie proved an excellent distraction, due mostly to her discipline in keeping focused on the screen and not allowing her mind to wander, but as soon as it ended, she made a crucial mistake. Two, actually.

Her first disastrous decision was to listen to her voice mail. It took almost twenty minutes to get through the thirty-three messages that had been left since the day of the Grammys. The shift from Sunday, when friends and family were calling to wish her good luck, to today — when nearly every message sounded like a condolence call — was astonishing. The majority were from Julian, and all included some halfhearted version of "I can explain." While they were appropriately pleading, none, noticeably, included an "I love you." There was one each from Randy, her father, Michelle, and Cynthia, all offering support and encouragement; four from Nola at various times wanting to know what was happening and giving updates on Walter; and one from Heather, the guidance counselor at Huntley she'd run into at the Italian bakery. The rest were from old friends, (ex) colleagues, and random acquaintances, and each made it sound as though someone had died. Although she hadn't felt like crying before she listened, there was a knot in her throat when she finished.

Her second, and possibly worse, amateur move was to check Facebook. She'd predicted that many of her friends would have posted excited status updates about Julian's performance — it wasn't every day someone they knew from high school or college performed at the Grammys. What she hadn't anticipated, perhaps naively, was the outpouring of support directed in *her* direction: her wall was papered with everything from "You're strong, you'll get through this" from one of her friends' mothers to "it just goes to show that all men are as*holes. don't worry, mrs. a, we r all rooting for u!!!" from Kaylie. Under any other, less humiliating circumstances, it would've been wonderful to feel so much love and encouragement, but this was just plain mortifying. With it came the incontrovertible proof that her private misery was being conducted very publicly, and not just in front of strangers. In a way she couldn't quite explain, it had been easier to think of the masses of nameless, faceless Americans examining the pictures of her husband and the Chateau girl, but the moment she realized it was also her friends and family, coworkers and acquaintances, it became almost unbearable.

The double dose of Ambien she took that night prophylactically was sufficient to make her groggy and hungover the next day but not quite strong enough to launch her into the blackout sleep she desperately wanted. The morning and early afternoon passed by in a fog with only Walter and the constantly ringing (but ignored) phone punctuating it, and were she not terrified of losing the Huntley job, too, she would have seriously considered calling in sick. Instead, she forced herself to shower, eat a peanut butter sandwich on whole wheat toast, and move toward the subway in plenty of time to get to the Upper East Side by three thirty. She arrived at the school fifteen minutes early and, after admiring for just a moment the ivy-covered stone facade of the town house, noticed a giant ruckus to the left of the entrance.

There was a small cluster of photographers and what looked like two reporters (one with a microphone, the other with a notebook), and they were surrounding a petite blond woman wearing an ankle-length shearling coat, a neat bun, and an ugly grimace. The photographers were so focused on the woman they didn't notice Brooke.

"No, I wouldn't say it's anything personal," the woman said while shaking her head. She listened for a moment and then shook it again. "No, I have never had any interaction with her — my daughter doesn't require any nutrition counseling, but . . ."

Brooke stopped listening for a split second upon realizing this strange woman was talking about *her*.

"Let me say that I'm not alone in thinking this kind of attention is inappropriate in a school environment. My daughter should be concentrating on algebra and field hockey, and instead she's fielding calls from reporters asking her to comment for a national gossip tabloid. It's unacceptable, and it's why the Parents' Association is calling for the immediate resignation of Mrs. Alter."

Brooke gasped. The woman caught Brooke's eye. The dozen or so other people in the circle — she could see now that there were another two mothers standing with the blond lady — all looked at her. The shouting commenced immediately.

"Brooke! Have you ever met the woman who appeared in the photographs with Julian?"

"Brooke, will you be leaving Julian? Have you seen him since Sunday night?"

"What are your thoughts on the Huntley Parents' Association calling for your resignation? Do you blame your husband for that?"

It was like the Grammys all over again, only this time without the dress, the husband, or the rope line that separated her from the paparazzi. Thankfully, she did have the school security guard, a kindly man in his late sixties who barely cleared five-six but who nonetheless held up an arm toward the crowd and ordered them to stand back, reminding everyone that while the sidewalk was public property, the stairs leading up to the front door were not. Brooke shot him a grateful look and bolted inside. She was equal parts angry and shocked, mostly at herself for not predicting — for never even suspecting — that all this hellish, unwanted attention would follow her to school.

She took a deep breath and headed directly to her office on the ground floor. Rosie, the administrative assistant for all counseling-related programming, glanced up from her desk when Brooke entered the anteroom to the suite where she, Heather, and the other three guidance counselors all had their offices. Rosie had never excelled at minding her own business, but Brooke guessed today would be worse than usual. She braced herself for the inevitable reference to the Julian photographs, the mob outside, or both.

"Hey, Brooke. Let me know when you're settled from all the, um, craziness outside. Rhonda wants to come in for a few minutes before your appointments begin," Rosie said, sounding nervous enough to make Brooke nervous.

"Really? Any idea why?"

"Nope," Rosie replied, clearly lying. "She asked me to let her know when you got here."

"Okay, can I take my coat off and check the machine? Two minutes?"

She stepped inside her office, only big enough to house a desk, two chairs, and a coat stand, and she quietly shut the door. Through the glass door, she could see Rosie pick up the phone, letting Rhonda know that she had arrived.

Barely thirty seconds had passed when she heard a knock. "Come in!" Brooke called, trying to sound welcoming. She genuinely liked and respected Rhonda, and while a visit from her principal wasn't the least bit unusual, she had been hoping to avoid any unnecessary contact that day.

"I'm glad you're here. I want to give you

an update on Lizzie Stone," Brooke said, hoping to co-opt the conversation by bringing up one of the students she counseled. Brooke barreled on. "I can't believe that Coach Demichev is trusted with the well-being of these girls. I mean, I think it's great he can just create Olympians out of thin air — no pun intended — but it's really only a matter of time before one of them starves to death."

"Brooke," Rhonda said, drawing out her name in an unusually long way, "I want to hear this; maybe you can write me a memo. But we need to talk."

"Oh? Is everything okay?" she asked, her heart rattling in her chest.

"I'm afraid not. I'm so sorry to have to tell you this. . . ."

She knew from the look on Rhonda's face. Of course it wasn't her decision, Rhonda said; she might have been the principal but she answered to so many others, especially the parents, who thought all this attention Brooke was receiving didn't reflect well on the school. Everyone understood it wasn't Brooke's fault, that of course she couldn't be pleased about the media scrutiny, which is why they wanted her to take some time off — paid, of course — until everything calmed down.

By the time Rhonda said, "I do hope you understand this is only temporary, and it's a last resort that none of us is happy about," Brooke had mentally checked out. She didn't suggest to Rhonda that the hostile mother currently holding court for press outside the school was the person drawing all the media attention, not her. She refrained from reminding her principal that she had never mentioned the school by name in a single interview and had never, ever compromised her students' privacy by so much as explaining her responsibilities to anyone outside her immediate circle of friends and family. Instead, she forced herself into appropriate-response autopilot, assuring Rhonda she understood, that she knew it wasn't her decision, that she'd be on her way as soon as she tied up a few loose ends. Less than an hour later, Brooke walked back into the anteroom with her coat on and bag slung over her shoulder and ran into Heather.

"Hey, are you done for the day already? I'm jealous."

Brooke felt a lump growing in her throat and coughed. "More like done for the foreseeable future."

"I heard what happened," Heather whispered, although they were alone in the room. Brooke wondered how she already knew and then remembered how fast rumors spread in a high school.

Brooke shrugged. "Yeah, well, that's part of the deal. If I were a parent paying forty grand a year for my daughter to go to school here, I guess I wouldn't be thrilled to have her harassed by paparazzi every time she stepped outside. Rhonda told me that some of the girls had been contacted by tabloid reporters via their Facebook accounts, asking what I was like at school and if I ever talked about Julian. Can you imagine?" She sighed. "If that's really the case, I probably *should* be dismissed."

"Vile. They are absolutely vile people. Listen, Brooke, I really think you should meet my friend. The one I was telling you about whose husband won *American Idol?* I'm guessing not a lot of people know what you're going through, but trust me, she gets it. . . ." Heather's voice trailed off, and she looked anxious, like she was afraid she'd pushed too hard.

Brooke had less than zero interest in meeting Heather's significantly younger friend from Alabama and comparing husband woes, but she nodded. "Sure, get me her e-mail and I'll shoot her a note."

"Oh, don't worry about it. I'll have her

get in touch with you if that's okay?"

It was absolutely not okay, but what could she say? She just wanted to get out of there before she ran into anyone else. "Sure, sounds good," she said awkwardly.

Brooke forced a smile and a little wave and bolted for the front door. She passed a group of girls in the hall and one of them called her name. She thought about pretending she hadn't heard, but she couldn't just ignore it. When she turned around, Kaylie was walking toward her.

"Mrs. A? Where are you going? Don't we have our appointment today? I heard there are a bunch of reporters outside."

Brooke looked at the girl, who was, as usual, twisting frizzy strands of hair nervously around her fingers, and felt a surge of guilt. "Hey, sweetheart. It looks like I'm, well, I'm going to be taking a little time off." When Kaylie's face fell, she rushed on. "But don't worry, it's only temporary, I'm sure, and you're doing so great."

"But, Mrs. A., I don't think that —"

Brooke interrupted her and leaned in closer to the girl, so none of the other students could hear them. "Kaylie, you've graduated beyond me," she said with what she hoped was a reassuring smile. "You're strong and healthy and you know — probably better than any girl here — how to take care of yourself. Not only do you fit in, but you're one of the stars of the school play. You look great and you feel great . . . hell, I don't know what more I could do with you."

Kaylie smiled back at her and leaned in for a hug. "I won't tell anyone you just cursed," she said.

Brooke swatted the girl's arm and grinned, although she could feel her throat constricting. "You take care. And call if you need anything. But trust me, you're not getting rid of me that quickly. I'll be back soon, okay?"

Kaylie nodded and Brooke tried not to cry. "And promise me: no more moronic cleanses, okay? We're over that, right?"

"We're over it," Kaylie said with a smile.

Brooke gave a small wave and turned back toward the building's exit, determined to keep moving past the handful of lingering photographers who launched into a shouting, questioning frenzy when they saw her, and she didn't slow down until she hit Fifth Avenue. She checked to make sure no one had followed her and then tried to hail a cab, a completely fruitless endeavor at four in the afternoon. After twenty frustrating minutes, she hopped a crosstown bus on Eighty-sixth Street and rode west to the 1 train, where she was grateful to find a seat in the very last car.

She closed her eyes and sat back, not caring that her hair was touching the place on the wall where so many people had rubbed their greasy locks. So this was what it felt like to get fired not once but twice in the same week. She was just beginning to feel really sorry for herself when she opened her eyes and saw Julian smiling down at her from an advertisement.

It was the same publicity headshot she'd seen a thousand times, framed by a photo of his album cover and the line "For the Lost," but she'd never seen it on the subway before, and she hadn't noticed how his eyes seemed to stare directly into hers. The irony that he was there with her, on that subway, despite never being *anywhere* with her, did not go unnoticed. Brooke walked to the opposite end of the car and took a seat where the only advertisements were for cosmetic dentistry and ESL classes. She sneaked a look back toward Julian and felt her stomach roil when, once again, he stared back at her. No matter which way she turned her body or angled her head, his eyes always found hers and, combined with his dimpled smile, made her more miserable. At the next sta-

tion, Brooke quickly switched cars, choosing one without her husband.

16
BOYFRIEND WITH A VILLA AND A SON

"Brooke, if you hear nothing else I say tonight, please hear this: I think this is worth fighting for." Julian reached across the couch and took her hand in his. "I am going to fight for our marriage."

"Strong opening move," Brooke said. "Well done."

"Come on, Rookie, I'm serious."

There was clearly nothing funny about the situation, but she was desperate to lighten the mood, even a little. In the ten minutes Julian had been home, they'd acted like complete strangers. Polite, wary, totally distant strangers.

"I'm serious too," she said quietly. And then, when he didn't say anything, she asked, "Why didn't you come home earlier? I know you had media obligations, but it's already Thursday. Was this just not important enough?"

Julian looked at her, surprised. "How

could you think that, Rook? I needed some time to think. Everything's happening so quickly, it feels like it's all unraveling. . . .'"

The teakettle began to sing. Brooke knew without asking that Julian wouldn't want the lemon ginger tea she was making for herself but would probably drink a cup of plain green if she prepared it for him. She felt a tiny bit of satisfaction when he accepted it gratefully and took a sip.

He twisted his hands around the mug. "Look, I can't even tell you how sorry I am. To think how you must have felt when you saw —"

"The pictures aren't the point!" she yelled, more sharply than she'd intended. She paused for a minute. "Yes, it was hideous and painful and embarrassing, there's no doubt. But it's *why* those pictures exist that I find way more upsetting."

When he didn't respond, she said, "What the hell happened that night?"

"Rook, I've told you: it was a stupid, one-time mistake, and I absolutely did not have sex with her. With *anyone,*" he rushed to add.

"So what *did* you do?"

"I don't know. . . . It started out as a big group over dinner, and then a few people left, and then a few more, and I guess by later on in the night, she and I were the only ones left at the table."

Just hearing Julian say "she and I" about someone else made Brooke feel queasy.

"I don't even know who she is, where's she from —"

"Don't you worry about that," Brooke said sarcastically. "The entire country is happy to help you out there. Janelle Moser, twenty-four, from a small town in Michigan. She was in L.A. for a friend's bachelorette party. How the hell they ended up at the Chateau is really the big mystery."

"I didn't —"

"And in case you were interested — although you could probably speak to this more authoritatively than *Last Night* — they are real."

Julian exhaled a long sigh. "I drank way too much and she offered to walk me back to my room." He stopped, ran his fingers through his hair.

"And then?"

"We made out, and she took her clothes off. Just stood up and stripped, like no pretenses or anything. It snapped me back to reality. I told her to get dressed. Which she did, but she started crying, saying she was so embarrassed. So I tried to calm her down, and we had something to drink from the minibar, I honestly can't remember what at this point, and the next thing I know, I woke up fully dressed and she was gone."

"She was gone? And you just passed out?"

"Gone. No note, no nothing. And until you told me, I couldn't remember her name."

"Do you know how hard that is to believe?"

"She got undressed — I never did. And, Brooke, I don't know how else to say it, or how else to convince you. I swear on your life and mine, and the lives of everyone we love, that that is *exactly* how it happened."

"Why did you do it? Why did you invite her in and kiss her?" she asked, unable to meet his eye. "Why her?"

"I don't know, Brooke. Like I said before, too much drinking, bad judgment, feeling lonely." He stopped, rubbed his temples. "It's been a rough year. Being so busy, me away so often, the two of us never getting any time together. It's no excuse, Brooke, and I know I fucked up — trust me, I know it — but please believe me when I tell you I've never regretted anything more than that night."

She tucked her hands under her thighs to keep them from shaking. "Where do we go from here, Julian? Not just this, but all of it. The never seeing each other? The fact that we are leading entirely separate lives? How do we work through *that?*"

He scooted closer to her on the couch and tried to wrap his arms around her, but Brooke stiffened. "I guess it's been hard for me, seeing how hard this has been on *you,* when I thought it was what we both wanted," he said.

"It might be what we both wanted. And I am genuinely, honestly happy for you. But it isn't *my* success. It isn't *my* life. It's not even *our* life. It is only *your* life."

He opened his mouth to talk, but she held up her hand.

"I had no idea what it was going to be like, couldn't envision any of this when you were in the studio every day recording your album. It was a one-in-a-trillion shot, no matter how talented and lucky you are, but it happened! It happened to *you!*"

"In my craziest, wildest fantasies or nightmares it never looked anything like this," he said.

She took another breath and forced herself to say what she'd been thinking for three days now. "I'm not sure I can do this."

A long silence followed her words.

"What are you saying?" Julian said after

what felt like an eternity. "Really, *what are you saying?*"

She started to cry. Not hysterical, gulping sobs but a slow, quiet weeping. "I don't know that I can live like this. I'm not sure how I fit in, or if I even want to. It was hard enough before, and now when something like this happens . . . and I know it will keep happening, again and again."

"You're the love of my life, Brooke. You're my best friend. There's no fitting in — you're the whole deal."

"No." She wiped her cheek with the back of her hand. "There's no going back."

He looked weary. "It won't always be like this."

"Of course it will, Julian! When's it going to stop? With the second album? The third? What about when they want you to start touring internationally? You'll be gone for months on end. What are we going to do then?"

With this, an expression of understanding registered on his face. He looked like he was going to cry now, too.

"It's just an impossible situation." She smiled a little and wiped away a tear. "People like you don't marry people like me."

"What does that mean?" he asked, a look

of total devastation on his face.

"You know what it means, Julian. You're a celebrity now. I'm an ordinary civilian."

They sat there and looked at each other for ten seconds, then thirty seconds, and then a minute. There was nothing more to say.

When she heard the knock at the front door at ten A.M. on Saturday morning a week and a half later, Brooke assumed it was the super finally coming to snake her clogged shower drain. She looked down at her faded, stained Cornell sweatpants and her hole-ridden T-shirt and decided that Mr. Finley would have to live with it. She even attempted a perfunctory smile as she opened the door.

"Good god," a horrified Nola exclaimed as she looked Brooke up and down. She sniffed in the general direction of the apartment and grimaced. "I think I'm going to throw up."

Nola, as usual, looked fantastic in high-heeled boots over dark skinny jeans, a tight cashmere turtleneck sweater, and one of those expensive down coats that somehow managed to make her look thin and stylish instead of someone who'd merely wrapped herself in a high-performance sleeping bag.

Her cheeks glowed from the cold outside and her wavy blond hair looked wind-tousled and sexy.

"Ugh, do you really have to show up here looking like that?" Brooke asked, returning the head-to-toe examination. "How'd you even get in, by the way?"

Nola pushed past her, shucked her coat, and took a seat on the living room couch. She made a face while she pushed away a days-old cereal bowl with her fingertips. "I still have my key from when I watched Walter. Christ, this is even worse than I imagined."

"Nola, please, I don't want to hear it." Brooke poured herself a glass of orange juice, downed it in one gulp, and didn't offer any to her friend. "Maybe you should go."

Nola snorted. "Trust me, I'd like that. But no can do. You and I are getting out of here today, and we're doing it together."

"Like hell. I'm not leaving." Brooke pulled her greasy hair into a ponytail and sat in the small armchair opposite the couch. The one she and Julian had bought at a vintage market on the Lower East Side because Julian said the cranberry-colored velvet reminded him of Brooke's hair.

"Oh yes you are. Look, I didn't realize

things were this bad. I've got to run by the office for a couple hours" — Nola looked at her watch — "but I'm coming back here at three and we're going for lunch." Brooke opened her mouth to protest, but Nola cut her off. "First, clean this dump. Second, clean yourself. You're starting to look straight out of central casting for the wretchedly depressed spurned lover."

"Thanks."

Nola picked up an empty Häagen-Dazs container by her nails and held it toward Brooke with a withering look. "Get ahold of yourself, okay? Handle all of this and I'll see you in a few hours. If you even think of disobeying me, you're not my friend anymore."

"Nola . . ." It came out as a whine, but a defeated one.

Nola had already walked back to the front door. "I'll be back. And I'm taking this key with me, so don't think you can run or hide." And with that, she was gone.

After learning of her enforced time off from Huntley and surviving that hideous conversation with Julian, Brooke had crawled into bed and barely gotten out. She did it all — the back issues of *Cosmo,* the pints of ice cream, the bottle of white wine per night, and the endless loop of seasons one through three of *Private Practice* on her laptop, and in a weird way she'd almost enjoyed it. Not since she'd gotten mono her first semester at Cornell and had to spend the entire five-week winter break in bed had she lounged and indulged so much. But Nola was right, it was time to get up and out, and besides, she was starting to grow disgusted with herself. It was time.

She resisted the urge to crawl back under the covers and pulled on her old fleece running tights and sneakers and went for a three-mile run along the Hudson. It was unseasonably warm for the second week of February, and all the gray slush from the previous week's storm had melted away. Feeling invigorated and proud of her motivation, she took a long, hot shower. Afterward, she rewarded herself with twenty minutes of luxuriating under her covers, allowing her hair to air-dry as she read a couple chapters of her book, and then fixed herself a healthy snack: a bowl of sliced fruit, a quarter cup of cottage cheese, and a toasted whole wheat English muffin. Only then did she begin to feel strong enough to tackle the apartment.

The massive cleaning took three hours and did more for Brooke's mental state than anything else she could have imagined. For the first time in months, she dusted, vacuumed, and scrubbed floors, countertops, and bathrooms. She refolded all the clothes in her dresser (but ignored Julian's), weeded out old and unworn clothes from their shared closet, organized both the hallway coat closet and the drawers of the living room desk, and finally, after what felt like years of procrastination, changed the printer cartridge, called Verizon about a mistake on their bill, and made a note to herself to schedule an annual ob/gyn exam for herself, dentist appointments for both of them (no matter how upset she was, she still didn't wish him cavities), and an appointment at the vet to get Walter Alter up to date on his shots.

Feeling like a goddess of efficiency and organization, she threw open the door when she heard a knock exactly at three and greeted Nola with a huge smile.

"Wow, you look human again. Is that lipstick?"

Brooke nodded, pleased with the reaction. She watched as Nola inspected her apartment.

"Impressive!" She whistled. "I have to say, I wasn't holding out a lot of hope for you, and I'm really glad I was wrong." She pulled a black peacoat from the hallway closet and handed it to Brooke. "Come on, we're going to show you what the outside world looks like."

Brooke followed her friend down to the street, into the back of a taxi, and, finally, into a banquette table at Cookshop, one of their favorite brunch places in West Chelsea. Nola ordered them each a coffee and a Bloody Mary and insisted Brooke take three sips of each before she'd let her say a word. "There," she said soothingly as Brooke obliged. "Doesn't that feel better?"

"Yeah," Brooke said, suddenly overcome with the urge to cry. She'd been crying intermittently for over a week now, and anything — or nothing — could set it off. Now it was the sight of a couple about her age sharing an order of French toast. They were mock-fighting over every piece, each pretending to spear a bite before the other could get a fork on it. Then they'd laugh and exchange that look. The one that said, *No one else in the world exists.* The one that Julian now gave to strangers in hotel rooms.

And there it was again. The mental picture of Julian and Janelle, wrapped in a naked embrace, kissing passionately. Gently sucking on that girl's lower lip, exactly the same way he would with —

"You okay?" Nola asked, reaching across

513

the table to put her hand over Brooke's.

She tried to suppress the tears, but she couldn't. Almost instantly, hot, fat droplets were coursing down her cheeks, and although she didn't sob or gasp for breath or shake, Brooke felt like she might never be able to stop. "I'm sorry," she said miserably, wiping them away as subtly as she could manage with her napkin.

Nola nudged Brooke's Bloody Mary closer. "Another sip. There you go. This is to be expected, sweetheart. Let it out."

"I'm sorry, it's so humiliating," Brooke whispered. She glanced around and was relieved that no one seemed to be looking at her.

"You're upset. It's only natural," Nola said, softer than Brooke could ever remember her speaking. "Have you talked to him recently?"

Brooke blew her nose as delicately as she could manage, immediately feeling guilty for doing so in the restaurant's cloth napkin. "We spoke the night before last. He was in Orlando, doing something for Disney World, I think, and he's getting ready to go to England for a week. A paid performance and some kind of huge music festival? I'm not sure."

Nola's mouth tightened.

"I'm the one who told him we needed time, Nol. I asked him to leave that night and said we needed some space to figure things out. He's only gone because I insisted," Brooke said, wondering why she was still defending Julian.

"So when will you see each other next? Is he deigning to come home after England?"

Brooke ignored the implication. "He's coming back to New York after England, yes, but he's not coming home. I told him he needed to stay somewhere else until we figure out what's going on with us."

The waiter came over to take their order and thankfully didn't pay them a moment's notice. When he left again, Nola said, "So what did you guys talk about? Did you make any progress?"

Brooke popped a sugar cube into her mouth and savored the feeling of it melting on her tongue. "Did we make any progress? No, I wouldn't say that. We had a fight about Trent's wedding."

"What about it?"

"He thinks we should cancel at the last minute out of respect for Trent and Fern. Thinks we'll 'overshadow' their big day with all of our drama. He just doesn't want to deal with seeing his entire family and every person he grew up with. Which I understand in theory, but it is something he needs to get over. It's his first cousin's wedding."

"So what's the outcome?"

Brooke sighed. "I know he called Trent and talked about it, but I don't know. My guess is he won't go."

"Well, at the very least it's good news for you. I'm sure it's the last thing on earth you want right now."

"Oh, I'm going. Alone, if I have to."

"Come on, Brooke. That's ridiculous. Why put yourself through that?"

"Because it's the right thing to do, and I just don't think you can cancel on your own family's wedding the week before for no good reason. Julian and I wouldn't even know each other today if it weren't for Trent, so I think I need to suck it up."

Nola stirred some milk into her refreshed coffee. "I don't know whether that's brave or admirable or just fucking stupid. All of the above, I suspect."

The urge to cry struck again — this time prompted by the idea of attending Trent's wedding alone — but she forced the thought from her mind. "Can we talk about something else? You, maybe? I could use some distraction."

"Hmm, let's see." Nola grinned. Clearly she'd been waiting for an opening.

"What?" Brooke asked. "Or should I ask 'who'?"

"I'm going to Turks and Caicos next week for a long weekend."

"Turks and Caicos? Since when? Don't tell me you're going for work. My god, I am so in the wrong industry."

"Not for work. For fun. For *sex*. I'm going with Andrew."

"Oh, he's *Andrew* now? How grown-up. Does that mean it's serious?"

"No, *Drew* and I are finished. Andrew is the cab guy."

"Stop it."

"What? I'm serious."

"You're dating the guy you screwed after meeting in the back of a cab?"

"What's so weird about that?"

"Nothing's so weird about it, it's just incredible! You're the only woman on the planet who could pull it off. Those guys don't call the next day. . . ."

Nola gave a sly smile. "I gave him good reason to call the next day. And the day after that. And the day after that, too."

"You like him, don't you? Oh my god, you *do*. You're blushing. I can't believe you're blushing over a boy. Be still, my heart."

"All right, all right, I like him. Big deal. I'm into it. For now. And I'm very into

Turks and Caicos."

They were interrupted again by the waiter, this time bearing their chopped Chinese chicken salads. Nola nose-dived at her food, but Brooke merely pushed hers around on the plate.

"Okay, so tell me how this came about. Were you lying in bed one night and he said, 'Let's go away together?' "

"Sort of. He actually owns a place there. A villa at the Aman. Takes his son there pretty regularly."

"Nola! You bitch! You didn't tell me any of this!"

Nola feigned innocence. "Any of what?"

"The fact that you have a boyfriend and he has a villa and a *son?*"

"I don't know that I'd call him my *boy-friend. . . .*"

"Nola!"

"Look, it's been fun. Very relaxed. I'm trying not to think about it too much, and you've had a lot going on lately. . . ."

"Start talking!"

"Okay, his name is Andrew, you know that part. He has brown hair and he's an excellent tennis player and his favorite food is guacamole."

"I'm giving you ten seconds."

Nola clapped her hands together and did

a little jump in her seat. "It's too much fun torturing you."

"Nine, eight, sev—"

"All right! He's about five-ten, maybe five-eleven on a good day, and he's got a six-pack, which I find more intimidating than attractive. I suspect that he has all his shirts and suits custom-made, but I don't have confirmation of that. He was on the golf team in college and spent a few years bumming around Mexico teaching golf before he founded an Internet company, took it public, and retired at age twenty-nine, although he still seems to do a lot of consulting, whatever that means. He lives in a town house on the Upper West Side, to be near his son, who is six and lives with his ex-wife. He has a flat in London and the villa in Turks and Caicos. And he is absolutely, positively inexhaustible in bed."

Brooke clutched her heart and pretended to collapse backward on the booth. "You're lying," she moaned.

"About which part?"

"About all of it."

"Nope," Nola said with a smile. "All true."

"I want to be happy for you, I really do, but I can't seem to overcome my own bitterness."

"Don't get carried away. He's still forty-one, divorced, and a father. It's not exactly the fairy tale. But I will say he's a pretty good guy."

"Please. Short of beating you or the kid, he can do no wrong. Have you told your mother yet? She might up and die on the spot."

"Are you kidding? I can hear it now. 'What did I tell you, Nola? It's just as easy to fall in love with a rich man as it is a poor one. . . .' Uch, knowing how happy it would make her takes the joy out of it for me."

"Well, for what it's worth, I think you'd make a great stepmother. You'd be a natural," Brooke mused aloud.

"I'm not even going to dignify that," Nola said, rolling her eyes.

It was getting dark by the time they finished, but when Nola went to hail a cab, Brooke gave her friend a hug and said, "I'm going to walk home."

"Really? It's gotten so gross out. You don't even want to jump on the subway?"

"Nah, I feel like walking." She took Nola's hand. "Thanks for making me do this, Nol. I needed a kick in the ass, and I'm glad you're the one who delivered it. I promise I'm going to rejoin the land of the living. And I'm so excited for you and your taxi lover."

Nola kissed her on the cheek and hopped into the backseat. "Call you later!" she said as the cab pulled away, and once again, Brooke was alone.

She walked up Tenth Avenue, pausing to watch the dogs play in the small dog run on Twenty-third Street, and then cut over to Ninth, where she backtracked a couple blocks to treat herself to a Billy's red velvet cupcake and another cup of coffee before continuing back uptown. It had started to rain and by the time she got home, her peacoat was soaked and her boots were covered in the city's special salty-dirty-slushy mix, so she stripped in the hallway and immediately wrapped herself in the purple cashmere blanket her mother had knitted years earlier. Six o'clock on a Sunday night, she had nothing to do for the rest of the evening and, weirder still, nowhere to go the next morning. Alone. Jobless. Free.

With Walter curled into a ball and pressed against her thigh, Brooke pulled out her computer and scanned her e-mail. Nothing interesting except for an e-mail from someone named Amber Bailey, which sounded familiar. She clicked on it and began to read.

Dear Brooke,
Hi there! I think my friend Heather

gave you the heads-up that I was going to get in touch, or at least I hope she did! I know this is super last-minute (and probably feels like the very last thing on earth you want to do right now), but a bunch of friends are getting together for dinner tomorrow night. I'll explain more if you're interested, but basically they're an amazing group of women I've met, and they've all had . . . oh, let's say "experience" with dating or being married to very famous men. Nothing formal, we just get together once every couple months and drink a lot! I hope you'll join me? We're meeting at 8 p.m. at 128 West 12th Street. Please come! It really is fun.

xoxo, Amber Bailey

Aside from the overly enthusiastic use of exclamation points, Brooke thought the e-mail seemed perfectly nice. She read it once more and then, without thinking or allowing herself to list the thousand and one reasons she shouldn't go, she hit Reply and typed:

Dear Amber,
Thanks for the invite. Sounds like just what the doctor ordered. I'll see you

there tomorrow.

Best, Brooke

"Might be a disaster, Walter, but I sure don't have anything better to do," she said, snapping the laptop closed and pulling the spaniel onto her lap. He stared at her and panted, his long, pink tongue hanging out the side of this mouth.

Without warning, he leaned in and licked her nose.

"Thanks, buddy," she said, kissing him back. "I love you, too."

17

GOOD OLD ED HAD
A THING FOR
PROSTITUTES

When Brooke woke up the next morning and saw it was nine thirty, her heart started racing and she jumped out of bed. And then she remembered: she wasn't late for anything. She had, at that moment, exactly zero places to be, and while this wasn't the ideal scenario — or a sustainable one — she was determined not to think of it as the end of the universe. Besides, she had a plan for the day, which was the first step toward establishing a routine (routines being very important, according to a recent *Glamour* article on being unemployed).

Number one on the *Glamour* to-do list was Get Your Most Dreaded Tasks Done First, and so before she even changed out of her robe, Brooke willed herself to pick up the phone and dial Margaret. She knew her ex-boss would've just wrapped up the Monday morning staff meeting and would be back in her office working on the next week's schedule. Sure enough, she picked up on the first ring.

"Margaret? How are you? It's Brooke Alter." The pounding in her chest made it hard to speak.

"Brooke! Good to hear from you! How is everything?"

It was clearly not a weighted question — Margaret was just making small talk — but Brooke panicked for a second. Did she mean how was everything with Julian? With the Chateau girl situation? With all the media conjecture about their marriage? Or was she just being polite and using a basic figure of speech?

"Oh, everything's great. You know," she said, immediately feeling ridiculous. "How are you?"

"Well, we're managing. I've been interviewing to fill your spot, and I have to say it again, Brooke, I'm sorry about what happened."

Brooke felt a glimmer of hope. Was she saying that so Brooke would ask for her job back? Because Brooke would beg for it back, do anything, anything at all to prove herself to Margaret. But no, she had to be sensible: if they were willing to hire her back right now, she wouldn't have fired her in the first place. *Just act normal. Say what you called to say and hang up the phone.*

"Margaret, I know I'm hardly in any place to ask you a favor, but . . . I was wondering if you would keep me in mind for any opportunities that come across your radar? Not at NYU, of course, but should you hear of anything else . . ."

There was a brief pause. "All right, Brooke. I'll certainly keep my eyes open for you."

"I would appreciate it so much! I'm very eager to resume working, and I promise you — and would promise any future employer — that my husband's career will *not* be a problem anymore."

Although she might have been curious, Margaret didn't ask any follow-up questions. They made small talk for another minute or two before hanging up, and Brooke breathed a huge sigh of relief. Dreaded Item Number One: complete.

Dreaded Item Number Two — a call to Julian's mother to discuss the travel details of Trent's wedding next weekend — wasn't going to be quite as easy. Her mother-in-law had taken to calling Brooke nearly every day since the Grammys to offer long and unsolicited monologues on how to be a supportive and forgiving wife. They usually included examples of Julian's father's tres-

526

passes (ranging in seriousness from flirting with his entire reception and nursing staff to leaving her alone many weekends a year to go on golfing trips with his buddies and do "god knows what" else), and they always highlighted Elizabeth Alter's abundance of patience and understanding of the male species. The clichés along the lines of "boys will be boys" and "behind every successful man there is a woman" were starting to feel not just repetitive but downright oppressive. On the bright side, Brooke wouldn't have guessed in a million years that Julian's mother cared one way or another if they stayed married, got divorced, or both simply vanished altogether. Thankfully, she got her mother-in-law's voice mail and was able to leave a message asking her to e-mail their travel plans since Brooke wouldn't be available to talk the rest of the day.

She was about to cross the next item off her list when her phone rang.

"Neha! Hi, sweetheart! How are you?"

"Brooke? Hi! I've got some great news: Rohan and I are definitely moving back to New York. By this summer!"

"No way. That is such great news! Did Rohan get an offer from a New York firm?" Brooke's mind had already begun cycling through all the exciting possibilities: what they'd name the company, how they'd recruit their first clients, all the different ideas she'd had for getting the word out. And now, it was one step closer to happening.

"Actually, *I'm* the one who got the offer. It's so crazy, but a friend of mine just signed on to cover for a staff nutritionist who's on a yearlong maternity leave. Well, my friend can't work right now since she's taking care of her sick mother, so she asked me if I'd be interested. Guess who it's for?"

Brooke cycled through a list of celebrities, just certain Neha was going to say Gwyneth or Heidi or Giselle, already in mourning for the business that wasn't going to be. "I don't know. Who?"

"The New York Jets! Can you believe it? I'm going to be the team nutritional adviser for the 2010 to 2011 season. I have less than zero knowledge about the nutritional needs of three-hundred-pound linebackers, but I guess I'll have to learn."

"Oh, Neha, that's incredible! What an amazing opportunity," she said, and meant it. Brooke had to admit that if something like that came up, she'd ditch everything else in a heartbeat.

"Yeah, I'm pretty excited. And you should see Rohan. The second I told him, he was like, 'Tickets!' He's already got the whole schedule printed and hanging on our fridge."

Brooke laughed. "I'm envisioning little five-foot-three you walking through the locker room with a clipboard and a bull-horn, batting Big Macs and tubs of KFC out of their mammoth hands."

"I know, right? Like, 'Excuse me, Mr.-NFL-All-Star-I-make-eighty-trillion-dollars-a-year, but I'm going to have to ask you to cut back on the high-fructose corn syrup.' It's going to be awesome!"

When Brooke hung up the phone a few minutes later, she couldn't help but feel that everyone's career was on track except her own. They weren't going to be starting a company together after all. Her phone rang again immediately. Certain it was Neha calling back to give her one more detail, Brooke picked up the call and said, "What, exactly, is your plan for when one of them hits on you?"

She heard the sound of a throat clearing and then a male voice asked, "Is this Brooke Alter?"

For just a moment — and for no good reason whatsoever — she was convinced it was someone calling to say Julian had been in a terrible accident, or was sick, or . . .

"Brooke, this is Art Mitchell calling from *Last Night* magazine. I was wondering if you had any comment about the piece in 'Page Six' this morning?"

She wanted to scream, but thankfully she was able to calm herself enough to close the phone and power it off. Her hands were shaking when she set it down on the coffee table. No one but her immediate family and closest friends had her new private number. How had this happened?

There wasn't any time to think about it, though, since she'd already grabbed her laptop and pounded in the web address for "Page Six." And there it was, at the very top of the page, taking up almost her entire computer screen. Two pictures: one of her crying the day before at Cookshop with Nola, clearly wiping tears away with her napkin, and the other of Julian, stepping out of a limo somewhere — judging from the old-fashioned taxi in the background, probably London — leaving an extremely attractive young woman behind in the backseat. The caption under her photo read, "Brooke Alter mourns the end of her marriage over a girls' brunch yesterday," and there was a circle drawn around her tearwiping hand, presumably indicating the absence of a wedding band. It continued:

" 'They are definitely over,' a source very close to Mrs. Alter says. 'She's even going alone to a family wedding next weekend.' " The caption accompanying Julian's photo was no less charming. "Scandal can't slow him down! Alter takes the party to London after his wife throws him out of their Manhattan apartment."

There was no stopping the vicious anger-and-nausea combo that felt so familiar now, but Brooke tried to take deep breaths and think through it. She suspected there was a perfectly logical explanation for that girl — delusional or not, she was absolutely positive that Julian would never be that disrespectful, or just plain *stupid* — but the rest of it was enraging. She looked at the photo of herself again and realized from the angle and graininess that it was probably taken by a fellow patron using a cell phone. Disgusted, she pummeled the couch with her fist so hard that Walter yelped and jumped down.

The landline rang and the caller ID showed that it was Samara.

"Samara, I can't take this anymore!" she said in lieu of hello. "Aren't you supposed to be managing his publicity? Can't you do something about pieces like these?" Brooke had never before shown even an inkling of

531

rudeness to the girl, but she couldn't keep quiet for another second.

"Brooke, I understand why you're upset. I was actually hoping to reach you before you saw the piece, but —"

"Before I saw it?" she screeched. "Some scumbag already called my cell phone asking for my comment on it. How do they have this number?"

"Look, there are two things I need to tell you. One, that girl in the back of Julian's limo was his hair and makeup person. His flight from Edinburgh was delayed and there wasn't time to get him ready before his performance, so she worked on him in the car. A gross misrepresentation."

"Okay," Brooke said. She was surprised by how much relief she felt considering her certainty that there was a logical explanation.

"Second, there is not much I can do when your people are talking to the press. I can only control so much, and it certainly doesn't extend to chatty friends and family."

Brooke felt like she'd been slapped. "What are you saying?"

"That someone is obviously giving out your unlisted number, and knows about the wedding this weekend, and is going on the record discussing your life. Because I can assure you, it's not coming from *our* end."

"But that's impossible. I know for a fact that —"

"Brooke, I don't mean to be rude, but I've got another call coming in and I need to run. Talk to your people, okay?" And with that, Samara hung up.

Too keyed up to concentrate on anything — not to mention feeling guilty from not having done it sooner — Brooke leashed Walter, dug her Uggs and some gloves from the hallway closet, and hit the pavement almost running. She didn't know if it was the pom-pom hat or the massively puffy coat, but neither of the two paparazzi she spied on the corner so much as glanced in her direction, and she felt a surge of pride for this small victory. They cruised over to Eleventh Avenue and then uptown, moving as quickly as they could through the week-day crowds. She paused only to let Walter drink from a water bowl outside a grooming shop, and he was panting by the time they hit Sixty-fifth Street. Brooke, however, was only just getting started.

In the span of twenty minutes, she managed to leave semi-hysterical messages for her mother, father, Cynthia, Randy, and Nola (Nola was the only one who answered;

her response: "Good god, Brooke, if I were really going to tattle about your life to the press, I'd have far juicier stories to share than freaking Trent and Intern Fern's wedding. Come on now!"), and was getting ready to dial Michelle's cell phone.

"Oh, hey, Michelle," she said after the beep. "I'm, uh, not sure where you are, but I just wanted to touch base about a piece in 'Page Six' this morning. I know you and I have talked about this *multiple* times, but I'm really concerned that you may have, um, accidentally answered some reporter's questions, or maybe told your friends something that found its way to the wrong person? I don't know, but I'm asking you — actually, I'm begging you — to please just hang up if someone calls to ask any questions about Julian or me, and to not discuss our private lives with anyone, okay?" She paused for a moment, wondering first if she'd been firm enough and then if she'd been too firm, decided she'd probably gotten her point across, and hung up.

She dragged Walter home and spent the rest of the day finalizing her already worked and reworked résumé, hopeful that she'd soon be ready to start sending it out. It was disappointing that Neha was out of a potential partnership, but she wasn't going to let it derail her plans: another six months to a year of clinical experience, and then hopefully a chance at opening her own practice.

Around six thirty, Brooke considered picking up the phone to cancel on Amber that night — the idea of meeting an entirely new group of women suddenly seemed like a very bad call — but when she realized she didn't even have her number, she forced herself to shower and put on her jeans, boots, and blazer uniform. *Worst case scenario, everyone will be hateful and horrible and I'll make up an excuse and leave,* she thought as the cab made its way from Times Square to the central Village. *At the very least I'll be leaving my apartment at night, something that hasn't happened for quite some time.* She thought she'd calmed herself, but Brooke felt a rush of nerves when she stepped out of the cab on Twelfth Street and saw a reasonably pretty girl with a pixie-ish blond bob smoking a cigarette on the stoop.

"Brooke?" the girl asked, exhaling a plume of smoke that seemed to hang in the cold, damp air.

"Hi. Are you Amber?" She gingerly stepped over some accumulated curb slush. Amber was standing two full steps above her, but Brooke was still an inch or two taller. She was surprised to see flame-red tights peeking out from under Amber's coat, topped by a fabulous pair of sky-high heels. That, combined with the cigarette, was not what she was expecting from Heather's description of her naive, sweet, churchgoing friend.

Amber must have caught her looking. "Oh, these?" she asked, although Brooke hadn't said a word. "Giuseppe Zanotti. I call them my man-stompers." Her Southern accent was sweet, almost syrupy in its slowness, completely at odds with her appearance.

Brooke smiled. "Let me know if you're renting those out."

Amber motioned for her to follow her up the stairs. "You're going to love everyone," she said, pulling open the door to a small foyer with a mini Persian carpet and two mail slots. "It's a great group of women. Added benefit being that whenever you think you have it bad, guaranteed someone here has had it *so* much worse."

"Gee, that's great, I guess?" Brooke said, stepping onto a small elevator after Amber. "Although after that piece on 'Page Six' this morning, I'm not so sure. . . ."

"Oh, that silly little bit with those amateur photos? Puh-lease! Wait until you meet Isabel. The poor girl's had her cellulite circled in a full-page bikini shot. Now, *that* sucks."

Brooke cracked a smile. "Yeah, that definitely does suck. So, you, uh, saw the 'Page Six' piece?"

The elevator opened into a plushly carpeted hallway softly lit with tinted glass sconces, and they both stepped out. "Oh, sweetheart, everyone read it. We all agree that it was nothing, a blip. The crying shot of you with your friend will be a total sympathy evoker — women everywhere can relate to that — and that ridiculous suggestion that your husband was getting it on in the back of a limo on his way to a very public performance? Come on. Everyone knows that must have been his publicist or hair and makeup girl. I wouldn't worry about it for a second."

With that, Amber swung open the apartment door to reveal one massive open room that looked a whole lot like a . . . basketball court? There was what appeared to be a regulation-size basket at the far end, complete with a shiny hardwood floor, sidelines, and a free throw line. The wall nearest them looked painted for racquetball, or maybe squash, and a giant bin of various balls and rackets took up the street-facing side between two floor-to-ceiling windows. A sixty-inch flat-screen hung on the only remaining wall, and parked directly in front of it was a long green couch with two brown-haired, mesh-shorted teenage boys. They were eating pizza and playing a football video game Brooke should've been able to identify, and each looked more bored than the other.

"Come on," Amber said, traversing the basketball court. "Everyone else is already upstairs."

"Whose apartment is this again?"

"Oh, you know Diana Wolfe? Her husband, Ed, was a congressman — I can't remember what district, but Manhattan somewhere — and he also headed up the Ethics Committee, of course."

Brooke climbed the open staircase behind Amber. "Okay," she murmured, although she knew exactly where this was going. You'd have needed to live in a cave for six weeks last summer to *not* know where this was going.

Amber stopped, turned toward Brooke, and lowered her voice to a whisper. "Yeah, well, you remember good old Ed had a thing for prostitutes? Not even high-end escorts, mind you, but full-on street-walking hookers. Double whammy because Diana was running for city attorney general. Not pretty."

"Welcome!" A woman in her early forties trilled from the top of the stairs. She wore an impeccably tailored mauve skirt suit, a truly gorgeous pair of black snakeskin heels, and the most elegant strand of chunky pearls Brooke had ever seen.

Amber reached the top of the stairs. "Brooke Alter, this is Diana Wolfe, the owner of this lovely home. Diana, this is Brooke Alter."

"Th-thank you so much for having me," Brooke stuttered, instantly intimidated by this older, extremely put-together woman.

Diana waved her off. "Please, it's nothing so formal. Come in, help yourself to some nibbles. As Amber surely filled you in, my husband has — had — or rather, I don't know whether he *had* or currently *has* since he's no longer my husband, but old habits die hard, so — my husband *has* a penchant for prostitutes."

Clearly Brooke was unable to disguise the shock, because Diana laughed. "Oh, darling, I'm not telling you anything the entire country doesn't already know." She leaned over and touched Brooke's hair. "Actually, I'm not sure if everyone knew how much he loved redheads. Lord, I had no idea myself until I saw the undercover FBI videotapes. After the first twenty-five or so girls, you can really start to detect some patterns, and Ed definitely had a type."

Diana laughed at her own joke and said, "Kenya's in the living room. Isabel can't make it because her babysitter canceled. Go say hello, I'll be in in a minute."

Amber led the way into the all-white living room and Brooke immediately recognized the statuesque African-American woman in stunning leather pants and a sumptuous fur vest as Kenya Dean, ex-wife of gorgeous leading man and lover of all underage girls Quincy Dean. Kenya immediately stood up and hugged Brooke.

"It's so nice to meet you! Come, sit down," she said, pulling Brooke next to her on the white leather sectional.

Brooke was about to say thank you when Amber poured Brooke a glass of wine and handed it to her. She took a long, grateful drink.

Diana walked into the room carrying a large platter of fresh seafood on ice: shrimp cocktails, all different size oysters, crab claws, lobster tails, and scallops, accompanied by little dishes of butter and cocktail sauce. She set it down in the middle of the coffee table and said, "No putting Brooke on the hot seat! Now, why don't we go around the room and tell her a little bit about our experiences, so she can feel at home, okay? Amber, why don't you start?"

Amber nibbled a large shrimp. "Everyone knows my story already. I married my high school sweetheart — who, by the way, was a huge dork back then — and the year after we got married, he won *Idol.* Let's just say Tommy didn't waste any time enjoying his newfound fame, and by the time he finished the Hollywood round, he'd slept with more girls than Simon has V-necks. That was really just a warm-up, though, because if I had to guess, I'd put his current numbers well into the triple digits."

"I'm so sorry," Brooke murmured, not really knowing what else to say.

"Oh, don't be," Amber said, reaching for another shrimp. "It took a while to realize, but I am so clearly better off without him."

Diana and Kenya nodded.

Kenya refreshed her own wineglass and took a sip. "Yeah, I'd have to agree, although I don't think I would've when I was still as early on as you," she said, looking pointedly at Brooke.

"What do you mean?" Brooke asked.

"Well, just that after the first girl, I didn't believe it would happen again — or even that he'd done anything wrong. I thought maybe he was being framed by some fame chaser. But then, as the accusations kept rolling in and then the arrests, and the girls were getting younger by the second, sixteen, fifteen years old . . . let's just say it's harder to deny."

"Be honest, Kenya. You were like me — you didn't believe anything was wrong after Quincy was arrested for the first time," Diana said helpfully.

"It's true. I bailed him out. But when *48 Hours* showed hidden-camera footage of my husband literally trolling a high school girls' soccer game, trying to chat them up, I started to accept it."

"Wow," Brooke said.

"It wasn't great. But at least most of the media horror show was focused on what a total and complete scumbag *he* was. Isabel Prince — she's not here tonight — didn't have it so easy."

Brooke knew she was referring to the sex tape that Isabel's husband, world-famous rapper Major K, deliberately released to the public. Julian had seen it and described it to Brooke. Apparently it featured Isabel and Major K in a rooftop hot tub, naked, drunk, kinky, and uninhibited . . . caught on Major K's professional-grade HD camera and soon thereafter sent by the Major himself to every media outlet in the continental United

States. Brooke remembered reading interviews asking him why he'd betrayed his wife's confidence and he'd answered, "She's fucking hot, man, and I think everyone deserves to experience one time what I get to experience every night."

"Yeah, she really got killed," Amber said. "I remember they were circling her fat in still shots from the sex tape. All the late-show hosts were joking about it for weeks. It must have been horrible for her."

There was a moment of silence as everyone thought about this, and Brooke realized she was starting to feel suffocated, trapped. The airy white apartment now seemed more like a cage, and these nice women — so welcoming and friendly just a few minutes earlier — were making her feel even more alone and misunderstood. She was sorry for their troubles, and they seemed nice enough, but she wasn't anything like them. Julian's biggest crime was a drunken make-out with a plain girl his own age — hardly the stuff of sex tapes, sex addiction, statutory rape, or prostitutes.

Something in her expression must have given away her thoughts, because Diana made a *tsk-tsk* sound and said, "You're thinking how different your situation is from ours, aren't you? I know it's difficult, dear.

Your husband had a little hotel room tryst or two, and what man hasn't had that, right? But please, don't fool yourself. That may be how it begins" — she paused and waved her hand in a semicircle around the couch — "but this is how it ends."

That was it. She'd had enough. "No, it's not that, it's just that . . . um, look, I so appreciate your hospitality and your inviting me here tonight, but I think I have to go now," she said, her voice catching in her throat as she gathered her purse and avoided eye contact with everyone. Brooke knew she was being rude, but she couldn't stop herself; she needed to get out of there *right then.*

"Brooke, I hope I didn't offend you," Diana said in a conciliatory tone, although Brooke could see she was annoyed.

"No, no, not at all. I'm sorry, I'm just not . . ." Her voice trailed off. Rather than think of something to fill the silence, she stood and turned to face everyone.

"We didn't even give you a chance to tell us your story!" Amber said, looking distraught. "I told you we talk too much."

"I'm so sorry. Please don't think it was anything anyone said. I'm just, uh, I guess I'm just not ready for this yet. Thank you all again. Amber, thank you. And I'm sorry," she was mumbling now, clutching her coat and purse, and had reached the top of the staircase, where she could see one of the teenage boys making his way upstairs. She had the crazy thought that he was going to try to detain her. Pushing past him harder than necessary, she heard him say, "Uncool," and then, a moment later, "Hey, Mom, is there any more Coke? Dylan drank it all." It was the last thing she heard as she crossed the basketball court and took the building stairs instead of the elevator and then she was outside, the freezing cold air whipping against her skin, and she could breathe once again.

An available cab passed her, and then another, and although it must've only been in the midtwenties, she ignored them all and began walking, almost running, toward her apartment. Her mind raced, going over every story she'd heard that night and discarding it, ignoring it, finding the holes or the details that didn't fit her narrative with Julian. It was ridiculous to think that she and Julian would end up that way, just because of a single lapse, a lone mistake. They loved each other. Just because things were difficult didn't mean they were doomed. Did it?

Brooke crossed Sixth Avenue, and then

Seventh, and then Eighth. Her cheeks and fingers were starting to go numb, but she didn't care. She was out of that place and away from all those hideous stories, away from those predictions about her marriage that held no weight. Those women didn't know her or Julian. She managed to calm herself, slowed her pace, took a deep breath, and told herself that everything was going to be fine.

If only she could get rid of that small, stubborn thought in the very back of her mind: *What if they're right?*

18

WE HIT CRAZY AT CHECK-IN

The phone beside the bed rang and Brooke wondered for the thousandth time why hotels didn't provide caller ID. But since anyone else would call on her cell, she leaned over, plucked the handset from its cradle, and braced herself for the onslaught.

"Hello, Brooke. Have you heard from Julian?" Dr. Alter's voice sailed through the phone as if he were in the next room, which, despite Brooke's best efforts, was exactly where he was.

She forced herself to smile into the phone so she wouldn't say anything truly nasty. "Oh, hi there!" she said brightly. Someone who actually knew her would have instantly recognized it as her fake friendly/professional tone. As she had been doing for the last five years, she avoided calling Julian's father anything. "Dr. Alter" was too formal for a father-in-law, "William" somehow felt too familiar, and he certainly hadn't ever invited her to call him "Dad."

"I did," Brooke said evenly for the hundredth time. "He's *still* in London, and he'll probably be there until early next week." They were aware of this information. She'd told them the moment they'd descended on her at the reception desk. They in turn told Brooke that although the hotel had tried to place them on the opposite side of the two-hundred-room hotel (Brooke's request) they had insisted on being in adjoining rooms "for convenience's sake."

It was her father-in-law's turn to *tsk* with disapproval. "I can't believe he's missing the wedding! Those two were born less than six months apart. They've grown up together. Trent gave the most touching speech at your wedding, and now Julian's not even going to be at his."

She had to smile at the irony of it. She'd given Julian such a hard time about missing the wedding, saying many of the same things to him that his father had just said to her, but the moment Dr. Alter uttered them, she felt compelled to leap to Julian's defense.

"It's a pretty big deal, actually. He's going to be performing in front of some incredible people, including the prime minister of England." She left out the part about Julian getting paid two hundred thousand dollars for a four-hour event. "He didn't want to steal attention from the bride and groom in light of, uh, well, everything that's been happening."

That was as close as either of them had come to acknowledging the current situation. Julian's father seemed content to pretend everything was fine, that he hadn't seen the infamous pictures, or read the articles detailing the apparent crumbling of his son's marriage. And now, despite having been informed a dozen times that Julian was not coming to Trent's wedding, he refused to believe it.

She heard her mother-in-law call out from the background. "William! What are you doing on the phone with her when she's right next door?"

Within moments there was a knock.

She heaved herself off the bed and pumped both middle fingers at the door while silently screaming, "Fuck you!" then carefully arranged her face in a smile, unlatched the chain, and said, "Why, hello there, neighbor!"

For the very first time since she'd met her mother-in-law, the woman looked uncomfortable, perhaps even ridiculous. Her fitted, cashmere sweater dress was a beautiful, rich shade of eggplant and looked like it had been custom-made for her trim figure. She'd paired it with the perfect shade of purplish stockings and a dynamite pair of high-heeled booties that, despite their edginess, did not make it seem like she was trying too hard. Her chunky gold necklace was cool but understated and her makeup appeared professionally done. All in all, she was the picture of urbane sophistication, a model for how women might aspire to look at fifty-five. The hat was the problem. Its brim was the circumference of a serving tray; while its color matched the dress exactly, it was hard to notice anything but the sprouting feathers, the sprays of fake flowers, and the crinoline pretending to be baby's breath, all held together by a massive silk bow. It perched precariously on her head, the brim dipping down to artfully obscure her left eye.

Brooke's mouth fell open.

"What do you think?" Elizabeth asked, touching the brim. "Isn't it fabulous?"

"Wow," she breathed, uncertain how to proceed. "What's it, uh, for?"

"What do you mean, what's it for? It's for Tennessee!" She laughed before switching to her best mocking approximation of a Southern accent, one that sounded like a weird combination of someone who spoke English as a second language and a cowboy from an old Western. "We are in Chay-duh-noogah, Bruck! Y'all must re-a-lize that re-ahl Southern ladies wear hats like this."

She wanted to curl up under the covers and die. This was humiliating beyond belief.

"They do?" she squeaked. It was all she could manage.

Thankfully, Elizabeth reverted back to her normal, slightly nasal New York pronunciation. "Of course they do. Haven't you ever seen the Kentucky Derby?"

"Well, yeah, but we're not in Kentucky. And isn't that, like, a special situation to wear the hats? I'm not sure it translates to other, uh, social occasions. . . ." She allowed her voice to drift off to soften her words, but her mother-in-law barely noticed.

"Oh, Brooke, you have no idea what you're talking about. We're in the South now, sweetheart! The one I brought for the actual wedding is even better. We'll have plenty of time tomorrow to go buy you one, so don't worry about a thing." She paused and, still standing in the doorway, looked Brooke up and down. "You're not dressed yet?"

Brooke glanced first at her sweats and then at her watch. "I thought we weren't leaving until six."

"Yes, but it's already five. You hardly left yourself enough time."

"Wow, right you are!" she exclaimed in a faux-surprised voice. "Let me run. I'm going to jump in the shower."

"Okay, knock when you're ready. Better yet, come on over and have a cocktail. William sent out for some decent vodka, so you won't have to drink that dreadful hotel sludge."

"Why don't we just meet in the lobby at six? As you can see" — Brooke stepped back and motioned to her ripped T-shirt and messy hair — "I have a lot of work to do."

"Mmm," her mother-in-law said, clearly agreeing. "All right then. See you at six. And, Brooke? Maybe consider a little eye makeup? It does a face wonders."

The hot shower and the episode of *Millionaire Matchmaker* that she had playing in the background didn't help her feel much better, though the single-serving bottle of white wine in the minibar helped a bit. It didn't last for long, though. By the time she'd put on her standby black wrap dress, slapped on some eye shadow like an obedient daughter-in-law, and headed to the lobby, she was back to being supremely stressed.

The drive to the restaurant was only a couple of miles, but it felt like an eternity. Dr. Alter complained bitterly the entire time: what kind of hotel doesn't have a valet, how could Hertz rent only American cars, who called dinner for six thirty in the evening, for chrissake, it was practically lunchtime? He even managed to complain that there wasn't enough traffic for a Friday night in Chattanooga — after all, what kind of respectable city had clear streets and plenty of available parking? Where on earth were other drivers so goddamn polite, what with everyone sitting at stop signs for ten minutes, frantically waving each other through? Nowhere *he* wanted to be, that was for sure. Real cities had congestion, dirt, crowds, snow, sirens, potholes, and other assorted miseries, he insisted in the most ridiculous rant Brooke had ever heard. By the time the three of them made their way inside, it felt like they'd been out all night.

To her enormous relief, Trent's parents were standing right by the door. Brooke wondered what they thought of her mother-in-law's absurd derby hat. Trent's father and Julian's father were brothers, extremely close despite a large age difference, and the four of them immediately retreated to the bar at the far end of the room. Brooke begged off by saying she was going to call Julian. She noted the relieved looks; women who called their husbands just to say hello didn't turn around and divorce them, right?

She scanned the room for Trent or Fern but didn't see them. Outside, it was in the fifties, which, compared to February in New York, was downright tropical, and she didn't even bother rebuttoning her coat. She was certain Julian wouldn't answer — it was midnight in the UK and he would've just finished his set — but she dialed anyway and was surprised when she heard his voice.

"Hi! I'm so glad you called," he said, sounding as shocked as she felt. There was no background noise. She could hear the excitement in his voice. "I was just thinking about you."

"You were?" she asked, hating the insecurity in her voice. They'd been talking once a day for the last two weeks, but each time it was Julian who initiated.

"It kills me to think of you at that wedding without me."

"Yeah, well, it's killing your parents, too."

"Are they driving you crazy?"

"Understatement of the century. We hit crazy at check-in. We are now on our way to self-annihilation."

"I'm sorry," he said quietly.

"Do you think you're doing the right thing, Julian? I haven't seen Trent or Fern yet, but I don't know what I'm going to say."

Julian cleared his throat. "Just tell them again that I didn't want to turn his special night into a media circus."

Brooke was quiet for a second. If she had to bet, she'd guess that Trent would rather risk a nosy reporter or two than have his cousin and lifelong friend miss his wedding, but she didn't say anything.

"So, uh, how'd it go tonight?"

"Oh my god, Rook, it was incredible. Just incredible. There's a town near the property, and it has this amazing medieval old city way up on a hill, overlooking the modern town below it. The only way to get up there was to take a little funicular to the top, like fifteen people at a time, and then when you step off, it's like a maze — all these huge stone walls with torches extending from the top, and little alcoves hiding shops and homes. There was an ancient amphitheater right in the middle with the most outrageous views of the expansive Scottish hillside, and I performed in the dark, with everything lit only by candles and torches. They served these hot, spiked lemon drinks, and there was something about the cold air and the hot drinks and the creepy lighting and the view . . . I'm not explaining it well, but it was awesome."

"Sounds amazing."

"It was! And then when it ended, they took everyone back to the hotel . . . resort? Country estate? I don't know what to call it, but this place is incredible, too. Picture an ancient farmhouse surrounded by hundreds of acres of rolling hills, but it's got all the flat-screens and heated floors in the bathrooms and the most insane infinity pool you've ever seen. The rooms are, like, two thousand a night and they each have a private fireplace with a separate little library, and they come with your own butler." He paused for a minute and then said, very sweetly, "It would be absolutely perfect if you were here."

It was nice to hear him so happy — really, it was — and so talkative. He was clearly taking the share approach; maybe he *did* have a crisis of conscience about their communications lately. But it was a little hard to stomach considering her own current circumstances: accompanied by her in-laws, rather than heads of state or international supermodels; strip malls instead of bucolic fields; a cookie-cutter hotel room at the local Sheraton with a decided lack of butlers.

And on top of it all, she was attending *his* cousin's wedding — alone. So while it was great to hear him enjoying himself so much, she would not be opposed to hearing fewer details about his current abundance of fabulousness.

"Look, I should run. The rehearsal dinner is about to start."

A couple about her age walked past her on their way to the restaurant's entrance, and they all exchanged smiles.

"Seriously, how are my parents?"

"I don't know, they seem fine."

"Are they behaving themselves?"

"They're trying, I guess. Your dad's all fired up about the rental car — don't ask — and your mother seems to think this is a costume party, but, yeah, they're fine."

"You're a hero, Brooke," he said quietly. "So above and beyond the call of duty. I'm sure Trent and Fern appreciate it."

"It's the right thing to do."

"But that doesn't mean a lot of people would've done it. I hope I did the right thing, too."

"It's not about us and what we're going through," she said quietly. "It's our responsibility to put on a happy face and celebrate their night. Which is what I'm going to try to do."

She was interrupted again by another couple walking past. Something about the way they looked at her indicated they recognized her. There would be assumptions when everyone saw she was there alone.

"Brooke? I'm sorry, I really am. But I miss you and I can't wait to see you. I really think that —"

"I've got to run," she said, aware that others were listening to her. "I'll talk to you later, okay?"

"Okay," he said, and she could hear that he was hurt. "Say hi to everyone for me, and try to have fun tonight. I miss and love you so much."

"Uh-huh. You too. Bye." She disconnected the call and was met with the all-too-familiar feeling of wanting to crumple to the floor and cry, and she may have done just that had Trent not walked outside. He was wearing what Brooke thought of as Boarding School Chic: white shirt, blue blazer, cranberry-colored tie, Gucci loafers, and — as a nod to the changing times — a daring pair of khakis (flat front instead of pleated). Even now, all these years later, she still flashed back to their date at the bland Italian restaurant and that intense, fluttery feeling she got when Trent took her to the bar where she spotted Julian.

"Hey, I heard a rumor you were here," he said, leaning in to kiss her cheek. "Was that Julian?" He nodded toward the phone.

"Yeah, he's in Scotland. I know he would rather be here," she said weakly.

Trent smiled. "Well then he would be. I tried to tell him a thousand times that this is a private residence and we would gladly hire security to keep away any paparazzi, but he kept insisting he didn't want to create a circus. Nothing I said could convince him. So . . ."

She took Trent's hand. "I really am sorry about all this," she said. "It's pretty hideous timing on our part."

"Come inside, let's get you a drink," Trent said.

She squeezed his forearm. "Let's get *you* a drink." She smiled. "This is *your* night. And I still haven't said hello to your lovely bride."

Brooke walked through the door Trent held open for her. The room was buzzing now, with people milling around with cocktails in hand, making the usual small talk. The only person she recognized aside from her in-laws and the bride and groom was Trent's younger brother, Trevor, a sophomore in college who was currently slumped in the corner, praying no one approached him, staring intently at his iPhone. With the exception of Trevor, it felt like the entire room stopped moving for a split second and looked up just as they entered; her presence — and Julian's absence — had been noted.

Unconsciously she squeezed Trent's hand. Trent squeezed hers back and Brooke said, "Go, go meet your public! Enjoy it — it goes by really fast."

The rest of the dinner was blessedly uneventful. Fern had been kind enough, without being asked, to move Brooke's seat away from the Alters and next to her. Brooke immediately saw her appeal: she told adorable stories and jokes, asked everyone questions about themselves, and had self-deprecation down to a science. Fern even managed to diffuse the awkwardness when one of Trent's med school friends drunkenly toasted Trent's past penchant for girls with fake boobs by laughing and pulling her dress away from her chest while glancing down and saying, "Well, he's certainly gotten over that!"

When the dinner was over and the Alters had come to fetch her for the ride back to the hotel, Fern linked her arm through Brooke's, batted her eyelashes at Julian's father, and turned on the Southern charm. "Oh, no you don't!" she drawled exaggeratedly, Brooke noticed with amusement. "This one is staying right here with us. We're sending all you old fogies back to your rooms, and we're going to stay and have a little party. We'll make sure she gets back safely."

The Alters smiled and air-kissed Fern and then Brooke. The moment they'd left the dining room, Brooke turned to Fern. "You saved my life. They would've made me get a drink with them back at the hotel. After that they would've walked straight into my room to ask another six thousand questions about Julian. There's a decent chance she would've commented about my weight, my marriage, or both. I can't thank you enough."

Fern waved her off. "Please. I couldn't let you leave with someone wearing a hat like that. What if people saw?" She laughed and Brooke was more charmed than ever. "Besides, I'm selfishly happy you can stay. My friends all love you."

She knew Fern only said it to make her feel good — after all, she'd barely had the chance to speak to anyone all night, although Trent and Fern's friends all did seem nice — but who really cared? It worked. She felt good. Good enough to do a tequila shot with Trent "in Julian's honor," and still good enough to down a couple

561

lemon drops with Fern and her sorority sisters (who, incidentally, could drink like no women she'd ever seen). She was still feeling good when the lights got turned off around midnight and someone figured out how to hook up an iPhone to the restaurant's stereo system, felt good all the way through another two hours more of drinking, dancing, and — were she to be completely honest — some fun, old-fashioned flirting with one of Trent's fellow residents. Completely innocent, of course, but she'd forgotten what it felt like to have an extremely cute guy focus on her the entire night, fetch her drinks, and try to make her laugh; that, too, felt good.

What didn't feel good, naturally, was the excruciating hangover the next morning. Despite not getting back to the room until almost three, she woke at seven and stared at the ceiling, knowing she would surely vomit and wondering how long she would have to suffer before it happened. A half hour later, she was on the floor of her bathroom, gasping for breath and praying the Alters wouldn't knock. Thankfully, she was able to crawl back under the covers and fall back asleep until nine.

Despite a crushing headache and a disgusting taste in her mouth, Brooke smiled when she opened her eyes and checked her phone. Julian had called and texted half a dozen times, continually asking where she was and why she wasn't picking up the phone — he was on his way to the airport for his flight home, he missed her and loved her and couldn't wait to see her back in New York. It was nice to have the tables turned, if only for a night. *She'd* finally been the one to drink too much, stay up too late, and party too long.

Brooke showered and headed to the lobby for some coffee, praying she wouldn't run into the Alters on their way out. They'd told her the night before that they were planning to spend the day with Trent's parents; the women had hair and makeup appointments scheduled and the men were playing squash. When Elizabeth invited Brooke to join them, she'd blatantly lied, saying she was thinking of heading over to Fern's house and having lunch with her and the bridesmaids. She'd just sat down with the paper and an extra-large latte when she heard her name. Standing next to her table was Isaac, the cute resident she'd been flirting with the night before.

"Brooke? Hey! How are you? I was hoping I'd see you!"

She couldn't help but feel flattered at this.

563

"Hey, Isaac. Good to see you."

"I don't know about you, but I'm feeling pretty banged up after last night."

She smiled. "Yeah, last night was tough. But I had a great time."

She was pretty sure this sounded as innocent as she'd intended it to — after all, the flirting was fun but she *was* married — so just in case, she blurted out, "My husband's going to be so upset he missed it."

A strange expression appeared on his face. Not surprise, but more like relief that she'd finally said something. Then she understood.

"So, your husband is Julian Alter, right?" he asked, taking the seat next to hers. "I'd heard everyone talking about it last night, but I wasn't sure if it was true."

"The one and only," Brooke said.

"That's the craziest thing ever! I can't even tell you, I've been following him since he used to play at Nick's on the Upper East Side. Then all of a sudden, he was everywhere! Couldn't open a magazine or turn on the TV and not see Julian Alter. Wow. You must be so excited."

"Thrilled," she said automatically, the realization dawning on her sickeningly. . . . She wondered how long she had to wait before she could get up without being overtly rude and figured a minimum of three more interminable minutes.

"So, I really hope you don't mind me asking. . . ."

Oh no! He was going to ask her about the pictures, she was certain of it. She'd had eighteen blissful hours where not a single person had mentioned them, and now Isaac was going to go ruin everything.

"Don't you want some coffee?" Brooke blurted out in a desperate attempt to distract him from the inevitable.

He looked confused for a moment and then shook his head no. He reached into the canvas messenger bag resting at his feet, pulled out a manila envelope, and said, "I was wondering if you wouldn't mind giving this to Julian for me? I mean, I can't even imagine how busy he is and everything — and let me say right off that I'm not nearly as talented as he is — but I've been dedicating what little free time I have to my music, and, well . . . I'd love to hear what he thinks." With that, he reached into the envelope, pulled out a CD encased in a sleeve, and held it out to Brooke.

She didn't know whether to laugh or cry.

"Um, sure, I'll — actually, why don't I give you his studio address? You can mail it to him yourself."

Isaac's face lit up. "Really? That's great. I just figured that with, uh, everything that's going on, I, well, I wasn't sure he was going to —"

"Yep. He's still there all the time, working on his next album. Listen, Isaac, I've got to run upstairs and make a call. See you tonight, okay?"

"Sure, sounds good. Oh, Brooke? One last thing. My girlfriend — she's not coming until tonight — actually has a blog. She covers, like, celebrity stuff and society parties, that kind of thing. Anyway, I know she'd *love* to interview you. She told me to ask you, in case you were looking for a fair and impartial place to tell your side of the story. Anyway, I just know she'd be thrilled to —"

If she didn't walk away that instant, Brooke was going to say something horrible. "Thanks, Isaac. Really sweet of her to think of me. I'm good for now, but thanks." And before he could utter another word, she bolted toward the elevator.

The maid was cleaning her room when she returned, but she couldn't risk going back down to the lobby. She smiled at the woman, who looked exhausted and in need of a break anyway, and told her to skip the rest. When the woman had gathered her supplies and left, Brooke collapsed back on the unmade bed and tried to psych herself up to get some work done. She didn't have to start getting ready for another six hours, and she was determined to spend the time researching job openings, posting her résumé, and writing a few generalized cover letters that could be personalized later.

She used the tuner on the clock radio to find a classical radio station, a small little rebellion against Julian, who had stocked her iTunes not just with his own music but also every other artist he thought she *should* be listening to, and she set up camp at the desk. The first hour she was supremely focused — no small feat considering the lingering headache — and managed to get her résumé posted on all the major job-seeking websites. The second hour she ordered a grilled chicken salad from room service and zoned out to an old episode of *Prison Break* on her laptop. Then she napped for thirty minutes. When her cell phone rang and showed "Out of Area" a little after three she almost ignored it, but thinking it might be Julian, she answered.

"Brooke? It's Margaret. Margaret Walters."

She was so stunned she almost dropped the phone. Her first reaction was fear — was she missing her shift again? — before logic returned and she remembered the worst had already happened. Regardless of why she was calling, Brooke could say with reasonable certainty that it wasn't to fire her.

"Margaret! How are you? Is everything okay?"

"Yes, everything's fine. Listen, Brooke, I'm sorry to bother you on a weekend, but I didn't want this to wait until next week."

"It's no bother at all! I'm actually sending out my résumé as we speak," she said with a smile into the phone.

"Well, that's good to hear, because I think I have somewhere for you to send it."

"Really?"

"I just got a phone call from a colleague of mine, Anita Moore. Actually, she's an ex-employee of mine, but from many years ago. She was on staff at Mt. Sinai for years, but she recently left and she's opening her own shop."

"Oh, that sounds interesting."

"I'll let her give you all the details, but it's my understanding that she received federal funding to open a kind of early intervention center in an at-risk neighborhood. She's looking to hire a speech therapist who specializes in children and an RD who has experience with prenatal, lactation, new-mother, and newborn nutrition. She'll be serving a community that doesn't have regular access to prenatal care, patients who don't know the first thing about nutrition, so there's no doubt a lot of it will be basic — literally, convincing-them-why-they-need-their-folic-acid type things — but I think in that way it'll be challenging and rewarding. She doesn't want to poach any of the current dietitians from Mt. Sinai, so she called to ask if I had any recommendations."

"And you recommended me?"

"I did. I'll be honest, Brooke. I told her all about Julian, the missed days, the hectic schedule, but I also told her you were one of the best and brightest I'd ever employed. This way everyone is going into it with eyes wide open."

"Margaret, it sounds like a wonderful opportunity. I can't thank you enough."

"Brooke? I only ask one thing. If you think your *hectic lifestyle* is going to continue in a way that will regularly impact your work, please be honest with Anita. What she's trying to do is too difficult without staff she can depend on."

Brooke nodded furiously. "I hear you, Margaret. Loud and clear. My husband's career will no longer be affecting my own. I can promise you and Anita that."

Barely able to keep from shrieking with joy into the phone, Brooke carefully copied Anita's contact information. Snapping open a fresh can of minibar Diet Coke, her headache magically cleared, she hit Compose on her e-mail and began typing. She was *going* to get that job.

19
PITY DANCE

Brooke smiled wanly at Dr. Alter as he held open the back door to the rental car and waved his arm gallantly. "After you, my dear," he said. Thankfully, he seemed to have gotten past his previous day's Hertz-directed rage and the ride was relatively rant-free.

Brooke was proud of herself for not commenting on Elizabeth's derby hat du jour, which today consisted of at least a pound of pinched taffeta and an entire bouquet of fake peonies. Paired with a sleek YSL evening gown, the most elegant Chanel bag, and gorgeous beaded Manolos. The woman was a lunatic.

"Have you heard from Julian?" her mother-in-law asked as they turned into the private drive.

"Not today. He left some messages last night, but I got in too late to call him back. My god, those med students know how to party, and they sure don't care if you're married or not."

Through the visor mirror that Elizabeth was peering into, Brooke could see the woman's eyebrows shoot up, and she felt a jolt of glee at her small victory. They rode in silence the rest of the way. When they came upon the imposing Gothic gate that surrounded Fern's home, Brooke could see her mother-in-law nod almost imperceptibly with approval, as if to say, "Why yes, if you *must* live outside Manhattan, this is precisely the correct way to do it." The drive from the gate to the house wove by mature cherry blossom trees and towering oaks and was long enough to warrant calling the property an estate rather than a home. Although it was February and chilly, everything looked lush and green — *healthy* somehow. A tuxedoed valet took their car and a lovely young woman escorted them inside; Brooke saw the girl sneak a glimpse at her mother-in-law's hat, but she was too polite to stare.

Brooke prayed the Alters would leave her alone, and the moment they spotted the bow-tied bartenders behind a massive mahogany bar, they didn't disappoint. Brooke flashed back to her single days. It was strange how quickly you forgot the way it felt to be solo at a wedding or a party where everyone else was paired up. Was this the new normal?

She felt her phone vibrate in her purse and, grabbing a glass of champagne off a passing tray as reinforcement, ducked into a nearby powder room.

It was Nola. "How's it going?" Her friend's voice felt like a warm, cozy blanket in this icy, intimidating mansion.

"I'm not going to lie, it's pretty rough."

"Well, I could've told you that. I still don't understand why you'd subject yourself to that. . . ."

"I don't know what I was thinking. My god, I haven't been single at a wedding in six, seven years. This just sucks."

Nola snorted. "Thanks, friend. Yes, indeed it does. You didn't have to go there to discover that on your own — I definitely could have told you."

"Nola? What am I doing? Not just down here, but in general?" Brooke could hear her voice high-pitched and a little panicky, and she noticed the phone beginning to slip in her sweaty hand.

"What do you mean, sweetie? What's wrong?"

"What's wrong? What *isn't* wrong? We're in this weird nowhere land of not knowing what to do next, not being able to just forgive and forget, not having any idea if we can move forward. I love him, but I don't trust him, and I feel really distant from him. And it's not just the girl, although that drives me crazy, it's *everything*."

"Shh, calm down, calm down. You'll be home tomorrow. I'm going to meet you at your front door — I don't love anyone enough to meet them at the airport — and we'll talk about everything. If it's at all possible for you and Julian to figure this out, to make it work, you're going to do that. And if you decide it's not possible, I'll be there for you every step of the way. So will lots of other people."

"Ohmigod, Nola . . ." She moaned with the misery of it. Having someone acknowledge that she and Julian might not make it was terrifying.

"One step at a time, Brooke. Tonight the only thing you have to do is grit your teeth and smile through the ceremony, the cocktail hour, and the entree. The moment they clear the plates from dinner, call a cab and get the hell back to your hotel room. Do you hear me?"

Brooke nodded.

"Brooke? Yes or no?"

"Yes," she said.

"Listen, get out of the bathroom and follow my instructions, okay? I'll see you tomorrow. Everything will be fine, I promise."

"Thanks, Nol. Just tell me quickly. How is everything with you? Andrew still good?"

"Yeah, I'm with him right now, actually."

"You're with him right now? Then why are you calling me?"

"It's intermission, and he's in the bathroom. . . ."

Something about Nola's tone sounded suspicious. "What show are you seeing?"

There was a pause. *The Lion King.*"

"You're at *The Lion King?* Really? Oh wait, this is a stepmother-in-training activity, isn't it?"

"Yeah, so we have the kid with us. So what? He's cute."

Despite herself, Brooke smiled. "I love you, Nola. Thank you."

"I love you, too. And if you ever tell anyone about this . . ."

Brooke was still grinning when she stepped out and slammed directly into Isaac — and his blogger girlfriend.

"Oh, hi!" Isaac said with the sexless enthusiasm of a guy who had spent the entire previous night flirting with someone for purely selfish purposes. "Brooke, I'd like for you to meet Susannah. I think I was telling you before how much she'd love to —"

"Interview you," Susannah said, extending a hand. The girl was young and smiley and reasonably pretty, and Brooke couldn't stomach one more minute of it.

Brooke summoned some long-forgotten reserve of confidence and composure, looked Susannah squarely in the eye, and said, "It's such a pleasure meeting you, and I do very much hope you'll forgive me for being rude, but I simply must get a message to my mother-in-law."

Susannah nodded.

Clutching her champagne flute like a lifeline, Brooke was almost relieved to find the Alters in the ceremony tent, with a seat saved for her.

"Don't you just love weddings?" Brooke asked as cheerfully as she could. It was nonsense, but what else was there to say?

Her mother-in-law peered into her compact and patted an invisible blemish on her chin. "I find it simply astounding that more than half of all marriages will fail, yet every single couple who walks down that aisle thinks it won't happen to them."

"Mmm," Brooke murmured. "How lovely to be discussing divorce rates at a wedding ceremony."

It was probably the rudest thing she'd ever

uttered to her mother-in-law, but the woman didn't even flinch. Dr. Alter glanced up from his BlackBerry, where he was checking stock prices, but when he saw his wife didn't react, he went back to staring at his screen.

Thankfully, the music started and a general hush fell over the room. Trent and his parents entered the tent first, and Brooke smiled when she saw how genuinely happy — and not the least bit nervous — he looked. One by one the bridesmaids and groomsmen and flower girls followed, and then it was Fern's turn, flanked on both sides by her parents, beaming in exactly the way brides do. The ceremony was a seamless blending of Jewish and Christian traditions, and despite herself, it was a pleasure to watch Fern and Trent gaze at each other with that knowing look.

It wasn't until the rabbi began explaining the chuppah to the audience, how this covering signified the new home the couple would make together, how it would shield and protect them from the outside world and yet was open on four sides to welcome in friends and family, that Brooke teared up. It had been her favorite part of her own wedding ceremony, and it was the moment in each wedding she and Julian had attended where they clasped hands and gave

577

each other the same knowing look Trent and Fern were now sharing. Now not only was she there alone, but it was impossible not to acknowledge the obvious: it had been a long time since their apartment felt like a home, and she and Julian might be on their way to becoming one of her mother-in-law's statistics.

At the reception one of Fern's girlfriends leaned over and whispered something to her husband, prompting the husband to give her a *Really?* look. The girl nodded and Brooke wondered what they were talking about until the husband materialized next to her chair, held out his arm, and asked Brooke if she'd like to dance. The pity dance. She knew it well, was often guilty of nudging Julian to ask solo women at weddings for a dance, thinking she was doing a good deed. Well, now that she knew what it felt like to be on the receiving end of such charity, she swore she'd never do it again. She thanked the husband profusely but begged off, claiming something about needing to find some Advil and could see his relief. This time when she headed for her favorite hallway bathroom, she wasn't sure she could make herself come back out.

She checked her watch. Nine forty-five. She promised herself that if the Alters didn't leave by eleven, she'd call a cab. She slipped back into the hallway, which was drafty and thankfully deserted. A quick check of her phone revealed no new messages or texts, even though Julian should have been home by then. She wondered what he was doing, if he had already gotten Walter from the dog walker and they were curled together on the couch. Or maybe he'd gone directly to the studio. She didn't want to go back into the reception yet, so she paced for a bit, first checking Facebook and then looking up the number of a local cab company, just in case. Fresh out of excuses and distractions, Brooke slipped her phone into her clutch, hugged her bare arms against her chest, and headed toward the music.

She felt a palm close over her shoulder, and she knew before she turned around, before he could utter a word, that it belonged to Julian.

"Rook?" His voice was questioning, uncertain. He wasn't sure how she was going to react.

She didn't turn around immediately — she was almost nervous she was wrong, that it wasn't him — but when she did, the onslaught of emotions hit her like a truck. There he was, standing right in front of her, wearing his only suit and smiling at her shyly, nervously, with a look that seemed to say *Please hug me.* And despite everything that had happened, and all the distance between them these last couple weeks, it was all Brooke wanted to do. There was no denying it: she was reflexively, instinctively ecstatic to see him.

After she collapsed into his arms, she couldn't speak for almost thirty seconds. He felt warm and smelled right and hugged her so tightly she started to cry.

"I hope those are tears of joy?"

She wiped them away, aware her mascara was running but not caring in the least. "Joy, relief, and about a million other things," she said.

When they finally pulled apart, she noticed he was wearing Converse sneakers with his suit.

He followed her gaze down to his shoes. "I forgot to pack dress shoes," he said with a little shrug. He pointed to his head, which was cap-free. "And my hair's kind of a disaster."

Brooke leaned in and kissed him again. It felt so good, so normal! She wanted to be angry, but she was just so damn happy to see him. "Oh, no one cares. They're just going to be happy you're here."

"Come with me. Let's find Trent and

Fern. Then you and I can talk."

Something about the way he said this calmed her. He was there, he was taking charge, and she was just so happy to follow his lead. He led her down the hallway, where a few wedding-goers did double-takes — Isaac and his girlfriend among them, she was pleased to see — and then straight out to the tent. The band was on break as everyone ate dessert, so there was no way they were going to slip in unnoticed. When they entered, the change in the room was palpable. People stared, whispered to each other, and a young girl of maybe ten or eleven actually pointed toward Julian and shouted his name to her mother. Brooke heard her mother-in-law before she saw her.

"Julian!" Elizabeth hissed, seeming to materialize out of nowhere. "What are you *wearing?*"

Brooke shook her head. That woman never failed to amaze her.

"Hi, Mom. Where's —"

Dr. Alter was only a second behind her. "Julian, where the hell have you been? Missing your own cousin's rehearsal dinner, leaving your poor wife alone all weekend, and now showing up looking like *that?* What's gotten into you?"

Brooke braced herself for conflict, but Julian just said, "It's great to see you, Mom, Dad. But you'll have to excuse me."

Julian whisked her over to Trent and Fern. They were busy making their rounds at all the tables, and Brooke could feel hundreds of eyes on her and Julian as they approached the happy couple.

"Trent," Julian said quietly, placing a hand on his cousin's back.

Trent's face registered shock and then joy when he turned around. The two of them hugged. Fern smiled at Brooke, and all her anxiety over whether or not Fern was angry at them for Julian's sudden appearance evaporated.

"First and foremost, congratulations, you two!" Julian said, clapping Trent again and leaning in to kiss Fern on the cheek.

"Thanks, buddy," Trent said, clearly happy to see Julian.

"Fern, you look absolutely beautiful. I don't know what this guy did to deserve you, but he's pretty damn lucky."

"Thanks, Julian," Fern said with a smile. She reached over and took Brooke's hand. "Brooke and I finally got to spend some time together this weekend, and I'd say you're pretty lucky, too."

Brooke squeezed Fern's hand.

Julian grinned at Brooke. "I'd say so," he

said. "Listen, you guys, I'm so sorry for missing everything."

Trent waved him off. "Don't worry about it. We're glad you made it."

"No, no, I should've been here for the whole weekend. I'm really sorry."

For a minute Julian looked as though he might cry. Fern stood on her tiptoes to hug him and said, "It's nothing a couple of front-row tickets to your next L.A. show can't solve. Isn't that right, Trent?"

Everyone laughed, and Brooke watched as Julian slipped Trent a folded piece of paper. "It's my rehearsal dinner toast. I'm sorry I couldn't read it last night."

"You could do it now," Trent said.

Julian looked dumbfounded. "You want me to read it now?"

"It is your toast, right?"

Julian nodded.

"Then I think I speak for both of us when I say that we'd love to hear it. If you don't mind . . ."

"Of course I don't mind," Julian said. Almost instantaneously, someone materialized with a microphone; after a few glass clinks and a couple hushing sounds, the tent grew quiet. Julian cleared his throat and appeared instantly to relax. Brooke wondered if the entire room was thinking how natural he looked with a microphone in his hand. Completely at ease and absolutely adorable. She felt a surge of pride.

"Hey, everyone," he said with a dimple-producing grin. "My name's Julian, and Trent and I are first cousins, actually only born about six months apart, so I think it's fair to say we go way back. I'm, uh, sorry to interrupt your fun, but I just wanted to wish my cousin and his beautiful new wife all the happiness in the world."

He paused for a moment and fiddled with his paper, but after his eyes skimmed over a few words, he shrugged and shoved it back in his pocket. He looked up and paused.

"Look everyone, I've known Trent for a very long time, and I can safely say that I have never, ever seen him this happy. Fern, you're a welcome addition to our crazy family and a breath of fresh air."

Everyone laughed except Julian's mother. Brooke grinned.

"What everyone may not realize is how much I owe Trent." Julian coughed and the room grew even quieter. "Nine years ago he introduced me to Brooke, my wife, the love of my life. I can't even stand to think what would've happened if their blind date had gone well that night" — more laughter — "but I, for one, am forever grateful that it didn't. If you would've told me on my own wedding night that I would love my wife even more today, I wouldn't have believed it was possible, but as I stand here tonight and look at her, I can tell you it's true."

Brooke felt the entire room turn in her direction, but she couldn't take her eyes off Julian.

"May you love each other more with each passing day, and know that no matter what obstacles life throws your way, you'll get through them together. Tonight is just the beginning, you two, and I know I speak for everyone here when I say how honored I am to share it with you. Please raise a glass to Trent and Fern!"

The crowd let out a rousing cheer as everyone clinked their glasses and someone called out, "Encore, encore!"

Julian blushed and leaned into the microphone. "Actually, now I'm going to do a special performance of 'Wind Beneath My Wings' for the happy couple. You two don't mind, right?"

He turned to look at Trent and Fern, both of whom appeared horrified. There was a split second of silence until Julian broke the tension. "I'm just kidding! Of course, if you really want me to . . ."

Trent was on his feet in a second, mock-tackling Julian, and Fern joined him a minute later and gave him a teary kiss on the cheek. Once again, the room laughed and cheered and Julian whispered something in his cousin's ear and the two embraced. The band began to play some soft background music and Julian walked over to Brooke and, without a word, led her through the crowd and back into the hallway.

"That was beautiful," she said, and her voice cracked.

He put both hands on her face and looked directly into her eyes. "I meant every word of it."

She leaned in to kiss him. It only lasted a moment, but she wondered if it didn't qualify as the best kiss of their relationship. She was about to wrap her arms around his neck when he pulled her out the front door and said, "Do you have a coat?"

Brooke eyed the small group of smokers at the other end of the walkway who were staring right back and said, "It's with the coat check."

Julian took his jacket off and helped her into it. "Come with me?" he asked.

"Where are we going? I think the hotel is a little too far to walk to," she whispered to him as they strolled past the smokers and around the side of the house.

Julian put his hand in the small of her back and nudged her toward the backyard. "We have to go back in, but I don't think anyone will mind if we sneak away for a little."

He led her through the yard and down a path toward a pond and motioned for her to sit on a stone bench facing the water. "You okay?" he asked.

The stone felt like an ice block through the sheer material of her dress, and her toes were beginning to tingle. "I'm a little cold."

He wrapped his arms around her and squeezed.

"So, what are you doing here, Julian?"

He took her hand. "I knew before I went away it was a terrible idea. I tried to rationalize that it was better to leave everyone alone, but it wasn't. I've had a lot of time to think, and I didn't want to wait another minute to talk to you about it."

"Okay . . ."

He took her hand. "I was sitting next to this singer, Tommy Bailey, that kid who won *American Idol* a couple years ago?"

Brooke nodded. She didn't mention the connection to Amber or the fact that she already knew all she needed to about Tommy.

"So we're, like, the only two people sitting in first class. I'm obviously going over there to work, but he's headed over for vacation. He has a couple weeks off from touring, and he rented some sick villa somewhere. And it strikes me — he's going alone."

"Oh, please, just because he was on the flight alone does not mean he'll be alone when he gets there."

Julian held up a hand. "No, you're totally right. He couldn't shut up about all the girls who were meeting him there, stopping by, whatever. His agent and his manager were coming over, a few so-called friends he'd rounded up by paying for their tickets. It sounded kind of pathetic, but I wasn't sure — maybe he loves that whole scene. Lots of guys probably do. But then he starts drinking, really drinking, and by the time we're halfway across the Atlantic, he's in tears — literally, crying — about how much he misses his ex-wife and his family and his friends from growing up. How there's no one in his life he's known for longer than a couple years and no one who doesn't want something from him. He's a wreck, Brooke, a total disaster, and all I could think was *I don't want to be that guy.*"

Brooke finally exhaled. She hadn't realized it, but she'd been holding her breath on and off since they'd begun this conversation. *He doesn't want to be that guy.* A few simple words, and she'd been waiting to hear them for so long.

She turned to look up at him. "I don't want you to be that guy, either, but I also don't want to be the wife who holds you back, who's constantly carping and making threats and asking when you'll be home."

Julian looked at her and raised his eyebrows. "Please. You love that."

Brooke appeared to think about it. "Yeah, you're right. I do love that."

They both smiled.

"Look, Rook, I just keep going over and over it in my head. I know it'll take time before you trust me again, but I will do whatever it takes. This weird no-man's-land we're in . . . it's hell. If you hear nothing else tonight, please hear this: I will not give up on us. Not now, not ever."

"Julian —"

He leaned close. "No, listen. You killed yourself working those two jobs for so long. I just . . . I didn't see what a toll it was taking on you, and —"

She took his hand. "No, I'm sorry about that. I wanted to do it, for you, for us, but I shouldn't have been so insistent on keeping both of them once everything started taking off with your career. I don't know why I did; I started feeling left out, like everything was spiraling out of control, and I was trying to maintain some normalcy. But I've thought a lot about it, too, and I should've at least quit Huntley when your album dropped. I probably should've requested to go part-time at the hospital. Maybe then we could have had some flexibility to see each other. But even if I only go back part-time now, or hopefully open my own practice, I still . . . I don't know how it can work."

"It has to!" he said with an urgency she hadn't felt from him in so long.

He reached into his pants pocket and pulled out a folded packet of papers. "Are those . . ." She almost blurted out "divorce papers" but managed to stop herself. She wondered if she sounded as irrational as she felt.

"This is our game plan, Rook."

"Our game plan?" She could see her breath in the air, and she was starting to shiver uncontrollably.

Julian nodded. "It's just the beginning," he said, pushing her hair behind her ears. "We're getting rid of poisonous people once and for all. First up? Leo."

Just the sound of his name made her cringe. "What does he have to do with us?"

"A lot, actually. He's been absolutely toxic in every imaginable way. Something you probably knew all along but I was too much of an ass to really see. He leaked a lot of stuff to the press and arranged to get the *Last Night* paparazzo into the Chateau, and he's the one who sent that girl to my table, all under the ridiculous rationalization that any press is good press. He orchestrated the whole thing. I was at fault — I absolutely was — but Leo —"

"Disgusting," she said, shaking her head.

"I fired him."

Brooke's head snapped up and she could see Julian was smiling. "You really did?"

"Oh, I sure did." He handed her a piece of folded paper. "Here, this is step two."

The single sheet looked like it had been printed from a website. It featured a headshot of a kindly older gentleman named Howard Liu, his contact information, and a history of the apartments he'd sold in the last couple years. "Should I know Howard?" she asked.

"You will soon," Julian said, smiling. "Howard is our new broker. And if you're okay with it, we have an appointment with him first thing Monday."

"We're getting an apartment?"

He handed her another wad of papers.

"We're seeing these. And anything else you want to look at, of course."

She stared at him for a moment, unfolded the papers, and gasped. They were more printouts, only these were of beautiful town houses in Brooklyn, probably six or seven in all, each featuring photos and floor plans and lists of features and amenities. Her eyes froze on the last one, the four-story brownstone with the front stoop and the little gated front yard that she and Julian had walked by hundreds of times.

"That's your favorite, right?" he asked, pointing to it.

She nodded.

"I thought so. We're seeing that one last. And if you like it, we're going to put in a bid then and there."

"Ohmigod." It was too much to process. Gone was all talk of the chic Tribeca lofts or the ultramodern high-rise apartments. He wanted a home — a real home — as much as she did.

"Here," he said, handing her a piece of paper.

"There's more?"

"Just open it."

It was yet another printout. This one featured a smiling headshot of a man named Richard Goldberg, who looked to be around forty-five and who worked for a company called Original Artist Management. "And this lovely gentleman?" she asked with a smile.

"Is my new manager," Julian said. "I made a few calls, and I found someone who understands what I'm hoping to achieve."

"Dare I ask what?" she asked.

"A way to have a successful career without losing what matters to me most — you," he said quietly. He pointed to Richard's picture. "I spoke to him, and he got it immediately. I don't need to maximize my financial potential — I need *you*."

"We can still buy that town house in Brooklyn, right?" she said with a grin.

"Yes. We sure can. And apparently, if I'm willing to forgo a few paychecks, I can decide to tour once a year, and even then put a cap on it. Six, eight weeks, max."

"And how do you feel about that?"

"I feel good. You're not the only one who hates me touring — it's no kind of life. But I think we could both handle six or eight weeks of it every twelve months if it's going to give us freedom otherwise. Do you?"

Brooke nodded. "I do, I think that's a good compromise. So long as you won't feel like you're cheating yourself . . ."

"It's not perfect — nothing's ever going

to be — but I think it sounds like a damn good start. And for the record, I don't expect you to drop everything to come with me. I know you'll have another job you love by then, maybe a baby. . . ." He raised his eyebrows in her direction and she laughed. "I can install a recording studio in our basement so I can be home with our family. I checked, and every one of these listings has a basement."

"Julian. My god, this —" She waved at all the printouts and marveled at all the thought and effort he'd put into it. "I don't even know what to say."

"Say yes, Brooke. We can make it work, I know we can. Wait — don't say anything yet." He pulled open the jacket she was hugging tightly around herself and reached into the inside pocket. In his open palm was a small velvet jewelry box.

Her hand flew to her mouth. She was about to ask Julian what was inside, but before she could say a word, he scooted off the bench and knelt beside her, his other hand resting on her knee.

"Brooke, will you make me the happiest guy in the world and marry me again?"

He flipped open the box. Inside was not some new fancy engagement ring with a huge diamond or a pair of sparkly studs, as she suspected. Tucked between two folds of velvet was Brooke's plain gold wedding band, the one the stylist had ripped off her finger the night of the Grammys, the same band she'd worn every day for nearly six years now but thought she might never see again.

"I've been wearing this on a chain ever since I got it back," he said.

"I didn't mean to," she rushed to say, "it just got lost in all the confusion, I swear it wasn't some sort of symbol. . . ."

He stretched up and kissed her. "Do me the honor of wearing it again?"

She threw her arms around his neck, crying once again now, and nodded. She tried to say yes, but she couldn't get the word out. He laughed and rocked her and hugged her back.

"Here, look," he said, plucking the ring from the box. He pointed to its underside where, right beside their wedding date, he had engraved today's date. "So we'll never forget that we're making a promise to each other to start over." He took her left hand and slid her own wedding band on her finger, and she didn't realize until it was back in place how naked she'd felt without it.

"Hey, Rook, I hate to stand on ceremony

here, but you haven't actually agreed yet."
He gave her a sheepish look, and she could
see he was still a little nervous.

She took it as a very good sign.

They couldn't solve everything in one
conversation, but tonight she didn't care.
They still loved each other. She couldn't
possibly know what the next months or
years would bring, or if their plans would
work, but she *knew* — for the first time in a
long, long while — that she wanted to try.

"I love you, Julian Alter," she said, reaching out to hold his hands. "And yes, I will
marry you again. Yes, yes, yes."

ACKNOWLEDGMENTS

First and foremost I want to thank my agent, Sloan Harris. I'm forever indebted to him for his tireless advocacy, his invaluable advice, and the calm, levelheaded way he handles every situation I throw at him. I wake each day thankful to be on Sloan's team. I also deeply admire the way he can work the word "kabuki" into almost every conversation.

Thank you to my very own Editorial Dream Team, in order of appearance: Marysue Rucci, Lynne Drew, and Greer Hendricks. Every author should know what it's like to be on the receiving end of such smart, savvy, and sensitive feedback. Sending a special hug to Lynne for her above-and-beyond cross-Atlantic voyage (annual tradition?).

Thanks to Judith Curr, whose energy and enthusiasm are contagious, and to David Rosenthal for always believing in me (and who surely loathes the phrase "always believing in me"). A huge thank-you to everyone at Atria, especially: Carolyn Reidy, Chris Lloreda, Jeanne Lee, Lisa Sciambra, Mellony Torres, Sarah Cantin, Lisa Keim, Nancy Inglis, Kimberly Goldstein, Aja Pollock, Rachel Bostic, Natalie White, Craig Dean, and the entire sales force. I'm thrilled to be part of the family!

Betsy Robbins, Vivienne Schuster, Alice Moss, Kate Burke, Cathy Gleason, Sophie Baker, Kyle White, and Ludmilla Suvorova: thank you. I simply adore you all. Special thanks to Kristyn Keene for offering wise and spot-on advice on everything from plot development to stilettos. You are always right. A big hug to Cara Weisberger for brilliant brainstorming sessions. Thanks to Damian Benders for my music industry briefing and Victoria Stein for educating me on all things nutritionist-related. Any mistakes in these areas are entirely my own.

Lots of love to Mom and Dad and the rest of my incredible family: Dana, Seth, Grandma, Papa, Bernie, Judy, Jonathan, Brian, Lindsey, Dave, Allison, Jackie, and Mel for enduring endless hours of blather about this book and doing it with so much love and support. Nanny, I know you're reading this somewhere, and I miss you so much.

And lastly, the biggest thanks of all to my husband, Mike. This novel (or my sanity) wouldn't exist without him. We talked characters at breakfast, plot at lunch, and structure at dinner, and not only did he never threaten divorce, he also made me laugh every step of the way. MC, I love you.

ABOUT THE AUTHOR

Lauren Weisberger is the *New York Times* bestselling author of *The Devil Wears Prada,* which was made into a major motion picture starring Meryl Streep and Anne Hathaway; *Everyone Worth Knowing;* and *Chasing Harry Winston.* A graduate of Cornell University, she lives in New York City with her husband. To learn more, visit www.laurenweisberger .com.

We hope you have enjoyed this Large Print book. Other Thorndike, Wheeler, Kennebec, and Chivers Press Large Print books are available at your library or directly from the publishers.

For information about current and upcoming titles, please call or write, without obligation, to:

Publisher
Thorndike Press
295 Kennedy Memorial Drive
Waterville, ME 04901
Tel. (800) 223-1244

or visit our Web site at:

http://gale.cengage.com/thorndike

OR

Chivers Large Print
published by BBC Audiobooks Ltd
St James House, The Square
Lower Bristol Road
Bath BA2 3SB
England
Tel. +44(0) 800 136919
email: bbcaudiobooks@bbc.co.uk
www.bbcaudiobooks.co.uk

All our Large Print titles are designed for easy reading, and all our books are made to last.